I0525560

STOLEN

Book 1
The Collectors Series

◇◇◇

S. M. Yair-Levy

DNYL Publications LLC

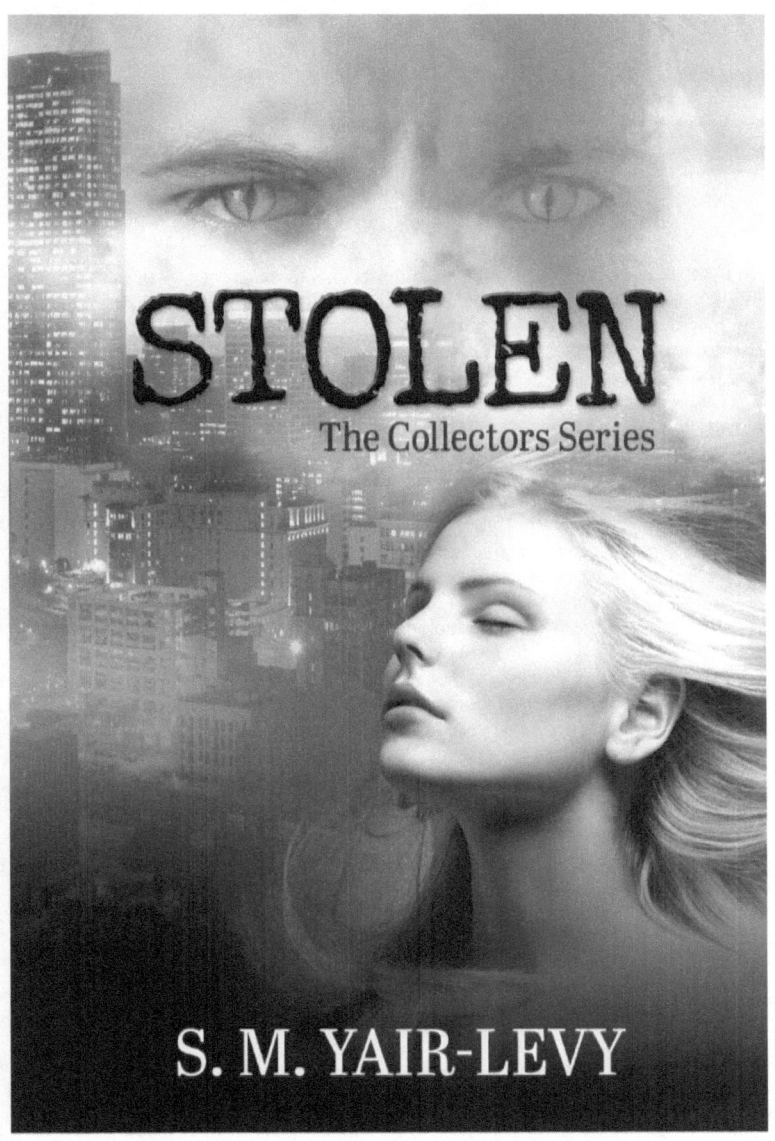

STOLEN

The Collectors Series

S. M. YAIR-LEVY

Published by: DNYL PUBLICATIONS LLC

Copyright©2016 S.M. Yair-Levy

Second Edition, -published 2016

ISBN:978-0692242674

Cover design by: Noa Yair-Levy

To my family,
my *soul*.

STOLEN

Book 1
The Collectors Series

PROLOGUE

"Remember tonight... for it is the beginning of always."
Dante Alighieri

THERE had always been something frightening about the wind. The power it harbored. As if it had the choice to kiss your heated flesh, or rip the air straight out of your lungs. Something you never saw coming until it was on top of you, gripping you intensely. Some say it has a choice because it's filled with the souls of your loved ones passed, while others claim the flowing air currents and shifting shadows are the ways demons travel.

As Dylan Prescott hurried alone down the small, cement path to her dorm, her backpack flopping against the back of her upper thighs, she wanted to believe the former. At nearly eleven o'clock at night, she refused to think of the possibility of demons lurking in those hollowed out corners that light refused to touch, ready to pounce and drag her kicking and screaming into the scorching depths of Hell. No, she chose to believe the soft lick of the wind against her skin was someone looking out for her... cradling her and curling nimble fingers through her long blonde hair as her mother used to do.

A succession of twinkling chimes lilted up from the large pocket of her bag. Stopping, Dylan unhooked one arm and flung her bag around to her belly, searching hurriedly for her phone. She dug her hand deeper, stabbing a finger on the unraveled metal spiral of her beaten up notebook, while sifting through enough highlighters to color the pages of all of her textbooks. She cursed when the ringing stopped just as she located the phone. It was her new roommate. A bubbly, albeit slightly stalker-ish girl that Dylan had nothing in common with. Well, besides the girl part.

Dylan sighed, letting her smartphone slip back down into the black-hole of her backpack and zipped up the side. It was only then that she realized the wind had stopped leaving phantom strokes down her arms and a dry heat to cloak her skin. The sprinklers had shut off too, their spray of water died down slowly to a light trickle as the heads retracted back into the plush green lawn around her.

She stood stock-still as an uneasy feeling trilled up her spine, prickling a wave of gooseflesh along her neck. It was that innate feeling of being watched. Her heart wound and coiled with the urge to run away.

She scanned the dark campus grounds, the buildings and trails that were only partially lit by downward cast street lamps or decorative landscaping fixtures.

Dylan began to hook her bag back onto her shoulder when she saw a slight shift in a shadow several yards in front of her.

"Hello?" she called out before she could stop herself.

The silence was deafening as it stretched out, causing her stomach to leap up into her throat. It was too silent.

Something moved again, and she strained her ears to listen over the pounding of her heart. It didn't seem to make any noise, and she started to wonder if it was just her cruel imagination, maybe a tree or post until it started edging quietly forward.

Dylan instinctively took a wobbly step backward. The figure reached the streetlight, basking itself in the amber glow. She squinted, making out a dark crown of hair and a tall build. With its head down, it looked like a wandering shadow detached from its human form. Yet even without any identifying features, one thing she did know for sure. *It* was a man.

Holy Hell.

Her mind contemplated the odds that this guy was another student or some kind of mugger, but before she could come to a conclusion, the person began to march straight towards her. His determined stride betraying his "shadow man" and she wasn't taking any chances. She quickly glanced behind herself at the empty pathway. Her step faltered as her eyes skimmed the area. As she snapped her attention forward, she slammed face first into a hard wall of male muscle.

Gasping and confused, she stumbled back, glancing at the vacant path behind her then back at *him*.

"P-please don't hurt me!" she whimpered, fumbling for her bag. "T-take my wallet—backpack, take my backpack! Just leave me alone!"

Catching the split heel of her converse sneaker on a crack in the pavement, she dropped her backpack with a *flop* and stumbled backward. The figure stepped over her bag, snatching her wrist with icy fingers as he pulled her upright. Dylan gasped as he stared into her with swirling, bottle-green eyes radiating around a four-pointed, star-shaped pupil.

A malicious grin grew along his face as his grasp caused a jolt of electricity to travel up her arm and throughout her body. It felt oddly cool, like slowly dipping naked into a pool filled with chilled, sparkling water. A strangled groan bubbled up in her throat sounding far and foreign as the strange effervescent sensation tingled her senses.

He stepped forward even further, bringing his body almost flush with hers. He cocked his head to the side. It was featureless from the dark shadows of the night. She had the strange feeling that perhaps he *was* night, the keeper of the stars and dominator of the sun.

He leaned down until his mouth was a breath from hers. She imagined her eyes were wells of terror, but she couldn't seem to look away from his penetrating gaze; or stop thinking about how at her current vantage, she could see the swirling depths of pain within his soulless eyes.

What is he doing?

What does he want?

She tried to pull from his grasp, but he held her to the spot by an insurmountable force.

A tiny spark of anger sputtered in her belly as she focused hard on trying to run, fight back, or God, even move. It didn't make sense that he could hold her down simply with a touch.

A wild wind suddenly slapped up against them. Her wild wind. It whipped their clothes and hair in violent thrusts and a steely resolve gripped her like a fist. She focused back on her attacker and noticed confusion in his eyes as his smile vanished. He dropped her wrist as if she'd burned him. He looked at her with a kind of disgust and twisted pleasure entwined together into a knot.

The moment he freed her wrist, her knees buckled and everything went black.

Coming to, Dylan squinted. Her eyes tried to open, blinded by a burning yellowish light in front of her. Shutting them again, she recalled what happened and gasped, trying to form words, but only air escaped.

"Shh, honey. It's okay. You're in the hospital. You've had an accident." Her mind immediately relaxed to the soothing sounds of her grandmother's voice and she drifted off into yet another slumber.

Green-eyes, wicked grins, and gliding black silhouettes haunted her dreams.

12

CHAPTER 1

Two Years Later

*"There will always be a reason why you meet people.
Either you need them to change your life or you're the one
that will change theirs."*
-Angel Flonis Harefa

"PLEASE hurry!" Dylan yelled up the wooden staircase. "I'm going to be late for class!"

"Found it!" she heard her grandmother, Isabel, sing as she padded barefoot across the attic above. "Come up here and get it. It'll take me forever to bring it to you down there."

Laughing, Dylan replied under her breath, "Uh huh, whatever."

Dylan took to the stairs, each old step complaining louder than the last. She reached the top and walked towards the attic stairs, passing her childhood bedroom.

Dylan's parents had died in a car crash when she was just seven years old. Everyone had been surprised that she had survived, but thanked God for sparing her life nonetheless. The crash had been a battle between the family's small SUV and a large cement truck.

The truck won.

She was told her parents were killed instantly, even though Dylan's nightmares begged to differ. The flash of headlights blinding her eyes, crunching metal, and the screams of her mother as her bones crushed and her sinews snapped, scarred Dylan's mind no matter how hard she tried to forget them.

Immediately after the accident, she moved into her only living relative's home: her father's mother, Isabel Prescott. She was a kind woman that went out of her way to make a home for the both of them. She was rather young for a grandmother and hated the term.

Making her way up to the finished attic, Dylan spotted her curvy grandmother hunched over some of her late son's boxes. Her long, curly, salt and pepper hair was thrown into a top messy knot and sweat marks darkened her navy tracksuit.

Isabel had hair Dylan often bemoaned she didn't inherit. Sometimes, when Dylan would look at photographs of her parents, she'd ponder what features she got from either of them. If it wasn't for the birth photos of her screaming, covered in red and white goo, Dylan would have concluded she was adopted.

Her father was what she referred to as a chic nerd. In every photo he was well dressed; but, his short, curly, black hair was always disheveled and his rectangle, black frames slightly askew. Her mother, on the other hand, was a French goddess. Always angelic with russet wavy locks and a towering willowy body. Obviously the genetics God didn't think Dylan were befitting. Dylan was short with extremely long, board straight, pale-blonde hair and ash-gray eyes. She was practically flat-chested and wire thin. Most of the time, she felt as attractive as a little boy.

Today was the fourteenth anniversary of the accident. Every year on this day, Isabel wandered up to the attic and sorted through her only son's possessions, lovingly examining each item. For the first five years, Dylan had joined her, sobbing for the entire day and sometimes for the entire week. When she was thirteen, Dylan stopped crying on these occasions, but still accompanied her grandma each year as she went over her late father's things.

This year wasn't different. The weeping had stopped for her grandmother too, and the act had become more of a ritual than mourning. Today, however, she had class and would have to let Isabel reminiscence without her.

As she closed the distance, Isabel rose and held out her hand. Dylan paused a beat before asking, "Where did you find it?" She eyed the antique golden ring with a red, oval, opaque stone easily the size of a quarter in diameter. There was a Latin engraving on the gold plate around the edges of the stone.

"I believe it was your mother's. I found it last night when I started going through The Boxes. I have no idea how we missed it for so many years."

"Wow," Dylan said, taking her eyes off the ring. "It's beautiful. Thank you." She kissed the small dimple that dotted the smiling woman's cheek. "I'll call you later in the week, but right now I'm very late!" Dylan declared dramatically, waving her hand above her head and bee-lining it to her car.

Jumping into her red Volkswagen Jetta, she was immediately assaulted by Sara Bareilles's spectacular voice in *Fairytale*. Smiling, she opened the sunroof and turned around in the dead end road on Leven Lane, driving back past her house. Not, however, without throwing a quick glance at the old, vine-covered Tuscan villa, complete with towering Magnolia trees and winding red brick pathway.

Driving along Sunset Blvd from her home in Brentwood, she opened the car's window to feel the cool, morning air across her face mixing with the sun's toasting rays. It was a delicious mixture, once again reminding her how much she adored summer mornings.

When she was young, she longed for the fairytale of the sad little girl uprooted from her sad little life by the handsome prince only to live happily ever after. But, with age came reason. She knew better now than to hope for something so... hopeless.

Up until she started college, Dylan's teens had been a long sequence of tears, rumors, pranks, and disappointments. She was happy to finally have that painfully boring life she always dreamed of—her very own fairytale. Other than the attack two years ago, not a lot had happened since, and she was more than fine with that.

The university seemed to become more proactive about security after several students were assaulted that same week she had been. For some reason, though, she was the only one that remembered anything from her attack. Not that she had readily forked over the information she held; worried they would throw her into some kind of loony bin. How could she tell anyone with a straight face that her attacker had alien eyes and seemed to be behind her in one moment and in front of her the next? Or, that his touch seemed to sink inside her like icy fingers digging for her soul? Perhaps that was how the other victims had felt as well … afraid they'd sound crazy, too. Despite the extra campus security, her naturally worried grandmother had pushed self-defense classes and demanded she carry pepper spray on her key chain. A small price to pay for Isabel's peace of mind.

Arriving on campus in record time, Dylan navigated her way through the maze of parked cars in the lot across from ROLFE Hall at UCLA. Locking her car, she jogged to the first class of her summer semester.

"Hey girl!" yelled Aria Wan from the middle of the stadium-style lecture hall.

Aria had been her roommate since freshman year and both were Cultural Anthropology majors. She was voluptuous and tall with multiple stud piercings and long, slick crimson hair, which typically hung loosely around the delicate features of her oval face. Today, she wore bright red overalls and a polka-dot tube shirt with a sweetheart neckline, showing off her cherry blossom tattoo that spilled down her right shoulder in beautiful bursts of prismatic color. It all gave her an edgy Pinup Girl look she wore so well. She was super smart, and unlike Dylan, Aria was a definite extrovert with *many* friends. She was just plain hard not to like, and equally hard to get rid of.

Sitting down, Dylan sighed, blowing her chunky, blonde bangs out of her eyes. Sometimes she felt like the outcast to Aria's cheerleader. The interloper in her own "best" friendship. What Aria saw in Dylan... she had no idea.

"What took you so long?" Aria asked, handing her a syllabus, and quickly getting back to work at assembling her binder and labeling the folders. "I thought you were going to get here early to help me sort through rush applications." The purse of her friend's lips told Dylan Aria had been worried. Even after three years of living together, Dylan still didn't know what made her friend so overprotective and didn't think she would ever ask.

"Come on. That's what your sorority sisters are for. *Remember*?" Dylan drawled. "Besides Isabel needed some help."

"Oh, yeah. I forgot that was today," Aria mumbled, halting her movements and giving Dylan her full attention. An uncomfortable, sad look took over her features.

Dylan winced at her friend's pity. Aria was usually good at keeping deep emotions around her at bay. She liked that her best friend was self-absorbed ninety percent of the time. It meant there were no heart-to-hearts deeper than the acknowledgment that the other was feeling like crap. For the past ten years, Dylan had worked hard to keep a numb exterior, which helped keep their shallow friendship so strong.

Redirecting the inevitable 'How are you feeling' conversation, Dylan added, "She also wanted to give me this."

She flashed the ring that fit snugly on her right ring finger. She wasn't even sure why she was sharing the small treasure with her friend. It was personal, and honestly, none of her business. "She found it in some of my dad's old boxes and thinks it was my mother's."

"That's really... old," Aria said dryly. Noticing the scowl on her friend's face, she quickly recovered. "I mean not bad old, but like expensive old. *Antique?*"

"Yeah, I assume it's a family heirloom," she murmured, eyeing the engraving once more.

The ring was heavy and dented, which made it slightly painful to wear. Nevertheless, it made her feel closer to her parents, and she'd take anything to have a piece of them with her again, even if it was a damaged, ugly ring.

"Good morning, class!" exclaimed Dr. Warjas, jolting Dylan out of her reverie.

Dr. Warjas was a short Filipino woman in her late fifties with very long, ashy hair who always seemed to wear strikingly sharp pantsuits.

"Welcome to Human Behavior Ecology," the professor called out as she turned to write on the projector. "Our classes will meet every Monday at 11:30 *sharp*," she added, underlining 11:30 multiple times in red. "Please turn to the syllabus for the course description, projects, and attendance policy. I *do* grade based on several factors and attendance *is* one of them. The lecture is three hours. This class is about the survey of research in human behavioral ecology. We'll be discussing the review of natural and sexual selection, kin selection, and reciprocal altruism. Emphasis on current empirical studies of modern human behavior from..."

Dylan felt her mind tune out and her focus turn to the trickle of students who continued to flow into the lecture hall, ignoring the professor's address. One of them looked familiar: a tall guy with hair the color of whiskey. It was mussed up as if he had just rolled out of bed or rolled around in one with someone. He occupied most of the same classes as Dylan, an obvious Anthropology major like her. He always seemed to be surrounded by friends wherever he went. And today, like every day, he wore a non-descript black T-shirt, dark-wash jeans and biker boots accented by black Ray-Ban sunglasses. He was strikingly good-looking with high cheekbones and a determined set to his jaw that turned heads wherever he went.

As he passed her, Dylan bit her lip, feeling the same hot butterflies his presence always evoked. To say she had a crush on him would have been a massive understatement. Nevertheless, she wouldn't dream of ever asking him out. She preferred the relationship she conjured in her fantasies as opposed to reality. She didn't want to taint his current perfection with how much of an incoherent tool he was bound to be.

She watched as he and a few other girls parked themselves on the top row. A brunette next to him was apparently a permanent fixture. *Probably his girlfriend.* The love in her eyes when she talked to him, or in the way her body always seemed angled towards his, was a giant mark of claim. Dylan often wondered if the same look of obsession reflected in his eyes. The thought sprang a twinge of pain in her chest. But that was all the more reason to stay away from him. At least from a distance, she could imagine he was completely hers.

Taking a deep, controlled breath, she brought her attention back to the boisterous professor and flipped through her syllabus, noting the multiple projects. She needed to focus on graduating and looking for a great internship. Dating was the last item on her checklist.

Oh, who was she kidding? Being near guys like him would probably give her hives. Not to mention kissing one might give her a heart attack. Yes, she'd steer clear and focus on school. Work first, *then* maybe boyfriend—preferably one that she could be articulate around.

"To begin the semester, those who have had me before know I usually have my students write about themselves on a note card and present to the class," the professor was saying, clearing her throat and sipping a glass of water. "But because of the doubling in size of this class this semester, I'm introducing the Color Game." The students started to murmur and shift in their seats.

"What do you think that's about?" whispered Aria.

"Not sure," Dylan said, giving her a quick, pained look.

"If you will notice, each row has a color and each seat has a number." Dr. Warjas pointed to the row in front of her. "I'm sure each of you are seated next to your friends. Natural Selection at work." She smiled, which looked strained against her usually austere expression. The room was still silent when she decided to continue. "All right, I'm going to pull a number and a color from this bag and match it with the complimentary color and same number. Then you will interview each other for one hour and present your findings at the end of class. And I don't want dry information. Get creative people!"

"Great," muttered Aria.

"Then, that person will be your partner for the rest of the semester's projects."

Everyone in the lecture hall seemed to groan at once. The professor, ignoring the reaction, called, one by one, the twenty-five students on the left side of the room, pairing them with the ones on the right. To Dylan's horror, she was paired with her Mr. Mysterious in the back of the room, Tristian Stewart.

Of course, right?

Turning her head slowly, while tucking her blonde hair behind her ear, she gazed in the direction of Tristian. He was slouched back into his chair and seemed to be impassively staring straightforward. Groaning inwardly, she thought she might actually be sick. How would this even work?

You can do this, she told herself. *This is for the grade.*

Before shifting her stare, she realized the brunette next to him was giving her a serious glare.

Great. Just great! The last thing she wanted was to get on anyone's bad side.

"Finally," laughed Aria, shaking Dylan's arm and yanking her down to earth. "Maybe now you can stop staring at his fine ass and just ask him out already." She boosted her eyebrows comically, then asked, "You okay? You look like you're going to throw up."

"Yeah, yeah, I'm fine. I just forgot to eat this morning."

"Right," she said slowly. "I'll see you at break." Dylan nodded listlessly as they stood to part ways, moving towards their designated partners.

Ascending the carpeted steps, she felt her blood pulsing from the adrenaline pumping into her veins. She took in a deep breath before shimmying past the glares of dissipating estrogen that flocked around him as she moved herself next to Tristian.

He stayed slouched in his chair, his legs slightly bent and spread wide with his head resting in his right hand. He looked relaxed, but something about him radiated aggression and dominance. She just wasn't sure what.

"H-hey," she stuttered, internally cringing at her inability to speak. "I'm Dylan Prescott, and you're Tristian Stewart... right?"

He remained silent, but turned to look at her.

"Okay..." Dylan continued, biting her lip and looking pretty much anywhere else but at him. "Look, I know I'm not your first choice in a partner... and the feeling's mutual, believe me. But... we need to work together, you know, for the *grade*."

He nodded once.

Taking that cue, she plopped down into the swivel chair next to him, fumbling for her notebook and favorite black fountain pen, the cap tipped with three red stones.

"So," Dylan croaked, trying to wet her dry mouth.

"Nice pen," Tristian smirked.

He speaks.

His voice was almost too perfect to be true. It was just the right amount of husk and honey making her heart flutter a bit.

Great.

"Huh? Oh yeah, I have a thing for pens, I guess," Dylan rambled, twisting the pen between her thumb and index finger, remembering the particular birthday when it was gifted to her.

Drawing her attention back to the assignment and trying to sound nonchalant, "So, where were you born?"

"How about I start," he interrupted.

"Er, sure," she replied, trying to pull some of the dead skin off of her chapped lips with her teeth, feeling nervous and suddenly very aware of her posture and hands. After fidgeting for a few seconds, she decided on a rigid, legs-crossed-at-the-knees-and-ankles pose, with a board-straight back.

Hopefully, this exuded confidence.

After she was situated, she noticed a look of suppressed wry curving his mouth.

"What are your hobbies?" he leered casually, positioning his body toward her, slightly hunched over the desk. The closer position granted her the aura of his masculine scent. He was all dark earth and buttery leather. It momentarily threw her off kilter. *Come again?*

"Besides pen collecting."

Scowling at his assumption, she set the pen atop her notebook. "I don't collect pens, by the way. A collection involves more than one, and I only have," she lifted the pen, "is one," she snapped, feeling too close to Mr. *Dark* and Mysterious.

He clenched his jaw in annoyance and she suddenly wanted

to rip off those infuriating sunglasses in order to catch a glimpse of what he was thinking. Or at least just see where the hell he was looking. She hated talking to people with blacked out shades. She never knew where she was supposed to look.

Sighing at the useless argument, she continued, "I like to read, and practice yoga. What about you?"

Ignoring her question, Tristian asked, "What do you like to read?"

"I have pretty eclectic tastes: romance and paranormal, maybe some mysteries and even British literature." She cracked her knuckles, suddenly needing air. "I'm currently reading "The Canterville Ghost."

"Interesting. Are you from LA?"

"No, moved here when I was seven," she said, rubbing her neck uncomfortably. She eyed his blank paper. "Aren't you going to write any of this down?"

"How old are you?"

"Twenty-one," Dylan breathed leaning back in her chair. "You know, you have to write something like we actually chatted."

"Do you have any siblings?"

"Do *you*?" she snapped.

Closing her eyes, she pinched the bridge of her nose; too much was happening today. The Boxes, the ring, adjusting to a new semester, and foremost—a new, amazingly hot but annoying partner that would most likely make her carry the load. She just needed a moment to get her bearings.

She threw her arms to her sides and looked at him.

"I need coffee. You want some? ...My treat."

"I don't drink coffee," he said flatly, grinding his jaw before moving back to his original position of ignoring her.

Who the hell doesn't like coffee?

"All right then."

23

Dylan squeezed back down the narrow aisle, exiting through the double doors at the top of the stairs. The farther she moved from Tristian the more air she felt entering into her lungs. He evoked feelings she didn't completely comprehend. Yes, he was extremely fine; but, in the short, five-minute chat she felt uneasy, annoyed, tense, and sadistically turned on. No wonder he had so many girls eyeing him.

Ten minutes later, Dylan felt more at ease as she made her way back to the spot where they had been sitting for the assignment, but Tristian was gone. She scanned the lecture hall and sat down, hoping he hadn't really left, but was only temporarily absent for a bathroom break. Looking down, she realized his stuff was gone.

Damn and I got nothing on him.

Packing up her stuff she also realized her pen was gone.

What an ass!

Dylan groaned at her growing hatred for Mr. Dark and Mysterious. Stomping down the steps to the professor's desk, she whined to the teacher that her partner had run off and she couldn't complete the assignment that day. Dr. Warjas unsympathetically handed her a copy of the student contact sheet.

"I suggest you track him down and get it done. For skipping the assignment, I'll need a two-page essay on the Evolutionary Approach to Behavior brought to me at the beginning of next class. Tell him to do the same." Looking at Dylan's coffee with a narrowed stare, she added, "Next time, don't blow off the assignment for a latte. I expect better from you, Ms. Prescott."

Sulking her way back up the stairs, she crumpled the contact sheet and shoved it into her backpack. Spotting Aria, Dylan filled her in on the current situation.

"Damn that sucks. Are you going to stick around?"

"I don't think so... I'll see you back at the apartment." She pushed herself upright. "You know what? I think I'll go to the gym. I could use some endorphins."

Aria grinned impishly. "Yeah, I think it's more like you need a dose of that sexy eye candy at the gym to take your mind off."

"No!" Dylan scoffed.

Turning to leave, she walked up the flight of stairs with a frown etched across her forehead and exited the double doors, willing to take an extra-long route just to avoid Dr. Warjas.

After running a couple of miles on the treadmill, Dylan's legs threatened to give out. She was so tired she couldn't have remained tense any longer if she tried.

Mission accomplished.

On her way out, she spotted her yoga instructor. The sexy eye candy apparently. He was the reason she took up yoga in the first place. She had stumbled into his class purely by accident. But he coaxed her to just try it out and she agreed, because honestly, it's hard to say no to him when your brain has turned into a pile of girly goo.

He ran most of the classes at the University gym, so it wasn't abnormal to run into him. She liked to casually flirt (if smiling like an idiot constituted flirting) or agree to take any or all of his classes to 'strengthen her core,' but that was about all she would do. He was way out of her league, towering around 6'3" with a bronzed, sculpted body and buzzed blond hair. Today he wasn't wearing a shirt with his basketball shorts, which left little to the imagination.

"Dylan!" he called over the group of sweaty students paddling hard on the stationary bikes.

"Hey, Garret," she warbled, already feeling her cheeks hurt as she shuffled over. "Sorry I missed this morning's class—had a family thing."

"No problem." He grinned. "I actually wanted to see what you were doing this Saturday." She must have looked shocked, because he quickly continued, "We're opening a Pilates class and I thought maybe you would want to join."

Talking through a forced smile, Dylan replied, "That sounds like fun."

"Yeah," he smirked, slightly narrowing his eyes. "Pilates should really help with your core body strength."

Right. "Sure, what time?"

"12:30?"

"All right, see you then."

He started to move to hug her but she held up a hand. "I'm all sweaty and gross." She grimaced motioning to her damp, white tee and gray capris. He laughed and swept her into a huge bear hug anyway, lifting her high off the floor. She felt his thick muscles wrap around her and cling to her dampened skin. Blood rushed to her cheeks and, as he sat her down, she turned her face away to hide her embarrassment.

"Oh! Don't forget, starting next week yoga classes are going to be in the afternoon," he said patting her arms platonically.

"Uh huh, bye," she mumbled over her shoulder, rushing out of the gym and feeling a bit flustered.

So much for relaxed.

Back at her off campus apartment, she took a nice, long shower. With her hair still wet, she found herself unraveling the crinkled paper of contact information from Dr. Warjas' class. Finding Tristian's number, she typed it into her phone and texted:

DYLAN*:* Hey, it's Dylan Prescott... from Behavior

Ecology. Sorry to bother you, but your not-so-swift getaway was noted by our professor. We still have to finish our assignment, but we also got an extra one.

She sure as hell wasn't going to mention it was because of her tattling on him that they had gotten the extra assignment. Tapping the 'send' icon, she threw her phone onto her bed. Just as she turned away, it chirped. She quickly scooped it back up and read the text.

TRISTIAN: 801 S. Hill St at 10 pm. Sharp.

DYLAN: Is that your place?

She held the phone waiting for a further reply, but he was obviously not going to answer her question. Tossing the device back onto her bed, she returned to the bathroom to finish blow-drying her hair.

A couple of hours later, Aria was ankles-deep searching Dylan's closet for something for Dylan to wear.

"It's too bad you're so short," Aria said, her voice muffled from the closet. "Otherwise, I'd just let you borrow some of my clothes."

Dylan wasn't that short, only about 5'5". Okay, okay more like 5'4 and three quarters. Dylan ignored her friend as she lay on the bed continuing to twist the ring around her finger, studying the Latin quote again.

"I don't think I need to dress nice for this guy. He barely looked in my direction the whole time he sat next to me. *And* I think that brunette is his girlfriend. She gave me one hell of a look."

Aria stumbled out of the closet to pick up her phone.

"Did you even look up the address he gave you?"

"No. It could be fake or an abandoned warehouse," Dylan laughed ironically while sitting up.

"Look, wear this—"Aria said, while inspecting the phone and handing Dylan her favorite pair of dark-washed skinny jeans, and a tight, black tube top, that Dylan hadn't worn since high school.

"Are you serious? This guy is definitely going to think I like him if I wear this to see him..." Then noticing Aria's sardonic face. "What?"

"The address," she answered, and then threw her phone at Dylan. She caught it just before getting smacked in the face. "It's a hot club downtown."

"You think he works there? At... *Spin?* " Dylan said reading the last word off her cell.

"Could be. Now you definitely have to dress up." Walking back into the closet and returning with some knee-high leather boots in hand. "Okay, put on that outfit *and* these. Meet me in my room for makeup!"

"Oh. Hell. No! I'm not wearing those!" Dylan said, grimacing at the five-inch heel and refusing to touch them.

"Why in the world did you buy them if you never plan to wear them?" Aria crossed her arms while clutching a long leather boot in each hand, looking quite authoritative.

"Isabel bought them for me at a Macy's Black Friday sale. I did never plan to wear them. I just didn't want to hurt her feelings."

"Just wear them," Aria sighed.

Half an hour passed as Aria played Barbie with Dylan's face. Pushing her friend away, Dylan finally peeled the liner and brush from Aria's happy hands, refusing any more maquillage.

"Please, go with me," Dylan pleaded. "Please!" She threw

in her best puppy-dog face.

"No way!" Aria responded, waving her off and cleaning up the makeup. "Try to get laid, though. I'm starting to think you've reclaimed your virginity."

Dylan bristled at the mention of her *virtue* and Tristian.

"What's that look?" Aria asked, twirling her finger in tight circles around Dylan's face.

"I, uh… I just don't feel comfortable going by myself, like this," she motioned to her sexy outfit, probably sounding just a bit too chipper. "I mean… maybe I shouldn't go at all. I can always just make something up about him. He did ditch me. I could be super mean in the paper." She wiggled her eyebrows mischievously.

"Trust me, Dylan. You need this. You look hot. Plus, you said he didn't look at you in class. Well, if he doesn't look at you now then we'll have to deem him gay."

Dylan couldn't contain the "Ha!" that erupted, but not at the thought of his sexual preference, even though she knew from the company he kept, gay was a bit far-fetched. She just wasn't delusional. Her looks weren't exactly *top notch*.

"Yeah, well think of this," Aria pointed to her shoes, "as a test."

Before leaving, Dylan returned to her room to stuff a few essentials into her pockets and grab her backpack. Walking past her full-length mirror, Dylan studied herself. The black outfit and smoky eye makeup accented her light-colored hair and brought out the gray of her unremarkable eyes. She just really wanted to lose the boots and wear her beloved Chucks; but, she knew Aria would have a fit.

Feeling mildly confident, Dylan left the apartment and headed to *Spin*.

CHAPTER 2

"Living is easy with eyes closed."
John Lennon

AFTER what felt like an hour trying to find a parking spot downtown, Dylan wobbled in her five inch heels to the club's small entrance bordered by a cliché rope. Showing her ID to the bored looking bouncer, she stepped in. As she entered the club, the combination of sweat and cologne instantly assaulted her senses. Taking a polluted breath, she began scanning the club for any signs of Tristian Stewart.

The place was dark and the dance floor was sunken in the middle along with the DJ station. A wave of colorful lights danced amongst the crowd and a DJ bounced to the beat, nodding in her direction as she passed overhead.

The place seemed quite packed for a Monday, not that she knew how packed clubs were on the weekdays. She'd been to the occasional restaurant or sports bar with Aria, but they'd never gone clubbing together. She couldn't deny that she felt a tad giddy as a ridiculous smile threatened to surface.

Inching her way through the mob of sweat, she moved into an open spot at the bar and ordered a drink.

"Vodka, water with lime, thanks."

The bartender nodded and she turned her gaze back to the techno beat of the club. She figured she'd enjoy a drink or two before texting him and submitting herself to the bittersweet torture of Tristian's presence. Besides, there was no way she'd be able to handle him outside of school while stone cold sober.

"That'll be five dollars," the bartender yelled, leaning over the bar. "You want to start a tab?"

"No tab," she replied, searching her pocket for a five.

She noticed a guy move in next to her and set down a five-dollar bill. Dylan eyed the artfully masculine hand that hovered over the bill and trailed her eyes up to the gorgeous blonde with thick, shaggy curls. He possessed large amber eyes, prominent cheekbones, and a long, slightly-crooked nose. He resembled the walking embodiment of the Michelangelo statue of David.

"Drink's on me," he stated while invading her personal space. She flinched as he held out his hand in the minuscule area between them.

"I'm Asher."

Shaking his hand weakly, she yelled above the music and into his ear, "Thanks."

"Your name?"

She assessed him a moment before muttering, "Dylan."

"Unusual name for a girl, Dylan."

"Yup," she said, feeling a bit indifferent to the same comment she got from most people. It wasn't her fault her parents were serious Bob Dylan fans.

She directed her attention to her drink, squeezing the lime. She took her first sip. It was cool and icy, slightly tart against her lips. She held the liquid in her mouth for just a moment and let it and a bit of lime pulp wallow against her tongue.

Mostly during her teens, Dylan relied on alcohol to numb her mind to the pain of living. Every sip now, seemed to do the opposite. The familiar burn instantly woke memories of sadness.

"Want to dance?"

"Huh?" she choked setting down her drink. She wiped the side of her mouth with the back of her hand. "Oh, no. I'm actually here to meet someone."

"Just one dance," he repeated, holding out his hand expectantly as she chewed her lip. "I'll have you back here in no time." Her mind flitted between jumping into his arms or pointing while yelling *"Stranger danger!"*

"Just a dance, Dylan. Not a contract."

She pulled her lips to the side, then smiled. "All right, just one." She took one last gulp of her drink before taking his hand and following him down the steps to the dance floor.

"See that wasn't so hard, was it?" he teased pulling her behind him.

Dylan didn't know what she expected or how to dance with him to the fast paced techno music. Maybe bounce along with the other bodies? He stopped on the edge of the dance floor. Holding her hand up and resting the other on her hip. He began to dance with her classically.

Moving her swiftly through the crowd, she felt on the verge of bursting into a fit of giggles at the absurd dancing, but his penetrating gaze kept her silent. The way he stared into her eyes was if he were searching her thoughts gave her a strange sense of connection to the amber-eyed guy. It wasn't lust, but something known… as if she looked hard enough, she would find the answers to her life's questions.

The pounding music and sultry bodies melted away as he spun her around and around with grace. A smile broke out across her face. She no longer felt awkward, nervous, or shy. His touch somehow made her feel comfortable and carefree.

Twisting her forward, he slowed almost to a stop, holding her close to his body while rocking back and forth. Closing her eyes and lifting her arms up and around his neck, she moved against him. She felt his fingertips grip along her torso and hips, like prickles of electricity connecting to its source. It was a remarkable sparkling feeling—familiar—but she couldn't place where she'd felt it before. His breath on her neck brought a line of goose bumps crawling down her spine. As if sensing her continuing ease, he held her closer, opening his mouth to whisper, "Temp-"

A drunken girl stumbled into them, forcing them apart. Before she could give the idiot girl a deathly look, she spotted Tristian on his cell walking toward the back of the club. As if she were sucked straight into a trance, she walked in his direction, forgetting all about the unusual blonde, sculpted guy on the dance floor.

Finally making her way out of the mob of bodies, she spotted a set of stairs leading down.

Huh, I guess he does work here.

Hobbling to the dark corner of the club, she peered over her shoulder then entered the even darker staircase. As she made her way down, the beat of the music became muffled before ultimately losing all but only the throbs of the base. At the bottom of the stairs, a damp, rock-lined corridor began. Sporadic lamps pooled light every few feet.

After what felt like five minutes of cautious walking, she considered turning around and forgetting the endeavor, when a cigar scent traveled to her nose. Squinting down the long pathway, she made out a brighter light and a vibrant red floor.

Finally, maybe the employee's lounge?

She arrived at the small, round room lit by lumpy, melting, black wax candles inside small shallow alcoves sprawled randomly across the wall to her right. Along the floor was a deep red carpet with washed out golden fleur-de-lis. The place seemed to be carved out of stone and the stuffy smell of fungi and cigars lingered in the air.

A young woman about Dylan's age was leaning against, what she guessed was, some kind of hostess station fashioned from the same rock of the walls. The girl seemed engrossed with her extremely long, ivory nails—her jet-black hair hanging loose like an onyx veil concealing her eyes.

Dylan spoke, "H-hey," her voice coming out a bit raspy. Clearing her throat, "Excuse me, I think my friend is in there."

The girl whisked her silky hair back revealing her unusually large, bored, blue eyes. "I highly doubt that," she smirked and went back to examining her apparently very interesting nails. "This is a private club," she added without looking up.

Dylan stepped forward, boldly, grabbing the cold stone of the desk. "Look, I'm pretty sure he went in there. Just let me look around. If I can't find him, I'll leave. You can even come with me if you want."

The girl looked at Dylan's hands that gripped her station. "That's a pretty ring."

Dylan yanked her hands back, examining her recent gift. "Thanks."

"You know what, go ahead and go in." The girl placed her palms over her eyes. "I didn't see anything," she giggled shrilly, shaking her head.

Weird. Dylan shuddered like trying to shake off a bad smell and walked over to the long, matching red curtain that pooled at her feet. She ran her fingertips along the soft fabric searching for the opening and parted the drapery.

Almost as if the fabric had silenced the room beyond, noise flooded her eardrums, causing her to start. Once the momentary shock subsided, she glanced around the extensive span of cavernous space packed with dancing people. Giant stalagmites jutted out of the floor and delicate stalactites hung from the ceiling, glistening like polished granite columns. A skeletal chandelier painted gold and black hung in the middle with ends illuminated by thick, dripping, red wax candles. The atmosphere was like getting hit with a heady dose of sex and virility. Leather, dark woods and deep hues decorated the space. Couples danced in varying styles on the dance floor or mingled at the bar. At a quick glance, Dylan assumed anyone would have thought they had walked into a high-end gentlemen's club.

34

Dylan descended several steps and stepped around a large hunk of glistening stone just as a group of girls with ashy blonde curls passed by laughing. Obviously inebriated. One of the girls looked at her and bared curved fang teeth in a snarl before releasing another bout of snorting giggles. Dylan watched the drunken girls exit the club and sighed.

Something else to put on Mr. Dark and Mysterious' list – 'into Goth clubs.'

Dylan inched around trying not to get in anyone's way, but her "excuse me's" died on the tip of her tongue as everyone moved out of her way, providing a clear path to the bar.

Taking a seat on a thin leather barstool, she observed the bartender with yet another frown. He had short brown hair and a thin trail of stubble sculpted into a goatee. He was a normal looking muscular man in a black, threadbare tee... Well, other than the red beady eyes and thick twisting horns glued to his forehead.

Wonder what it's like here on Halloween...

"I like your horns," Dylan yelled over the haunting tune, making a tall gesture above her head. "They're very big. Do they get annoying?"

Chuckling the bartender yelled back, "Only on days that end with Y."

Sitting down she smiled at his line, then belatedly widened her eyes. "You have to wear them all the time?"

Shaking his head and continuing to laugh, he set down a shot of golden liquid.

"Here, it's on the house." He garnished the glass with a lime wedge.

Smelling the obvious Tequila, she thanked him, downing the cool burning liquid while scrambling for the lime wedge.

Spinning around on the bony barstool, she rolled her body rhythmically to the intoxicating beat of the music and scanned the unusual club for Tristian, once more taking in her surroundings.

Along the other side of the club were alcoves embracing booths. The same thick velvet as the club's entrance hid the occupied rooms. As a waitress exited a booth, Dylan noticed bodies packed in, multiple laughing girls sitting on the laps of a few guys that had pointy ears and red eyes like the bartender. Creasing her forehead even more, she peered up, noticing half-naked girls with sagging, lacy, black wings dancing in steel cages to the unique melody.

A pair of hands landed on her shoulders and she jumped at the sensation. Turning quickly, her eyes landed on Asher, his long, golden curls and distinct amber-eyes unforgettable. It was only then that she noticed his pupils were in the shape of some kind of long star.

"Are those contacts?" she pried.

A coy smile played on his lips at her expression. "You left," he stated, ignoring her question.

"Oh… sorry about bailing," she lied, clearing her throat.

"No problem… Didn't know you come down *here,*" he said, letting his eyes fall from hers then down her body, drinking her in.

"I don't." Crossing an arm over her chest, she rolled her eyes at his presumptuousness. "Like I said, just looking for a friend."

"Where is this friend? If you have spotted her… or him?"

"I lost him again," she shrugged with one shoulder.

"Don't you think it's a bit odd down here?" he volunteered, lifting an eyebrow.

"That's an understatement," she mumbled, and then held up her hands. "I mean, sorry if you like to dress up too. But I don't see the point in pretending to be vampires or werewolves."

"There are no wolves here," he stated seriously, looking

around the club before pausing with a smile. "Come on, let's dance."

"I should really be looking for my friend." She glanced at her watch, noting it was close to eleven.

"Oh come on, please?" He held out his hand once more. "We were having such a good time upstairs," he pouted.

"Fine," Dylan smiled and took his hand.

He tugged her to the middle of the room, noting the music was more suited to his style of dance. A woman's voice bellowed a song in another language across the room, very throaty and rock soul with an uneven tempo. Asher led Dylan into a warm embrace, the patrons giving them a wide berth again. They danced hand and hip the same way as upstairs, twirling her around and snapping her back to his broad chest.

"I've never heard this music before, have you?" she asked, trying to lighten to mood and keep her mind off the fact that *many* people seemed to be staring at them.

As Asher dipped her, she saw the club upside down and caught a glimmer of Tristian. Popping her head back up and continuing to twirl, she kept her eyes focused on her mysterious classmate and watched as he headed to an empty alcove and shut the curtain.

"Yeah, it's a usual down here."

Dylan shifted her gaze back at her dance partner.

"Wow," she breathed. "Where'd you learn to dance?"

"My parents."

"Well, you're very good."

"Thanks," he smirked, spinning her around and slamming her body into his. "You aren't so bad yourself."

She smiled tightly in return.

He glanced down at her lips and Dylan's face immediately pinked, unable to decide if she wanted this stranger to kiss her, or not. Just then he flipped her around and they started to grind

like the others around them. She let out a lungful of air. So...
maybe she did.

"Who are you looking for?" he breathed against her neck.

"Oh," she blinked, turning her head to the side. "Tristian
Stewart... you know him?"

He flipped her around again, a distinct hardness overtook
his face.

"Yeah, what are you doing with him?" he asked gripping
her hand just a bit too tight. "How long have you known him?"

"I don't." She curled her lip, trying to free her hand. "We're
in the same class and have an assignment," she offered, "He told
me to meet him here."

What's it to you anyway.

The music changed and he dipped her, landing a startling
kiss. She locked up, but he pulled away before anything more
embarrassing could happen.

"Thank you for the dance," he growled with an impish grin.

She opened her mouth trying to form words, any words,
other than a squeak. He smirked and lifted her back up.

Clearing her throat, she pulled up her top out of habit and
started nodding without restraint. Stopping herself, she touched
her lips and turned to scurry away.

"It was nice meeting you, *Dylan*," he called after her.

Making her way through the gyrating bodies, she came to
the closed curtain into which she had seen Tristian disappear.

Taking a few deep breaths, she steeled her nerves from her
first kiss with a guy. It felt nice... but not what she thought it'd
be. Her romance novels scripted fireworks, lust, and a pop of
electricity. With Asher it felt... *nice*. Like kissing your friend.
She didn't think kissing Tristian would be nice. No, she had
already experienced a violent lust and crippling chemistry just
sitting near him. It would definitely not be *nice*.

Standing there, she pondered if she should go take another

shot of tequila. She had a feeling she'd need it to deal with Tristian's moodiness and sexual presence.

Pursing her lips, she decided she had had more than enough liquid confidence to last the night. She parted the thick material and peered in.

"Tristian?"

She saw a brunette girl straddling him in a tiny black dress that barely covered her rear. She was gripping the small, tufted sofa with painful fists as she ground herself against him in sensually rhythmic movements, sucking on his neck. Tristian's head was thrown back and his fingers seemed to dig into her hips. Dylan's lips parted, her eyes unable to look away from his pleasured expression.

Not even a second passed before the woman snapped her head around and hissed at Dylan through clenched teeth and curved fangs. Blood oozed out her mouth and down her chin.

Stifling a scream, Dylan tripped over herself. Her face hot from embarrassment from what she just interrupted. Tristian seemed to at least have the decency to look mortified as he shoved the girl off his lap in one swift swoop.

Thank God, he was clothed. She almost thought...

Jumping up, at an impossible speed, he grabbed Dylan's arm, yanking her into the adjacent, vacant booth and drawing the curtains. He paused a beat with his fingers steepled at his lips then turned around fiercely, seizing her arms with force.

"What are you doing down here, Dylan?" he practically screamed in her face.

"You invited me, remember!" she yelled right back at him, trying to squirm out of his embrace. "What the hell, Tristian. Let go!" He let go of her and started pacing the tiny space. "No wonder you're always wearing black! You think you're a vampire, or get off pretending with your girlfriend." She stood, accusingly, her hands on her hips. "Was she really drinking your blood? *God*, you're really into this crap, aren't you?"

Tristian stopped and stared at her with a question mark playing his face.

Dylan continued, noticing his blank expression. "You know, playing vampires and stuff?"

"*Playing?*"

"Yeah, like, make believe?" she said slowly, lifting her eyebrows and nodding at the idiot. "I mean, don't tell me you actually believe you're a vampire."

Shaking his head and bursting into a short fit of laughter, he reached for her hand. "Come with me."

Evading his touch, she continued despite his deride, "It's not funny. Your girlfriend can get sick ingesting blood or get an iron overdose or... I don't really know, but it can't be good."

"She'll be more than fine. If anything just a bit pissed. And she's not my girlfriend," he laughed. "I'll tell her you said that though."

Oh? She had noticed that behind all that oozing blood and makeup had been a different brunette than the Miss Glare she had visually confronted in class.

Oh, shoot. He was cheating.

"Wait, you're bleeding still. Sit," she commanded, eyeing his oozing wound from a slight distance. She knew she should stay far, far away from him. He was dangerous and obviously screwed up in the head. But he was too damn magnetic. Even without realizing it, she had already stepped closer.

"No, it's okay. Really," he breathed, patting his neck, and eyeing the blood on his hand with a wince. "You shouldn't be here. You need to go."

"Just sit!" Dylan said again, louder.

When he didn't move to the couch, she grabbed him by the arm and yanked him to the seat. Falling onto the leather booth, his eyebrows shot up from under his Ray-Ban's as she slid behind the table and crouched on her knees beside him.

She flicked a finger in his face with a bone chilling look.

"Don't even think about it, Stewart."

"What?" he grinned, then tried to mask it horribly. "No, no thoughts, I promise."

She smirked and grabbed a cocktail napkin off the half-moon wooden table. He was enjoying the roughness too much *not* to have any thoughts.

Taking hold of his hair, she pulled his head to the side exposing his neck, ignoring the glorious feeling of her fingers gliding through his tresses. Shaking her head in disapproval, she took the napkin to his neck and dabbed gingerly. His cheek twitched with each touch as Dylan talked.

"Look, let's go get some coffee… *or tea* … or whatever you drink and do our project. We can just forget all about this."

A gush of blood slipped out of the wound when she released the pressure of the napkin. Pressing the napkin back down, she slapped the back of his head and he growled. "God, you're so dense, Tristian! Can't you see it's not all about sex? Can't you see that things like this are *dangerous*? I mean, for a while I actually thought you were smart, kind of an ass, but a *smart* ass."

He jerked his face in her direction.

"Oh, don't give me that look! She cut you deeply and was actually sucking your blood. Your blood, Tristian! Seriously, how stupid do you have to be?" Dylan scolded shaking her head again, knowing he was going to need to see a doctor. She lifted the napkin again and watched as more blood trickled out the opening. "This is too deep; I think she punctured something. You're going to need stitches or…" Dylan trailed off, noticing the two small holes starting to knit back together right in front of her eyes.

Blinking, she inhaled a sharp breath and let go of his hair, abandoning the task. *The wound is gone, healed!*

She sat back on her heels and frowned, looking around and wondering if she was hallucinating.

Staring listlessly, Dylan felt as if her spirit were disembodied, floating up to the open plenum and looking down at the scene. Suddenly, the whole club made sense. The unusually large, blue eyes, twisting horns, pointed ears, and wicked curved fangs. Everything looked insanely professional, "too *real,*" she thought aloud.

Tristian slowly looked up at her with the annoying Ray-Ban's still hiding his eyes. Apparently noticing her rattled expression, he felt his neck then cursed.

"You're right, we should leave. There's a lot I need to explain."

Still in a half-shock, Dylan sat unmoving. Tristian grabbed her forearm, tugging her up and out of the booth. As he guided her back into the club, half pushing, half pulling her, everything seemed to be rolling in slow motion. Time stood still as the girls in cages licked their fingers while slinking their bodies to the haunting tune; organic wings sunken into their porcelain skin like black, shallow tree roots. Men and women were being bitten in the alcoves with sickening pleasure, and the bartender threw fire from his hands over a line of shots for an applauding crowd.

No wonder they had been staring at her. She was a human encroaching on an inhuman space. Dylan, afraid to look anywhere else, stared straight down.

Just as they were close to making it to the entrance, Asher suddenly stepped out of the crowd in front of them.

"Whoa," he drawled. "What's going on here?"

"It's none of your concern. Step aside."

Dylan remained silent, slowly moving her gaze up from the polished floor. Asher shifted his glare towards Dylan as his face fell with uncertainty, then immediately hardened.

"What did you do to her, *Collector*?"

Dylan narrowed her eyes at Asher.

Tristian straightened his shoulders, instinctively gripping Dylan tighter. "Nothing. She's just realizing what this place is."

Asher took a half step forward, blinking his star-shaped pupils like a reptile. Dylan flinched at the small alien act. Tristian gripped Dylan even tighter. "I need you to step back, she's *mine* now."

As if placed on fast-forward, Dylan seemed to snap back into herself.

"What? I'm not yours!" she screamed, squirming in his hold. "Let go! LET... GO!" She elbowed Tristian in the gut and he released her with an *oof.* Dylan took this opportunity to run, while silently thanking Isabel for the self-defense classes.

Sidestepping Asher, she heard him mutter, "Good hit," as she bolted toward the curtain containing the entrance to the paranormal club.

Sliding through at a speed so fast she barely had time to register the need to breathe, let alone figuring out how she was running in these God-awful boots.

She darted past the small red lounge and into the long dark corridor. The hallway seemed to tilt as she willed herself to run faster. Using the cold, stone walls for support, she heard a faint giggle from the strange hostess echoing dementedly all around her. Reaching the metal stairs, she grabbed the handrail and jumped, taking three steps at a time until she arrived at the top. Trance music and musk hit her senses like a wall.

Stumbling, she managed to stand, smoothing her hair and pulling her tube top up. Spying the little black door she came through at the beginning of the night, Dylan raced towards the entrance, bumping into and passing the lot of drunken humans.

Bursting through, she felt the rush of sweet night air and

silence. Feeling like she had escaped a nightmare, she fell against the side of the brick building, willing herself to gather her thoughts.

Listening to her slowing pulse, Dylan couldn't help but analyze her soundings. Streetlights changed, cars honked, billboards blazed, and the moon glowed. Everything was so *normal*, it made whatever had just occurred seem dream-like and… hysterical. A moment passed before a small giggle erupted from her mouth.

Had that really just happened? No…

Composing herself, she pushed off the chilled brick and returned to her normal gait in the direction of her car, choosing denial as her best bet. However, before she was able to get very far on her self-imposed cloud of ignorance, Tristian appeared out of the mouth of the adjacent alleyway, halting her in her tracks.

Her smile vanished as she watched him step toward her, holding up his hands out in front of him.

"Dylan, please. Just let me explain. Let's go get some coffee like you said."

She abruptly turned, only to find herself, once again, face to face with Tristian. A charge of emotions engulfed her. Everything from the night of her alleged mugging came bubbling to the surface. She gasped as he grabbed her wrist in the exact same spot and everything swallowed into blackness.

CHAPTER 3

"The truth does not change according to our ability to stomach it."
Flannery O'Connor

DYLAN woke her mind fuzzy, the last remnants of a dream being chased away by the awareness of her surroundings. She smiled against the pillow she was spooning. It was a nice dream, cuddling on the grass with her mother. She could still feel the warmth of the autumn sunlight behind her childhood home, and hear the sounds of the rustling fallen leaves in the wind, but the details were fading fast even as she tried to recall them. With a mental sigh, Dylan allowed her brain to focus and cautiously opened one eye.

Where am I?

She jerked upright on her elbows. The room was large and dark, and shadows seemed to swallow up the corners. The only sound was a faint buzzing from the ceiling fan.

Straining her eyes to focus, she made out a desk in the corner complete with chair and computer near a large floor to ceiling wall of glass. Bookshelves lined the adjacent wall filled to the brim with novels and notebooks. The very large bed she was lying on had a faint scent like soap, musk, and leather, *like male*.

Dripping bloody fangs, piercing eyes, and porcelain flesh flashed inside her mind's eye and she shrank back, yanking the duvet over her head and giving herself a false sense of security.

What was she even doing here? She had passed out after Tristian had caught up with her... Was this his bedroom? Or had he left her, letting someone—or, some*thing* else grab her instead? She shivered and pushed the dangerous thought from her mind; not that being in Tristian's bedroom was any safer. After seeing him in that club, who knew what the hell he was! Despite whomever's room she was in, she needed to get home, now!

After a couple more seconds of considering her limited choices, she peeked out from under the covers. Her mind continued to flip and tumble with a thousand scenarios—mostly those she had seen in horror films and now wishing she had opted for comedy instead—when she noticed a vague, sliver of light spilling onto the carpet from beyond the cracked doorway.

Throwing off the comforter, she brought her feet to the soft carpet, noting her boots placed carefully beside the bed along with her things. *My phone!*

She snatched up her keys and searched around for her cell. She would call the police then Aria then Isabel. No way was she letting some vampire freak use her as a feeder or ship her off to be some blood slave. She suddenly stopped and examined her naked keys. *Of course.* What kind of kidnapper would he be if he didn't take away her source of communication? And on top of that her pepper spray was gone.

Damn it!

She sat back onto the bed and thought about Plan B, which

basically consisted of running as fast as she could out of here and never looking back. She started to pull on her horrible boots, but found herself observing a spiky heel instead. She stood, aiming them in front of her like a weapon. She probably ran better without them anyway.

Tiptoeing carefully across the room to the door, Dylan peered out into the empty hallway. As she opened the door, it squeaked. The small noise sounded like an explosion compared to the quiet.

After a long, stomach churning moment, she continued down the hallway, gingerly keeping each step light and soft against the floor. Just then Dylan spied a red front door looking like the light at the end of a very dark and creepy tunnel.

"I can't let you leave yet," said a deep voice from behind her, bringing Dylan to an immediate stop mid-stride.

Her stomach dropped at being caught; but, once her mind placed his voice, her body's immediate reaction was to relax and drop her guard. It was just Tristian. Her partner in class. Someone she knew and had a crush on for years. A guy she had thought about touching and kissing in those rare moments they had crossed paths. No, he wasn't a bad guy, he couldn't be...

She felt him step closer. It was the knock in the head that she needed to remember the club and how he had been the one to kidnap her.

He couldn't let her leave, yet? Well, too bad!

Adrenaline pumped hard into her veins, clouding all her thoughts except for one: *run*.

She took off towards the door, but Tristian was quicker. He threw both of his arms around her body, locking her against his hard chest. Dylan thrashed from side to side, screaming at the top of her lungs. He slapped his hand over her mouth, muffling her incessant shrieking. After several seconds of useless moving, her jerks became less and less vigorous as reality sank in. With this strength, he really had to be supernatural.

"You get it out of your system, yet?" Tristian asked, never relenting even a fraction from his immense hold on her. Dylan thrashed once more, for good measure, only making him tighten his grip. "I can stand here all night," he sighed.

She stilled, feeling each hot pant of his breath in her hair.

"I'm going to remove my hand. Are you going to scream?"

Dylan shook her head tersely and his hand slipped from her mouth.

Puffing, Dylan grit her teeth. "What do you want from me?"

"To just listen, but you need to promise to chill out. I have neighbors. And I don't feel like explaining to them why I have a girl exhibiting a psychotic break in my apartment."

Dylan relaxed her features. "*Fine.*"

Tristian released her.

Like hell I'm sticking around for this!

She threw her foot back, knocking him in the groin then darted for the door, dropping her boots along the way.

Slamming into it at full speed, she winced, but immediately realized it wasn't budging. She continued to turn the locks back and forth repeatedly in hopes they'd eventually work. Panicking, she flipped her body in the direction of Tristian.

He chuckled, getting to a slow stand. "You. Stubborn. Girl."

Walking toward her, Dylan's stomach knotted. She was cornered.

Shit! Shit! Shit!

"Stay back or I'll scream," she whimpered, pressing her body against the corner of drywall.

Do not cry. Do not cry, she chanted to herself repeatedly, willing the floodgate of tears to hold.

He frowned slightly and, surprisingly, halted.

"What do you want from me?" she asked again.

He didn't say anything in response. He only tilted his head as if taking her in or sizing her up. She pressed her back further against the wall. His silence scaring her even more.

He suddenly appeared next to her and she screamed, spinning around him and running deeper into his apartment.

She dashed around a large column and found herself in his kitchen that opened up like a fan to a formal dining and living room. She panted and stumbled into the quartz countertop. Realizing her dead end, she spun around only to find Tristian standing opposite the kitchen island.

Dylan sucked in a startled breath and grasped blindingly at the knife rack behind her. She whipped out a bread knife and waved it at him.

"WHAT DO YOU WANT?!"

Tristian leaned against the island counter and sighed as if the entire situation bored him.

"Dylan... I really do just want to talk. That's all. I promise to arrange a cab to take you to your car or where ever you want."

Dylan stared at him for a moment. It was hard to believe that was all he wanted. If he only wanted to talk then why not do it somewhere comfortable, somewhere public. And why on earth did he bring her here unconscious? Had he been the reason she'd fainted?

Her chest heaved quickly and her knife-laden hand shook. She glanced around at her surroundings then back at him. "*Why?*"

He straightened and held his hands up in surrender. "I need to—"

"Explain what I saw," she finished for him. "How am I supposed to believe a word you say after you kidnapped me?!" she trilled.

He smirked at her coldly. "*Kidnapped*? This coming from the girl who passed out in my arms? I would have expected a "thank you" for the grand gesture of not leaving you on the street," he snapped.

She worked the grip on the knife as an inkling of doubt entered her mind. Was it possible she was over exaggerating?

No.

"*Thanked you*?" she hissed incredulously.

"Dylan," he rubbed his lips uncomfortably, "Please. Let's go to the living room. It's right around the corner." He pointed behind himself.

"Let me leave," she pleaded. "This night never happened. We never have to see each other again!"

"You can… but not yet. It's not very hard. I'll do all the talking."

"Fine," she called as his shoulders visibly relaxed. "But here. You can tell me right here." She didn't know what he had in store for her in this living room or why he was so adamant about talking there.

"Dylan," Tristian sighed again. "I'm starting to lose my

patience." She flicked her eyes up to his surprisingly weary expression.

Dylan took a long look at him. Despite the circumstances, she realized there was something about him that she wanted to trust. For the second time that night, she couldn't explain the kindred feeling that seemed to draw her to another....

But then he continued, "Now, sit on the couch and let's talk like civilized creatures before I give you something to actually be frightened of."

She gasped. "That's supposed to convince me you're not evil? That you're someone whom I can trust?"

"Ah," he laughed once, "see, I never told you I wasn't evil, but I swear my intentions are sound."

God, she hoped she wouldn't regret this. Perhaps she was going insane, but she decided to do something she worried she would hate herself for, later.

"Okay," she said hesitantly.

He looked surprised at her assent, but only for a second. "After you," he said, motioning to the living room.

"Nu-huh. You go first." She pointed the knife higher, wondering if it were really true that you needed to steak a vampire in the heart.

He remained hauntingly still for a moment. She worried she'd finally angered him beyond repair with her demands before he turned and walked leisurely away. She followed and thought about running with his back turned, if only she could get the door to work-

"I'll just catch you, Dylan," he singsonged, catching her off guard once again.

Had he heard her thoughts?

He stood next to his black, leather couch, eyeing her. It was then she realized she had stopped following him once she had left the kitchen.

"Might as well get this over with, because you're not leaving until we do."

Holding her eyes on Tristian, she inched closer, passing a beautiful marble table with raw edges and leather chairs in the dining room, then entering the open living room perfectly encased by the stunning LA skyline. His apartment was truly beautiful—all concrete, dark wood, and glass. Her mind briefly wondered how someone in college could afford such a place as she confirmed the room wasn't bound in plastic nor any notes displayed about 'playing a game'; then she felt stupid for thinking such a thought. He was probably much older than he appeared being a "vampire" and all.

She stopped a couple feet away from him and opened her mouth, unable to keep it to herself any longer. "What are you?" she asked, wide eyed.

He smiled creepily as if she'd finally asked the secret question he had been dying to answer.

"What do you think I am, Dylan?"

The way he said her name sent a shiver across her body. She thought about the night as a whole, and even though her answer was the same every time, saying the words: "I think you're a vampire" just sounded idiotic.

He took a step closer and she tensed up, fighting the urge to scream and run.

"Say it, Dylan. I want to hear it from those pretty lips."

"You're a vampire..."

His lips worked as a strange emotion crossed his face that she couldn't name; yet, as quickly as it commenced, it faded— his expression sobering as he leaned even closer. She gulped.

"I'm worse, little girl. I'm a demon."

All the blood quickly drained from her face.

He was a demon. A creature from Hell. The danger that stalks inside shadows and consumes anything living. She should have known. She had felt that darkness radiate off of him in waves of death. Oh God. She wanted to run, to stab him, or even just scream, but she couldn't. She was so scared she was speechless and unable to move. Even if she could run, she knew it would be useless. He had her captive deep in his home and that was that. She didn't stand a chance, not even when she thought he was a vampire. She had only been deluding herself.

She was unequivocally trapped.

He grabbed her hand that held the knife and easily disarmed her, tossing the weapon across the room. He then pulled her shell-shocked body abruptly to the couch and looked down at her harshly.

"Good," he said. "Now listen and *never* forget."

◇◇◇

Now that he had her somewhat shocked enough to subdue her, Tristian sat on the farthest side of the couch and studied her. His eyes roamed over her tight clothes. Her tiny, slender body heated with passionate hate, and her terrified eyes smudged and smoky, highlighting the youthful grey of her eyes. He focused in on the raging pulse in her throat. Having her here, terrified and vulnerable, pleased him so much his own adrenaline picked up. He couldn't tell if it was from the earlier events or the mere fact that she was in his private space.

She was kind of cute, all frazzled and angry in his kitchen, waving the most useless knife he owned at him. He'd never seen her wear makeup like this and the way she manhandled him at the club, crawling along the couch wearing those fuck-me boots, made her look intimidating, domineering, and every bit as powerful as expected.

He wanted more than anything to rip off her clothes and lick the light sheen that blanketed her skin… but knew anything more than a platonic relationship with her would just make things severely unpleasant. Besides, she wasn't like the usual women he slept with. Dylan was reserved, almost frigidly so. Obviously not someone to play with.

Tristian continued to sit silently for a moment, reveling in the way not talking seemed to escalate her fear. He eyed her wary expression, suddenly remembering her remark about him being a vampire. Hah! The thought had been so absurd, he'd almost lost it right then and there.

Still holding back a small smile, Tristian cleared his throat, figuring he had to get it over with. Whether she liked it or not, she was a pawn in a very dangerous game and it was up to him to gain her trust, no matter how much he loved scaring her.

"All right," he breathed. "I'm sure I don't have to explain much…" Tristian stopped. What all did he really need to tell her? The club pretty much explained it all for him. Vampires, sirens, warlocks. Her eyes had been opened enough… yet, she still didn't *know*.

"I get it," she suddenly cut in annoyed, only making him

emit a flicker of a smile at her hostility. "Who was Asher, and why did he call you a Collector?"

Bingo. He pursed his lips into a thin line wanting to convey a sense of betrayal from Asher. Even though, he hated the other demon, he wanted Dylan to think she was one step ahead of him.

"Ah, the basics." He smiled tightly. "Would you care for a drink?" *I know I could*, he mentally added, needing something strong and straight. He started to get up.

"No." She seized hold of his sleeve to halt him. Her fingers grazed his flesh searing the skin with the simple touch. It surprised him so much he felt his mind go blank. Had she intended this reaction? He assessed the moment, noticing she seemed startled as well—quickly withdrawing her hand to her lap and backing further away. "I only want to leave."

Do you now... He lifted an eyebrow.

Clenching his jaw, he continued to the small hutch across the room and pulled out two glasses and a decanter, filling each with two fingers of whiskey. He turned back around to find her eyeing the bread knife across the room before quickly looking away.

Tristian sat and handed her a tumbler. She took it, shooting it back as if she were at a kegger and not sipping a vintage Dalmore.

Oh, screw it, he thought throwing back his as well.

"You're a demon," Dylan said, wincing through the burn in her throat. "What exactly does that mean?"

"Well, I'm not just any demon, but a Soul Collecting Demon," he said with pride.

She suddenly stood and he started to get up, too, when she headed straight for the liquor cabinet and started shakily refilling her glass.

He relaxed against the back of the couch. "We, demons, live off of life Essence. We consume the souls of humans.

She flinched and took a large gulp, polishing off her second glass.

"...Because we are soulless, they naturally become something of value to us, but in the most basic sense, it's our sustenance."

Tristian watched her lean against the hutch and nod, as if the conversation wasn't ludicrous to her human, conditioned mind. Though he did appreciate her receptiveness, as he honestly hadn't known how she would react to the new information. Perhaps she knew about her real life all along? Although, he was fairly certain the liquor helped.

Whatever the reason, she seemed more comfortable around him, even if it was only a fraction. He did need her to trust him, after all.

"We are typically created, not born by conventional means anymore-"

"Created?" she asked, straight up grabbing the decanter and returning to the sofa while cradling it, looking tired and resigned.

"Yeah. It's actually a lot of work to raise a damned spirit, then form it into a body with black magic—but highly profitable if you know how." He shrugged and Dylan's face compressed humorously. Yeah... maybe he'd touch on that subject another time. "Anyway, those who are created are generally weak and have purposes in mind by their creator and can do nothing else, like slaves.

"Wait," Dylan frowned. "Why, if it's a lot of work, do demons create instead of birthing? Can you not procreate?"

"The law isn't exactly keen on powerful, free demons," he said reaching for the decanter. She glared and took a long pull from the crystal top. Tristian decided to forget it and leaned back, rubbing his eyes. Hopefully she'll wait to vomit after she's gone. "Therefore, they regulate this by having the demon 'parents' meet a certain criteria to be allowed to reproduce."

Were they really discussing birthing? They had gotten off track. He didn't really care if she understood anything about the underworld. Maybe, just maybe, he was delaying the inevitable, because telling her this would snowball his objective. Twenty years of anticipation thrown into the balance of a single question: Would she want to know her parents? He didn't know what he'd do if she didn't. "If two extremely powerful demons wanted to make a child, most likely they would be forbidden."

"What if they just did it anyway?" He couldn't stop the smile trying to contort his lips. It was just too easy.

"They'd have to hide or give the child to the Law for their uses—"

"So you're created?"

"My parents were powerful, but not that powerful. I am born, so is your friend from the club—Asher… and well, so are *you*."

Tristian braced himself for a reaction at being a demon, but she was utterly blank. His eyes narrowed in disbelief. He didn't know what he had expected, but no reaction at all? Well, that hadn't even crossed his mind. He almost needed her tears, her horror to cement the omen.

Maybe, no reaction was her reaction. Over the course of his surveillance, he had noticed her lack of emotion. She would smile, laugh, and frown politely, as if she were expected to, but the most emotion he'd ever seen spilling out of her occurred in the club and here in his apartment. It made him wonder if that was how she prevented herself from an outpouring of inexperienced power.

"There are many different races of demons. We are the Collectors. A Collector is contracted out to collect souls for all of the demon worlds. Demons working outside of a legal contract are deemed rogue, and actively hunted by the Shadow Horde and killed.

"So, who dictates all of these laws? Is there like a council or president? Or is it this Shadow Horde?" She took another large swig and licked her lips.

"Ultimate power lies within the Law. They call themselves the Omnipotence or Three Kings. They are the most powerful and keep the populations at a disadvantage by limiting our soul intake." Tristian yawned feeling the heaviness of exhaustion and checked his watch. That went quicker than he thought and surprisingly, Dylan hadn't tried to flee again, which in his book was as good as trust. "Any more questions?"

"So, let's just say I believe all of this," she whispered. "How does a demon take a soul?"

"Through very close contact, a touch, a kiss... depends on the demon."

She touched her lips with a frown. "Are you going to take

my soul now?"

Apparently, he hadn't made himself clear. Tristian closed his eyes and took a deep breath before removing his sunglasses and revealing the horrendous green-eyes complete with the distinct demon-shaped pupil.

"There is a reason you can remember *that* night."

He watched Dylan study his eyes for a moment, feeling a bit awkward and exposed, itching to get this part over with.

"You," she hissed. He almost sighed with relief at her reaction. Pressing herself against the far end of the couch, she pointed the decanter at him and waved it aggressively, sloshing the brown liquid inside. "You attacked me two years ago!" She jumped up, her voice raising an entire octave making Tristian cringe. "W-why?"

Dylan brought the bottle to her lips again and Tristian was suddenly up, towering over her and stopping her from any more self-medication. She didn't even fight him this time. She just crossed her arms and looked... sad.

"You already took it, didn't you," she asked. He realized that was what she thought was going to happen tonight after he'd told her he was a demon. Sucking her blood was one thing, but taking a fundamental piece of a person forever...

"In my defense, I was collecting and I mixed you up with a different contract." He smiled good-naturedly in hopes to lighten her plummeting mood, but the act seemed to have the opposite effect. He added quickly, "There's this aura that resonates around a person when you're designated for their soul. I signed a contract to bring you to the Elementas. I didn't think at the time that the same aura would resonate around you.

Anyway, during the extraction I realized you had no soul, my Unda wasn't working, and you just seemed pissed…"

"I have no soul?"

He cursed under his breath before hastily continuing, "But then I simply knew why. You're Temperance."

Flicking her eyes up. "What? What's a… Temperance?"

"You, your name. Well, before you were called Dylan."

Noting the confused look on her face, he decided for blunt before he completely screwed up.

"Uh, I hate to break it to you, but you're one of us. Your parents are two very powerful demons. The Omnipotence wanted to regulate you, their offspring, for the Law's use-"

"My parents were demons!" she shrieked.

"Not the ones you knew as a child," he blurted before she hyperventilated.

His face compressed with anxiety—he was messing this up. You'd think after many years of anticipating this moment, he'd finally have the whole conversation planned out.

"Your biological parents wanted to protect you from the role you were destined to live out. They hoped that one day you would find that ring," as he gestured to her pink hand with a significantly swollen finger, "in the hopes you would want to find them again. Your real mother gave you to a baby-snatching demon and you, Temperance Elementa, were then switched with a human baby, Dylan Prescott. Of course, when the Omnipotence got a hold of the real Dylan, they realized the child was human, took the soul and eliminated it—"

"Wait up." She blinked rapidly as her eyes glassed over.

He felt like she was about to cry and really didn't want to be here for that. "You're saying I have parents who aren't dead?" she whispered, looking nowhere in particular. "And that I'm a Soul Collecting Demon placed here and no one knows where I have been, except you, for the past twenty-one years?"

"Yes," he sighed a smile, thanking the worlds that at least that part got through to her—who gave a shit about the rest? "But showing up at that club, with that family ring, you made yourself known to quite a few talkative creatures." Cocking his head to the side. "Where did you get that anyway?"

Staring at the ring, she ignored his question. "And I'm in danger from other Collectors? Of being enslaved by the Omni-?"

"Omnipotence, and yes, but as long as you stay with me and we find your parents, you'll be okay," he said as gently as he could, hoping it didn't sound as fake as it felt. She looked down and pressed her hands to her face making odd sounds that Tristian believed to be crying. He reached out to take her swollen hand, but when she looked up he realized she was laughing. She suddenly stopped and recoiled from him as if his touch were acid.

He grit his teeth wondering if she thought this was all some kind of joke. Except the next words that came out of her mouth were anything but.

"You said my parents were two powerful demons, and the power is inherited, well… why am I so normal?" she asked. "I mean, I'm not powerful at all. I barely passed my self-defense class," she chuckled sadly, then frowned.

"I have a hard time believing that. You landed a pretty good kick back there."

Tristian winced pulling on his pants near his groin. He didn't want to tell her her lack of strength confused him too, but he hadn't ever made a point to study the habits of a youth before; other than himself that was, and even his childhood had been an exception.

"Sorry," she whispered sheepishly.

He stepped closer to her and she stiffened. He made a surrendering gesture with his hands as if to show her he wasn't going to bite. Well, he smiled inwardly, maybe not tonight... No, he chastised himself; he couldn't think these thoughts about her.

He mentally erected a wall between them, finding the comforting, yet horribly false words he was searching for.

"You're more powerful than you give yourself credit for," he said cautiously moving to wipe the mascara-lined tear trail from her cheek with his thumb.

She didn't jerk away this time, and he had to bite back a smile. "Most of us begin intensive training at sixteen, steal our first soul at eighteen, and when we turn immortal at twenty-five is when we crescendo at our peak of abilities and stay there as long as we continue to consume Essence. So, don't expect to take over the worlds, just yet."

She released a single laugh, but sobered quickly. "Wait, immortal?" She licked her soft lips.

Tristian suddenly felt the need to taste her lips to feel if they were as soft as they looked. Shaking his head at the unnecessary thought, he moved to the hutch, returning the half empty decanter—needing space because he actually might kiss her if he got too close.

"We don't grow old in the mundane sense. However, we look and feel physically twenty-five years-old and stay forever that way."

"How old are you?"

Tristian looked back at her. "I'm much older than you. Can I see your hand? It seems swollen."

Dylan, accepting his deflection, nodded and slowly lifted up her hand as Tristian began to inspect it.

Flipping her hand gingerly, "It doesn't hurt?" he asked.

She shook her head while shifting her gaze between him and her hand.

"Huh. Oh…" He leaned in. "You're bleeding."

Dylan withdrew her hand promptly and examined the lacing cuts on her finger around the ring. "It must be the band." She wiggled it off with a wince. "Why don't I heal fast like you?"

Snatching the ring out of her grip, he eyed the dented band. "A lot changes when you turn."

Unlatching the silver chain from around his neck, he slid the ring on and placed it around her neck.

Her entire body went rigid and he sensed her increasing breath. Staying within an inch of her face, he plucked a loose strand of hair dangling near her astonished eyes and pushed it behind her ear. Her face in turn seeped to crimson as he continued to examine the soft lines of her delicate features. It kind of amused him how uncomfortable she got around him.

Bringing himself back down to the present, he tightened his lips and sat down feeling for his sunglasses. When he didn't immediately touch them, he panicked before remembering that he took them off deliberately. He must be exhausted because he had never forgotten to put his sunglasses back on in front of another creature before.

Setting them back in place, "It's going to be okay," he sighed slightly out of breath. "Your life hasn't changed; only your awareness of it. I'll help keep the others away."

"Why do you wear sunglasses all the time?" she asked, sitting down next to him. "Was it to keep me from recognizing you?"

"Yes and no. If I stare a human in the eye, it's easy to get lost and start stealing their Essence. I'm skilled, but still not quite able to control that part." He laughed inwardly. Sometimes even he was surprised at the bullshit that flowed freely from his mouth.

"Why wear them now, then?" Dylan reached up to slip them off, but he evaded her and quickly stood again.

Dammit. It was time for her to leave.

"It's habit," he lied, now suddenly the uncomfortable one.

She felt for the ring now dangling around her neck and bit her lip, making him look away and run his fingers tersely through his hair.

"So, what now?"

He turned back to face her. "Whatever you want. Like I promised."

"I want to meet my parents. How do we do that?"

He grinned at her obvious answer. "Okay but first-"

"Ah crap, are they like super evil overlords or something?"

He smirked, shaking his head. "Not exactly. I just need some sleep, then maybe some coffee? Plus," he cocked his head to the side while narrowing his eyes, "don't we have some papers to write-"

Dylan laughed nervously then let her head fall in her hands, groaning.

"Are you all right?" He crouched at her feet, but her head instantly snapped up causing him to jerk at the almost collision.

"Oh!" She reached out and grabbed his shoulders making him flinch. Clearing her throat, she withdrew her hands and crossed them over her chest. "I'm sorry, I didn't realize you were that close." Her face turned bright red again.

He stood and held out a hand. "Come on, it's already four in the morning. You can have my bed. I'll sleep in the library."

"What happened to calling me a cab or taking me wherever I wanted to go?" she lilted in jest.

Her light attitude surprised him enough that it took him a moment to realize she was probably just drunk.

"You're more vulnerable at night. I'd feel better if we traveled around during the day."

"We?"

She took his outstretched hand and he pulled her up to a standing position close, almost too close, to his body. He could feel the heat rise from her skin as the smell of her shampoo assaulted him. The concoction was insanely intoxicating.

"Get use to me," he rasped. "I'm not leaving your side from now on."

"I don't have a choice in this? Er... staying, I mean."

"You always have a choice, Dylan."

She nodded, but didn't look too convinced.

"Do you want to leave?" he asked genuinely curious. He knew she should, but he couldn't make himself tell her to.

Not surprisingly, her face turned bright red again, causing him to ponder briefly how many times she needed to blush before she became permanently red like that.

She opened her mouth about to say something, but shut it again. He cleared his throat and rubbed his neck before running his nails across his chin.

"I'll stay," she whispered looking into his eyes. "If that's okay with you."

He felt her words were pregnant with more meaning, but brushed it to the side as a useless thought.

"Yeah, this way." He pointed back the way they came with his head maintaining eye contact. She offered a small smile, pulling her honey hair to the side and exposing her long neck. Yet another place he wanted to taste.

Damn, she's beautiful.

"Hey," Dylan said. "I thought you said you didn't drink coffee."

"I lied," he said dryly.

CHAPTER 4

"Last night I wept. I wept because the process by which I have become woman was painful. I wept because I was no longer a child with a child's blind faith. I wept because my

eyes were opened to reality..."
Anaïs Nin

DYLAN awoke in the same king-sized bed she had been in earlier that morning, but now had a feeling of more security despite the unusual scent. Not quite ready to get up, she spooned the fluffy down pillow, recalling her disturbing dreams of vampires, werewolves, demons, and angels.

After a few minutes, she began blinking her eyes in the direction of the sun. Sitting up, she looked around while taking in the details of Tristian's large minimalist bedroom. Besides the wall packed with books everything was very... bare. The bed had a tufted leather headboard that matched a desk chair and dresser. All of the furniture seemed very expensive.

I guess soul collecting pays well, she thought as she moved to the edge of Tristian's bed and stretching wide—curling her hands and feet.

Smiling at the seductive scent of coffee, she got up and walked to the wall of glass, where she spotted a button for the power shade. Brilliant rays flooded the bedroom as the beige shade retracted into the tall ceiling. Gazing at the hazy Los Angeles morning skyline, her eyes shot wide at the sheer drop.

Whoa.

They were really high up. Her stomach dropped and Dylan took a deep breath as she slowly backed away. Heights were never her thing.

Ambling to the opposite side of the room, she found herself at a junction of three doors. She tried the one on the right, which opened to reveal row after immaculate row of suits, t-shirts, jeans, shoes, and dress shirts all on wooden hangers and organized by color. You know, if you considered, black, white, and gray colors.

Feeling as if she was treading on private space, she vacated the closet and opened the opposite door; another closet. This one was empty but for her clothes from the night before which had been hung neatly.

Hmm, when did he do that?

Quickly yanking her jeans and top off the hangers, she then tried the third door. Finding a light switch, she stepped into the spacious en-suite bathroom. Quartz vanities lined both sides of the bathroom with "his" and "hers" stone bowl sinks. A very large glass box, or shower, stood in the middle with a Jacuzzi tub. A water closet was positioned on the other side.

Locking the door behind her, she caught a glimpse of herself and gasped.

"Oh, dear God," she groaned.

She really hoped she didn't look like this last night. Demon or not, Tristian was still a hot guy and hot guys weren't supposed to see girls like this; and *this* was just horrifying—her hair was a giant mess and the once sexy, smoky eye make-up now dripped down to her chin from sweat and tears. Pursing her lips, she snatched Tristian's toothpaste and used her finger to brush her teeth with a scowl. Oh well... it wasn't like he was interested in her anyway!

Peeling off the large T-shirt and boxers Tristian had loaned her, she stepped in the shower. It had one of those large rain shower-heads, much nicer than the generic ones at her apartment. Down at her feet were a few green bottles. Flipping open the cap on one, she inhaled the '*Morning Mint*' aloe, mandarin, and mint infused body wash.

She lathered her body and thought of the previous night. After he had escorted her back to his room and tossed her some of his clothes, it gotten awkward. Really awkward.

It was almost like he didn't want to leave or get too close. He just stood there, making small talk. They talked about school, their majors, living in LA; hell, they even talked about the thirty percent chance of rain for the next day. All the while, he stood next to the door like a curious, but scared, cat. She didn't know whether to be flattered or creeped out. Was he looking for an invitation? Or was he simply nervous about leaving her alone in his bedroom?

Probably the latter.

He was miles out of her league. She couldn't imagine him wanting her. Particularly, if she looked like a hooker that had gotten caught in the rain.

Toward the end of the conversation, she could barely keep her eyes open thanks to liquor. He seemed to take the hint because that was when he bade her goodnight. The last thing she remembered was the highlighted morning sky bleeding through the window shade.

Ten minutes later, and smelling insanely like Tristian, she slid on her skinny jeans and tube top. Still feeling a bit naked, Dylan snatched the t-shirt off the floor and slipped it on as well. Fingering her bangs, she pulled her long, blonde locks into a messy bun at the top of her head using the elastic band on her wrist.

Looking at herself once more with a sigh, she left the luxurious bathroom and followed a savory scent down the hall—her mouth watering as she neared the kitchen.

"I hope you like breakfast tacos," Tristian muttered without looking up from dicing tomatoes with an unusual knife. The hilt was made out of some kind of white stone and the tip looked sharp as hell.

"They're my favorite, thanks," she said with a small smile while gingerly sliding onto one of the circular barstools at the middle island. Dylan eyed the knife rack behind him, noticing it was conveniently bare. "Hope you don't mind. I used your shower."

"Not at all." He wiped off the blade and set it down far away then set a plate of fruit in front of her. "I was going to offer it anyway."

"Your place is amazing. Business must be good," she mumbled around a full mouth of strawberries while trying to steer the conversation away from her complexion... that apparently needed washing.

"You could say that... Do you want some coffee?" He set down the French press returning to the eggs. "Milk? I don't have any sugar."

"I'll get it." Moving to the glass front of his Subzero fridge, she spotted the milk and made her coffee.

"I usually don't eat this much in the morning. Mostly fruit and coffee," she rambled.

"Oh," he froze slightly, "I don't get to cook much. This is actually the first time using the pans."

"Really?" She gestured wildly with her coffee spoon, "Then I plan to eat a lot!" He returned her smile while buttering some tortillas. "I just hope you washed the pans first. Aria, my roommate, kept forgetting to do that when we moved in together," she teased while taking a sip of her coffee and watching him through the thick, delicious steam. "I kept finding bits and pieces of dust or plastic in our food. Every time I found a hair, she'd just tell me to shut up and accept the extra fiber." Dylan giggled and shook her head at the memory.

Looking at her, he cocked his head to the side, then turned his attention back to the eggs. He seemed to be contemplating something as he stared at the sizzling pan for a moment and scratched the nape of his neck. With his arm raised, her eyes roamed down to the exposed flesh of pure muscle just above his jeans. Heat hotter than her coffee crawled up her cheeks; but, before she had a chance to avert her eyes, he picked up the skillet and dumped the contents into the adjacent trash compactor.

"What are you doing?!" she sputtered incredulously as he turned on the faucet and began rinsing the pan. "Did you-"

"That was just the test batch," he interjected casually as he slid the skillet back on the flame and cracked several eggs, finishing off the carton. She bit her bottom lip to stifle a laugh but her smile couldn't be contained.

He glanced at her a couple times. "Yeah," he shrugged, "I forgot to clean the pans."

Dylan shook her head still laughing at him. The atmosphere was instantly lighter and she pushed off from the counter to help as he restarted the eggs. She toasted the tortillas and seasoned the Pico. Working around him was oddly comfortable. She was almost able to forget about the whole situation that occurred the night before. Except every time she looked at him, her fingers itched to remove those ever-present sunglasses. He always seemed to catch her looking and would smile suspiciously, boasting the most adorable dimples.

Sitting at the island, Tristian assembled two tacos and set them on her plate. Unable to contain herself any longer, she boldly slid off his sunglasses, setting them down on the white quartz countertop above his plate. Tristian tensed slightly, but didn't object, only frowning before picking up his taco—slightly fumbling its contents.

At that moment, Dylan wished she knew what he was thinking. Why did he feel compelled to constantly wear his sunglasses? She didn't buy the lame explanation he gave her the night before. Other than the unusual pupils, his eyes were breathtaking. She couldn't imagine ever wanting to hide them.

"Um…"

"Yeah?" he mumbled through a full mouth, glancing at her and making eye contact. She felt herself melt slightly in the deep green abyss of his eyes.

She cleared her throat, breaking the connection to stare at her plate. "How come you guys have those eyes? Mine are just normal and *gray*." She crinkled her nose as she moved to take another mouth-watering bite. First time cooking or not, he was amazing at making tacos. He set down his taco and faced her, wiping his mouth with a paper towel.

"We get the color of our eyes after collecting our first soul."

"Oh." She didn't know what she expected but that wasn't it.

"Part of the first soul you collect becomes a part of you. It stays with you forever and can give you strength or define the basis of who you are."

"It changes your personality?" she asked.

"Not always."

She nodded, despondently, picking a piece of cilantro off a tomato.

"It's not something you need to worry about now. Your eyes are anything but normal…"

She found herself returning to look at him.

"I think they're beautiful."

She felt heat blossom across her face from his complement as she quickly turned her head back in the direction of her half eaten taco and muttered, "Thanks."

His elbow brushed her arm and the air seemed to grow thick at their close proximity. She thought she could actually see the sparkling electricity wafting between them; shocking her skin with each casual brush of his skin. Her heart pounded, causing her chest to leap with each pressing throb. Hunching her back, she tried to hide her obvious nervousness, eating like Quasimodo over her plate.

Ugh! Why can't I be normal? Or just plain indifferent to my "Mr. Dark and Mysterious" ... Wait... My? He's not mine!

She groaned inwardly as they finished their meal in the mutual awkward silence. Her mind was swamped with a series of incoherent, rambling thoughts that she couldn't seem to stop.

Leaving the apartment, they stopped at the infamous red door from the previous night. She was about to ask why the door didn't budge, *what magic he used,* when she saw him turn the lock and throw his body into opening it.

"This thing sticks all the time." He grinned playfully while holding the door for her. They stepped across a small foyer to elevator doors. After traveling down from the 33rd floor, Tristian drove her to her car that was still parked down the street from *Spin*.

Unlocking her Jetta, Dylan fondled her keys, feeling more secure with her pepper spray and phone.

Pivoting around to face Tristian, she said, "Um, thanks for everything," as she waved her hand in the air to accentuate the 'everything'. "I guess, I'll be seeing you later?"

He smiled back through the open, black Audi S4 window. "Yeah, I'll call you," he smirked, then sped off leaving Dylan silently cursing herself for sounding so *needy*.

Pulling onto the 10, Dylan's mind was turning at supersonic speed with all the new information she had attained. Part of her still wanted to laugh it all off as insanity, but what about the eyes, the disappearing vampire bite, or his speed? Or the fact that a "vampire" anything was in the equation. There was just too much to believe otherwise. Part of her had always believed in angels and demons, just as much as she believed in heaven and Hell. She just never imagined them with normal bodies, walking around on the streets where she lived.

Deep in her thoughts, Dylan flicked on her blinker and switched lanes. A horn blared and she jumped, jerking the car back in her original lane.

"Shit!" she screamed only slightly surprised at her piercing retaliation as the driver of a silver Miata zoomed into her line of sight flipping her the bird.

"Oh, real classy, lady!" Dylan yelled at the closed window. Her adrenaline surged as she tightened her hold on the leather steering wheel. A loud ringing reverberated through the car's speakers at first startling her then causing her to laugh exhaustedly as she hit the "pick up" button on the steering wheel.

"Hey," she breathed.

"Hey, sweet pea!" squealed an overly excited woman on the other end. Her grandmother.

"Hey, Isabel. What's up?"

"Not a lot. On my way to the supermarket and had some time to kill in the car. Thought we could chat if you're not too busy…"

"No, I'm not busy, just on my way home," *from a boy's house and you definitely wouldn't approve.*

"Oh good! How was your first class yesterday?" *Ah, damn! I forgot about the assignment.* Dylan groaned.

"Uh oh. That bad?"

"N-no, the class was fine. The semester is based on group projects and the teacher thought it to be *fun* to pair us with someone we don't know…" She bit at her chapped lips as she wove through traffic. "Anyways, long story short, he bailed and so I had to meet up with him last night to do the assignment." *And apparently I'm a demon!*

"Were you both able to work things out?"

"Uh, yeah."

"Hmph," her grandma grunted.

"What? What, *hmph*?"

"You're just now coming home?" *Oh crap.* "Dylan," her voice suddenly stern, "You were with him all night? Are you being safe?"

"Isabel!" Dylan shrieked, horrified and feeling the urge to run her car into the silver Miata in front of her just to divert the conversation. "This is not a conversation I'm going to have with you!"

"Sweetheart, I'm only looking out for you because I love you. Getting pregnant or an STD is a serious ordeal. You still have college to finish, your masters, PHD *and* a career. Please be smart and use protection."

At a stop light Dylan started pounding her head against the steering wheel. Making little bleeps with the horn.

"You're probably trying to rip your ears off right now." She heard her grandmother sigh. "I just haven't heard you talk about a boy since that Jacob Mancuso in the sixth grade. So, it must be more than *just* a boy."

Dylan grimaced at the mention of the little twit's name. She was right about one thing, Dylan hadn't mentioned a guy to her grandmother since middle school. But Jacob Mancuso had been the last person she had tried to date because he had made her middle and high school days a living hell. He was that older "Mr. Popular": blonde, tan, bleached smile, outrageously wealthy and sickeningly beautiful. His father was a fashion photographer, his mother an empty-headed model.

Jacob had set his eyes on Dylan and after a whole week of holding hands and sitting together at lunch, yes true love, he had asked her to the Spring Fling. She had said yes and met him at the auditorium on that Friday at eight p.m. She wore a jean skirt with rhinestone detail and a dark purple silk halter with cascading ruffles down the front. Her hair was styled in an array of tight curls with a matching purple gem barrette. He took her hand, as always, and led her to the center of the dance floor where they slow danced to *Hoobastank*.

Towards the end of the song, his hands slid down her back and grabbed her butt. Not in a gentle, 'this is a slow dance and you're my girl way', but full throttle *'you're my bitch'* ass grab. She freaked more out of shock than anything else and pushed him away, turning around to hide her blazing red cheeks. Just before she turned back to face him, he yanked her jean skirt down and whispered in her ear something along the lines of, "Nobody says no to me, *bitch*." As if the world was working against her, the heart shaped spotlight that illuminated random couples had shone at the precise moment on their little spectacle.

Jacob howled with laughter and pointed. To her horror everyone turned and gawked at 'Dirty Dee.' Dylan had worn underwear that spelled "Wednesday" in large letters across the butt.

Like who really wears those things on the right day?!

From then on she was relegated to the less popular side with no boyfriends and less friends, and that was putting it mildly. Thank God, she had a chance to start over in college. A blaring car horn yanked her out of her reverie.

"Yeah, well there was a reason I stayed away from the Brentwood boys," she told her grandmother while being purposely vague.

She had never told Isabel about the hazings she had endured through her formative years; but, she had a suspicion that Isabel already knew. Especially, after repeatedly coming home crying sporting various foods and, once, super glue stuck in her hair.

"But it wasn't like that last night. We met at a bar and I, uh, drank a bit too much and he let me crash at his place, which was right down the street. He even gave me his bed and slept on the couch."

"That's nice," Isabel said dryly, almost as if she didn't believe her. "So, what's his name? He's an Anthropology major, I'm assuming, so you both have that in common."

"Yeah, same major," Dylan sighed. "His name is Tristian Stewart. He's... foreign, tan, has dark hair and absolutely *stunning* green-eyes." She felt her stomach flip at the mention of his eyes. That guy had no idea how beautiful he was... or maybe he did. Taking a fistful of the white tee he loaned her, she brought it to her nose relishing his unusual scent.

"Foreign? Where is he from?"

"Um... somewhere in Europe. I didn't ask," Dylan frowned. "He doesn't really have a distinguishable accent."

"Well, if he's caught your discerning eye, then I say he's a keeper. You just better bring him by for some savory banana muffins so I can meet him," her grandmother crooned.

"Sure thing, Isabel," she smirked. "We're still getting together for lunch next week?" Dylan asked, as she turned into her apartment complex.

"I think so. We may have to do it the following week, but give me a call Monday and we'll set a day and time that works for us both."

"'Kay, Love you."

"Love you, sweet pea."

Once she had gotten back to her apartment, Aria was there and practically jumping up and down asking how her night was. She made sure to leave out most of the details except for the dance with Asher, the kiss, and staying at Tristian's. She had told her best friend the same story—that she had gotten way too drunk and Tristian, who lived nearby, took her back to his place and gave her his bed to sleep it off. It seemed like a plausible story. Even perceptive Isabel seemed to believe it. After Aria had essentially planned their wedding, Dylan waved her off and the girls went back to their boring lives.

The next week went by pretty routinely. Tristian had said he was never leaving her side, yet the strange guy seemed to have disappeared. Not even a text or pocket dial… if phones still did those. She felt a tad ridiculous stewing over if he'd call or not. He'd never made any promises or declarations of love that would signify any reason, at all, for this sudden infatuation.

It was Saturday morning and Dylan was trying to think of any excuse to miss the Pilates class. Her body ached and her head pounded from attending the Chi Alpha Delta sorority's first of many rush parties that summer. Not that she was rushing. But, Aria had pleaded with her to go and keep her company and also help fill the place. Dylan drank herself into an incoherent stupor and passed out on one of the sorority sisters, Emily Lam's, bed. Around six a.m. she had made her way home and collapsed into yet another black hole of sleep.

At eleven a.m. Dylan's head felt heavy, but better than it had earlier. She rolled out of bed and threw on her blue yoga pants, yellow tank and unclasped Tristian's silver chain, letting it land on the dresser atop her ring.

On her way to the university gym, she stopped at the local coffee shop to grab a latte and relax her mind before the strenuous class. Sitting at one of the outside tables, Dylan held the steaming cup with both hands and closed her eyes, taking in the soothing, bitter aroma and warm breeze. Her senses were sharpening, thanks to the caffeine, and she let her thoughts wander to Tristian's delicious scent. She hated that she didn't smell like him anymore, and hated even more that he hadn't called. Yes, hate was an easier emotion to deal with over whatever it was she felt for him.

The adjacent chair yanked from her table caused her eyes to flick open.

"*Daniel*, right?" the girl spouted with a gigantic condescending smile slapped across her face. Great. "Miss Glare" from class. Dylan just sat there dumbfounded. She was never good at confrontation. Every time she was picked on in school, Dylan clammed up. Like right now.

"Well, *Daniel*." She clasped her hands together and rested her elbows on the metal table, pointing her two index fingers at Dylan. "I know you didn't have a choice other than to be partners with Tristian but I need for you to know he's mine, and I have no intention of sharing."

"It's Dylan," Dylan whispered, rolling her eyes. Of course he had a girlfriend. She was probably pissed Dylan had stayed the night there.

"What?"

"Dylan," she enunciated louder, with pride. Anger boosted her confidence and before she was able to filter her thoughts, words came pouring out. "Not *Daniel*… I'm sorry if you feel threatened about me staying there on Monday... but we're partners in class, nothing more—and like *you* just stated… not my choice." Her heart was racing and she knew she needed to get out there fast.

The girl's perfectly shaped eyebrows shot up. "You stayed at his apartment?"

Shit.

"Why else would you be sitting here, staking claim?" she asked honestly.

She opened her mouth and Dylan didn't doubt she had some stuck up retort, they all did, but Dylan was way too hungover for this. She glanced at her watch and decided she would be a few minutes early for Pilates. "Look," Dylan's voice seemed to shrink back into its usual protective hiding place, "there's nothing going on between us, but I have to go. Enjoy your coffee." She quickly got up and retreated towards her car with her tail tucked between her legs.

Once she was out of sight, she threw her back against her car and sighed a huge smile. *That felt good,* she thought still chuckling at the look of horror on the girl's face. Whatever her name was just seemed speechless after hearing Dylan had stayed at Tristian's. She probably didn't believe the 'nothing happened' and thought they had slept together.

Her mood suddenly sank. He had a girlfriend, he'd cheated on her at the club and Dylan had just rubbed it in the girl's face. So maybe he hadn't cheated with Dylan, but that girl didn't know that.

Look who's the bully now.

Yanking her car door open, she landed inside and jammed her key into the ignition. Tristian was making it very easy to hate him. Jerk.

Walking past the weary students working hard on the equipment, Dylan arrived to the mirrored studio where she attended her weekly yoga class. Her anger had died down on the way as she reminded herself: he wasn't someone she would ever allow herself to date anyway, so why be mad?

Stepping through the threshold, Dylan frowned and glanced at her watch—*12:20.*

I'm not that early, she thought as she scanned the dark empty room. *Damn, maybe I got the day wrong—he did say Saturday, right?*

"You made it!" called a familiar voice from behind her.

Dylan turned, not exactly relieved, and started smiling like an idiot.

"Hey. Am I too early or something?" she asked glancing at her watch again. "I mean it's only ten minutes before the time you told me." Garret walked past her flipping on the lights while juggling an arm full of foam mats.

"It's possible you may be the only one who showed."

"Oh, I guess I'm just a sucker for a good workout," she

deadpanned. *Why am I here?* She groaned inwardly. So far the day had proven a failure and she couldn't decide which poor decision to blame.

"Really?" Garret asked while laying two of the mats out. "Because you look hung over."

Dylan walked to the mirror. "Is it that obvious?" she asked examining her face while pushing at the dark circles under her eyes, realizing she did look like hell.

"I'll take it easy on you today then." He sat down on a mat and tapped the other, motioning for her to sit. "So, where'd you go last night?"

They both lay down and he lifted one of his legs flexing and pointing his toes. Dylan mirrored his moves as a soothing melody of rainwater and piano filled the room.

"A rush party-"

"A rush party?" he interjected with a wry look. "You don't come across as one of those girls."

"I'm not!" she scoffed. "Do you know my friend Aria?" Garret then switched legs, as did Dylan. "I pulled her to a couple of your yoga classes."

"Is she the loud redhead?"

"Yeah, tall, Asian, pretty obnoxious."

"Yeah," he laughed. "She's hard to miss." They switched to bicycling their legs.

"Well," she puffed, "She's in a sorority and dragged me along to act like I'm rushing."

"Why?"

"Probably to just help make the party more of a success, I guess." He switched to one pointed leg moving in painfully slow circles.

"You didn't ask?"

"No… she asked for my help and I said sure. What are best friends for, right?"

Switching to the other leg. "You're a better person than I am. I hate those rush parties, even if it were my own brother begging me to go."

Setting their legs back down, Garret started to instruct her by kneeling beside her. Even though his perfect body was hovering over her, she felt only a slight flush. Nothing like what she experienced around Tristian, and that made her frown. Was he ruining other guys for her already?

"All right. Bring your legs up, keep your back flat and stretch your arms past your body."

She nodded and did what he said.

"Uh, you okay?" he asked.

"Yeah, why?"

"You were kind of... glaring at me."

Her face scorched and she pulled her bottom lip to the side. "I'm s-sorry. I just have a lot on my mind, I guess..."

"Fair enough," he mumbled, suddenly serious.

He checked her posture, pulling her arms a bit higher while resting a hand on her stomach. Her muscles involuntarily contracted at his touch as she focused on the ceiling and breathed slowly. Okay, so maybe Tristian hadn't totally ruined her. Garret finally gave her a curt nod before moving into the same position.

"Now keep flexing your abs and bicycle your legs."

"I don't think you're going easy on me anymore," Dylan joked, but Garret just continued to huff while counting down.

Dylan had her mouth agape, already feeling the trembling effects of her hangover. "So, what does Garret do on Friday nights?"

"Uh... I, uh, usually just hang out with a few friends." She looked over at him. It almost seemed as if he were uncomfortable talking about his life. Or maybe he just didn't like getting glared at.

"Sorry, I didn't mean to ask about your personal life. I just… I know nothing about you. Well, except for the fact you seem to be really good at all things fitness."

Setting his feet back down he looked at her collapse. "No, I asked about your night, so it's only fair you get to know about mine. To be honest, I'm not that open with anyone, so don't take it personally."

She raised an eyebrow, but figured he probably didn't want to elaborate with a stranger. A stranger that he hugged and dragged to all his classes. But she decided to drop it for now.

"So… what's next teacher?"

He smirked and guided her through a few more moves. After thirty painful minutes, Dylan's body had completely transformed into Jell-O and seemed to be sweating alcohol from every pore.

"All right, let's do the same meditation as in Yoga class."

"Thank, God," she groaned, dropping her arms and legs flat to the mat.

They moved into the Savasana yoga pose, which was basically a laying position with your arms and legs spread eagle—her now favorite part of Pilates.

"Remember to breathe in and out deeply, keeping your attention within your body."

They were both silent in meditation for a bit, which gave Dylan time to think about her unusual personal discoveries. Her hectic summer schedule and time away from demons, mythical creatures, clubs, and dazzling skyscraper palaces kept her from pondering it too deeply; almost to the point of forgetting it even happened. How did she know, really know, everything Tristian said was true? That she didn't bump her head or accidentally get slipped acid at the beginning of the night? Or what if it was all a huge prank? Definitely kind of elaborate, but she was sure Ashton Kutcher could pull it off. It wasn't the first time the thought had come to mind, and the more time away, the more it seemed plausible.

She licked her lips, tasting the saltiness of her sweat and feeling even more uncomfortable; not from the floor, awkward conversation, or even from the nagging hangover, but because she knew, without a doubt, she hadn't been drugged or pranked.

"Relax your feet," Garret's voice broke her thoughts.

"Huh?" she snapped jerking her head in his direction and instantly regretting the movement.

"Your feet. Relax them," he said with a low laugh.

"Oh," she tittered and repositioned herself back to spread eagle or Savasana pose, "Right."

"Relax your legs."

"Relax your abdomen."

"Relax your chest.

"Relax your arms."

"Relax your face."

"Continue to breathe in and out. Feel your body become as light as a feather."

They breathed in comfortable silence for several minutes and Dylan realized this was just what she needed after last night.

"Dylan?" Garret said

"Hmm?" She still had her eyes closed, unwilling to move any of her now jelly-filled limbs.

"I brought you some water."

Dylan cracked open one eye. "Oh, thanks." She stretched and sat up feeling like a real life 'Gumby'.

"That meditation really relaxes me," she giggled tremulously, taking the water.

"Have you eaten?" Garret asked while rolling up his mat. Dylan got up and started to roll hers.

"Um, No. I only had time to grab some coffee before

coming here." Standing she gave him the mat and finished the miniature bottle of water he had brought her. Dylan frowned as he fumbled the mat. "Are you supposed to eat before or something? Because this is my first time practicing Pilates..."

He chuckled under his breath. "No, I just figured it's lunch time and maybe you would want to check out this new organic café down the street called *Fresh*?"

"Oh, sure, um..." A flashback of her hideous school days and the date that brought it all on passed through her mind. Wait... was this a date? She recoiled inwardly, scared to have her college days ruined as well. But she was older. He was older. They weren't in high school anymore. Smiling to herself and feeling cautiously optimistic, she figured it was probably about time she started dating.

"I definitely need to shower first." She held out her hand. "Give me your phone."

He hastily dug into his pocket to fish for his phone. After a few scrolls and clicks, Dylan handed it back.

"I put my phone number in there with my address, pick me up in like thirty?"

A smile spread across his face as his shoulders visibly relaxed. "Sounds good. Pick you up at 1:30."

They started out the door and Dylan boldly turned to Garret. "There wasn't any Pilates class, was there?"

"There was." He fumbled the foam mats again as he reached for the light switch. Dylan nodded like she didn't just make an ass of herself. Damn, she was on a roll today... "But you might have been the only one who knew about it."

She giggled again as her face peaked to an optimum shade of red. "I'll see you soon," she said, feeling like this was someone who she should pursue—someone single and... well... human.

CHAPTER 5

"I desire the things that will destroy me in the end."
Sylvia Plath

DYLAN went on the non-eventful lunch date with Garret. The beginning had been slightly uncomfortable and, at one point, she had actually danced around him when he tried to pull out her chair. After that, she told herself to relax.

Although she had been initially attracted to him, their conversation flowed and she found herself wanting him more as a friend than anything else. They just didn't have the *spark* that Tristian evoked—which irked her. She wanted to like sweet, calm, *single* Garret.

Surprisingly, they had a lot in common. He had been in a camping accident when he was just a kid and lost his family as well. But, unlike her, he didn't have an awesome grandmother to take him in. As a result, he bounced from foster family to foster family until he was seventeen and became emancipated. He kept a close relationship with his most recent foster parents, even after leaving for college. He considered them his adoptive parents and they considered him their son, even though they had never made it official.

Just knowing someone else had gone through something similarly horrific helped Dylan open up about her past a bit more than she normally did. For the past ten years, she'd perfected the act of hiding her emotions; relying on the façade that got her through hell and back. It was strange talking with someone who wasn't charging by the hour and willing to listen—wanting to listen—without judging her. She could feel her armor cracking a bit more each day and feared the moment it would be broken… causing her to be vulnerable to life again.

Garret and Dylan had agreed to another date. She just couldn't seem to get Tristian out of her head but she needed to. He had a girlfriend he had cheated on… definitely not someone she should even associate herself with. So, even if Garret ended up being the means to rid her mind of those beautiful green eyes, so be it.

"You think he'll tell you why he hasn't called?" Aria asked, while she grabbed a cup of coffee at the small beverage and snack cart near their Behavior Ecology class.

"Keep it down," Dylan hissed. "What if he's around here… or better yet one of his *followers*."

"Oh, shut up. At least then he'd be forced to tell you," her friend chortled, stirring her coffee with a cluster of wood stirrers.

"Well, he doesn't *owe* me an explanation. He did me a favor, that's all. Plus, he has a girlfriend. He shouldn't call me." Dylan didn't know who she was trying to convince. She had thought there was something between her and Tristian, maybe something small, but still something. Perhaps she was wrong. She must have said or done something that turned him off that morning. After removing his sunglasses, he had begun acting weird and, she thought, almost cold. Maybe that was why he was keeping a distance. She frowned. Since when did she dwell on guys? Let alone cheating guys like him?

"Don't down play this, you totally dressed up for class today," said Aria, leaning in. "You even said because of him your 'date' was spoiled." She threw in some air quotations around the word date.

Damn the payback of confiding.

Yes, she did dress up slightly. She wore her favorite black Chucks and jeans, but switched it up with a white racerback tank that was embellished with sequins. This was miles ahead of her usual jeans and sweatshirt ensemble.

"Fine! What do you want me to say? That I think he's sexy as hell and I even pondered buying the same body wash because I like his scent so much? Now would you let it go already?" Dylan said, maybe a bit too loud. She didn't understand why her friend was pushing this.

"I like your *scent* too," said a husky male voice from behind her. "What is it? Coconut and magnolia?"

Aria's eyes bulged, rounding as wide as a fish. Dylan cringed, knowing exactly why and who it was. Prickly fingers of heat traveled up her neck and slapped her cheeks. What was she thinking? She liked his scent?!

Oh no. I think I'm going to throw up... Now wait, did he just admit to smelling me?

Mentally she smacked herself on the head.

Girlfriend. He has a girlfriend!

She took a deep breath and turned around slowly, only to find Tristian leaning lazily against the wall wearing Ray-Ban's, dark jeans, and a black tee that stretched deliciously over his muscles.

She felt her knees weaken. *Oh God, I am ruined.*

"Morning, gorgeous," he said, as an impish grin flirted his full lips. She couldn't deny the intense wave of emotion that stirred within her at the sight of him. For reasons she couldn't fathom, Dylan felt the urge to touch him, to trace her finger along the edges of his collarbone and wrap her arms around his chest where she knew she'd fit perfectly. Snapping herself to the present, she blinked and gave an uneven smile.

"Hi," she squeaked, willing the color to drain from her reddened face. She stood there shy, shocked, and unable to form a coherent, complete sentence. Hearing Aria clear her throat, Dylan broke her trance.

"Oh, this is my roommate-"

Aria stuck her hand out cutting Dylan off mid-sentence. "Best friend, Aria Wan."

Tristian smiled and nodded a silent 'hey' then shifted his attention back to Dylan. Aria withdrew her hand, slowly darting her eyes back and forth between Dylan and Tristian.

Tristian boasted those infamous dimples and held out his elbow to Dylan. "May I escort you to class?"

She nodded, holding back a girly giggle that was sure to come out hoarse and all kinds of wrong.

Turning to Aria. "I'll see you after?"

Aria had the goofiest grin slapped across her face and said, "Oh, you know it." She winked and sashayed into their class. Dylan knew what that statement meant. It meant she expected *all* the details.

Looking back at Tristian, Dylan swatted his elbow down and headed to the lecture hall.

◇◇◇

Walking up the steps to his usual spot after turning in their papers, Tristian turned to Dylan.

"I meant to call."

"I'm sure you did," she mumbled, halting slightly. Her eyes squinted like she was trying to figure him out.

He wanted to elaborate, but there was absolutely nothing to elaborate on... well, besides the one very big, blinding reason, but he very well couldn't tell her that without blowing his entire plan.

Finally opening her mouth and then shutting it again, she sighed, "I... you don't owe me an explanation."

She pushed passed him, cutting off the opportunity for a retort. He grunted, grasping at the fact she just might be a bit angry.

They sat down, rummaging through their backpacks. Setting up his laptop, he noticed Natalie giving Dylan a death stare from across the room. Clenching and unclenching his jaw, Tristian ignored the jealous human and felt the strange urge to make Dylan understand.

"I still told you I would. I want you to trust me and I already-"

"Look," she swiveled her chair towards him, leaning close, and gazed at him through her long dark lashes. "It's not like we slept together and you didn't call me-" he watched her olive skin seep to a deep shade of red, which made him hold back a smile. She was so innocent and the thought of them sleeping together aroused a reaction in her that he wanted to figure out.

She inched even closer and lowered her voice. "You held me *hostage* for half the night and didn't call me." Her breath just grazed his lips and he found the sensation surprisingly exhilarating. She raised an eyebrow. "I should be relieved."

"Are you?" he snapped, his voice coming out in a hoarse whisper.

She studied his face for a moment as if considering his words for the first time. "No."

His heart skipped a beat. He immediately frowned at his body's responses to her as she sat back and focused on the chatty professor; sporadically glancing in Natalie's direction— as if she hadn't just rocked his world with a simple answer.

Fuck.

This wasn't like him. He took a deep breath, unable to focus on anything but her. She baffled him. Whenever he thought he had a good grasp on things, she'd throw in something like that; or would casually touch him or remove his sunglasses—

completely oblivious to what she was doing to him. Perhaps there was a siren taint in her bloodline; that could be the only logical reason for the insanity she inflicted on his body.

Tristian continued to study her even though he faced forward. There were multiple reasons why he liked to wear his sunglasses, and this was one of them. She absent-mindedly twirled her finger around his silver chain that held her Elementa ring. He hadn't planned on giving it to her. It was his father's and one of the few items he had left, but it did look good on her.

"So, what did you end up writing about?" He didn't really care what she wrote. It could have been about his passion for worms or living in a cave. He just didn't want her to stop talking. Her words were addictive.

She suddenly fumbled her pen and her breath caught. Okay, so maybe now he wanted to know.

"Um," she waved her hand in the air. "Just really boring stuff. I couldn't tell too many truths, you know."

"Yeah… but I'd like to meet the boring Tristian, if you don't mind."

She pursed her lips together trying to smother a smile. "All right… but don't judge me. I may have been a little mad at you for—just a bit mad is all." He only raised an eyebrow, maybe now even a bit more curious.

"Okay, I said you were from Transylvania," she chuckled under her breath. "I said you moved here when you were five with your parents—who now live back there with your relatives. That you are into Goth clubs with your girlfriend and you like playing vampires in order to connect to your roots." Dylan finally looked at him and burst into a single, boisterous laugh then slapped a hand over mouth.

Beneath his sunglasses he narrowed his eyes at her youthful amusement. At least, she was entertaining herself. Though, he had to admit, the boring Tristian was probably more compelling than the real Tristian.

91

Dr. Warjas immediately halted her lecture on the "evolution" of behavioral ecology to clear her throat and glower at them.

"Crap," she whispered, turning so red she rivaled a tomato.

"I told you I don't have a girlfriend," he clarified, ignoring the professor's scowl.

She glared at him and shook her head, glancing at Natalie again, causing him to wonder if the human had said something to her.

"Does she know that?" Dylan whispered.

"Who?" he inquired, even though he already knew who.

"The brunette that keeps staring at you." She nodded her head in the direction of Natalie. "She had quite the different story when we ran into each other over the weekend," Dylan scoffed.

Tristian grabbed her wrist, yanking it slightly and forcing her to face him.

"Natalie isn't my girlfriend. I don't *have* a girlfriend." His eyes somehow found their way to her lips and he watched her purse them as she yanked her hand back.

"Fine."

"You don't believe me?" he growled as he started to get up. "I'll make sure she knows, right now."

Suddenly, it was her hand on his wrist. He fell back into his chair with a raised eyebrow. Damn, he loved it when she manhandled him.

"I said fine," she hissed rolling her eyes. "That means I believe you."

He grinned wickedly. "Sorry, my vampire relatives must have passed on a bad temper."

She shook her head smiling and continued to scribble some notes. "So, what'd you write about me?"

"That you were a pleasant surprise."

She frowned and looked at him, giving it her full attention. "That's it?"

"That you are athletic and have a passion for fairytale endings; are open-minded, kind, and take family and friends seriously, because you never know when you'll see them next. You worship your parent's legacy and will keep anything, no matter the size or beauty close to you, because it brings you closer to them... Oh, and that you moved here when you were seven from San Diego."

He went back to his computer and typed some of the notes off the projector like what he had just said was no big deal. She was still staring at him. He didn't know why he romanticized the truth instead of downplaying it. But he kind of liked disarming her. He watched the yearned for words sink into her like the first drops of rain into the parched earth.

"Non-truths?" she breathed, sitting back in her seat a bit pale.

"Yeah... I couldn't tell too many truths, you know," he said, echoing her earlier statement.

About thirty minutes later, the tension between them had grown so palpable, he thought that if he stuck his hand up, the air might slap him back.

Glancing at her notebook and the cheap pen she was using, he remembered accidentally swiping the fountain pen during last class. Well, accidentally might have been a bit of a stretch. Hoping to lighten the mood, or possibly test her a bit more, he brought it out and started to write with it. As he suspected, her eyes snapped to the pen making him hold back a wicked grin.

Suddenly she stood up, looked left and right, then stormed towards the back exit. With a deeply furrowed brow, he watched her, appreciating the tight uptilt curve of her ass. As the doors flapped shut behind her, he blinked and quickly jumped up to follow her, keeping a slightly annoying mortal pace.

"Dylan," he called looking around and stepping up his pace

to a jog. He was trying not to be too vociferous in the large atrium, but she didn't turn, so he yelled a bit louder despite the echo.

"Dylan!"

She halted next to the alcove under the stairs that lead to the upper levels, but still didn't turn around. Her shoulders were hunched and her fists clenched.

"I'm sorry about the pen," he immediately blurted while gingerly stepping forward. He knew it was just a pen, but now he had a feeling it held special meaning, a sentiment, perhaps, to her parents. Damn, he was such a dick. He couldn't seem to do right by this demon.

"I don't know why I took it before. I brought it out now just as a joke. It was stupid." He got within an arms distance, reaching for her shoulder. "Dylan?"

Just then she snapped around, her face burning with fury and eyes glistening with tears. He took off his sunglasses and pushed them into his back pocket. An act he hoped would evoke a sense of bondedness between them.

"Dylan, I'm sorry."

Stepping closer, he brushed a lock of hair behind her ear, and her eyes closed. A single tear traveled down her trembling cheek and he found himself cupping her face, brushing away the errant drop with his thumb. She moved slightly into his touch. He felt himself suck in a sharp breath as he worked hard to keep his lips off hers.

Oh, what the hell.

Taking a risk, he claimed her mouth, holding her by the nape of her neck. He hadn't a clue what he was doing. She was just a contract and the daughter of two very powerful, and quite frightening, demons. But he couldn't ignore the affection he'd developed for her. He had enjoyed watching her from a distance for the past two years; but, ever since that night they had spent

94

together, he couldn't get her out of his head.

The way she had smelled like him the morning after she spent the night, how sexy she looked in his boxers spooning his pillow, her constant blushing, and how she demanded to remove his sunglasses... all made him desperately needy for more. Hell, even his apartment wasn't the same without her presence! Because of those thoughts, he hadn't been able to be around her, afraid he'd make this very mistake.

His pulse thundered. She seemed startled at first. She gasped and yanked her lips away, breaking contact. Staring intently, gray to green, he worried for a brief moment that she had rejected him. He needed to appease the situation—apologize for his mistake.

"Dylan, I-" she quickly pressed a finger to his lips silencing him. Her finger was soft and palatable. Dauntingly so, that with every inch of effort inside him, he kept himself from closing his lips around it.

She slowly removed it, letting her finger drag over his bottom lip and down his chin as she leaned in slowly. Her sweet breath, the first sensation he noticed before her mouth graced his like she was testing the temperature of his mouth; worried it might burn her.

Her kiss was gentler than his and more exhilarating than he'd ever imagined. He wanted to take hold of her small frame and rake his fingers through her hair, but he was afraid any sudden movement would scare her away.

Parting her lips almost apprehensively, she allowed him to enter. The small taste was almost too much to bear. He wanted to dive into her mouth and throw her against a wall, to hear her scream, to taste the tears of her pleasure—but he refrained. He wanted to follow her lead and keep her comfortable, which was a first for him. He'd never cared about whether the chick would want him again.

She brought her arms up and around his neck, working her

fingers through his hair. The act was simple, something he was familiar with, but it felt new and weakening. Along with her sweet kiss, he was having a very hard time keeping things chaste.

A low growl erupted in his throat and she gripped tighter. No longer in charge of his actions, he proceeded on impulse. He immediately picked her up by her thighs and rushed them to the nearest secluded location, which turned out to be the alcove under the stairs.

With her legs wrapped around his waist and her ankles locked, they hit the wall, hard. She gave a strangled yelp, but didn't give any indication of wanting to stop. In fact, she kissed him harder. One of her legs hit the ground, keeping her upright while the other wrapped around his hip in a vise-like grip.

He continued to explore her mouth viciously as if she were the drug to this furious addiction. A moan escaped her as he bit down on her bottom lip then flicked her tongue with his. He wanted to savor every second that passed and devour every inch of her.

He traveled his lips down her neck—sucking light bites hungrily along the silver chain he loved that she wore; and ran his fingers fervently up her body, caressing each and every curve, line, and angle. He felt her grind against him and it took everything within him not to take her right then and there.

Her seductive touch set his body aflame, simmering excitedly as her nails dug into his shoulder blades. Everything was so much more intense with her. He'd never felt this way with a woman, or creature. He couldn't quite put his finger on it; it was just astoundingly different. He wanted to brand her, to stamp his mark into her flesh for the entire world to see that she was his-

A door slammed nearby, causing them to break contact. She instantly dropped her legs, moving to a full stand. He could feel her chest heaving against his as they waited for the intruder to exit.

Turning his attention back to Dylan, he noticed a look of pain etched across her face. Her breathing was rigid and she stared wide into his eyes. He knew deep down the deer had been spotted. The prey tensed for flight. But he still felt perplexed. He didn't want to accept what was in front of him. Opening his mouth to speak, she threw up a hand.

"I'm *so* sorry."

"I'm not," he whispered cocking his head to the side and not wanting to let her go.

Staring at her mouth, he needed more of her succulence. Licking his lips, he started to move closer, telling himself to ignore the warning light burning into his brain.

She pushed him back. Snapping his arms up to brace himself, his head nearly collided with the stringer under the middle of the stairs. Her strength surprised him as it did her.

Shaking her head and holding a tense hand to her lips, she stumbled around him and scurried down the adjacent steps. Tristian watched her exit through the side doors leading to the outside parking lot, leaving him burned and still clutching the fountain pen.

◇◇◇

A week dragged by. Dylan had barricaded herself in her apartment. Tristian tried calling her repeatedly. He even left her pen in a black box on her doorstep with a note asking her to call him, but she had continued to ignore him. She was entirely too embarrassed at her actions to face him. Surely he had to think she was unstable or just completely nuts.

Not to mention those awful words he wrote about her in his assignment. It couldn't have been further from the truth. Where did he get off saying that bull? Okay, so maybe her Transylvania story wasn't any better, but the person he had described, Dylan wished she was. It hurt her to think that was who he saw. She only hoped he didn't expect her to be that person, because for the life of her, she couldn't get him out of her head and for the first time all week, she didn't want to.

Closing her eyes, Dylan touched her lips musingly. Never in a million years did she think her first make-out would be that intense. She just couldn't believe *she* kissed him. She wasn't even sure what she was doing, if she was any good, or if it was just as earth shattering for him. But while their lips were linked, none of that mattered. Everything melted away. She felt free, whole, and for the first time in several years, vulnerable. That feeling terrified her.

Breaking away from him, reality set in and everything came crashing down like an ominous tidal wave, wiping away all her happiness. She had no idea what to do or say, or what he expected from her. So, she did the one thing that popped into her brain, she had fled.

Tristian's warm touch and delicious kiss played like a broken record in her mind. Whenever she thought she had fixed it, the phone would ring setting the stylus back on the scratch. He hadn't tried to call that day and a strange emotion had knotted in her throat. Too proud to face him, she had decided to skip Monday's class, despite the lecture from Aria.

"I just need a few days to myself," Dylan said, returning from the bathroom with her toiletries to pack to take with her to her grandmother's house until at least Monday night. "And besides, I have like a mountain of laundry."

She turned to her overflowing linen laundry bag, tossing in a few spares and pausing on the white tank with ink stained on the back.

"Why won't you tell me what happened?" Aria asked maternally. "It must have been bad to warrant that kind of reaction from Tristian."

Dylan cringed, still unable to form words on what transpired between them.

Right after class Aria had come bursting into their apartment like a frightening whirlwind of red and flung Dylan's backpack at her. Apparently, Tristian had stalked back into class, threw a temper tantrum while collecting his and Dylan's things, dropped Dylan's bag next to Aria and her partner, and then proceeded to make a scene in front of Natalie; telling her, not so quietly, to, *"Think twice next time."*

Dr. Warjas demanded Tristian grab some fresh air and cool off. He left, but never returned. After hearing that, Dylan cried and completely clammed up.

Aria sat on Dylan's bed, waiting a beat before trying a different approach.

"Don't forget Warjas grades on attendance. You've basically skipped out half way through the first two classes. If you miss again it's going to be two absences and you only get three before losing ten percent of your grade."

Dylan chunked the shirt in the trash and picked up her two bags and phone.

"I'm just going to skip this one time. Let me know if she adds any new projects for the following week or anything. If I send you my paper in an e-mail, can you turn it in for me?" She gave the best smile she could muster given the immense weight on her chest.

"Of course, princess!" Aria rolled her eyes, waving the air. "Now get out of here. I'm sure you'll clue me in when you're ready. Just try to do it before I die of suspense."

"You're the best!" Dylan called over her shoulder.

Leaving her friend in the organized mess of her bedroom, Dylan let out a deep sigh as she navigated through the hall and out of their tiny apartment. She had evaded yet another heart-to-heart, thank God.

It was just passed sunset on Saturday night, the humid air already cooling from the sun's absence. Checking her rearview mirror, Dylan pulled out of her parking spot and drove towards a small coffee shop in Brentwood. There she planned to finish her paper and then head home.

The comforting aroma of coffee, vanilla, and warmth filled her senses as she scanned the quaint coffee shop. The whirl of a blender sounded and jazz music played, complementing the frantic chatter and laughs of the patrons. The place was crowded, as it had been a staple in the neighborhood for as long as she could remember. After ordering her latte in a large ceramic mug, Dylan snatched a vacating, secluded table near the rear of the cafe and got to work.

An hour passed by and she tapped the curser sending her paper to Aria. A familiar energy tingled the back of her neck. Immediately turning around, she expected to see Tristian. Instead, two luminous amber eyes stared back at her from the adjacent table.

"Hey, gorgeous," Asher leered.

A paradox of feelings from disappointment to relief passed through her. Pursing her lips into a thin line, Dylan muttered, "Is this some ridiculous common greeting all you demons use?" Okay, so maybe she was just a tad bitter today...

"Whoa, who pissed in your cheerios?" Asher asked widening his beautiful cat-like eyes. "And isn't that like calling the pot black or something?"

"Sorry," she sighed. "And it's kettle."

"Huh?"

"Never mind."

"Anything you want to talk about?"

"With you? No."

"Ouch." Asher shifted in his seat, rubbing the back of his neck and looking uncomfortable.

Dylan squeezed her eyes shut for a moment.

"Sorry… again." Scrunching up her face to look at him. "It's just… I was trying to get away for a few days from demons, boys, and paranormal crap, and here you show up. Oh God, now I'm continuing to be an ass. How can I make it up to you… Oh!" She snapped her fingers. "Let me buy you a coffee, or scone? They have the best scones here-"

Asher grabbed her arm as she tried to stand, tugging her back to a sit.

"You're cute when you ramble." He got up and moved to the opposite seat at her little round table. Pushing aside her laptop, he grinned. "So, I'm guessing Tristian filled you in on all the details?"

"Yeah," she said, drawing the word out. Looking up at him Dylan asked, "Did you know when we were dancing at the club? When you… kissed me?"

"I had my suspicions, but I wasn't sure until I kissed you."

"So, you did it just to see my soul? Or should I say lack thereof…" She gave an uneven smile while looking down, ever so slightly creasing her brow.

Asher grabbed her chin to move her gaze back up to his.

"There are other ways, *easier ways,* to check, but I wanted to kiss you." Flicking his eyes down at the ring she still wore around her neck. "I see you're not wearing your ring on your hand," he stated, changing the subject and dropping his hand from her chin.

"Huh?" Looking down at the delicate silver chain Tristian gave her, sadness rose up in her throat stunting her speech. Swallowing several times, she finally found her voice. "Y-yeah, the band is bent and it hacked up my finger." She picked up the ring examining the three sharp dents on the band.

"Your family's ring. You should always keep it with you. It will remind you of who you are."

But what if I don't know who I am?

Looking back into her eyes skeptically, he drummed his fingers on the wooden table. He seemed antsy or nervous, but maybe she just brought that out in people. "So, why isn't Tristian following you around? A lot of people are looking for you."

"Are you?"

"Me?" he leaned his chair back feigning shock. "Nah, you are not on my contract. But I've heard the rumors. I guess you could say I was just passionately curious at the club." He gave her a smooth wink, setting his chair back down.

"Yeah, I'm supposed to be this big powerful demon, right? You were probably disappointed."

Asher seemed to think about this for a moment. "Not disappointed, more like... intrigued." He blinked his pupils on reflex. It made her think of a reptile.

"How do you do that? The eye thing." She had seen him do it at the club, but was in too much shock to ask. "Can all demons do that? Can I?" She twirled Tristian's necklace around her finger, unintentionally drawing Asher's eyes there.

He continued to stare at her ring. "If you haven't done it yet, then you probably can't. It's a taint in the bloodline," he explained as he flicked his gaze up to her eyes. "Then again a lot of things change after you steal your first soul."

"Huh." She dropped the necklace letting it slap back in place.

Strumming his fingers some more, he slapped his palms on the table making Dylan start.

"You seem to have a lot of questions. It's Saturday night and you're here doing *homework*," Asher sneered playfully, then broke into a smile. "Let's go out."

Dylan weighed her options for a moment then figured she didn't have anything to lose. She felt like she was embarking on a new chapter in her life; demons, dating, kissing, emotions...

"Why not," she said dryly, taking his hand to a stand.

"That's the spirit." Asher pulled her out the door, apparently amused.

CHAPTER 6

"Never open the door to a lesser evil, for other and greater ones invariably slink in after it."
Baltasar Gracián

ASHER led Dylan to his Ducati motorcycle. It was gorgeous, shiny, and slightly intimidating. The black and silver chrome glittered in the moonlight, accented with a twisting red pipe giving the bike an added edge. *Perfect for a demon*, she thought, running her eyes along the fine leather seat; noting the limited space for two riders.

After they left the café, she had dropped off her computer and changed in the back of her car. She chose a simple, blue, racerback tank and jean jacket with numerous black zippers. It didn't take her long, but it was nice to have nearly her entire closet in the backseat of her car.

He pushed off from the motorcycle and handed her the passenger helmet. He had slipped on a thick, matte-leather jacket while he waited for her. It had a red lining and two reflector silver arrows, like thick upside-down check marks mirrored on both sides of his chest. The black accentuated his blond, curly hair and amber cat eyes. For the first time, she could see past his exceptionally handsome looks to the demon that lay just underneath. She wondered if she, too, had that side—that side that could haunt someone's dreams.

"I've never been on a motorcycle," Dylan muttered while fumbling with the pink passenger helmet. "Pink? Really?" she boosted an eyebrow. Chuckling, Asher moved to help her snap it on, but she evaded him and snatched up his black Shoei helmet in the process.

"Why do you have a pink helmet?" she laughed, twirling around him as he lunged once more.

He huffed while planting his feet and spinning to face her. "Well... because only chicks get on the back of my bike," he said as if it were a given.

"Well, I'm not wearing this girly thing that resembles half a watermelon."

He watched her dance around him with a slight curl to his lip before quickly snatching the black helmet out of her hands so fast she barely had time to blink. Pouting, and about to relent to the goofy gear, Asher popped the black helmet on her head.

"Fine," he scoffed, plucking the other helmet from her hand and setting it on his head. "I'm not afraid of a little color."

Snapping the buckle, he held both hands out to his side. "How do I look?"

She laughed using both hands to push the visor up. "Very dapper!"

He bowed, while whirling his hand in the air. "Why, thank you, me lady. And doth not worry, I'll take thee slow. Just shout if thou too aghast," he cooed with a bite of mockery.

"Yeah, yeah. Whatever you say, *my lord*," she murmured sardonically while pulling her jean jacket on and stuffing her keys, cash, and phone in the zippered pockets. "You know, you rolled with that frighteningly well."

"I do have some knowledge of the fifteenth century."

Her eyes rounded as Asher jumped on his Ducati, tapping the remainder of the seat twice before flicking the kickstand up, releasing the fold up pillion pegs and grabbing the clutch. He roared the exceptionally loud engine to life making Dylan start. She quickly praised the heavens for masking her embarrassing squeal with the growl of the engine.

Stepping closer, her nerves responded in a way similar to the feeling of being next in line for a roller coaster. With a quick breath, she popped her leg over the rumbling leather and slid on awkwardly behind him. He grabbed her hands, firmly positioning them on his thick leather belt with slightly worn edges. He revved the engine and glanced down the dead street while yelling something over the deafening sound.

"What?" she yelled back, just as he took off, making her hold tense. He snickered, as he steered down the street.

Realizing the pain in her fingers, Dylan relaxed slightly, positive that she had put permanent dents into his belt from the severe grip of her nails. Shifting closer to his body, she moved her hands promptly up to his abdomen for a more secure hold. Peeking open her eyes, she felt her stomach flip. This didn't feel safe at all.

"Where are we going?" she forced out of trembling lips.

"A beach party. You need to loosen up a little. Have some fun."

She couldn't deny that. The last two weeks had taken its toll on her physically and mentally. She was so overwrought because of Tristian she couldn't even stay for the end of yoga class and had headed for the treadmills—evading Garret when the class was over. She felt so mentally messed up, she didn't want to drag someone as nice as Garrett along for the ride anymore. Letting him think there was any chance with her at this point would just be mean.

"I'm due for some fun." She took a deep breath, daring another look at the road.

Okay, so maybe it's not so scary.

"Where to? Santa Monica?"

"Get comfy! It's about a twenty-minute drive depending on the lights."

She repositioned her body again, laying her head against his back. The rear of the bike was jabbing into her butt and the way her legs were stacked on the extra pegs made her thighs ache. Figuring *'comfy'* was out of the question, she shifted her gaze to the mature oaks and massive brick and iron gates as they sped down San Vincente Blvd.

A scent tickled her nose of something floral and sweet mixed with... bergamot? She frowned, taking a sniff of Asher's back. It was an odd combination, but not unpleasant.

"Don't fall asleep!" he called over his shoulder.

"I'm just getting *'comfy'*!" she called over the rush of night air, squeezing his stomach through the thick gear.

"Hey, no abusing the driver! Otherwise, I'll have to pull over and give you a spanking." She felt his laugh even if she didn't hear it.

"Ha. Ha," she rolled her eyes, "Somehow, I think you'd enjoy that just a bit too much." At that, he seemed to laugh even harder.

The cool night air was starting to bite into the exposed skin on her hands. She slid them into his jacket pockets without thinking.

"Damn, groping me already? I usually demand dinner first!"

Now she was laughing. "Don't get any ideas! Just keeping my hands out of the wind."

Asher was posing as someone she didn't mind being around. He was funny and seemed to try to make her comfortable, while simultaneously pushing her outside her perfectly constructed safety box. Maybe one day she could add him to the growing list of friends. For now, he was just a hot guy taking her to a party.

Dylan was curious about the kind of parties demons went to. She tried to imagine, but the only things that came to mind were from vampire and werewolf movies, neither of any relevance.

Her mind somehow shifted to Tristian. Like it always did. It didn't matter what she was doing, Tristian always found a way to snake into her thoughts. Those startling verdant gems claimed residence in her mind long ago. Squeezing her eyes shut, she willed herself to focus on the guy she was straddling. Asher was very cute and yet, she still thought of Tristian. His delicious full lips, heady touch, and heavenly aroma. She shuddered involuntarily at her reverie.

"You cold?" Asher called over his shoulder.

It took Dylan a moment to understand why he was asking the question. Her face flushed, thankful he wasn't able to see her.

"A little bit, but I'm fine."

About fifteen minutes later they traveled past the glowing festive lights of Santa Monica Pier and turned onto the small paved bike path that lined the beach. Asher wove them through several street performers and a few pedestrians who shouted obstinacies for riding his bike on the walkway. After a few more minutes the path cleared. The engine rumbled to a stop as Asher parked behind a large boulder. Dylan immediately jumped off, welcoming the solid ground under her sneakers.

The salty breeze stung her eyes and stirred her hair as she pulled off the helmet. Her first long motorcycle ride and she definitely felt it in her butt and thighs. Rubbing her sore muscles, she began doing a few simple stretches while listening to the soothing crash of the waves. Something about the beach seemed to call to her. It was soothing, always making her feel closer to her parents.

"We made good time," he said, leaning casually against his bike while watching her touch her toes.

"Yeah?" she said popping back up. "Am I supposed to be

this sore?"

"That's what she said," he smirked.

"Ha. Ha." She rolled her eyes at his lame derisive comment.

"But yeah if you're not used to riding one," he chuckled.

"This was my first time, remember?"

"Then you're definitely going to be feeling sore tomorrow." He burst into another boisterous laugh and Dylan suddenly felt like she was with a twelve year-old.

"Hmm, let me guess... *That's what she said?"* Dylan mocked.

"Hey now," he tilted his head in mock seriousness. "Get your mind out of the gutter."

She only narrowed her eyes at him, holding back a wide smile.

"Come on." He motioned with his head as he started walking further down the beach.

Leaving the helmet neatly perched on the seat, Dylan followed Asher as he led her on a long walk, during which she took full advantage and asked anything that came to her mind.

"...Yeah I knew they were two powerful demons, but what were their strengths?"

She suspected Asher was being purposely vague to piss her off. She just wanted to understand a bit more about her family and about herself.

"Elementa," Asher spoke like it explained everything.

"My last name?"

"We don't have last names, but the types of powers we possess or the combinations of powers from our parents." Asher glanced at her then continued, "Well, at least that's how it used to be. We all have a seriously long name that's available if we please. But most of us just continue with our patronymic name these days."

"Okay…" she spoke slowly, hoping he'd continue.

"Your parents before they mated went by Atticus PyroVentus and Constance HydroTerra. Both of which had been shortened immensely already."

Dylan stopped and grabbed Asher's arm.

"Laymen's terms please."

Sighing he said, "Instead of naming you PyroVentusHydroTerra, your parents changed it to Elementa. They also call themselves the Elementas." He scanned her face.

"You don't know a lick of Latin do you. Fire, Wind, Water, Earth '*may your powers combine*'…" he said in an exaggerated voice and raised his eyebrows as he waited for the light bulb above her head to illuminate.

"Oh! Elementa… elements!" She clapped her hands like a proud child. "Duh," she laughed. "I guess I should have been able to get at least pyro and hydro. She shook her head, feeling like an idiot.

Asher smiled, "Yes, you can manipulate the elements. Now, can we continue to the party? It's still like ten minutes down the beach… at your pace."

"My pace, huh?" she muttered, starting to walk again. "So, how come I haven't been able to do anything with the elements, yet?" she asked, stopping again. "Because, I need to steal a soul or become immortal first?"

As he halted, Asher growled, apparently getting annoyed.

"Some demons can before they take their first soul. Others train until they turn and then can use their powers at full. I am a bit surprised though… a demon as powerful as you hasn't accidentally released in some way."

She nodded feeling bothered, but continued to walk. She wasn't sure why he was getting so irritated. He had to have known she would bombard him with questions. This was why he took her out… wasn't it?

With her head tilted to gaze at the sprinkle of heavenly bodies, wisps of dark clouds glided ominously through the night, she pondered if she could literally move the world. How much strength she would need to lift an ocean or save a city from an earthquake. The elements were infinite. Everything she touched, tasted, *breathed* was something tangible—something she was supposed to be able to manipulate. Even the body was made up of elements… could she manipulate herself? Others? She smirked inwardly. There was no way she was *that* powerful. When Asher said elements he probably meant grains of sand not whole beaches.

Asher, looking like he accidentally kicked a puppy, grabbed her arm to stop her.

"Look, ah…" He let go, to run his fingers through his blonde locks. "I can teach you how to use your *Unda* if you would like."

She sighed a little annoyed with all the Latin.

"The *what*?"

"The current that we use to absorb Essence. It's generally used to numb the victim into a state of oblivion. It's how we use our powers on physical objects."

"I would like that, thanks… Hey, what do you do with the soul after you take it?" She really hoped they didn't just eat it. That reminded her of that old movie *Soylent Green*, yech!

"Our bodies harbor it. The more souls you consume, the greater your strength. The law gives us a fifty-year window to release the amassed and a limit of souls during that time frame, dependent on your personal strength. Their goal is to keep the population at a disadvantage as well as guarantee constant production."

"How do they take them out of you?" she asked trying to keep composure to her voice. It all seemed so technical, unnecessary, and frankly… gross.

111

"It's pretty easy... We place our right hand fingertips to this device and that's it. No pain or anything."

She pursed her lips together with a nod. "But I'm guessing taking the soul is painful, if you need to numb a human."

He let out a huff of laughter. "You could say that... Imagine using a strong vacuum to slowly rip out your intestines through your mouth."

Dylan's mouth fell open. How horrible.

Asher nudged her chin. "And not all demons numb their victims."

"There are some pretty evil ones, aren't there?" she said, starting to understand why Tristian insisted on hanging around.

"You have no idea," he breathed. And with that, both of them walked in silence towards the lighter horizon bleeding into the pitch-black sky.

Getting closer to the flame lit sky, the thick smell of musky smoke, cedar, and something sweet filled the air. Dylan's mouth fell open when they arrived at the gigantic bon-fire. Logs, the width of her car, were stacked like a tepee, with chunky flames licking the wood. The top of the fire flicked green and purple sparks towards the sky. Hisses and sizzling pops sounded over the reggae like music as hundreds of creatures danced, drank, and mingled around the inferno. Strangely enough, the heat she felt wasn't scorching but comfortably warm against the cool ocean breeze. Easily a couple stories tall, Dylan couldn't help but wonder what the locals thought.

As if reading her mind, Asher leaned into her ear. "It's black magic. Any humans passing by might feel a bit warm, but would never notice it."

She looked up at him. "Oh? What happens if they walk straight into it?"

He shrugged. "Let's hope we don't find out... but I don't

think the vampires would let them get that close." He winked menacingly.

"Crazy demons," she muttered, silently praying no humans felt the urge to meander the beach at midnight.

He pulled her towards a large log like the ones in the heap. Half sunken into the beach, it allowed partygoers to relax on it. She wondered how exactly this was all set up and if she could watch next time.

A few pickups were parked on one side of the party where some dwarfs spun turntables and hopped to the heavy bass and offbeat percussive guitar rhythm.

"So, what do you think?" Asher said nudging her chin again. "Better close that thing before a bug flies in."

Snapping her mouth shut, she scowled at him—confused.

"You've been gawking at everything with your mouth wide open since we arrived."

"Oh! Sorry, it's just... wow... I've seen beach parties before and the bon-fires were nothing like this." Clearing her throat. "I guess I should just stop being surprised, right?"

"When you stop being surprised life tends to get boring." He paused for a moment. "I'll go get us drinks."

Eyeing a small green and purple man with three small horns, tapping his flat head to the music, she mumbled, "Good idea."

"Those are the only ones I have," he crooned. Giving her a wink, Asher then sauntered in the direction of one of the pickups posing as a bar. Just as he left, a guy, no a vampire, came and sat next to her. He was all thick muscles and sharp lines like an overstuffed, ken doll. His luminous skin accented his short, black hair and hazel eyes. It made him appear almost black and white in a world of color.

Smiling, he exposed his unusual curved fangs. Not that she really knew what normal fangs looked like. Her paranormal knowledge pretty much started and ended with movies and fictional books. His out-stretched pale, porcelain hand broke her train of thought.

"Hey, I'm Datu."

She grabbed it with a small gasp at the lack of warmth to his skin. Quickly pulling it smoothly to his lips, he kissed the back of her hand.

"Kaya matamis," he cooed caressing her skin and glancing through thick lashes.

She cocked her head to the side as he lingered for just a bit too long and *was he smelling me?* she wondered as with a grimace spread across her face. Just as she was about to yank her hand back, Asher stepped forward with a bored expression. Like he expected to find an over-friendly vampire making out with her hand.

"Trying to steal my date already, Datu?"

Datu instantly let go, causing her hand to drop in midair as he sat back with a fake look of surprise.

"Asher, y*our* date? She's way too lovely to be with the likes of you." He ended the sentence in a snarl, then leaped at him. They started tumbling through the heavy, white sand. Sprays and clumps of white powder kicked around them. Dylan quickly stood frightened, about to shout for help, but just as fast as it started, it ended with the boys breaking out into a fit of laughter. She looked down with a scowl as they stood brushing off the sand.

Asher strutted up to Dylan and gave her one of the red plastic cups he'd set down conveniently before the brawl. She took it, and dusted some sand off his shoulders.

"It's a vodka, water with lime."

She smiled at his recall of the drink she had at Spin.

"Thanks." She took it and sipped. "What are you drinking?"

"Whiskey neat," he said, taking a gulp, then hissing the

sting through his teeth.

She stared off into the distance, taking a mental note, for whatever reason, when suddenly Asher shook his head violently letting sand spray off his hair.

"Hey!" she squealed, guarding her eyes, and lifting her drink in the air. "You're getting sand all over me!" Dylan pushed him away playfully then downed her drink.

"*Damn*, girl knows how to party!" Datu sang still brushing sand off his shirt.

After swallowing she nodded at Datu. "So, you're a vampire, right?"

"What gave me away?" he smiled letting his fangs drop. "It's the hair isn't it? It just hasn't been the same since the *change*."

She laughed. "Yes. Yes, it's definitely the hair."

He floated very close to her and breathed a long inhale. She watched as his eyes briefly flicked to red.

"You know, for a demon, you smell rather nice."

She raised an eyebrow and Asher cut in. "Yeah, yeah, he smells everyone. Datu, Dylan, Dylan, Datu," an introduction lacking severely in enthusiasm. "Now come." He pulled on Dylan's hand, tugging her away from the odd vampire. "Let's dance."

After shrugging off her jacket, they bounced through the sand to the dancing bodies that swayed like an undulating mass of water licking the sand. Joining the tide, Dylan instantly felt way out of place. Creatures all around her moved seductively, beautifully. She wanted to let loose but something about being in the lion's den made her sweat. What was stopping the vampire to her right or the devil-goat *thing* to her left from devouring her whole? Not to mention, her hips just didn't roll like that.

Eyes of all colors and shapes seemed to swing to her, when

she realized not moving was drawing more attention than dancing badly. Possessive hands landed on her hips.

"Dylan," Asher yelled over the music. He closed the distance between them and lowered his voice. "Don't worry about what everyone else is thinking." He licked his lips. "The sexiest women I know do exactly what they are afraid to do."

She smiled with her eyes cast downward. His delicate fingers lifted her chin and she found herself swimming in a pool of golden irises.

"See that Sprite with the scales?" He asked nudging his chin to her left.

Her eyes found a gorgeous woman with green and blue glossy scales covering her tiny body, save for her face and magenta hair, which was styled in a pixie cut. She seemed to be dancing with herself; her legs bounced aggressively, her eyes squeezed tightly, and her fists appeared to be glued to her chest in almost a painful fashion.

"I don't see how that's sexy-" The words died on Dylan's lips when she caught sight of Asher. His lanky build hunched left and right, his entire face scrunched awkwardly, and his teeth ground visibly—over exaggerating the sprite's moves.

Before she could help it, a laugh shot through her lips causing her entire body to convulse with hearty sobs.

"Stop it," she panted, hunching over. Her eyes teared up as she bellowed giggles, which only seemed to motivate him further. Gasping for air, she threw a hand up, unsuccessfully, several times before getting another, "Stop!" out.

He chuckled slowing to a stop and motioned for her to find a creature to copy.

Her chest was still heaving with sporadic contractions, when she set her eyes on a man. Honestly, on any other day Dylan might have wet herself from fear. *It* came up to her waist. Its eyes were chartreuse orbs and its skin charred and broken like old leather. Basically what she thought a demon was supposed to resemble. Instinct had her backing away but his style of dance had her... intrigued.

She met Asher's eyes with a leering smile before jumping into a crouch and wiggling her arms out in front of her. She glanced up to see Asher howling with laughter. Upon seeing her, the small "demon man" began rippling his arms at her. Asher seemed to laugh even harder. She continued to return the dance when she felt Asher's arm drag her away.

"My apologies! But she is my date."

The creature shrugged and began wiggling his tentacles in the direction of other creatures.

"You are so lucky I saved you," Asher stated.

"Why?" She giggled sarcastically, "We were having such a good time! Couldn't you tell?"

"Sure!" he said. "Feel free to return to the mating dance of the Deber!"

"The what!" she choked.

"It's not a big deal. I'm sure you made his night."

She rolled her eyes, faintly aware she no longer felt self-conscious. She threw her arms up and let her body feel the beat, surrendering to the fluid music.

After dancing for a while and working up a quite a sweat, the music slowed and they continued to sway as he pulled her close. With her back to him, she interlocked her fingers around the back of his neck and he rested his head in the crook of her neck. Asher pulled her closer and nerves flooded her belly at the thought of his hands on her the same way they had been at the club. She moved against him and his hands gripped her torso igniting a current of energy although not the same as before.

Closing her eyes, she let her mind relax, letting all her stress bleed out into the night air. Dylan couldn't keep her mind from retreating to her kiss with Tristian. She never knew such passion existed outside of fiction.

Popping her hips to the seductive melody, she traced her fingers south from their spot behind the neck of her dance partner and down her body, interlacing her fingers with his. His hands slid along her stomach and her skin sizzled with heat.

The way Tristian bewitched her mind and claimed her body that morning during class, she felt she could never be anyone else's ever again.

She ground further back as a manly groan vibrated against her neck—running a searing jolt down her spine. She imagined Tristian's muscular body wrapped around hers, skin against skin. Oh, she wanted to taste him again and to revel in his scent. A small moan traveled through her lips as rough fingers bit into her hips grinding her harder. She needed him closer, needed Tristian to kiss her like she needed air. She flipped around and gasped.

Crap! Not Tristian!

Where the hell had she gone? She let out a huff of frustrated air and smiled sheepishly. Of course she wasn't with Tristian. She was ignoring him. She was here with Asher—who now had desire written all over that smirk. He leaned in and she closed her eyes, hoping to feel some fireworks that would prove her earlier theory wrong—when a girl clearing her throat stopped Dylan mid-thought.

They looked over and Asher laughed incredulously shaking his head. "Livia, what-"

"Asher, I need to talk to you," snapped a beautiful, lanky blonde in skin-tight white jeans and a teal, cotton tunic that hung over one bony shoulder. Her face came across as bored or annoyed but her eyes were pure anger. Just then, she crossed her arms and lifted an eyebrow.

"Well?"

"I'll be right back," Asher said with an apologetic smile.

Dylan, confused, seemed to have forgotten how to speak properly. All that came out was, "Who? What?"

He leaned down and whispered in her ear, "I'll explain when I come back."

Dylan nodded while Livia smirked. She watched them walk away from the party towards the water. Livia glanced in Dylan's direction multiple times while talking close to Asher.

"Hey," said Datu appearing suddenly at her side. "Don't fret. Livia gets jealous over her Ex."

"Ex, huh," said Dylan with a frown. Looking towards Datu she found her smile. "Let's go get a drink."

"Sure, Sinta." He held out a muscular elbow and she took it.

"What's Sinta mean?"

"Huh? Oh, didn't even realize I said it." He smiled, shaking his head a bit. "It's just a term of endearment for a friend or sister." She nodded as they walked to the makeshift bar. Dylan, unable to hold it in any longer, didn't beat around the bush. "So... Ex. Spill."

He glanced at her with a sympathetic look. "Well, they've been together for a long time. Her name is Livia Mutatio. She's a demon too, but not a Collector like you guys."

"What do you mean a long time?"

"They were mates off and on about a century ago for about forty years. She was way too jealous and Asher gets contracted out a lot. She couldn't handle it, so he dumped her." Somehow, that last statement caused a faint smile to flash across Dylan's face. "Look, I've known Asher for over two hundred years, and that woman has this invisible hold over him. I was actually pretty psyched when I saw him with you. I thought he was moving on."

"Maybe he's trying to... Just because she showed up doesn't really mean anything, right? Maybe she just needed to talk."

He nodded. "Maybe… but in my experience they usually hook up whenever they get around each other."

Dylan felt a bit played. Not that she foresaw a future with Asher or anything; but inviting her to a party, dancing quite heatedly and then ditching her a second that demon showed her face? Yeah, that made her feel just great. Datu continued despite her silence.

"I mean, you do know the saying, never trust a demon."

"I'm a demon," she sneered narrowing her eyes. "Should I not trust myself?"

"Hey now, it's just a saying," Datu said cautiously. "But… unless you know who and what you truly are... then no, I guess, you can't trust yourself either."

Dylan pursed her lips and moved up in line to the bar.

"Do you only drink blood?"

Datu answered her question by cutting in front of her and ordering himself a 'Bloody' Mary and two shots of Tequila for Dylan.

"Cheers," she said wanly and downed the liquid, wincing through the recollecting burn. She sucked on the lime wedge and stomped her foot.

"So... call me crazy, but I want to go check and see what they're doing for myself."

Datu raised a perfect eyebrow. "Really?"

She perched her small hands on her hips in an *I'm-an-evil-demon-so-don't-get-in-my-way* look. She hoped it was somewhat believable.

"Suit yourself, Sinta," he laughed sadly.

She knew it sounded more than pathetic, but she had a weird feeling and needed it validated. Her internal warning bells were flashing. If they were in fact hooking up, then so be it; but, neither of them looked happy to see the other. Something was definitely up.

He ordered two more shots and handed them to her. She raised her eyebrows in question.

"I have a feeling you'll need these as well."

After mustering probably too much liquid confidence, Datu pointed the way towards Livia and Asher. Stumbling through the thick sand, Dylan moved as stealthily as she could in her current state of mind. Inching around a large rock, she heard two people arguing.

"-Call me here to make me jealous?" shrieked Livia.

"No. But apparently, I called at the wrong time of the month."

"*Ass*!" she growled. "It's been half a century, Asher. I'm trying to move on. I have a mate now. I can't be here for you whenever you want me. And personally, it looks like you don't need me at all!"

"Please, would you just shut up and listen to me, Livia?" Asher snapped sounding tired and annoyed.

It was silent for a moment and Dylan's heart rate soared. She was worried they were going to round the corner at any moment. Her ears scorched just at the thought of being caught eavesdropping. On the verge of retreating, Asher continued calmly.

"I called you because I trust you… because Temperance Elementa is the girl out there."

"What!" Livia screamed.

"Hell, Livia, calm down."

"What the *hell* are you doing with her?" she hissed. "Are you trying to get yourself killed?"

"She's been raised mortal. I feel sorry for her, okay? She has no education or training in our worlds. I'm trying to teach her some of the basics because Tristian Effingo—"

"Knows where her parents are," Livia finished for him.

"That's your contract isn't it?"

"Look, you know we can't discuss our contracts."

"It is!"

Dylan could practically hear her smile from around the boulder.

"So what, you're trying to gain her trust by making her fall for you? So she'll lead you to them? You know what, that's actually very brilliant on your part. If she loves you she'll spill everything."

Dylan started to see red. Asher was just a demon trying to get something from her, to fulfill his contract. *You can never trust a demon...* She had been so naïve.

"I need you to talk to her about your mother."

"Ziri? What-"

"I'm almost positive she was the one that switched Temperance as a baby."

Livia growled, "Don't accuse my family of disloyalty to the OP! Are you not only accepting their personal contracts, but hunting too?"

Despite Livia's raised voice Asher kept calm. "I doubt the Law cares about Ziri. I want you to talk to Temperance and persuade her to push Tristian to continue the search. I thought he knew where they were, but he's dragging his feet and I don't know why. Her parents will be furious if their daughter shows up with no training so close to the turning age.

Livia's voice composed, "Maybe he likes it here. Once he completes his contract, he won't be able to come back. You know, if he really is with the Elementas."

"All the more reason to get her to push him."

"Hmm."

"What?"

"Are you afraid he's competition?" snickered Livia.

"What? No-"

"Or is the OP's patience on your little bargain running thin?"

Asher snarled as Livia continued to laugh. "What? Did you really think that deal was so secret?"

"I've been looking for them for twenty years. Of course it's running thin! I thought I would've found them earlier. After searching for sixteen years to no avail, I heard about Tristian's contract through rumors within the Omnipotence. I knew I needed to follow him to her parents. And what do you know, I was right."

Dylan's eyes widened as she pushed herself away from the sharp boulder, unable to withstand any more. She stumbled back to the party knowing she needed to get out of there quickly.

Wiping at her face, she looked down at her hand with a frown. She had been crying. Her heart rate reached a crescendo as panic seeped in. She needed to regain control over her emotions. These demons were hacking through the brick walls perfectly assembled around her heart. Before she knew it, she would be back on Prozac and seeing her therapist three times a week. Looking up, she saw Datu and ran toward him.

"Ah man, see I didn't want you to see that." He threw an icy arm around her. "They're freaks, you know."

Sniffing, she started to feel dumb for crying, but it was so hard to stop once she had started. She shouldn't expect high values from these people- these *demons*. Tristian even told her how conniving demons could be when their contract was within reach.

Datu pulled her to sit on the large log, wrapped his strong arm around her, and patted her shoulder. She knew something was up and now she didn't know who she should lean on. Everyone seemed to be working towards a personal agenda. Dylan Prescott or Temperance Elementa was just a pawn, a piece to play in their twisted game.

"No, it was worse." She held out her hand. "Give me your phone."

He gave it to her reluctantly.

"Uh, Dylan-"

"I'm getting out of here… please tell Asher I disappeared in the crowd."

He boosted an eyebrow. "Sure, Sinta. Whatever I can do."

"Just try and stall him as long as you can." Handing his phone back. "I put my number in there… Give me a heads up if he starts in my direction."

"Sure," he said, still keeping a cautious attitude.

Dylan kissed his cold cheek and stood up. Brushing debris from her jeans, she trudged back the way she'd arrived.

CHAPTER 7

"Our actions are in our own hands, but the
consequences of them are not. Remember that, my dear,
and think twice before you do anything."
Louisa May Alcott

MOVING farther away from the party, Dylan began to feel the cold clawing at her exposed arms. The wind seemed to have picked up even more just five minutes into her walk back, whipping her hair into her eyes and mouth.

"Stupid, stupid... stupid," she huffed spitting clumps of hair.

Wrapping her arms around herself, her calves began to burn from her pace and the long distance. Rocks scratched her toes and it felt like the entire beach had piled in her sneakers.

"So. Damn. Stupid," she muttered punching each syllable.

Arriving to where Asher had parked his Ducati, Dylan sat on the cold pavement directing her frustration at her shoes while shaking out the sand.

Grunting, Dylan got up. "What did you think would happen? Huh? So stupid."

The long walk gave her a lot of time for deliberation on the night as a whole. She felt like a serious idiot in many ways. It wasn't like her to just jump on the backs of motorcycles with strange boys or crash parties like she owned the place. Who did she think she was? She gnashed her teeth together as that thin thread of self-confidence earlier gained shriveled within the flame of reality.

Reaching into her pockets for her phone to call a cab, she ended up screaming and stomping her feet like a child. Her jacket was still at the party along with her phone and cash! Practically growling, Dylan climbed the large rocks lining the main road above the beach.

It was almost four a.m. so she wasn't all that surprised no one was traveling along the feeder. She didn't even know which way to walk, but chose to go right.

Because right was right... right?

There had to be some kind of gas station or truck stop open. Five minutes down the dark, deserted road, every business she'd come across had been closed.

Dylan spotted car lights traveling in her direction and threw a hand up in the air. Looking at her waving hand, she switched to a hitchhiker's thumb instead.

"Come on, come on, stop. *Please*."

A beat up white 4Runner slowed to a stop next to Dylan and a man rolled down the passenger window.

"Ya need a ride, Darlin'?" slurred a hefty middle-aged man with a thick country accent. Apparently, she hadn't been the only one drinking.

In the back of Dylan's head, a siren was sounding again, *Danger, Run!* But she told herself, she was cold, aching, and out of better options. And over all, the thought of crawling back to the party for a ride burned her pride.

"Yeah, just to an open gas station?"

"Sure thing." He reached over to open the passenger door and Dylan jumped in.

Shutting the door, she immediately took in the overwhelming musky scent of Old Spice and cigarettes. She never understood what induced men to want to smell like cinnamon potpourri.

"So, why's a fine thing like yourself doin' out here at this late 'our?" he bellowed as he turned around the SUV, heading back the way he came.

"Oh, um, car trouble."

Dylan felt instantly uncomfortable. She shifted on the split leather seat and looked out the window. "Thanks for the ride. I really appreciate you taking the time out of your night."

They traveled in silence for a few minutes listening to Lee Brice sing something on the radio about partying. The fact that she knew it was Lee Brice made her laugh, thinking of Isabel and her affection for brawny men in cowboy hats.

Passing a few closed businesses and an old motel that looked like something Norman Bates would own, Dylan began to worry nothing would be open. The man took a turn down an even darker road.

"I saw an open gas station down her' earlier."

Dylan glanced at him but he didn't look at her. She started to remember the pepper spray on the keychain in her jacket. The doors suddenly locked and her stomach clenched. He slowed to a stop near a vacant lot.

Blood pumping, she dared another look in his direction. His face was cast in a series of shadows, playing up thick wrinkles and an insidious smile. His eyes were hidden like two black pits gouged out to cover his inner demons. Sweat dotted his upper lip and plastered his stringy, dark hair to his forehead. He moved his hand onto her inner thigh, grabbing her with bruising force way too close to the V in her legs.

"Wh-what are you doing!" she stuttered, blinking in shock while trying to free herself from his advance.

"Oh, don' act like that ain't what you were doin' along the road at this late 'our. I ain't see no broken car." He leaned over the center console, reeking strongly of whiskey and stale cigarettes. Dylan threw up her hands in defense and struck his jaw, but it did nothing but make him obviously angry.

"So that's how it's goin' be, hunh." He hastily grabbed a chunk of her long hair at the nape of her neck and threw her head against the window. A cracking pain erupted in her head followed by a deafening ringing. A warm gush trickled down her forehead and into her right eye. Holding her head and gasping, she was in too much pain to notice he had gotten out of the car until her door opened, forcing her to spill out the side and onto the ground. She felt gravel and asphalt grind into her palms, elbows, and knees.

She started to sob when the man grabbed her hair yet again and began to drag her across the asphalt. Rocks tore into her jeans and sliced her knees. Her hands found his trying to pry him off as she kicked her legs in desperation, but he held her too tightly. Her self-defense training appeared to be useless, as all she seemed to be able to do was cry, kick, and scream. Shoving her into the back seat, he grinned.

"You know you wan' it rough."

"N-n-o!" she squeezed out as she tried to kick and squirm, knocking him in the gut a few times. He seemed completely unfazed—if anything, he *chuckled*.

He soon pinned down her thrashing legs with his weight as he began to rip off her jeans. She let out a blood-curdling scream when she felt the night air kiss her thighs.

"You don't have to do this! Please, don't do this!" she cried as tears blurred her vision. Suddenly, his dirty thick fingers were in her mouth, silencing her. She bit down and he reared his hand back.

"Stupid 'hore!" he yelled cracking a backhand her across the face.

She cried out, slapping both hands to her face and trying to roll into the fetal position but he yanked her hips back in place. She lay there limp, as the world seemed to blur in and out of focus, hoping to once again become numb. But the man's sadistic chuckle, as he yanked her jeans the rest of the way off, snapped her back to reality. No one was going to hurt her or walk all over her without a fight. She was a demon; a force to be reckoned with.

Mentally holding a finger to the universe, Dylan flipped her head up and looked hard into his eyes, with all her might, while she snatched his arm. She wanted to hurt him, maim him permanently and scream until his ears bled.

A sensation flickered within her body, like a spark of electricity grasping for fuel. Suddenly it lit, blazing forth. A hum so shocking she gasped at its sheer force swelling inside her. It continued into a long inhale. The hick started to scream and scratch at his head, drawing blood and shaking it quickly from side to side in terrifying agony. Anger rushed her veins as she listened to a scream so shrill she had never heard anyone, let alone a man, make—but she couldn't *stop*. She didn't want to stop. She was hurting him, as he had done to her, and it made her happy inside.

Still inhaling, a mist began to form in front of him, like the heavy mist of morning, but this wasn't harmless vapor, this was, she realized, *a soul*.

His eyes flipped open, bulging like two blood-shot marbles cracking with brown irises. His mouth had morphed into a full on gape, but his shriek has ceased into a silent scream. His expression reminded her of The Scream by Edvard Munch.

Trembling and beyond scared, she couldn't seem to stop inhaling. *Help!*

The mist began to form the face of the bug-eyed man, blindingly bright, yellowing, and sickly.

With all the strength she could muster, she released him and threw both hands against the chipped leather seats to brace herself, to stop the extraction. Dylan managed to squeeze her eyes shut inadvertently making the truck jump. A crunch exploded and glass shattered, sprinkling a torrent of tiny shards on top of her.

Feeling the man drop limp onto her lap, she opened a cautious eye. Flipping both open in horror, she gawked at the man passed out on her bare stomach. His blood smeared like skid marks against her pale skin.

Without a second thought, she kicked at the open crumpled door and shoved the scum off of her. She jumped out of the SUV—a shower of glass raining off her body. Immediately dipping down, she tested his pulse that still beat strongly. Sighing with relief, Dylan stood and tugged on her ripped jeans and laced her sneakers. She winced slightly at the gravel still stuck to her torn knees and raw palms. Looking down at the disgusting excuse for a man, she started to kick his still body.

"You think you can rape me! Pig! You picked the WRONG girl!"

Dylan's mouth ran yelling profanities even she was surprised were in her vocabulary. She kicked him once more in his large gut, causing her to stumble on a dip in the ground. Examining the cause of her fall, she realized there was a small crater surrounding the SUV. Her eyes moved to the blown tires, the crushed metal on the sides, and every piece of glass— windows, lights, mirrors—shattered.

Blinking in astonishment, Dylan whispered, "Did I…" she trailed off comprehending the seriousness of her actions.

Her eyes darted around the deserted road. Treetops stirred and leaves rustled. The area felt alive and watchful. A low rumble of thunder sounded in the distance, startling her. Shadows seemed to loom up all around her, like thick, black, featureless forms awaiting her demise. Tristian's words came to mind, *demons working outside of a contract are deemed rogue and actively hunted by the Shadow Horde…*

Scrambling to stand, Dylan located the man's wallet and kicked him one last time for good measure. Taking off in the direction of the entrance to the deserted street, she thought of the old, creepy motel they had passed. Never stopping, she started to feel her legs move at new speeds.

What's happening to me? Adrenaline coursed through her veins at her will to live. *It was an accident*, she cried to herself. She didn't mean to take that man's soul.

Rounding the corner on the dark street, Dylan spotted the grimy motel. She slowed her pace as she hit the parking lot not wanting to alert anyone. Her shirt and pants clung to her body, sullied with sweat, dirt, and blood.

Power walking to the main office, she smacked her bloody palm against the window. An old, stocky man with uneven stubble and a thick, greasy comb-over walked up, eyed the bloody handprint, and then casually slid the window open.

"Can I help you?"

Panting, Dylan breathed, "A room please."

She nervously glanced around a few times as a bead of sweat traveled down the length of her nose. The old man looked at her skeptically, eyeing her bloodied body and the print on the window once more.

"One bed is forty dollars a night."

She fumbled the rapist's wallet, almost dropping it twice before she was able to count out forty dollars and slapped it on the man's desk. He quickly replaced the money with a key, never asking a single question about her appearance.

Finally in the motel room, Dylan locked the door and kept the lights off. A sudden shrill ringing jarred her nerves. Jumping, Dylan stared at the phone.

Why would anyone call this room? Who would know I'm here except for the Shadow Horde?

Letting it ring, Dylan scanned the room for any kind of weapon. Her eyes trailed to the bedside lamp. She unscrewed the light bulb and hit it against the nightstand leaving a sharp edge. Making her way to the corner of the room, Dylan slid down the wall and stared at the locked door. The A/C's buzzing seemed to cloud her hearing and her body shook uncontrollably as she sat in the secure darkness.

Did I really steal a soul? Crush a car? Were my powers starting now that I had taken a soul?

Her fingers traveled up her crusty cheeks to her eyes.

My eyes.

Too afraid to move from her protective corner, she remembered Tristian's words.

"We get the color of our eyes after collecting our first soul. Part of the first soul you collect becomes a part of you. It stays with you forever and can give you strength or define the basis of who you are..."

"Oh God," she whispered as horrible images of the rapist sinking his dirty hands in her body flashed through her mind's eye.

A loud pounding sounded at the door jerking Dylan out of her haunting reverie. A tiny scream bubbled up in her throat, muffled by the bloodied knuckles of her free hand.

They're here.

Tears started to really stream down her cheeks. "I didn't do it on purpose!" she cried. "I don't want to die."

"Dylan!" said a muffled voice. "Open the door!"

"Wh-who are you!" she yelled from her corner.

"It's me... Tristian." Her heart leaped at his name. "Open the door."

She started to get up. "Wait." She swallowed against the acid in her throat. "How did you find me?"

"Open the door and I'll tell you all about it."

She moved slowly to the door. Her logical side screamed for her to run back into the confines of her protective corner, but her hopeful side longed for Tristian's secure embrace. She knew she hadn't exactly been the greatest judge of character lately...

but she *needed* him. If only to hold her.

The air was silent and thick as her hand shook so violently she could hear a dangling piece of glass tinkle within the broken light bulb. Her heart pounded as she caught a glimpse of her chest visibly quaking as she peeked out the peephole.

Tristian.

Exhaling a giant stressed breath, she threw open the door, instantly jumping into his arms.

"You're here." Tristian's intoxicating manly scent numbed her pain, more than any substance ever could. "You're really here," she said again as tears continued to spill down her face.

He hugged her back equally as hard then pulled away, cupping her face. "What were you thinking?" Even through his sunglasses she could tell his vivid stare searched her new, wet eyes.

"How did you find me?" Dylan panted while tugging him into the room and quickly shutting and locking the door.

"Asher called me after you disappeared from the party," Tristian said, flicking on the lights and moving to a sit on the bed, pulling Dylan next to him. "He asked if I knew where you were. He was worried some creature got to you or worse…" He trailed off gently grabbing her hand, which still clutched the broken light bulb, and took the improvised weapon. He paused a beat as he noticed her raw palm. "I drove down here to help him look when I saw the Radiance," he mumbled distantly.

Dylan blinked. "*Radiance?*"

"Whenever a soul is released from a body, it shines so intensely it highlights the area, like a spotlight that's only noticeable to the underworld. I followed it to the wrecked truck and the man still there lying passed out. I figured you probably tried to go somewhere safe, and I thought of the motel I'd past. The old guy at the front office initially lied for you. But I saw the bloody print and knew you were here." Tristian smiled, his eyes returning from their glaze. "But after some *convincing* he told me which room you were in."

Dylan blew out a shaky breath. "I didn't mean to do it." She looked up and automatically removed his sunglasses and set them on the bed. "I didn't mean to steal a soul."

"You didn't."

"What?" she squeaked. "But I wrecked that truck. I ran *really* fast."

"I checked the man, he still had his soul. You must have stopped midway, which is nearly impossible to do for your first time. It's not uncommon to have powers before you mature."

She took a ragged breath thinking about the rapist's face as the soul seeped out of him. A shudder overtook her from just the thought.

"Are you cold?"

"He tried to rape me," she said, knowing that wasn't what he asked. Tristian tensed. "Everything that happened, I…" She took another deep, shaky breath and looked to the ceiling, her lids fluttering through impending tears. "I have no idea how I did anything back there. It all just *happened*." Before she could stop herself a river of words spilled forth from her mouth. "God, I've made a series of moronic decisions… I forgot everything at the party and tried to *hitch-hike* to a gas station. Yeah, real smart. I just ended up getting the shit beat out of me. I remember at one point being enraged and the next thing I knew, I was taking that asshole's soul and he was screaming in agony." *And a part of me liked it.*

She glanced up and Tristian looked slightly impressed, or possibly horrified, before shifting her stare back to the floor. She couldn't watch him judge her; not then and not ever. "I just… had no idea what I was doing while I was doing it."

"If it makes you feel better," he spoke softly, moving a lock of hair behind her ear and trailing his fingers to her chin lifting her eyes to his again. "Soul extraction without numbing the person is probably the most painful experience a human can have."

She nodded, already knowing that. The vacuum scenario Asher painted, ever so vividly, was forever seared into her mind.

"Are *you* okay?" he asked with worry contorting his face. She shook her head and laid it on his shoulder trying to compose herself. A place where she should have been all night, all week.

"Dylan?"

"What's going to happen now?" she asked, lifting her head off his shoulder and looking into his serene eyes.

Tristian wrapped a firm arm around her, drawing her close. "We'll stay here tonight. Tomorrow we'll go back to LA. No matter what, I'm not leaving you this time. You can ignore me all you want, but I won't change my mind."

She bit at her bottom lip and looked away, could she trust him? He had said this before and broken it.

Never trust a demon...

"What's going on in that mind of yours?" Tristian asked.

"Nothing, really... I guess, I just hope you actually stick around this time. That's all."

She saw his eyes cloud over with something she couldn't name, hurt or regret maybe?

"I shouldn't have let you leave the morning you left my apartment." His voiced dropped to a whisper, "Or let you run away when I had you in my arms last week."

Her heart clenched as she listened in silent awe, his forehead resting against hers. "If I had been with you, you wouldn't be here." He picked up a bloodied hand that looked like she raked her palm over a cheese grater. "You wouldn't look like this." He swallowed, his voice distant as if he was far

135

away in his mind. Before she could tell him something, anything, he squeezed her and let go, creating distance between them.

"Maybe you should take a bath, get some sleep."

"What about the Shadow Horde?" Dylan said looking up at him. Partly wondering why the sudden cold-shoulder.

"You didn't take a soul so they don't have a reason to intervene. All they know is a soul was extracted then replaced."

"I know you are contracted to find me and Asher is contracted by the Omnipotence to find my parents..." Tristian seemed suddenly rapt. "Er, that's why I left the party. I overheard him talking to Livia-"

"Livia was there?" Dylan nodded. "I figured Asher was contracted to hunt your parents, but it was only a guess."

"Hunt?"

"Yeah..." He cringed slightly. "They're fugitives, with death warrants."

"Because of me?"

"Because of what *they did* with you."

Dylan, still trembling violently, tried to slip off her sneakers. She didn't care about anything anymore. She just wanted to go to sleep. Tristian, sensing her struggle, immediately crouched down by her feet, helping her tug the shoes off and stand up.

"Where all are you hurt?" he asked.

"Other than the obvious..." She lifted her palms, "here," then her elbows, "here," and looked down at her knees and pointed to the large, torn red circles, "and there." He nodded, looking her up and down with his head cocked to the side.

"Wait here a second."

Before Dylan could reply, he darted to the bathroom and returned before Dylan could reply with a washcloth and the motel's complimentary water glass filled with warm, soapy water. He pulled her to the side of the bed and sat the cup down on the nightstand.

"Sit," he commanded. She obeyed and he immediately brought his fingers to her chin. "Close your eyes."

Squeezing them shut, he brought the towel to her face and wiped off the runny mascara, tears, and blood. She felt him grasp her right hand and gently dab her palm—picking out pieces of gravel and glass. Dipping the cloth, he squeezed the water over her palm. Her eyes flicked open from the stinging burn of the soap sterilizing her skin. The murky water dripped to the floor as she found herself watching him. He seemed to be taking controlled breaths as he concentrated deeply—making sure not to hurt her. She could see his pulse throbbing thunderously in his neck and his brow severely furrowed.

When he was done, he looked at her as he blew lightly across her tender flesh to suppress the sting. The act was so sensual and raw, she had almost forgotten pain radiated at the surface. Their eyes locked and his clouded over, the color reminding her of a seaweed-filled ocean during a storm. She suddenly felt something shift between them. The act was so simple, yet she somehow knew anything leading up to that moment was insignificant and that everything from then on would be different. After a few seconds, he looked away— shattering the moment.

He moved to her other hand and then her elbows, continuing the delicious ritual. He started to put the towel away when she boldly said, "Turn around."

He rubbed the back of his neck and reluctantly turned, looking a bit confused. She peeled down her jeans, almost falling twice, but caught herself on the bed before divesting herself of them completely. She sat down on the bed and covered her purple, lace-trim boy-shorts with a thin sheet, unveiling her tattered knees.

"Okay," she spoke softly, quite surprised at her actions. She was never this forward, but with Tristian, all of her inhibitions were pushed to the back of her mind, her body desiring only him.

He turned around and registered what she had done. His eyes darkened, as he seemed almost stuck in place. She shifted her legs up to her chest gingerly and patted the bed. He slowly sat and pulled her legs over his lap by her ankles. His hand traveled from her ankle up to her swollen knees. He let out a long, slow, and tortured breath.

Resting his right hand lightly on her thigh, he seemed nervous. She reasoned with herself that he couldn't possibly be as nervous as she was. She handed him the cup of red murky water and their fingers brushed, sending exhilarating shocks straight to her core.

Leaning back against the headboard, she tightly held his silver chain, running it across her lips listlessly while concentrating on not jumping at each point of contact. He took another deep breath and dipped the cloth, squeezing the water over her knees—letting it drip on him and the bed, but neither of them seemed to care.

He brushed it along her skin lightly, wiping off the excess dried blood and asphalt. She let out a rush of air as the sting pinched her, making something between a whimper and a moan escape. He stopped as his hooded eyes flicked to hers. His hand that rested above her knee clenched tighter and their chests heaved in sync. The moment took reign over her body and what made her tremble now was how close they were and how little clothing she was wearing.

With her lips slightly parted, she dropped the chain, letting it slap back into place. His hand twitched and for a fleeting moment she thought he was going to slide it up and under the white sheet.

But he didn't.

He looked away with a frown and finished the job, leaving

her blinking, completely hot and flustered. *What just happened?*

She chastised herself by biting her lip to distract her thoughts. He probably didn't want to be with someone who resembled Rocky after a fight. Plus, she shouldn't even want this. Not after what just happened. But she did. Badly. She wanted him all the time, and right now the distraction was exceptionally tempting. Blood trickled into her mouth, salty and metallic, when she realized she'd bitten herself too hard.

"Damn." She held up her hand to the wound thankful the pain cooled down her sudden libido.

Where was all of this coming from?

"You okay?" he asked, his voice grating.

"Yeah, fine," she muttered.

She licked her lip and patted the cut with her middle finger. He seemed to hurry up—finishing with her knees rather quickly. But she didn't care. She felt utterly spent.

"Thank you," she managed to whisper, worried if she spoke any louder she might spontaneously combust.

Inner turmoil was evident on his face, but she couldn't think of anything he could be conflicted about. She lifted her legs slightly, careful not to bend her tender knees, as he swiftly slid backwards onto the middle of the bed beside her. She lay down and faced the wall—the spot where she had sat waiting for the Shadow Horde.

As death had stared her straight in the face, the one thing that enveloped her mind was that she was going to die alone. That no one had a clue where she was or *who* she really was. All her life she had been alone. Abandoned by her biological parents, left by her mortal parents, isolated in school, and to top it off as incredible as it was, she wasn't even human. It was a realization that shook her to her core. She was alone, because she made it that way. She'd alienated herself, keeping her walls up to ward off heartache, but it was only hurting her more. She needed to change, to open up, to tell her friends and family finally what was eating at her heart. She needed to be a better person.

She squeezed her eyes shut as tears pricked the backs of her lids. Suddenly she realized Tristian hadn't moved. She looked at him and smiled weakly, patting the bed beside her. Looking back at *the* spot, she felt thankful that at least she had him right then, even if it was for only the night.

He paused for a moment, then kicked off his shoes and cautiously moved to a sit beside her.

"What happens to you after you bring me to my parents?" Dylan asked.

He cleared his throat. "My contract will be up."

She turned her head to look at him. "Yeah, but will I see you again?"

Dylan noticed a flicker in his eyes. "Yes."

She nodded, turning back over. He was lying. She couldn't explain how she knew. It could be a mixture of what Asher and Livia said plus common sense. When things were too good to be true, they generally were.

Without thinking, she grabbed his hand beckoning him to hold her. She just needed contact, to be held like she meant something to someone, anyone. He stiffened for a second and she worried she was coming on way too strong. That this, whatever *this* was, was either pity or his job. Then, before she could sink deeper into her negative mind, he slid down to cradle her tense body. The thin sheet still marked a barrier between them. She enjoyed the warmth of his breath on her neck way too much.

"Thank you for finding me," she whispered as her muscles finally released.

He held her a bit tighter as her trembling slowed. His lips slightly brushed her ear as he whispered, "Do you want a blanket?"

The simple act immediately sent waves of desire rippling through her.

No. "Yes, but I think it's also my nerves from almost dying," she said.

He nodded, his nose grazing her neck as he wrapped his feet around hers and pulled the comforter at the end of the bed over the both of them.

Despite the pain, she felt like she was floating on the high that was his body heat. There was this strange feeling in her chest that she could only describe as vines crawling out of her heart towards him, trying to wrap them tighter, needing Tristian to be closer, on top of her, touching her, licking her... No, what she needed was a bucket of ice water, so she could dump it on her head! Goodness, she needed to change the focus off her body.

"C-can you tell me something about my parents?" she panted, somehow completely out of breath.

"When I was a child..."

"When was that?"

"A couple centuries ago." Her eyebrows shot up. *Two hundred years ago...?*

He moved back slightly and propped himself up on his elbow. Stroking her entire arm lightly with the tips of his fingers—igniting a trail of goose bumps.

"When I was a child, I heard this story about two powerful demons who wanted more than anything to be allowed to have a child. I didn't understand why they weren't allowed to procreate. I was only eight years old, a youth, and still naïve to most of the Laws. These two demons called on the Three Kings over and over again pleading and arguing their right to have a child. They argued that they shouldn't be punished for falling in love with each other. My parents then explained to me about the

Law regulating the actions of the strong and powerful. During each hearing with the Court, all of their alliances and friends filled the halls supporting their right, including my parents. Each hearing attracted millions of demons, of every kind, wanting to witness the 'Elementa Dilemma'. Even now, I don't know how they were able to keep the interest of so many worlds after centuries and thousands of court dates. It's possible the population just really wanted to believe in the power of love." He smirked as if it was a joke to believe in such things.

"Nonetheless, that seemed to help tremendously in their favor, as well as the constant protesting of a close group of friends. Finally, twenty-two years ago, they were given approval with one clause: they had to give their child to the Omnipotence for their use. This generated a new law for any of those wanting to reproduce that previously couldn't before. Your parents obviously agreed, but the night you were born... I guess, your parents couldn't let you be enslaved for the rest of your life. So, they switched you.

"The day you were announced, twenty-one years ago, I was working in Elon. Many demons gathered to see you. No one knew how you would look or if you would come out using your powers on everyone." He chuckled lowly, remembering something in particular.

"A carrier delivered the baby, which was strange, although accepted. Zirk took the infant and found the baby to have a soul. The baby was then handed to Vashti. She reached into the child's mind and discovered the baby was indeed human. They took the soul of the child and killed it. Zirk announced the findings to the populous and sent the Shadow Horde after your parents and anyone associated with them. Only to find they were gone and have been since."

Whoa, all because of me?

"Who are Zirk and Vashti?" Dylan asked.

"Two of the three kings of the Immortal Court."

142

"Where's Elon? It's a city?"

"It's a world and our home. It's considered the capital of demon worlds."

"Why would my parents want to have a child if they weren't going to benefit from raising it?"

"Well, the day you were born, the OP needed to secure your destiny, so to speak. Basically, you would only be there for the ceremony binding you to the Omnipotence and return to the law at age sixteen for training."

Dylan thought about her life at that age and how starkly different everything would have been if her parents hadn't hid her.

"Where are my parents?"

"I don't know for sure. My guess is somewhere between worlds."

"If you don't know where they are, how do we find them then?" She asked, turning her head to look into his stormy green-eyes.

"Leave that to me." He looked at her for a moment then let his eyes roam up to her aching forehead, down to her sore cheeks, and then to her split lip where he frowned before returning eye contact. "You should try and get some sleep. It's already almost six."

She looked away shyly as a small smile teased the corner of her mouth. "Yeah."

She knew sleeping platonically next to a boy was no big deal, but sleeping next to Tristian, well, that just made her nervous as hell. She tried to ponder the most casual way to sleep because she suddenly couldn't remember how she normally did. Which way? Did she sleep on her back or her side, with one pillow or two? Taking a deep breath in an attempt to steady herself, she took a chance and quickly turned into him. Cuddling against his warm, granite chest, immediately it felt right.

He sucked in a sharp breath, but didn't jerk or push her away. She heard him let out a surge of air as he wrapped his arms around her, pulling her closer, holding her tighter, and resting his head on hers. Passion seemed to prickle the air around them as emotion seeped from her every pore. It was beautiful and warm, and for the first time, she felt *alive*.

In that moment, she didn't care about the Shadow Horde, the rapist, or even her embarrassment the week before. It was just the two of them, in their own world, and all she wanted to do was stretch the feeling of possibilities that ran through her mind while in his arms. Tristian woke her heart in ways she never considered possible and she only hoped she invoked the same feelings in him.

Perfectly content, she listened to his heart beat and steady breathing as she drifted into a blissful sleep.

CHAPTER 8

"Only in the darkness can you see the stars."
Martin Luther King Jr.

CRUNCH, crunch. All Datu could hear for the long twenty-minute walk was the howl of the whipping cold wind and ice, and the crunch of snow compacting beneath his sneakers. If Datu had been able to feel the cold, he held no shadow of a doubt both hypothermia and frostbite would have set in long ago.

He had been blindfolded and escorted by two very tall hairless men with vacant white balls for eyes and missing lips—keeping their rotting, fulvous teeth showcased at all times. Their skin was a metallic bronze that glistened in the moonlight, and their fingers were long, blood-encrusted, sharp talons. They were called "worms" after the vile beings that burrow in soil and feed on decaying organic matter. Their life purposes limited and dependent on their masters—feed, defend, attack, and serve. '*The scum of the underworlds*' as the creatures would say. Neither of the worms could speak, not that he felt the need for conversation with the creepy beings, but the silent walk was starting to feel excessive.

Datu stumbled on a change of plane. Sharp rocks sliced through the soles of his shoes as the two creatures halted. He heard the loud groan of a door and a rush of warm air slap his body. An inhuman odor tingled his heightened sense. Scrunching up his nose in disgust, the vampire was pushed into

145

a wide room.

"Remove its blind fold!" demanded a booming voice that seemed to originate all around him. As commanded, the worm slaves removed the sack from around Datu's head.

Blinking to focus against the harsh light, he looked around at the vast marble palace. Broad soaring columns with dark orange veins and blazing torches lined the middle of the fortress, marking a path to the booming voice. The walls appeared to be plastered but cracked with something alive, and throbbing inside, something *blood red*. Whatever it was, made the blood in Datu's veins pulse at a feverous rate.

"Step forward, vampire!"

As if struck by fear, Datu's legs seemed unable to respond to his mental instructions. He began to panic, wondering if he was making a huge mistake. A worm then shoved him forward towards the ghastly demon. The being was one of the most powerful demons in all of the worlds. He was quite a bit older with burn scars wrapping his body and bald head, that boasted his deep-set dark-orange eyes. Slits marked where his ears and nose used to reside and long, white, rigid scars lining the shriveled flesh above his herculean muscles.

The demon sat severely upon an ornate metal throne atop rows of thick marble steps. Each breath he took flexed the walls and Datu realized the red organ throbbing in the plaster was connected to the demon's every movement.

Gripping the throne with bone crushing force, his muscles flexed shoving his blue veins outward.

"Why have you begged for a visit, vampire?" crackled the voice. "It better be good. I don't take kindly to surprise guests." He hissed the last word as seething as a viper.

"I," Datu's voice quivered. He cleared his trembling throat and spoke stronger. "I know where Temperance Elementa is."

The creature sat back, relaxing, and tilted his head up. A

smirk flirted his split lips. "And where is this?"

"Los Angeles, California."

A wicked smile broke his face. "And why are you telling me this information, vampire?"

"Rumors have it, you've been looking for her and I want to be human again," Datu blurted, straightening his shoulders to exude confidence.

The demon tapped his black nails against his raised chin and lifted an eyebrow. "You do not wish to be immortal?"

"I want to walk in the sunlight and be free of the bloodlust." Datu swallowed against the burn in his throat. The thought of blood, no matter how much he had just consumed, churned his stomach violently, always wanting more.

"I see," the being said as he seemed to ponder this a moment, picking at his fingernails that were shaped like long, black ovals with a sharp tip. "And what makes you think I can grant you this freedom?"

"You have done it for others. Granted life, released curses, and given freedom to slaves-"

"All right," the demon interjected.

"Yes?" Datu couldn't believe his ears. A brilliant smile made its way across his face. He would be human again. Blood would no longer rule his life. He couldn't wait to start his utterly boring life as a mortal. To age, to bear children, and most importantly to live *free*.

An acidic voice broke his muse, "One condition."

Datu's face fell, then immediately hardened to feign indifference.

"Bring me this Temperance Elementa."

Datu thought of the sweet, broken hearted girl at the party. "She has powerful Collectors following her every move. I can point her out... maybe pull her away from them for a short time, but she will not go anywhere with me. I'm sure of it."

"Fine." The demon waved a lazy hand. "Kill him."

"No!" shrieked Datu as the worm slaves moved towards him with large rusted axes gripped in their claws. Their gigantic feet scraped on the marble and their expressions were pure excitement like large jungle cats lunging at their prey.

"I'll do it!"

The scarred demon held up a lazy hand to the worms. Drool sloshed out of their lipless mouth as they halted mid-sprint, letting their axes droop to the hard floor.

"I'll do it, just... d-don't kill me," Datu panted while darting his large, hazel eyes between the worms and demon.

"Two days." He straightened his shoulders. "I give you two days. Bring her to me, vampire."

"You will then set me free?"

Faster than Datu could blink, he was standing face to face with two terrifying blood-orange eyes holding his head at a neck-breaking angle. The demon's nails bit into his skin spilling a trickle of clotted blood.

Datu's life didn't flash before his eyes. He didn't see his lover, or even the slipping memory of his parents. All he could feel, taste, and see was the white-hot, blinding pain evoked by the disfigured demon in front of him.

"I," roared the demon while widening his shadowy eyes. "I will decide if and when you get any reward." He bent the vampire's head just a fraction more. "Not you."

Datu blinked back the searing pain as his mouth hung open, his curved fangs slipping out—reaching for blood. The being smirked and released him.

"Bring her to me, vampire," the demon hummed wickedly as he bounced back to his throne. "Or I will find you and *end you*."

◇◇◇

The chilling wind whipped Dylan's hair in her eyes as she

strained to see in front of her. The scenery was distorted, as if someone smeared charcoal across a finished canvas. The wind changed direction and she gasped at the sight she beheld. She was balancing on the ledge of a skyscraper, looking down at the glittering red and white lights of the traffic below. She was so far up, the cars resembled glowing ants crawling to their destinations.

Waving her arms in frantic, large circles trying to maintain a good balance, a deep voice stole her attention. She planted her feet on the stone ledge and looked at a winged figure crouched next to her resembling a shadowy gargoyle.

"You shouldn't be here," he whispered against the wind.

She didn't say anything only studied the figure, wondering why it looked and sounded so familiar, until he turned. Swirling verdant gems glowed through the shadows, illuminating his set features.

"Tristian?" she heard herself hiss over the howling wind.

His hair flowed like liquid silk with the wind, and his bare, tan, chiseled chest heaved with deep breaths. He smiled, baring fangs similar to a Piranha's and lifted a stiff hand with black, sharp nails tipping each finger. She continued to stare, feeling confused at what she was witnessing. He cocked a long finger, beckoning her closer.

Without a second thought, her legs moved as he unrolled up to a standing position next to her. His wings flapped around them halting the wind, and Dylan noticed, the world. She looked back at him, feeling her knees tremble at his close proximity.

He blinked and his eyes morphed from their gorgeous green to an unusual orange. He brought up a black talon and slid it down her cheek and over her bottom lip.

"Are you scared yet?" he spoke softly cocking his head to the side. She furrowed her brow as he brought both hands to her chest and shoved her off.

Dylan jerked awake from the sensation of falling. Squinting at the blinding sunlight through the drawn window, she swept her eyes across the half-made, empty bed and touched the spot next to her reminiscing their night together.

Sucking on her split lip, she shifted onto her side and glanced around the empty room, still mostly covered by the other half of the comforter. She pondered for a moment if she had imagined Tristian coming that night at all.

"Tristian?" she called out, but all that responded was silence because she was alone. He had left her again.

Sighing, she rolled over and winced at the intense pain that seemed to throb across her entire body with emphasis on her head. Taking a few minutes to muster enough confidence to move, she glanced at the nightstand where a bottle of water and two ibuprofen sat.

Well, that was nice even if he did leave again, she thought smiling bittersweetly.

Pushing through the pain, she sat up still slightly tangled in the sheet and blanket, then downed the pills and water. She picked up her jeans and made her way into the rusty bathroom with yellowing linoleum floors and a generic Formica vanity, the edges chipped with age. She turned on the faucet, thankful the liquid came out clear, and splashed cold water on her face.

Taking a deep breath, she took a closer look at her face and examined the damage: A self-inflicted split lip, a few cuts, and a gigantic purpling bruise the size of her fist and split in the middle, hovered over her right temple and poured into her disheveled, blood-encrusted hair.

Dylan whimpered, trying to think of any logical excuse that would make sense to Aria, her grandma, or even Garret. Her thoughts provoked a never-ending abyss of tears. She let the drops rain down on her raw cheeks. She didn't understand how her life had become so chaotic in such a short time. How had she let this happen? And who was this blubbering mess staring back at her in the mirror? The Dylan she knew didn't cry or break down. Her therapist had been right. It had all caught up with her. One of the reasons she quit therapy was because the woman kept insisting Dylan needed to open up. That if she didn't it would all pile up and pile up until she broke. Was this what broken looked like?

Despite the condition of the shower, Dylan stepped in letting the scolding water wash away the blood, bruises, and chaos. Using the tiny bottles of shampoo and conditioner, she watched the red suds swirl down the drain from her hair. Her blood and *his blood*.

When something inside her snapped.

Unwrapping the bar of lavender soap, she scrubbed at her skin with vigor. Dirty fingers and whiskey from the rapist felt imprinted on her body and she didn't know how to get it off. She scrubbed harder then accidentally dropped the soap causing her to scream in frustration and punch the tile. Large chunks of porcelain and grout fell, littering the bottom of the tub. Cradling her hand, she fell against the side of the shower and slid down to sit directly under the rain of water. Her pulse roared as she fought to keep composure. Closing her eyes, she tried to relax her sobs and convulsing limbs when she thought of Garret's soothing voice.

Continue to breathe in and out...
In and out...
In and out...

The water began to run cold when Dylan realized she had been in the shower for over thirty minutes. With her impassive mask placed neatly back into place, she got out.

She gently wrung out her hair and dabbed the stiff towel across her red and raw body, avoiding more injury. Deciding against wearing the stained jeans and tank, she wrapped the towel around her torso.

Feeling like she should call Aria to come pick her up, she ventured out of the misty bathroom. Opening the door, she froze at the sight of Tristian holding coffee and a large, brown paper bag. He seemed more relaxed sitting there on the bed in his soft gray tee and jeans. Dylan had never seen him in any color other than black. The gray really brought out his silky dark-brown hair and natural tan. He wasn't wearing his sunglasses and his eyes were as green as lush meadows in the wet springtime. She couldn't help but smile. If he hadn't been staring at her, she probably would have lost herself in studying his features.

Dylan sighed solace. "Hey," she said padding over to sit next to him acutely aware she was wearing close to nothing.

"Coffee?" He handed her the paper cup. She took it willingly and carefully removed the plastic lid, letting the bitter notes of steam waft up her nose—waking up her senses. It was delicious and calming, and half of the reason why she loved coffee so much.

"Thanks," she breathed.

"I've also got some bagels and," accentuating her favorite dimples, "New clothes."

"You didn't have to do that," Dylan said still smiling at the fact he hadn't left.

"I did." He opened the bag, fishing out a smaller brown bag holding the two bagels. "It's the least I can do. Besides, you'll scare people if you wear that around." He gestured to the crusted shirt she had set on her lap.

"You're not wearing your sunglasses," Dylan blurted.

"You'll just take them off of me if I do," he said matter-of-factly. "I'm saving you the effort."

She narrowed her eyes slightly. "Why do you hide your eyes, really? They are so beautiful." She started to reach up to touch his face, but he flinched, causing her to drop her hand and crease her brows together. He was so hot and cold it was hard for her to gauge his feelings.

"No. Your eyes are beautiful." He looked away. "Mine are only a reflection of the soul I took."

Dylan could tell there was a story behind this, something painful in his past. But she was uncontestably hitting a nerve by asking him about it. She figured he'd tell her when he was ready.

"Well, thanks again." She took another whiff of her coffee and set it on the nightstand. "I'll go change."

"I'll meet you outside." Tristian stood while slipping his sunglasses back in place. "I have a few phone calls to make."

"Sure," she mumbled over her shoulder as she proceeded to the bathroom, inspecting the bag carefully.

She pulled out a thin, white button up—the long sleeves rolled to three-quarter length, a white racerback tank with a metal stud embellishment, and light-wash, skinny jeans complete with some leather wrap bracelets adorned with steel studs and matching earrings. At the bottom was a pair of Ray-Ban sunglasses.

She couldn't deny she felt a tad giddy when she saw the completed outfit, almost as if the night before hadn't occurred. But what made her smile even more was the top happened to be strikingly similar to the one she wore to class the week before. Her giddiness was short lived, though, when she caught sight of her reflection in the mirror.

Quickly wrapping her damp locks into a top chignon bun using the elastic at her wrist, she ran her fingers through her bangs—trying to hide the disgusting bruise; the evidence of her weakening armor.

Dylan felt better despite the wreckage on her face and legs; and Tristian had done that. He had turned her looming shadow into a shaft of optimistic light.

After slipping on her favorite—now stained—Converse sneakers, she grabbed her clothes and coffee, and peered out into the walkway surrounding the stark parking lot.

She spotted Tristian's dark chestnut hair against the azure sky. The beautiful morning was nothing compared to the fine specimen resting against the concrete column. The way he leaned with his back to her, leg crossed over the other, and his thumb hooked in his back pocket, reminded her of a James Dean poster she had in her room back at Isabel's. Except she'd much rather have him on her wall instead.

Tristian continued to talk on his phone, unaware of her presence. She strained to hear the conversation for a few moments—maybe still cautious around her new demon friends, but all she could make out was something about Topanga and a dirt road. Passing him into the blinding sunlight, she grazed his shoulder playfully. She heard him clear his throat and mutter something under his breath before ending his call.

"You look great… and it all fits okay?" he asked as she turned to walk backwards. He pushed off the column towards her. "I described you to the saleswoman and she picked everything out. Well, almost everything. I chose the shirt."

"Yeah, it's actually perfect. I even have my own Ray-Bans now." Giving him a wink, she slid on the sunglasses and turned back around sashaying over to his Audi.

"Glad to see you smile. We have a lot to do today."

Snapping her head back in his direction. "Oh?"

"I want to take you to meet someone."

Dylan reluctantly nodded and slid into the car. They pulled onto the main road leaving the old motel behind like a nightmare soon to be forgotten.

They drove along the Pacific Coast Highway for a few minutes. Dylan rolled down the window allowing the rush of warm, fresh air to blanket her face. She closed her eyes wishing life could be this simple. Coffee, salty breeze, cute boy... Why did it have to be tainted with so much ugly baggage? Hadn't she suffered enough for one lifetime? Perhaps not. Perhaps she was destined to live out a life saturated by disappointments. Which only piqued her curiosity to what would be next. She took a sip of her now cold, extra-sweet latte. She looked at the coffee with a grimace, snapping out of her tranquil state. Perfect.

"Dylan?"

"Hmm?"

"You okay?"

"Yeah, well as much as I can be with what happened last night." She set the coffee back in its cup holder. She could do without coffee... maybe.

"All right, you're just so…"

She cocked her head to the side. "What?"

"Quiet," he quickly stated. "I'm used to you bombarding me with questions or chatting about something random."

"Oh." She pursed her lips and picked at the chipped red nail polish on her thumb. She never knew why Aria insisted to do her nails each week. Dylan always just picked it away.

"I'm actually not all that chatty or curious... usually. It's just this new life I knew nothing about. My life had been perfectly planned out after I left high school. College, internship, masters, doctorate, career—I *wanted* to travel between third world countries to live and study modern tribes. Witness the Surma stick fights for love and worship with the Fang Tribe— to see the powerful, old bones of their ancestors-" Dylan quickly stopped herself. She could chat about her passion for the beautiful civilizations for hours on end, and she didn't want to bore him with her flight off-topic. "Anyway, then life… if I could have one with that job… you know husband, kids, et cetera.

"I only have one friend that I keep shallow tabs with, because I don't like emotions, opening up, or the unexpected. I've kind of made peace with the fact that my parents are dead, and I felt my best when I was numb. But now... for the last two weeks, I feel like it's been turned upside down. My dreams seem silly—paling in comparison to what's possible now... I have parents who are *alive*. I look forward to what the next day might bring—*who it might bring*." A small smile crossed her lips. "Gosh, just last week I stood up for myself! I started to feel invincible-" she paused. "I'm not. When faced with death, all by myself, in the shittiest motel possible... I realized I'm still the same, sad little girl. And no one really knows the real me, or even the old me. No one. If I had died, what would they say at my funeral? "Great girl, studied hard-""

"Blushes a lot," Tristian added, causing her to blush. She held back a small smile.

"Just a lot of realizations have hit me. I'm a *demon* for goodness sakes. And I say goodness sake!" She shook her head. "Not to mention, last night I really stumped myself. I mean to tell you the truth, part of me really thought you were full of it." She positioned herself to face him and began whispering, "But I crumpled that car, I rippled the earth, and ran at an inhuman speed. I saw a soul. *An actual soul.*"

"Why are we whispering?" Tristian whispered back at her, letting his sexy dimples show. *Hmm...*

She narrowed her eyes and continued despite his mockery. "You know, I thought high school bullying was bad. If this is a preview of what my infinite years ahead hold, I'm afraid I just can't do it. I don't think I'm strong enough." Her voice dropped below her breath. "Even the coffee people hate me." She knew this was the most she'd dished out of her heart in way too long, but in a way it felt great.

Tristian burst out laughing.

"What! It's serious!" She rolled her eyes, but he wouldn't

stop. He glanced at her frown and laughed harder.

"Why are you laughing?"

"What did the *coffee people* do to you?"

"They made it too sweet!" she barked, trying to hold back the giggle that was threatening to erupt. This was insane... He was insane! But his laughter was just too contagious and she quickly joined in, much to her dismay.

After a few moments their laughter died down to sporadic chuckles. Wiping his tear filled eyes with the collar of his t-shirt. "That's not serious, Dylan," he breathed through a smile.

"No, I know the coffee people don't actually hate me. It's more of a... metaphor of my life." She took a deep breath and slouched back against the seat. The air grew silent and the sudden realization that she probably said too much pecked at her mind like a bird pecking at a piece of stale bread. Tristian was becoming so easy to talk to that it always seemed all the good and bad spilled uncontrollably from her mouth. Along with last night's events, even the week before, jumbled together like spoiled food in her stomach. He definitely had to think she was nuts. He'd be nuts not to think so.

"I-I'm sorry, I think I just unloaded, like years of pent up crap on you in less than five minutes." She gave him a slim smile then turned on the radio, so he didn't feel the need to reply or console her. *Avicii, Wake Me Up* was playing, she huffed inwardly, *how appropriate.*

Tristian took a deep breath and grabbed her hand lacing his fingers with hers.

"Don't be sorry. I shouldn't have laughed. I like knowing what lies in that gorgeous head of yours. Whether it's profound or silly, knowing you is better than just assuming. So relax, I'll get you one *without* sugar."

"You don't need to get me another coffee," she said seriously.

"No, it's okay, really. I'll even make sure the *coffee people* stay in line. I don't need you unleashing your new found powers on the innocent civilians of this fair city." He smiled, bringing her hand up to his mouth and kissing the back of her hand. It sent a zap of energy up her arm. Her mouth went dry and she glanced down at their interlocking fingers as a fire of emotion sizzled her nerves.

"There's a place right up the road."

"Tristian, I'm perfectly functional without caffeine."

"Nu huh. I know how you get when you're deprived of your latte," he taunted with mock disapproval.

Her mouth fell open. "Sure! Like you're really one to talk," she laughed.

"Yeah, yeah. Whatever you say, beautiful." He shook his head with a smirk as they pulled off the highway and into a drive-thru coffee chain, still keeping a secure grip and rubbing his thumb lightly across her knuckles.

Her mind flipped that word over and over. Beautiful. He had called her beautiful. He wasn't talking about a particular body part or naming her gorgeous like guys do when they're flirting. But beautiful, and he was holding her hand and caressing it. He freaking kissed it, too! For the first time, she was jealous of her own hand. She wanted him to kiss and caress her, like he did back at school.

She sucked on the scab forming on her lip, wondering what all of this meant for him. It was surmounting to an inexplicable moment for her. But what if this was all in her head? Maybe his gentle touches were how he acted with every girl? Her chest suddenly ached and her eyes widened at the sensation. What was that? The simple thought of him not reciprocating her feelings and touching other girls actually brought on physical pain. Real pain. Since when did emotions inflict bodily harm?

Burying her confusion, she looked over at him as her eyes lingered on the ripples of his chestnut locks tousled from the wind and roamed down the edges of the dark stubble sculpting his jaw and neck. She thought about that first night at the club when she'd walked in on him and the vampire. She felt her brows dip as she searched for a scar, blemish… anything to mark validation of what she witnessed. But his neck was perfect and scar free. So why was she still torn and raw, healing like a human, when she watched Tristian's vampire bite heal almost instantaneously?

"Tristian?"

"Yeah?"

"So after I turn of age… My injuries will heal like yours did at the club?"

He let go of her hand to grab his wallet out of the center console, sending an instinctive sigh to hum through her lips. His eyes flicked to hers momentarily and her eyebrows shot up at her apparent reflex.

Oh. My. God… I can't believe I just did that, she groaned inwardly as her face seared.

She wanted to shrink down into the seat and become invisible. Looking away nervously, she was suddenly very aware of her body, how awkward she must look.

The barista at the drive-thru window interrupted his daze, clearing her throat and holding out the steaming cup toward Tristian. He clenched his jaw and grabbed the cup tossing his change in the tip jar.

"Well," he said, clearing his throat and handing her the coffee. "Vampire bites heal quickly. So, no matter who gets bitten the wound will always disappear soon after. When you interrupted the, uh, woman, she hadn't finished… that's why it took that long to heal. Usually it is quite instantaneous when they're… done."

His words were chopped and hasty, and Dylan pondered for a moment if he was embarrassed talking about it. She still didn't understand why anyone would intentionally ask to be bitten. Maybe he was doing her a favor?

"However... I have a special ability to heal myself and others." He pulled around the coffee shop and navigated back onto the main road.

"You do?" she asked, craning her neck towards him. Slightly shocked he hadn't offered to fix her wounds. "Can you heal me?"

"I would have volunteered my powers earlier if it were something more serious. As much as I *hate* seeing you roughed up, healing takes too much out of me. I become weak. I'll have to absorb Essence or hibernate for days or weeks at a time to recoup. Although, if I get hurt, minor bruises and cuts always heal fast without effort."

"Well, I guess I'll just have to get used to the color purple for a few days." His hands tightened on the steering wheel at her statement. "Oh, I'll pay you back for all this when I see you in class." She gestured to the clothes and coffee. "I just need to visit an ATM."

"Don't worry about it," he mumbled, keeping his attention to the road.

"No, just tell me how much it all is. I can't let you buy me clothes and food."

She saw his brow wrinkle above of his sunglasses.

"Why?" Tristian asked, glancing in her direction.

"It's just too much. We barely know each other."

"Well, I feel like I know you more than just barely..."

"I still can't ask you to buy me entire outfits." She fiddled with the button on her shirt. "I know Diesel is expensive. I mean these jeans must have been at least two hundred and fifty bucks."

"Think of it as a gift," he grinned. "I get paid very well, Dee. Besides I like buying you things."

Dee? Usually that particular nickname made her scream in frustration, but it sounded nice coming from him. She nodded and whispered, "Thank you."

"So, where's this friend at?" she asked, changing the subject and looking out the window as they traveled into Topanga Canyon. Deciding she'd bring the money anyway, even if she had to slip it into his backpack.

"Only a few more minutes up the road."

She nodded and took a moment to study the details of his body and the angles of his face through the corner of her new sunglasses—conveniently concealing her voyeurism.

His hair was styled in his usual messy shag that gave him a sexy, bad-boy vibe. He seemed lost in thought, almost desolate, lonely. Like he held a great weight that she couldn't even begin to understand but wished she could. She wanted to be let into that mind filled with over two hundred years of wisdom, adventures, love, and loss. It was what made him who he was and she wanted all of him—every pained piece. His easy stature, though, was the epitome of cool and controlled, the opposite of his burdened expression. She marveled at how well he held himself together. Her lips parted slightly as her eyes continued down his fit body, sending shocks to her core. Squeezing her thighs together, she remembered how those strong hands felt running hungrily along her body and how his flexed muscles felt under her palms as he gripped her roughly.

Feeling the familiar sensation of heat rising into her cheeks, she took a deep breath and quickly slipped her hand in his, locking their fingers.

He glanced at her as a beautiful grin spread across his face, wiping away any disheartening thoughts. She couldn't help but return the contagious broad smile, wondering if she had finally found her fairytale.

"I feel like I know you more than just barely, too," she added, leaning back with a sigh. Knowing this man was going to be her undoing because she was falling helplessly. She only hoped, in the end, he'd be there to catch her.

CHAPTER 9

"A dream you dream alone is only a dream. A dream you dream together is reality."
John Lennon

DRIVING through the cracked and pot-hole filled winding roads of Topanga Canyon, Dylan had her head pressed against the window. Her eyes lost in the forest like an excited puppy, just waiting to be released into the boundless unknown. They turned down a deserted, weed-lined, gravel road. Bumping along, Dylan watched Tristian's face grimace and jerk with each flying rock. As if the rocks weren't hitting his car, but actually flying at his head instead. *Boys and their toys* she thought, rolling her eyes and returning to the lush landscapes.

They pulled up to a modern cabin nestled on the side of the canyon. Sliding out of the fine leather seat, Dylan had her mouth agape as she looked up at the tall Oak trees, towering over the small home like a green shield concealing a good part of the sky. Tristian strode up beside her after he had assessed the damage to his bumper. She ignored his hovering and continued to gaze at the thick Elderberry bushes, dotted with White Sage, and purple Chia blossoms. The preserve was striking. Such nature just didn't exist in the city.

The cabin had large windows, smooth, brown wood siding, and a slanted matching roof. She found herself walking mindlessly up the low concrete steps. The house was supported on stilts—cantilevered over the gorgeous canyon.

"Whose house is this?" Dylan asked, leaning over the metal

railing and looking down at the breathtaking drop.

Tristian quickly peeled her away from the edge and held her close. "An old friend."

"Aren't all your friends old?" she teased, looking up into his eyes and feeling safe in his grasp.

Tristian smirked, "You have no idea." He interlaced their fingers and pounded his other fist against the wide, metal door with horizontal panes of frosted glass.

"Old man," Dylan grinned, inching back towards the vast overlook and feeling his grip tighten, halting her venture.

"Watch it. I may be old compared to you but I'm like a child compared to this demon. She's been around for a few millennia."

"You make me sound like a sickly old woman," said the *friend* in the open doorway. He immediately dropped Dylan's hand as their eyes flew to the stunning woman who somehow seemed young and old concurrently. She had long, jet-black hair and vivid aquamarine eyes. She wore a white cotton tank with thin linen pants. Her features spoke of another time and her smile was warm. Dylan instantly didn't like her.

"Please, come in," she said, beckoning them to follow.

Dylan raised an eyebrow at Tristian who only smiled coyly. "After you."

He guided her by the small of her back into the open home. Pushing her sunglasses up on her head, she gawked at the view. The entire back of the house was lined with floor to ceiling windows. Giving the illusion of an unobstructed drop. Near the windows, vertigo swirled her head like a wave pulling her for the plunge.

"I see you like the view?" the woman asked appearing at her side.

"It's wow…" Shaking her head in hopes to process a sentence. "Sorry I'm-"

"Temperance Elementa, correct?" her voice flowed like silk.

"Y-yes, well I go by Dylan." She held out her hand to the woman who only bowed her head instead. She heard Tristian chuckle under his breath.

"You'll have to forgive my customs. I am as old as your friend said." She flicked her hair, narrowing her eyes at Tristian. "I am Sansvi." Cocking her head to the side. "You don't like the name Temperance?"

Dylan sighed and forced a smile. "It's just kind of... odd, don't you think?" she said backing away from windows, and Sansvi.

"It's a very powerful name," Sansvi said matter-of-factly. "It means to contain, control, and have balance. Very fitting for you, I think."

"Yeah well, I guess it'll just take some time getting used to."

"Yes." She motioned to the living area. "Please sit. Would you like some tea?"

Tristian pulled himself away from the windows. "No tea. We need to get down to business."

"Yes, my apologies." She bowed toward him.

They all moved to a sit on the thin white leather sectional. Dylan sat with the windows to her right as Tristian and Sansvi took residence on the other side. Tristian sat lazily with his arm sprawled along the back of the couch and behind Sansvi, but Sansvi sat rigidly on the edge with her legs crossed.

Dylan felt something bloom in the pit of her stomach as she watched him with his arm around the other demon, but before she could fume aloud, she became distracted by the strange energy of the room. Squinting her eyes at her surroundings, Dylan noticed lines blurred, similar to looking under water and she had the constant feeling of fullness in her ears. Moving her

165

mouth open and shut to pop the odd feeling, Sansvi stared at her with an amused expression.

"What you are feeling is the *Pocket*."

Dylan blinked rapidly. She couldn't help herself, she felt totally lost on what was going on.

"A Pocket?" Dylan's eyes darted between the two demons. "And how *do* you two know each other?" She narrowed her eyes at Tristian then directed her questions to Sansvi. "And what's the business? Do you know my parents? Are you going to bring me to them?"

Sansvi smiled at Tristian almost as if to share a private joke and held up a lazy hand. "Dear child-" before Dylan could snap back a retort on *not* being a child, Tristian jumped in.

"She tends to ramble," he spoke to Sansvi. Dylan suddenly wanted to punch him for the condescension. He turned his attention to Dylan. "A pocket is an inter-dimensional bubble that brings a platform, such as this house, between worlds. Sansvi doesn't actually live here in Topanga. This is just a vacant lot in the mountains. She's from the world of Baal."

Sansvi cleared her throat in annoyance. "I am just an affiliate of your parents. No one important. I know Effingo through their connections. This is the first step in alerting your parents to Effingo's completed contract-"

Dylan blinked, "Effingo?" She had heard that name last night too, in Asher and Livia's conversation.

"Oh yeah, my last name isn't Stewart." Tristian shrugged.

She felt her brow continuing to crease more and more with each passing statement.

Sansvi said, "I don't know how much you have been told, but your parents are fugitives and will ultimately have to be found."

Tristian said, "Remember I told you no one knew where they were?" He leaned forward, resting a hand on her knee.

Goose bumps attacked and a shiver passed through her body. Oh she really hoped nothing was going on between them...

"Well, they've been hidden very well for the past couple decades. I have a certain protocol to go through, so they can be confident it's not a trap and that it's the real you."

Dylan felt suddenly uneasy, like she was being examined through a magnifying glass only to reveal she would ultimately fail.

Shifting in her seat, she nodded. "All right, so the first step was coming here..." Dylan understood the need for her parents to stay hidden, but no one knew where they were? Not even close friends? "What are we supposed to do?"

"I am an Oracle, or prophetess, dream connecter. Whichever you prefer. You have a link in your mind. I'm going to help you retrieve it."

"Then we'll go from there." Tristian tried to give her a reassuring smile but it did nothing to cool her nerves.

Taking a deep breath, Dylan nodded again. "Let's get it over with."

Sansvi and Tristian had been conversing heatedly for a few minutes on the side patio near the kitchen. She watched as Tristian gestured violently while Sansvi looked bored, unrelenting on whatever the argument was. That didn't make Dylan feel any less anxious. She closed her eyes and focused on dousing her simmering tension.

"It's good you meditate." Dylan cracked open a heavy lid to see Sansvi standing over her. "I'm sure it helps you gain control of your developing senses."

"I never thought of it that way." Dylan sat up. "Are you ready?"

"I should be asking you that." Sansvi smiled briefly and gracefully sat down next to her.

Dylan regarded the demon skeptically. The casual clothes

looked forced and unnatural as if she was really meant to wear elegant pencil skirts with six inch heels. Sansvi started to raise a hand to her forehead.

"Wait." Dylan evaded her touch. "Where's Tristian?"

"I asked him to step outside."

Now she understood why he looked heated. "Sorry, continue."

Sansvi raised her palm to Dylan's forehead. "This might hurt."

Before Dylan could ask why, an excruciating pain rippled down through her body. It felt like thousands of tiny needles pricking at her insides and ripping her open. It touched the tips of her toes like shoots of bamboo under her nails and began to move back up to her head. She felt a scream tear through her and as soon as the pain registered completely, it stopped.

A serene, salty breeze licked her skin, spraying her hair across her face. She heard the gentle lapping of water to her left as she moved her hair aside, gaping at the deep sapphire dome in front of her. She sat up, blinking a few times. Looking around, her mouth fell even more agape.

It was so beautiful.

An illuminated translucent skyscraper surrounded by delicate, skeletal structures sat in the distance. The small city spilled an array of colorful lights, like haunting rainbows, into the vast dark waters. To her right blanketed a slim greenbelt that bled into a thick forest with twisting trees and exuberant leaves exploding with vibrant yellows and greens. It was just past sunset, and an orange and purple haze dotted where the sun must have been. Even the sand under her palms felt soft as silk. The place was a dream, more than anything she could ever imagine.

Then she saw them. They walked hand in hand over the grassy dunes salted with white sand—her parents.

Dylan's heart began to beat in excitement but all she could do was stare. She was the spitting image of her mother—the same olive skin-tone, oval face, striking eyebrows, and almond shaped, hazel eyes. However, where Dylan was blonde her mother was dark. Her wavy coffee-colored hair fell past her chest, accentuating the same slight figure. Although small, she exuded towering confidence, somehow shadowing the 6'6" demon next to her.

Her father was a statuesque, broad-chested man with slightly tanned skin and honey-blonde hair. Loose strands framed his heart shaped face accenting his wide blue eyes and structured jaw.

Dylan stood dusting the crystals of sand from her sore palms as they stepped forward. Her mother broke away from her father's grasp to take Dylan's hand. Her caress was warm and motherly, something she had missed *so damn much*. She blinked droplets of tears and her mother wiped them away as she seemed to examine Dylan's injuries with displeasure.

"Mom?"

The woman suddenly smiled as she beckoned Dylan's father over. The three of them held hands for a moment as Dylan sniffed away her tears.

"My name is Constance and he, your father, is Atticus."

"Where are we? Is this real?" Dylan asked, afraid to look away. As if they might vanish into thin air with the simple turn of her head.

"Elon. Our home, the one you were born in, is just beyond the hills," Constance said, while pointing the way they came. "And yes, we are truly meeting in the minds. It is but a connected dream." Her voice seemed to echo a bit like a radio, tuning in and out of focus. Dylan felt like she needed to strain to hear but her mother kept speaking without pause. "We cannot wait for you to come home. You have no idea how long we've waited for this moment."

"How do I come home?" The gentle breeze off the ocean blew stronger, whipping Dylan's hair.

"Don't you know?" Her mother asked skeptically.

"No, I don't. I was told you have a message for me to follow."

"You already know everything," spoke her mother placidly. "It is all there." She lightly brushed a finger across Dylan's temple.

Her father spoke, "Only when you seek the truth will it come to you. *The Energy flows where the Balance lies.*" He squeezed her hand with a stern expression, conveying the importance of the statement.

"I don't understand." Dylan felt the wind pick up even stronger, deafening her ears. "But I don't understand!" She wanted to stomp and cry like a toddler but the ground began to quake and the sky clouded over with heavy, black clouds broken by streaks of white crackling lightening. Large trees slapped to the earth, stealing her attention. When she looked back, her parents were gone and just as it had previously formed, an agonizing pain radiated from her head rippling down her body.

Throwing her hands to her temple, she fell to her knees. The pain began to crawl back up and Dylan strained her eyes to see one last glimpse of her true home. The scene immediately shattered into a million pieces of falling glass as the pain reached her scalp throwing her back into Sansvi's cabin.

Dylan gasped. She scrambled to an unbalanced stance suddenly staring at the glass coffee table. Realization of her inevitable destination into the glass, she threw her arms up to protect what she could, as a warm embrace of dark earth hit her like a welcomed wall. Relaxing against Tristian's chest, she smiled as his strong arms wrapped around her tightly. A few seconds passed as she focused on calming her heart. Finally opening her eyes, she studied the second-rate view of Topanga in his embrace. It was sunset and the sun's rays bled through the room covering everything in a rainbow of red, violet, and orange.

"How long was I out?" Dylan whispered, still clutching tightly, never wanting to let go nor extinguish the heat passing between them. His rapid heartbeat bounced in sync with hers while she rode the soothing rise and fall of his breath.

"Several hours," he mumbled, giving her a kiss in her hair and setting his head atop hers. She hummed at the simple and sweet gesture making him hold her tighter.

"Did you get the message?"

"It was so beautiful… I've never seen anything like it, not even in pictures." A flash of cerulean sky and delicate towers then the warm smile of her mother moved across her mind's eye. "*They* were so beautiful."

Sansvi cleared her throat prompting Tristian to break their muse.

"We should go. It's already 8:30."

Dylan dropped her arms and nodded impassively. She turned to Sansvi who seemed a bit pale.

"Thanks," Dylan said to her with a polite smile as Tristian grabbed her hand.

The strange woman bowed, looked at their interlocked hands, and narrowed her eyes at Tristian for a very brief moment before sliding to an exhausted pose on the corner of her couch. Dylan didn't really know what to make of that. Was she jealous?

Tightening his grasp, Tristian led her back to his car. Opening the car door, Dylan felt an electrical charge in the air— like the feel of static during a storm. She turned to look back at the small cabin. It started to vibrate. The wood shuddered and the railings clinked like wind charms. The structure expanded like a balloon then sucked in on itself, leaving a puff of smoke in a lush vacant drop. Dylan heard Tristian laugh.

171

Snapping her head in his direction. "Did you *see* that?" she said, looking at him, then the lot, and back.

"Think about having to travel that way," he grimaced a shudder as his body continued to shake with silent laughter. "Come on, we have a bit of a drive back to my place."

Sliding into the passenger seat. "Your place?"

Tristian shifted into drive carefully turning the car around. "After what happened last night, I don't feel comfortable leaving you out and about by yourself. I'm not leaving you... remember?"

"Okay... I understand last night was absolutely my fault, but one: I doubt I'll be *out and about*." She air quoted the out and about. "Two: Aria is going to flip a switch if I don't get home soon. I'm almost positive. Especially after trying to call my lost phone, then my grandma's house. You know, I'll be surprised if her sorority hasn't issued a search."

He cocked an eyebrow apparently amused. "I don't think the world has stopped," Tristian said, holding back a chuckle. "It's only been one day, and you can call her and your grandmother now if you want." He held out his cell phone but Dylan ignored it.

"I want to go to my apartment." She crossed her arms across her chest with a frown. Dylan knew she was acting twelve, but felt like she had lost all control of her life. Even if it was something as silly as demanding her next destination, she wanted to be the one to choose.

"Fine, but let's grab some food?" Dylan's stomach growled at the sound of nourishment. "I'll take that as a yes."

Traitor... She thought looking at her belly.

"Yes, I'm starved."

CHAPTER 10

"I should have judged her according to her actions, not her words... I should never have run away! I ought to have realized the tenderness underlying her silly pretensions...

But I was too young to know how to love her."
Antoine de Saint-Exupéry

TRISTIAN knew her actions were a result of her trying to cope with the mere fact that her entire world was changing, but he couldn't help but wonder, if he was the cause of her melodramatic mood swings. If he itched her the wrong way. Except, the way she watched him when she thought he wasn't looking, clung to him that day and the entire night, or the way she was clearly jealous at Sansvi's—it couldn't be him. He hoped.

He glanced at her through the corner of his eye. She was staring out at the beach with that permanent frown etched on her face. He wanted to stop the car, drag her to the beach, and toss her into the crashing waves just to see her smile and laugh—his favorite sound these days. Damn, he didn't know what was going on with him. He noticed his feelings had deepened as he watched someone as trusting as Sansvi set his worry aflame.

Taking a deep breath. He knew nothing good came from these thoughts. She was only a contract and he had already broken so many rules. Even Sansvi acknowledged *the* broken rule right before they left, but he couldn't stop touching Dylan.

It was addicting and he needed more.

Last night had been the ultimate test of his will. So, maybe giving her a sponge bath wasn't the brightest of moves for the most unusual relationship, but he just wanted to take care of her, to make everything better. He didn't know she'd undress and want to be held all night.

Damn, his inner self bellowed.

He wanted her so badly. He almost took her right then and there when she moaned as he cleaned her knees. It all seemed as if she was throwing herself at him, but it would have been taking advantage if he'd complied. To keep his distance, he chanted the mantra: *Just a contract, just molested, just upset,* over and over again until the words possessed no meaning. She was only vulnerable and in need contact. He was sure if anyone else had been there, they would have received the same treatment... right? Reminding himself once again this was for the Elementas, for his *family*, not for himself. He raked tense fingers through his mane and turned onto Sunset Boulevard.

The sun had just vanished behind the horizon, causing the air to chill through the open sunroof. An array of lights from traffic, street, and neon signs danced across her absolutely beautiful, solemn face. Tristian grumbled to himself and pursed his lips. This was going to be harder than he thought. Maybe he'd call Monica, or even Natalie, later to take the edge off. He hadn't enjoyed their company since the morning he'd spent with Dylan, but they were at least mediocre distractions that jumped when he gave the word.

Tristian spotted a Mexican restaurant and glanced at Dylan. "Tacos again good for you?" he asked. He knew she favored the cuisine from a couple years of observation. He smiled to himself; of course she didn't need to know that. Who knew, maybe he'd be able to convince her to go to his place after some filling food mellowed her edge. Even if he couldn't stay with her, at least she'd be safe in his refuge.

"Perfect." She smiled forcefully through the stubborn attitude she had been exhibiting for the last ten minutes. You had to admire her tenacity. "Actually… use the drive-thru. I know of a place we can eat."

After receiving their order, Dylan navigated them back onto 'PCH' and to a vacant parking lot along the beach. He immediately knew where they were headed. Dylan came to this spot several times a year as well as on the anniversary of her human parents' deaths. Tristian didn't know its significance, but he knew it was a place to remember.

Dylan stepped out of the car and into the night as if she just assumed Tristian would follow. He cringed and got out of the car, nearly resentful of the power she held over him. Just as he was about to shut the car door, he paused for a split second then plucked off his sunglasses, tossing them on to the seat.

Catching up with her, she led him to a grassy patch just before the white sand crested on the beach. An old, rusted, Spanish fountain trickled near the sidewalk, sandwiched by two cement benches. Light from the pier hit the mosaic, bathing the ground in a sprinkle of dancing light. Dylan wrapped her arms around herself and plopped down on the soft grass. Her back was to the black ocean as she patted the area next to her, motioning for him to sit.

"My mother used to bring me here," Dylan began as Tristian moved next to her still holding the bag of food. "After recitals or random days we felt like doing something—just the two of us. We would pick up ice cream at a local truck and come here just to watch the sunset, or make fun of the tourists." She smiled distantly while harshly ripping shards of grass. "They were such good people, my parents. They cared for me immensely and would do anything for me." Dylan paused, staring at the easy flow of the fountain's water and shook her head. "And here I am, a *demon*. I took away their real daughter, used up all their life's Essence. I was their pride and joy." He watched as her eyes glazed over with tears and her right hand clutched his chain securely. He wanted to pull her into him, to hold her, to whisper sweet nothings in her ear, anything to chase her desolate thoughts away—but knowledge of their foreseeable destination kept him away.

"When I was in that dream, or whatever it was, with the Elementas, for the first time since the accident I had forgotten all about my parents. I know they weren't my biological parents but I can't forget about them." She finally looked at him. "Don't ever let me forget where I came from, where I really grew up. No matter what happens or what world or dimension I end up in. Don't let me forget them."

Tristian felt a pang of empathy in his chest for the ache of bewilderment she felt.

"I won't," he spoke sincerely, handing her a bottle of water. "What did the message say, Dee?"

Her eyes returned from their glaze, "Huh?"

"Your parents. What was the message?"

"Oh… Energy flows where the balance lies." She grabbed a foil wrapped taco, ripping it open as a puff of steam escaped up and over her head. "They said I already know what it means, that I need to *seek the truth*." They took bites of their tacos, the spicy Pico itching his nose. "I have absolutely no idea what they're talking about." Dylan muttered between starved bites.

Tristian pondered the message for a moment. "*Energy flows where the balance lies*." The only place he knew where the energy flowed was back at Elon in the glass Tower of Souls. Surely her parents didn't want her to go marching into the same building that housed the Immortal Court looking for a balance. No, that wouldn't be what they would want.

"What are you thinking about?" Tristian focused back on Dylan, who was staring at him intently.

"Just about the message." He took the last bite of his taco, wiping his hands on a limp napkin. "It doesn't make sense to me either."

"So, Tristian Effingo-" Dylan started.

He smiled coyly, really liking the way his name sounded on her lips, "Yes?"

"What's up with the Stewart?"

"I was trying to be covert in my operation. Less creatures knowing where I am, who I'm trying to find, less interferences."

"*Covert in my operation*," she echoed in a low voice, mimicking his stature.

Tristian shook his head. "What have I gotten myself into," he asked the heavens. She slapped him in the stomach, playfully, causing a laugh to burst through his lips.

"Whatever, Mr. Dark and Mysterious…" Wide-eyed, she snapped her mouth shut for a moment before continuing. "But why Stewart and not something common and generic like Smith or Jones?"

"Truthfully, I didn't put too much thought into it. It was the first name I saw when the admissions director asked me my last name." He laughed realizing how idiotic that sounded out loud. "I probably should have gone with Dark and Mysterious, but somehow I think that would have given me away…"

She tittered. "Yeah I have a feeling that'd be quite obvious." Worrying her split lip drew his attention there. He heard her continue, but all he could think about was the sickening *thing* that had left its mark on her face. If it weren't for the way she had left him, he would've probably killed the bastard himself after hearing what he did or tried to do. An instinctive growl rumbled in his throat.

"Tristian?"

"Hmm?"

"I said, did you do tomorrow's assignment?"

He frowned, looking up into her chaste gray eyes. Suddenly

feeling lost and powerless, he wondered if she knew how much she weakened him.

"Are you even listening to me?"

At that, Tristian brought his hand up to the curve of her face, he felt her tense at his touch. He chose to ignore it—the doe still cautious of something new. Leaning in, he brushed a soft kiss across her swollen lips. He heard a faint gasp as he sent a surge of his *Unda* through the slight contact. A shudder woke her body and he begrudgingly pulled away, resting his forehead against hers, unable to open his eyes just yet. For some reason, he wanted to relish the contact. Opening his eyes, they locked with her dilated gray ones for just a beat. He then sat back and took a deep breath.

Touching her lips. "What was *that*?" she asked, blinking and breathless.

I have no idea... "The force we use to numb a mortal for soul extraction-"

"*Unda*," Dylan whispered.

"Yeah, how did you-"

"Asher-"

"Oh, right." He snarled at the thought of another Collector using his *Unda* on Dylan.

"Nothing happened," she retorted. "I mean, we danced and he kissed me at the club but before-"

"He used his *Unda* on you at the club?" Tristian's voice was clipped as he felt his ire blaze, building in his veins and ready to combust.

"No." She sucked on her healed lip. "Did you-" She held up her fingers feeling for the cut.

"I couldn't help myself," he stated while mentally planning to confront the demon.

"I thought healing took too much out of you?"

"It does. But I couldn't stand to see your lips marred," he

said while seething to himself, *Asher kissed her. He used his Unda on her.*

"Thank you, I guess," she muttered, looking down at her taut hands.

He stared at her a moment, regaining placidity. She was obviously reacting to him positively every time they were around each other. Which didn't make sense given that she had freaked out the week prior.

"What happened the other day with the pen," he blurted out of pure curiosity before he could consider his words.

Dylan snapped her eyes to his then looked away. "Oh." She cleared her throat. "I was just overwhelmed, you know, with all the new information."

Lying.

She chuckled nervously. "That was my dad's pen."

True but still not the reason.

She picked at the scab forming on her palms. "I guess it just hit me that he wasn't my dad at all, it was silly. I'm sorry you must think I'm completely nuts."

Did she think of him as a fool?

"Not at all, I think you're handling it all very well." *Unique but well.* "But, why did you run away?" He mentally urged her to answer truthfully.

Dylan squirmed in her seat nervously. "I was embarrassed by my advance... the way I acted, the words we had shared. I felt like I had," she stopped and shook her head, letting her words hang there.

"Huh," he said believing her, *so it wasn't me...* He didn't know what to do with that information. Part of him was elated she didn't harbor ill feelings toward him, but the other part. The part that stemmed logic into his brain, told him none of it was possible. That one or both would end up hurt or worse... dead.

"What I feel... with you... is so new to me." He watched as

she struggled to explain. He wanted to stop her, to keep her from the obvious pain that spilling her guts involved, but he was selfish. He wanted to know more about what exactly she felt with him. So, he remained silent, inwardly pushing her to proceed because he needed it validated. Needed to know what he was feeling too.

"You're very intense…" Okay, now she was just spouting off words. "I mean…" She scratched her eyebrow unable to look him in the eye. "Every time I'm with you, I feel exposed. And after I kissed you, I realized I didn't want you to think of me as just another one of those girls ogling over you." She cautiously met his speculating gaze. "Because… Because, I never felt that way with anyone. I pushed you away because the realization rocked me."

The moment she stopped speaking, Tristian became aware of the fact that his heart had been beating at an incredible rate. But what was he supposed to say to that? Of course he felt the same way, but she couldn't get attached to him. It would create severe complications in his future endeavors. He opened his mouth on the verge of repeating her exact words, but all that spilled out was sarcasm.

"Ogling?" he leered.

She seemed to let out a gigantic breath and smiled.

"What, you don't notice the flock of chicks that track your every move?"

He frowned and looked around hoping to make her laugh.

"Not now, you dork!" she laughed. "I mean at school. Could be other places as well, just clearly not when you're alone with me." He could swear she was blushing but it was too dark out to really tell.

"Yeah… they are pretty friendly there aren't they?" he winked. "So are you apparently."

"Huh," she grunted. "If we're on the topic of the pen… I

have to know… Why'd you take it in the first place?" she asked narrowing her eyes as if she were trying to read his thoughts. Evidently it was his turn to squirm.

"I wanted to make sure you had a reason to talk to me again." He watched her expression soften. "I didn't expect you to show up at the club." Mostly because he hadn't didn't asked her to come.

He didn't want to tell her his cellphone had been swiped that morning. That Asher had wanted her there for a particular objective. A motive he could easily guess, now.

"Why wouldn't I?" she asked.

"Well, it just seemed out of character for you…" He searched for the right words. "You're just really… good."

She quirked a brow and smirked, "Good?"

"Yeah, you're not like the majority of the human college students. You don't go looking to get wasted every night, attend parties, or go clubbing." He frowned, remembering how she had easily drank the liquor at his apartment, and added, "although, you do handle liquor quite well."

"You obviously don't know me that well."

He frowned deeper. That seemed impossible. Yes, he wasn't on her tail 24/7 but he had kept a distant eye on her for the past two years.

"I actually did all of those last week," she said. "The club was with you, a bonfire with Asher, and I attended a rush party."

"A nerdy rush party doesn't count." He smiled, thinking about how he watched her dance with Aria and her friends as if no one was watching—but he was. He'd gotten really good at slipping in and out of places to make sure she was all right.

"It was not nerdy! Wait how do you-" She crinkled her forehead then with a shake of her head, released her hair from its tight hold—letting the soft strands cascade over her shoulders.

He felt his fingers burn with a need to touch, to *seize*. He wanted to run his fingers up her neck and grab her hair as he pulled her mouth to his. Tristian took a deep breath reining in the titillating thoughts that swam laps around his head. How had this contract become so personal?

"Besides you said party, nerdy or not it was still a party."

She was so adorable the way she defiantly set her chin.

"Stop laughing at me!" She feigned anger, but couldn't hide the smile. With a sigh, she tossed her hair away from the wind and sat back, her arms propped behind her.

Tristian only shook his head and rubbed the back of his neck, drawing his nails along the stubble on his jaw. Knowing this woman was going to be the death of him because he'd do anything for that smile.

"Can you show me how to use the *Unda*?"

"Sure."

He shifted to sit in front of her as his hair blew across his forehead from the strengthening breeze. Grabbing her hands, he gently pressed his fingertips to hers. At her touch, Tristian felt lighter. It was like he was meant to be connected to her in some way. How was it the one person you shouldn't have... turns out to be the one person you couldn't imagine living without? Clearing his throat and trying to maintain focus, he instructed her in a hasty, flat voice.

"Close your eyes and imagine releasing all of your stress in a steady stream to each point where our fingers touch." He needed to get this over with, quickly. Despite his new revelation he needed space. Just grazing fingertips wasn't going to be enough once he touched her.

Yeah, maybe taking Dylan to her apartment is best.

She closed her eyes and he watched her bring her brows together and her muscles bunch. She was definitely concentrating hard.

"Don't pull a muscle," he joked.

She slapped his hand playfully, keeping her eyes closed.

"How will I know when I do it? Will it feel the same way yours felt?"

"Not the same, more like a cool breath at the point of contact." Dylan straightened her shoulders and took a deep breath, inhaling through her nose.

"I don't think I'm doing it right," she said, slouching and blowing her bangs from her eyes.

He grabbed her hands forcefully and looked straight into her eyes. "Don't think about anything else, *only* my touch." As he spoke his voice came out huskier than he intended.

She nodded, swallowing, and closed her eyes again.

A slight wave of current just barely grazed his fingertips when her eyes flew open. "I did it...?" He smiled a confirmation. "I did it!" she yelped while throwing her arms around him. He almost fell over but caught himself wrapping his arms around her and relishing her rousing heat. He absent-mindedly nuzzled his nose in her hair, grazing her neck. She shivered pulling back slowly.

He looked into her hooded gray eyes where the crescent moon reflected, creating the illusion of infinite space. Using both hands, he pushed back loose strands of her hair, cupping her face, then leaned in to brush a kiss over the bruise on her right cheek and the scratch on her left cheek. He pulled back slightly and her eyes danced between his as they both paused holding onto the moment.

Her breathing was heavy when he dipped to her trembling lips. She immediately sighed against his mouth as if she were finally at home in his embrace. Passion rushed his body as their tongues collided fervently. He felt absolutely possessed by her. Holding back the past twenty-four hours had gotten the best of him, and now, all he could think about was getting even closer and having those legs wrapped around him again.

Grasping the back of her neck, he forcefully entwined his fingers in her long, silky hair, just as he'd imagined. He immediately realized he didn't think he could ever be apart from her now. Each moment was incredibly intense, and he didn't know if he could *feel* without her. The thought scared him, but not as much as letting her go did.

Moving his other hand along her shoulders, he sent a steady stream of *Unda* through his fingertips, mending any and every injury he came in contact with. It felt fantastic to finally heal her; it had been absolute hell watching her be in pain all night and day.

He felt her tremble. "Tristian," she moaned as his lips traveled the curve of her neck, nipping at the delicate skin of her earlobe. He growled in response to his name breathless on her lips and kissed just below her ear before making his way back to her luscious mouth. She scratched along his spine, leaving trails of fire in their wake.

He deftly moved his hand down her blouse, flicking each button aside. She quickly shrugged off the shirt, letting the sheer fabric billow to the ground. She then rolled back on the grass boasting the sexiest smile he'd ever seen.

Her hands roamed under the thin fabric of his shirt and traced the outlines of his abs. He watched her take in each reaction of her touch with a patience he didn't know he possessed. Pulling off his tee with one arm, he used the other to brace himself over her. Tossing it aside, he covered her with his body and claimed her mouth once more.

"I've never needed. Anyone. Like I need you," he admitted against her mouth between kisses. He carefully grazed his fingertips up her stomach and under the cotton tank, caressing her creamy skin. He wanted to touch and memorize her every curve. He smiled inwardly as he sensed her gasp from his declaration. Flicking his tongue in her mouth, he worked his way back down towards her jeans. Running his fingers lightly along her waistband and underwear, he felt her stomach flex and her body shiver.

Shit, is that lace?

Damn, she was insanely sexy. He not only wanted to touch every inch of her, but he wanted, no, he *needed* to taste too. He *needed* to hear his name shouted from her full lips in ecstasy. He *needed* her in his bed that still smelled of her, not here, but he didn't want to stop. He couldn't. Pulling away from her the first time felt like something inside him broke.

He felt down her leg and wrapped his arm around her thigh cocking her right leg up and around his waist. She moaned locking her ankles as he continued to explore her mouth aggressively. He grabbed her ass, hard, and moved against her slowly showing her just how much he needed her.

She sucked in a sharp breath as her nails bit into his shoulders, keeping him pressed against her. The pain shot straight down into his core and he groaned, moving faster against her as her head fell back.

"Don't... stop," she rasped, clenching her legs around him and squeezing her eyes shut. He knew she was close. Hell, he was close even with their jeans still on.

Tristian scooped her head up in his hand and forced her to look at him. "Open your eyes, Dee," he hissed against her slightly parted mouth.

Her eyes flicked open as a fire flashed behind them. Her body stiffened and she cried out his name as intensity washed through her. He smiled wildly as his forehead rested against hers. That had to be the single most satisfying experience of his life, but he couldn't deny how much he ached for her.

Perhaps they could hurry back to his place and keep it going, the right way, for the rest of the night. There was no doubt in his mind she would accept his invitation now.

Grunting, he forced himself away from their heated passion. Her hands snatched the hem of his jeans, halting him.

"Tristian?" she breathed, looking surprised and lost. "What-"

"Do you have any idea how incredible you are, Dee?" he interjected, searching her wide moonlit hungry eyes, and down the long sweep of her neck. He didn't want to give her a single moment to second-guess what they'd done. She had been a proven flight risk and for the life of him, he'd die if she bolted now.

She smiled, with a slight frown puckering her forehead, and shook her head no. Opening his mouth, he wanted to tell her that they were heading to his apartment—when he heard the heavy tread of footsteps.

He didn't need to look up to know the intruder was male and approximately two hundred pounds of sweating meat. But he did anyway. Flicking his eyes up, a bright light blinded him. He held up a hand to block the blaze.

"All right, you two, get up." The man motioned sternly with his torch.

Tristian yanked her top down with an annoyed grunt and pulled a wide-eyed and flushed Dylan up next to him.

The uniformed man tossed Tristian his shirt and said, "I need to see some identification-"

Tristian pulled on his gray tee and suddenly felt an insatiable hungry pull towards the thick Essence that seeped off of him. He had drained too much energy healing Dylan.

Feeling starved and pale, he surged forward. He threw the large man down with ease and growled a sinister smile. Staring into the officer's terrified eyes, Tristian surged his *Unda*, drawing the succulent soul out slowly, savoring the delicious energy. It smelled sweet as honeysuckle in summer, bringing a thick line of saliva to his lips. To consume souls for nourishment always felt insanely satisfying. He could just imagine the glorious high, a feeling like no drug ever created.

Part way into the extraction, his senses started to still like the calm before a storm. Instantly aware of his surroundings, he heard Dylan's whimpers and heavy breathing.

◇◇◇

She didn't know what to do.

Was he allowed to do this?

Was this man on his contract?

If not, what about the Shadow Horde?

Dylan's mind swam with questions as she watched him pull the gaping officer's soul out of his mouth. A bright light emanated from the soul like a searchlight fixed straight above to the sky. *The Radiance,* she thought wide-eyed and terrified— just as she had been when almost collecting the night before, but this time she was terrified for Tristian.

Oh God, what had she gotten herself into? Dylan's eyes darted around for something to stop him, a stick, anything. Unable to think clearly she rushed at his back and began pulling at his shoulders.

"Tristian! Stop! Please!" she screamed into his ear, slapping her palms on his back. "The Shadow Horde!"

That seemed to break his focus and he looked at her, his green eyes swirling around the hard onyx of his star-shaped pupil. He let go of the cop and the soul slapped back into his victim like a sling shot, blinking out the radiant light and leaving the officer unconscious, like a fallen tree after a storm.

The area was darker and colder than she remembered. Tristian's breath was rigid and a fiery rage was apparent on his features. She shivered and backed slowly off of him, hands up in surrender. She swallowed against the bile of dread, suddenly very scared of the one person she felt the safest around.

187

"Tristian," she whispered. "Let's go." She held out a trembling hand, hoping to try and calm him with her *Unda*.

In a blink, he had stepped back and crouched over the officer, growling like a feral animal guarding his prey from her. She snapped her hands back up in surrender.

"I don't want the soul. Let's just get out of here. And forget it… Okay?"

She saw the cloud suddenly lift from his eyes. Tristian blinked repeatedly as if waking from a trance and frowned. Glancing at the officer and back, he cleared his throat.

"Yes, let's go."

He looked back at the limp officer again. Then forcefully grabbed her outstretched hand and rolled upright, pulling her away towards the car. They silently power-walked through the islands of lamplight in the empty parking lot. She glanced at his austere expression, wondering what possibly could be going on in his head. He had told her it was nearly impossible to stop midway in an extraction. She wondered if that had been the first time he was able to.

Tristian looked unnervingly pale, like he had lost an insane amount of blood, but was still able to walk where a mortal would be dead. Unable to think of a way to help, Dylan continued to send a steady stream of her *Unda* in hopes of keeping him calm and numb as they made their way back to the car. Once they got closer to his car, Tristian wiggled out of her hold as if it was an irritable feeling.

"You don't need to use your *Unda*," Tristian muttered staring ahead like he was lost in thought. "It doesn't numb demons like it does mortals."

"Oh." She frowned. There was still so much she didn't know. "Do I need to drive?" she asked warily.

Tristian blinked and looked at her like he had forgotten she was there. "No."

She opened the car door. "All right…" she trailed off, unable to shake the horror of what just happened.

They slipped inside and he roared the engine to life. Switching gears, Tristian peeled out of the abandoned parking lot. She tensed as he rushed into oncoming traffic.

Scrambling through the contents of his cup holders, Tristian searched for his sunglasses. He grunted, then reached underneath himself and found them. With a forced sigh, he slid them on. She shook her head at his absurd obsession and shifted to stare out the window.

Even though she had known about this life for a couple of weeks, it hadn't felt real until today. Passing the professionally lit lawns that lined Sunset Boulevard, Dylan thought about all the people unaware of their surroundings. Everyone tucked securely into his or her homes without a real care in the world. Satisfied with their state of the art security systems thinking the worst they'd need to keep out was another human. Not knowing that those things we all thought were just stories, the Boogie Monster, things that go bump in the night, are real, just waiting for their next innocent victim. Nothing felt safe anymore, and she didn't think she could trust any more demons.

The Collectors reminded her of a savage tribe she studied once—the Majerónas. They constantly battled and fed on the conquered victims of their opposing tribes and unsuspecting visitors. Eating their flesh and grounding their bones into a drink in pursuit of immortality and supernatural powers—to absorb their life's Essence and fuel their settlements.

She just couldn't imagine doing that—acting like Tristian, fighting over souls like a starved jackal in the wild. It was barbaric and terrifying. If it weren't for the sudden manifestation of her powers and the dream of her parents, she'd doubt her identity as Temperance Elementa. Part of her didn't even want to be this other girl. Those demons weren't her real parents. She was only still hurting and looking for a replacement to fill the gaping void.

Could she run away from this life and forget about demons, collecting and the underworlds? Chewing her lip, she knew it would only be a matter of time before someone else, *something* else, found her again. How could she be a Soul Collecting Demon and not collect souls? What happened to a demon that didn't collect before the immortal age? Did they even turn? Grow old? Die? Had a demon ever done that before? Surely, someone else had to feel about taking souls the way she did...

Oh God, what am I going to do?

Does God even listen to me since I'm a demon?

Is there a God?

She squeezed her eyes shut, halting her rambling thoughts and willed herself to swallow her imminent tears. Her life felt like an emotional roller coaster, flying closer and closer towards the twisting corkscrew, all the while knowing her harness was disengaged and scrambling for something to hold on to.

Just wait until you're alone, don't cry in front of Tristian.

She mentally chanted this over and over again, taking several cleansing breaths, then glancing at Tristian. Her breath caught at his defeated stance. He looked so tired and ill. His shoulders were hunched as he laid his weight on the steering wheel. His skin was glossy with sweat and ghostly pale as dark shadows enhanced his protruding cheekbones. He looked as if he hadn't eaten in weeks! Dylan clenched her hands, holding back, as her fingers yearned to touch him. She wanted to help him, cure him, and hold him until everything was right again.

"Tristian," she whispered. He flinched at the noise and shifted his head in her direction. "Are you okay?"

"I healed too much of you." He swallowed forcefully. "I need to pick up Essence soon."

"Sure." She smiled thankful her body didn't ache anymore. Tristian had healed almost everything, erasing the hick's touch from the night before even more. "We can do that, then we can go to my apartment."

She watched as his eyebrows yanked together. "This is something I need to do by myself. I'm taking you to my apartment, and that's final."

"I need to go to my apartment. I'll be fine, Tristian."

"No. *Temperance*." She jerked from the verbal slap. She was beginning to really hate that name. "You're not safe at your apartment. If I need to leave for the night, I need to know you're going to be safe, and safe is my place."

"I promise not to leave," she spoke knowing she sounded whiny. "I'll probably go to sleep within an hour of being home."

She would ask him to stay at her place, but that thing—that demon—that had appeared only moments ago scared her and she didn't know if she wanted to be with him anymore that night. She needed some space and time to think.

Tristian itched the stubble of his jaw vigorously. "Fine," he growled.

"Don't call me Temperance," she added quickly.

"That's your name."

"No. It's Dylan, Dylan Prescott. *That's* my name." She glowered at his face, slicing two imaginary slashes with her knife like stare.

"Whatever." He rolled his eyes like a petulant child.

"And Tristian?"

"What, *Dylan*?" Tristian retorted with a glare.

Picking at a loose string at the hem of her shirt. "Was that the first time-"

"What? The first time I attacked someone? No," he lectured. "The first time I stopped in the middle of an extraction? Yes." His knuckles were white from the intense grip he held on the steering wheel. "You have no idea the void it

191

leaves." Tristian continued his narrow stare forward and straightened his shoulders. "To see it right there. To know how good it will feel to course through your veins." He snarled at her for the last statement, "*and it gets interrupted.*"

"What was I supposed to do!" she fumed. "Let you take that innocent man's soul?" She watched as he clenched his jaw and gripped the steering wheel at the top with even more force, popping his knuckles.

"You wouldn't understand," he snapped refusing to look at her.

"Try me," she challenged facing him and crossing her arms for added effect. He pursed his lips and shook his head, smirking condescendingly.

And the ass returns! She thought. What the hell was his problem?

"I'm not so frail that I can't handle the Goddamn truth!"

"You're right, Dylan, you aren't." She only raised an eyebrow at his response.

"You're a demon, I'm a demon. This, that back there is what we *do*," he sneered. "You're so damn guileless. You think you won't be taking souls once you reunite with the Elementas?" He laughed hollowly. "Not every person we're contracted is a rapist or murderer." She swallowed as he ran his fingers through his hair and pointed tersely to his face. "These fucking eyes that you're so damn attracted to aren't mine. They belong to an innocent child in Persia. Sure he grew into a murderer considering how he was raised, but every day when I look in the mirror, I see the horror and pain in that little boy staring back at me... I barely knew how to use my *Unda*," he strained the last statement.

She gasped silently but quickly reined in her shock at his confession. She wanted to reach out, clutch his face and force him to look at her as she kissed each eyelid. To remind him those eyes were a part of him, stolen or not, she couldn't love any part of him less, even if she tried—but she held back. There were still too many unknowns and she was terrified he'd push her away, reject her, or worse, tell her he didn't love her.

"This life is going to harden you in ways you never imagined. So, it's about time you grew the fuck up, Temperance."

"Sorry, I-"

"Don't," he interrupted shaking his head. "This was a huge mistake." He chuckled to himself. "No sorry… a *gigantic* mistake." He flicked his finger between them. "Nothing is going to come of this. You do know that, right?"

The knife of his words plunged into her stomach. She gasped but instantly felt anger gush out of the emotional wound.

"Why?" she barked back. "Because you're scared when things get real? Is that why you never let anyone in? God, you're like this giant jigsaw puzzle. Shifting from hot to cold. I can't figure you out! But I do know you feel it too. It's probably the one thing you can't keep from me." She brought a shaky hand up to her face and muttered more to herself than him, "There's no way I'm alone in this."

She was slightly surprised at herself. She was always so careful to ponder her words before allowing to spill from her lips, but she couldn't seem to shut up. A recurrent theme around him. "You know this is so damn real, it probably terrifies the crap out of you too," she said on the verge of tears again.

He screwed up his face, still staring at the road, then finally shook his head and licked his parched lips. "I don't know what you're talking about. You don't know anything about me."

His response knocked the breath right out of her. How could he not feel it too? Was it possible to feel this strongly about someone and have them not reciprocate it? She thought she knew him, even if they had just met a couple weeks ago. He was sweet, kind, sexy, and fun to be around. She felt like she could talk to him about anything. She'd never experienced these

193

emotions with anyone else and she didn't want to.

"Liar!" she screamed into her tense hands slightly muffling her voice. "Stop lying… please, just tell me the truth for once."

"I am telling you the truth," he growled. "You're just too fucking stubborn to let it sink in."

She snapped her head up to look at him, but he was too much of a coward to meet her stare. God, she was so mad. She wanted to hurl herself at him, pinch him until he told her the truth and break those damn sunglasses. Embarrassment and rage scorched her face.

"Stop the car," she voiced acerbically.

He laughed once, "Not a chance."

"Stop the car!" She couldn't stand another second around him. She knew she was only seconds away from a complete breakdown.

He clenched his jaw, and continued to drive. She stared at him in utter disbelief. He was ignoring her! Ignoring her! Suddenly, as if body snatched by a crazed woman, Dylan flung herself across the center console and ripped off his sunglasses. Tristian swerved the car, just missing the bumper of the minivan to his left.

"Wh-what the hell!" he yelled over the blaring horn righting himself in the lane. "Are you trying to get us killed?"

"Stop the car!" she yelled straight to the side of his face.

"No!" he yelled right back at her. Their noses were a whisper away from each other, as she shifted between each breathtaking eye. He glanced at her lips then rolled his eyes, returning to the road.

Clutching the sunglasses with implacable force, she huffed and threw herself back in the passenger seat. He chuckled and she craned her neck slowly to glare at him. Fumbling for the power window switch, she pressed the button. The window rolled down as the cool night air spilled in violently, tossing her golden locks and drying her tear stained cheeks. Tristian glanced at her multiple times, confusion contorting his handsome features. An impish grin grew along her face as she held up the sunglasses. Recognition of the inevitable washed over him and she blew a kiss before tossing them out onto Sunset Boulevard. Tristian jerked his head to the side mirror watching several drivers crush his beloved sunglasses.

"FUCK!" He punched the steering wheel making Dylan start. "Crazy fucking... Arrgh!"

Her ears scorched as she suddenly felt extremely foolish for her actions. He growled low in his throat then took a deep breath to regain placidity. He pressed the window switch and tapped the child lock.

Her chest heaved with a sick realization at how insane he made her. He didn't love her; she couldn't punish him to do so, and just like that locking feature, she was acting like a child. She brought both hands down her face with an exasperated sigh. He was right. It hurt deeply that he didn't want to be with her. Her chest twisted in pain as her heart finally tore in two.

"You're right," she squeezed out really needing air, and space, *lots* of space. "This has been a mistake. We obviously don't know each other at all."

"D-"

"Don't!" she pleaded through the thickness of her tears. It was her turn to cut him off. She didn't want to hear any more of his harsh words that were eating away at her from the inside out. She was reluctant to acknowledge that she had in fact fallen hard for this guy—a demon who didn't feel the same. She had inferred his feelings all-wrong. She thought he cared for her deeply, but maybe it was only physical. He was still that player she had walked in on at the club and was forced to work with in class. This was probably how he acted with Natalie, Sansvi... and to think what could have happened on the beach. *Oh God,* she groaned inwardly. She felt like vomiting. How could she have been so stupid? Of course, he didn't love her. Who could love her?

Swallowing against the lump in her throat, she wished her mom were here so she could run into her arms and cry. Not Constance but Léa Prescott. Dylan needed her mom to wipe the tears and mend what she had so stupidly opened to the wrong person. The worst part was he was right—she was too inexperienced, too trusting to the demon life.

Taking a deep breath, she hardened her face the very way she'd perfected over the years that helped her not allow anyone to see her pain, and turned to stare out the window. He finally pulled the car in front of her apartment building.

She felt broken, scarred, irate, and bereaved of her life and dreams. He touched her hand and she promptly jerked away from his touch.

"Just tell me one thing." She breathed against the severe ache in her chest and forced her emotions back down within her. "Why'd you wait so long?"

"What?" he asked, looking puzzled.

"Two years," she said calmly, maybe too calm, as she looked straight into his fiery eyes. "You waited two years to tell me who I was."

Tristian's voice came out strained and laced with sadness. "You seemed happy. I didn't want to be the one to tear your world apart." He averted his eyes like he couldn't bear to look at her any longer.

She couldn't contain the incredulous laugh that burst through her lips. Shaking her head slightly, she looked at her stressed hands. He thought she was happy? Damn, she had to give herself credit. She put on a better show than she thought.

"What's so damn funny?"

"I wasn't happy." Part of her didn't even know why she was still there talking. Maybe she just needed him to know. She figured this would be the last person she ever opened up to, so what'd she have to lose?

"I may have acted like my world was torn in the beginning, but I've never felt more like myself than I do now… than I did with you." She bit her lip. "What you wrote about me for class. It couldn't have been further from the truth. Life's full of too many disappointments to believe in happily-ever-afters. I keep everyone close to me at an arms distance because I'm afraid of how I'll handle another tragedy. If I'm not close to the person, then I can't break; and *believe* me, I've been broken and pieced back together too many times. I don't think I'll be able to repair myself the next time.

"I do worship my parents and hold on to everything that connects me to them—that part was true but not for the reason you think. I do it only because I feel it's my fault they're dead. So, no. I wasn't happy. I'm sorry I'm not the person you thought I was… so, I guess you're right. This was a mistake. Just… don't call me anymore." Why did these words taste toxic as they left her tongue?

"Dee-" he started, but she cut him off.

"I'll ask for a reassignment tomorrow in class. If you need me for anything Elementa related, I'm sure we'll figure it out, but otherwise." She finally looked into his pained face. "Just leave me alone." A lone tear fled down her cheek.

Opening his mouth to say something, she gave him a look that said she dared him to say something… anything. Oh, how part of her wanted him to recant everything and pull her into his arms and kiss the pandemonium away. But that was wishful thinking. He was a jerk, who didn't give two shits about her, or her happiness.

A moment of silence wafted through the small space of the sedan before she gave him a sign that suggested what he go do to himself and quickly stepped out of the car. Wrapping her small arms around herself and holding the loose pieces together, she braced against the certain reality that finally hit.

CHAPTER 11

"I care for myself. The more solitary, the more friendless, the more unsustained I am, the more I will respect myself."
Charlotte Brontë

"HOLY crap, Dylan!" yelled Aria as Dylan sulked into their small living room. Tossing her new Ray Ban's on their distressed wooden coffee table; a flea market find that the girls cherished. "I was about to call on a search party!"

See! She wanted to turn around and scream out the door at Tristian as if he could still hear her—as if he was still even there.

"Where the hell were you?" she waved her finger aggressively. "I called Isabel to make sure you got home okay because you were acting weird. She told me she *never* saw you! It was the next freaking day, DYLAN. And then I had to lie to her when she asked me why on earth I was asking! She started freaking out!" She threw her hands up in exasperation then let them fall to her sides with an over dramatic sigh. "I hate lying to sweet old people."

With a sigh, Dylan flopped on their couch pinching the bridge of her nose. She counted the throbs of her pulse through her fingers trying to gain some placidity but Aria wouldn't take the hint.

"I had two random guys *and* Garret show up looking for

you-"

"Two random guys?" Dylan asked, slightly curious.

"Yes, and when did you become so popular with the guys?" she inquired before holding up a hand. "You know what? I don't want to know." She shook her head and stepped toward Dylan. "The first guy that was looking for you, a hot blonde, but completely arrogant, said you ditched him at a beach party."

"Asher."

"Sure. The second guy, another *total* hottie, introduced himself as Datu and brought your abandoned jacket with phone and cash." She hooked her hands on her hips. "Seriously, Dylan! I thought you were lying in a ditch somewhere!"

"You sound like my Grandma."

"Good! ...Uh, you need to give her a call. I think," she smiled sheepishly, "I freaked her out." Aria laughed, flinging herself on the couch next to Dylan.

"So, Datu came by?" Dylan thought about the nice vampire and figured he probably came not too long ago after sunset. "When?"

"Like an hour ago." Aria beamed. "You know he asked me out."

Now Dylan was smiling. "Really?"

"Yeah, he wants to go grab a drink and see a midnight movie. He has a *friend,"* Aria sang the last part.

"No, definitely not!" Dylan swept her bangs mistakenly revealing her new multicolored accessory that Tristian hadn't healed.

"What," Aria grabbed her friend's head jerking Dylan's forehead close to her eye, "is that!"

Dylan winced shoving her friend away. "A bruise."

"No shit, Sherlock! How though?" Aria sat back and gestured with her arms. "Spill."

Dylan gave her a watered down version of her night with

Asher, Datu and Tristian. Leaving out, once again, a majority of the events.

"That guy, Asher, sounds like a total jerk, leaving with his ex after bringing you there... But Datu sounds like a good guy, covering for you and all. So, tell me more about Tristian, you spent the whole day and night together." She waggled her eyebrows.

"Yeah, well after the gross hick-"

"I can't believe you hitch-hiked!" Aria shook her head in disapproval. "Seriously, Dylan."

Dylan grimaced, she had divulged his advance and the severe crash against the window but skipped the rest. It was unnecessary and she didn't want any more sad eyes or pity.

"Well after that, I ran into Tristian." Even saying his name made her stomach bottom out. "Yeah, small world," she muttered. "He took me to a motel to bandage me up-"

Aria frowned. "A motel?"

Dylan was unsure how to go about this. She couldn't tell her best friend that she hid there from a mythical group of bounty hunters because she thought she stole an unauthorized soul.

"Uh, yeah, it sounded good at the time." *Damn, I'm really not good at lying.* "We were both drunk and I was really shaken up." *Yeah, that sounds better.* "Anyway, nothing happened that night. We just talked and *sleep* slept together." God, that was such an understatement. She had fallen in love with him that night. "Then the next day, he bought me these clothes, and took me... sightseeing in Topanga. Then we had dinner watching the sunset on the coast. That's when things got hot and heavy-" Aria's eyes widened making Dylan blush. "But a cop came and busted us up." *Thank God ...I think.* "Not sure if we would have gone much further or not."

"You ho," the redhead nodded with a Cheshire cat grin. "So, he just dropped you off? Are you guys going to start seeing each other now?"

Dylan thought about their 'heated chat'. "No. You know how he is with girls." She tried to play it cool, not letting her friend see how she was utterly dying inside. "I'm probably just another chick spreading her legs." Dylan rolled her eyes.

"Yeah, he is a ho. Well," Aria said, drawing out the word with a wide smile. "If you're still single, let's go on the double date. Please, pretty please!"

"Fine," Dylan sighed immediately regretting her agreement, remembering her promise to Tristian about leaving her apartment. But that didn't matter now did it? Promises didn't matter between acquaintances and he had absolutely no say in her life anymore. Plus, Datu was a good guy. Surely he would look out for her if Tristian couldn't.

Aria jumped up. "Awesome! Let's get dressed, they'll be here in like thirty minutes."

"What did Garret want?" Dylan asked as the girls walked down the hall to their bedrooms.

"You know, I have no idea. He just stopped by, asked for you. I said you were out and he left. Super strange guy."

Dylan knit her brow, "Hmm, bizarre."

Dylan walked into her room, passing her pearl-lined, oval, full-length mirror. She halted just beyond the mirror then jumped backwards, gaping at the huge grass stain with something black covering her rear.

Shaking her head, she marched toward her closet remembering the majority of her clothes were crumpled in the linen bag sitting in her abandoned car. Her favorite jeans bloodied and stained in the back of Tristian's Audi.

Tristian... She bit her lip hard. The painful sensation temporarily masked her shattering heart. Was what they had really so insignificant he felt he could dismiss it so easily? Was she that easily fooled? Damn her for opening up to him. All she got in return was emotionally pantsed by Tristian Effingo; which turned out to be a thousand times worse than actually getting pantsed. Taking a deep breath, she stepped into her closet and gingerly shut the door. Laying down into a fetal position, she finally broke the dam of tears and let them fall. She sobbed like the damn fool she apparently was.

Ten minutes later, and slightly dehydrated, she considered bearing through the Aria inquisition just so she could stay home and mend her heart with wine, spoonfuls of Nutella, and Emily Brontë.

Then she heard a light tap on her closet door.

"Dylan, are you all right?"

Dammit!

She didn't want her friend knowing how fast and hard she fell for such a huge player. Sniffling, she quickly tried to wipe her face of her tears but realized it was useless. Her face felt puffy and red. Aria would have to be blind not to notice. Feeling trapped, she sat up and opened the door.

Aria's face crumpled. "Omigod! What's wrong?"

"Oh, you know, falling for boys who don't like me back," she laughed hollowly, wiping at her running nose with the tail of her tank, "like usual."

Aria sat down on the carpet and gave her a huge hug.

"Tristian?" she asked, pulling back to look into her eyes.

Dylan nodded. "Ugh, I'm so stupid," she sniffed again feeling her tears bleed down her cheeks like an open vein.

Aria pursed her lips and crossed her legs. "No, you're not stupid. Don't even think that. You know how words have an underlining effect on our bodies… But I can tell Tristian is… easy to love. He's very charming, and if you don't have a lot of experience with guys, it can be easy to mistake that for genuine feelings." Dylan nodded. "Plus, you're probably not in love with him… more like smitten... captivated? You're in lust with him. You've only spent one day with him, and yes, a lot of what you told me was pretty romantic, but he could have just been trying to get into your pants."

"We've spent more than a day and…" Dylan trailed off knowing the argument was futile. "You're right. I just got my feelings hurt. The worst part was I even told him how I was feeling, that's when things got hot on the beach. He told me he never needed anyone like he needed me. I thought… I thought he meant figuratively but maybe he was just being literal. Like a 'right here, right now', sense…" Dylan thought about how good he made her feel on the beach and how he didn't seem to care about his own needs. If he just wanted in her pants, then why didn't he try harder? In that moment, she probably would have said yes to anything.

Stop twisting his actions, she chided herself. *He told you he didn't feel the same.*

"On our way here, we got into a fight. He told me that it was all a…a," she swallowed, suddenly unable to voice the words. "That I was a *gigantic* mistake and that nothing more would happen between us…. I don't care what you say, Aria. I'm extremely stupid."

Aria's eyes bugged either at his words or how much Dylan had just opened up to her for the first time.

"What a giant turd! *You* are not a mistake, Dylan." She pursed her lips like she was trying to hold back her fists of fury from flying out the door and after him. "He's the fucking mistake. You hear me?" Dylan nodded appeasingly as Aria seemed to clear her head with a sigh. "Wanna skip the date? Stay in, get plastered and prank call that asshole? We can even egg his car?" Aria was now grinning so wide at the thought of beleaguering him, but there was a tinge of sadness to her eyes that Dylan couldn't handle to look at.

Dylan laughed, "As tempting as that sounds, I don't want that *turd* to ruin my night. Let's go out. We can still get plastered, but at least this way it's on Datu and his friend." She winked accidentally releasing a tear. Her last tear, she promised herself.

"Are you sure?" Aria asked looking worried.

"Yes… and please, no more sad looks. I'll get over it…" she smiled. "Now that *that's* behind us, did you need something?"

Her friend seemed to study her for a moment, seemingly perplexed, before shaking off the errant thought.

"I brought you my bag of make-up and was just wondering what you're planning on wearing."

The girls stood and Dylan wiped her entire face with the tail of her shirt and shook the nerves off her body.

"I'm thinking something just above casual since we're going to a movie."

Fingering through what was left of her pathetic collection of clothes, Dylan selected a thin, gray, flyaway tank and a pair of skinny jeans that she hadn't worn in a few years.

"Cool, I was thinking something similar." Aria smiled and gave her a quick hug and darted back to her room. "Ten minutes!" she called over her shoulder.

Dylan chuckled, feeling surprisingly lighter after talking about the situation with Aria. Maybe that was why her therapist insisted on talking to someone.

Stepping into her jeans, she looked at the hole in the right knee. She had bought the jeans like this, bleached, ripped, frayed, generally looking like it should have been the aftermath of what happened the night before. Minus the debris. Minus the blood. Before knowing her true identity, the jeans didn't feel right. Like she was posing as this other person: a more confident, badass. Now looking in the mirror they somehow fit. Not that she felt like a badass. Far from it. But she felt darker; perhaps it was the known vacancy of her soul.

She pulled on the gray flyaway with a black bandeau underneath and the infamous black leather boots. She looked and felt tough. Well, she was a Soul Collecting Demon, right? She flexed her arms like Mr. Universe, "HAuhh," and burst into a fit of giggles. With a shake of her head, she left to wash her face and straighten her bangs. Sitting down on her bed, she laid out Aria's makeup like a deck of cards and drew thick liner on her upper lid. After bronzing her cheeks, concealing her bruise, and blinking on some mascara, she surveyed herself in the oval full-length mirror in the corner of her purple bedroom.

"You don't need anyone to become who you truly are," she sighed to herself with a wistful smile. Wondering how long it took to mend a broken heart, she didn't know how long she could withstand this stabbing ache in her chest. Dylan started at the light tap sounding at her door. Rolling her eyes, *Yeah, really hardcore, Dylan.*

"Come in," she called.

Aria walked in wearing a loose, white, silk button-up with a strip of silver sequins in the center, coral skinnies, and beige heels. Even though she was nearly 5'9", Aria wore the tallest heels, nothing below four inches otherwise they were 'flats' as she would say.

"Good thing Datu's like 6'3"," Dylan muttered while fixing her long hair into a loose, side, French braid.

"You know I wouldn't agree to the date if he wasn't."

She wasn't joking.

Dylan plugged her almost dead cell into the vacant docking station. She figured since she went almost twenty-four hours without it, she could do a few more.

Aria's phone chirped. "They're here."

Just as she was about to leave her room, Dylan's phone vibrated. Backtracking, she opened Tristian's text message. Like morphine straight to her shattered heart, she instantly felt herself smile. She started to text back when Aria called from the front door.

"Dylan! Get your hot butt out here... now!"

On reflex Dylan clicked the home button and hurried out the door.

◇◇◇

Tristian watched as Dylan gave him an obscene gesture then slammed the car door and left to walk to her apartment. His eyes lingered on her tiny frame; her hair blowing casually as if invisible fingers dallied through her tresses. He probably would have apologized or jumped out to walk her to her door if the gnawing hunger wasn't pinching his sides and pissing him off. He didn't know why he told her it was a gigantic mistake. If she was any mistake, he never wanted to be right. He brought both hands down his face before punching the dash.

"Fuck! Why did I say that?"

But he knew exactly why he said it. He had been going back and forth, ever since that first morning on how he should or shouldn't be around her, when what he needed was to just be there in the moment. She was a prize worth cherishing and he didn't know why he kept trying to convince himself otherwise. Obviously willpower towards her wasn't his strong suit. So, why fight it? Yes, dating her made the original plan messy, but he couldn't deny his feelings for her any longer. There was still a remote possibility that everything would work out.

The worst part was the look on her face when he basically told her he didn't feel anything for her. That had to be the biggest lie of his existence.

Grabbing the door handle, he pondered a moment if he should rush after her and make everything right again, but he *needed* Essence. Everything fucking irritated him when he was this hungry, and he didn't quite trust himself to talk to her like this without making the entire thing worse. They were both just upset, in need of some time apart to simmer down. Yes, a night away should really put things in perspective for both of them. Besides, after what had happened the night before, he felt confident she wouldn't be wandering about at night without him. Or at least he hoped. Dylan was so stubborn and unpredictable. Most of what made her so appealing.

He told himself he would see her in the morning. He'd bring her coffee and breakfast. Hell, he'd bring her the worlds if she'd only forgive his stupid words.

Grudgingly pulling out of the parking lot, he couldn't help but fantasize about their night if she hadn't interrupted him, but he understood her reluctance to take a soul outside of a contract. She didn't know that he had done it before and possessed connections to make the claim disappear, even if it was quite inconvenient. He would much rather jump through hoops than go crawling to the Soul Society for energy, but there wasn't a choice. He'd stored all the souls his other contracts had going and he needed to grab a new set of indentures for the remaining time needed in this world.

Tristian drove towards Downtown LA on the 10 to *Glesia de Nuestra Señora la Reina*. An old church built a couple hundred years ago, maintained as a front for the Covenant Portal. Its use was for all species of the underworlds. As he got closer to the ancient building, he started to shift against the Nappa leather that bound his seat. He hated going to the Soul Society, making nice, plastering a fake smile; all the while trying to keep away from the speculating eyes of the Omnipotence.

He wasn't exactly on their bad side, but definitely not on their good side either. Tristian knew if anything came to light, they wouldn't think twice before bringing him in. They felt threatened by him for dropping his prestigious title after the birth of Temperance, but he couldn't work for something he no longer believed in. Now according to them, Tristian was in somewhat of a 'freelance limbo'; never letting anyone in on his objectives, and that angered the OP. It was rare to have a demon refuse the help of a family, so that unfortunately made him that much more *interesting*. He didn't mind them thinking whatever they wanted as long as they could never prove for whom he was working.

His interest in the Elementas had proven helpful on more than one occasion and he would go down making sure the OP stayed away from them, even more so with Dylan. She held a special place he couldn't deny. Not that he completely understood what all he felt for her, other than a sudden infatuation. The car still smelled of flowers and the beach. Taking in a deep whiff, he was cognizant of the fact he didn't want it to leave, ever. He thought of her whimpers, her gentle but rough caresses, the look in her eyes when he did something so simple as hold her hand, making him feel like *such* a dick for the way he treated her.

He shook his head; this wasn't like him at all. He never dwelled on the feelings of women, let alone, cared how he treated them. But she was spectacular, intriguing, and damn sexy. He couldn't seem to ever get enough. He just wanted more and more Dee. He laughed to himself. He didn't even know where that nickname came from, but he kind of liked it and she didn't seem to mind.

Her words on never wanting to talk to him again suddenly sliced through him, ripping a gigantic hole straight through his chest. He should have just kissed her, so she'd shut up. But after hearing her thoughts on what he wrote only made him feel more connected to her on a deeper level and it stunned him into silence. They were the same in many ways and it was unsettling.

Tristian parallel parked in front of the old building and dug into his glove compartment searching for the key every member of the underworlds had registered in Los Angeles. An old pair of Ray Ban's fumbled into his grasp washing a wave of relief over him. He burst into a loud laugh; unable to believe she had tossed his sunglasses out the window.

Wiping off the dirt and grime with his shirt, he slid them into place and hopped out into the humid night air. The putrid stink of left over egg rolls and miso from the nearby restaurants filled his nose as he walked toward the wooden courtyard door. Tristian freed the latch, making his way to the basement door on the side of the building. He knocked five times, alerting the keeper to his presence.

A stocky dwarf answered clad in jeans and a yellow t-shirt. His long, gray beard rustled in the intruding wind. Tristian lazily held out his key. Rolling his eyes, the man stepped up on to a stool to examine it. He nodded and stepped off leading the way for Tristian to follow.

They trod down a narrow, winding rock staircase. The light tapping of water sounded in the distance and large metal candelabras lit the way. He couldn't help but feel like he was descending into Hell. Which wasn't all that far off, considering.

At the bottom the dwarf halted. Knowing this was as far as the creature would go, Tristian slid past him into the small room. The only light emanated from the glowing arched doorway in the middle of the room, blanketing the damp stone walls in a soft blue. He felt his phone buzz and looked 'Asher.'

What the hell does he want?

Just knowing he touched Dylan in any way curdled his blood; but the fact that he kissed her, made him seriously want to rip his face off. Declining the call, he texted Dylan.

TRISTIAN: I'm sorry... None of this was a mistake. I do feel it too. I hope you'll forgive me. I'll be there to pick you up in the morning before class. We'll talk more then. Please, stay put, beautiful.

He stared at the text before sending it. He wanted to write her an entire letter on just how much she wasn't a mistake, but knew everything he needed to say should be said in person. Pressing send, he returned his phone to his back pocket as the voicemail tone sounded. He'd get back to Asher later.

Moving towards the glowing doorway, he patted his body down for anything liable to fly off. Removing his sunglasses, he set them in the same back pocket as his phone. Tristian began to close his eyes as his phone sang again.

'Natalie'—fuck, she was persistent.

He almost regretted taking her soul during a weakened moment. She became clingy and bothersome. Fallacious, unrequited love, an unfortunate side effect of the sudden hollowness in her chest. Feeling like he needed to rip off the band-aid, *again*, he answered in a short clipped tone.

"What?"

"Hey, Baby!"

He cringed at her term of endearment. She really wasn't getting it, but at least she was staying away from Dylan.

"What?" he repeated to the incessant human.

"Er… Lauren and I were heading out. Thought you'd want to join?"

"Can't," was all he said.

"Can't?" she asked him incredulously. "Are you with *her*?"

Her? "Not at the moment."

"So, it's true?" He moved his head to both sides, popping it to relieve tension.

"Natalie, I need you to be a little less vague," he snapped. "What's true?"

"You're with her now?"

"I'm not *with* anyone," he smirked. "I need to go." He hung up without giving her the opportunity to continue. He definitely needed a break from this world. He just wasn't sure Elon would be any more of an alleviation.

Sighing, he thought carefully about the details of his destination. He walked through the blue glass feeling his stomach instantly drop as the ground gave way. This was the worst part of falling through a portal. It was never comforting no matter how many times he had done it in his two hundred and twenty-three years.

Tristian felt a surface solidify underneath his shoes, stagnant air, and the unmistakable scent of lilac.

Home.

◇ ◇ ◇

Wobbling down the three flights of stairs from their apartment, Aria and Dylan spotted a brand-new, black Mercedes G-Wagen rolling towards them.

Aria hummed, "Someone's got money."

Dylan, knowing Datu and his friend could probably hear them with their heightened senses, only smiled at her friend.

The car stopped and a very fit Datu jumped out the passenger side wearing a taut *Red Hot Chili Peppers* concert tee hugging his ripped cords and low riding jeans. He gave Dylan a friendly hug.

"Hey, Sinta."

Facing Aria, he kissed her on the back of her hand.

"Mmm… ikaw ay kaya matamis," he purred.

Speechless, Aria swooned so hard she practically fell over. Dylan snorted a laugh.

He too smirked at her reaction. "You both look lovely."

"Thanks," the girls said in unison.

Just then his very tall and equally chiseled friend walked from the driver's side. He was stunning. Thick brown curls rained around his structured features and ice blue eyes. He wore a simple, black tee with similar jeans as Datu. Dylan felt goosebumps break out across her chest where his eyes lingered.

Vampire, she thought as he swaggered over.

He seemed to have heard her thoughts because she could have sworn he nodded in response. He took her by the hand as Datu had the night before, and inhaled deeply.

"I'm Erez."

Dylan blushed and pushed a couple of nonexistent fly-away strands behind her ear.

"Dylan. Nice to meet you."

"Likewise," he said with a wicked grin.

He opened the passenger door for her while Datu and Aria slid into the back seat. The new car smell of leather and soap brought the immediate thought of Tristian kissing their interlocked fingers with a dimpled smile during their drive to Topanga.

Shaking the memory, she suddenly felt cold. The pain in her chest rose and she considered running back inside for her phone just to read the text again. Part of her was terrified in anticipation of the next morning. She knew it wouldn't take much for her to forgive him and want for everything to be right, but part of her would always wonder how much of everything he said in their argument was actually true. Dylan looked back at her apartment with a sense of longing. She felt like she should go back inside. She didn't want to be here anymore; it didn't feel right.

"So, what's the plan?" Erez asked as he jumped behind the wheel. They started to pull out of the parking lot and Dylan relaxed against the leather seat, figuring not too much could go wrong in a movie.

Aria poked her head between the front seats. "We were thinking drinks then a midnight movie. That new comedy about a night in Vegas?"

Erez shrugged, "Sure, I know a good place for drinks."

Dylan thought of the underworld club on Hill Street and wondered if he would actually take them there. Particularly with Aria, a mortal, a human. She would be like a walking feast. She looked to Erez skeptically, but again as if reading her thoughts shook his head with a smile lurking near the corner.

"It's a lounge called Silk in West Hollywood near the theater. The DJ is badass."

"Sounds good to me!" Aria beamed patting Dylan's shoulder with a suggestive look, then sat back under Datu's extended arm. They chatted quietly about the movie and if it would be as funny as its reviews posted. Dylan glanced at Erez and pondered if he could really hear her thoughts. She supposed it wasn't too far fetched. Just then Erez started to really smile and she widened her eyes at him.

You can, can't you, she thought.

Erez shrugged, taking a swig of his aluminum water bottle.

Well, this could put a damper on the whole elusive act to lure you to my bedroom, she joked and possibly still testing him.

Erez immediately choked on his drink spraying a bit of red on the dash. *Blood.*

Dylan started to chuckle as he scrambled to wipe off the evidence with his hand, before Aria poked her head forward again.

"What's so funny? Both of you were just so quiet."

"Oh, uh-"

Erez cut her off, "Aria, have you been to this bar before?"

She gave Dylan an incredulous glance and turned to Erez. "Nope, what's it called again? Silk?" Aria started to talk about the places she had been in West Hollywood while Dylan continued to talk to him mentally.

So... Can all vampires hear thoughts? Should I be worried about Datu listening in?

He glanced at her and shook his head.

"So, how do you and Datu know each other?" Aria asked stealing his full attention.

Erez seemed to think about it for a moment, and then glanced in the rearview mirror.

"I guess you could say we grew up together."

Dylan thought for a fleeting moment about the possibility it was so long ago, they don't even remember.

Datu piped up, "Yup, back in the day as you'd say."

"Yeah, he even saved my life," Erez said vacantly like he was somewhere else deep in thought.

Before Aria could bombard Erez and Datu about how exactly Datu saved his life, Erez swerved into a parking spot and the guys jumped out. Aria raised an eyebrow, but surprisingly dropped it. As the girls slid out of the SUV they hooked arms and walked to *Silk*.

"So, what do you think of Erez?" Aria whispered. "Hot, right?"

"He's pretty interesting," Dylan said having several flashbacks of her fight with Tristian… *No a gigantic mistake…* She suddenly needed more reassurance from him. The simple text just wouldn't do.

"You like Datu?"

"Well, I don't know if I can say that I *like* him yet." Aria glanced behind at the two vampires whispering to each other. "I *can* say he's nice to look at."

"You haven't noticed anything weird yet?"

Aria knit her brow. "What do you mean?"

"Oh, nothing. I meant more like no faults so far?"

"Oh," Aria laughed. "I thought you were going to tell me he had webbed feet or something totally freaky."

"Definitely no webbed feet." *I don't think.*

"You're sure you're okay here?" Aria asked looking

worried again.

"Yeah. Definitely. Don't worry about me." She gave a sad smile knowing it was probably unconvincing but Aria accepted it nonetheless. "Hey, can I borrow your phone?"

"Sure—nope."

"What, why?"

"Dylan, I'm not letting you call him. Not drunk, not sober, not ever. So, forget about it."

Dylan exhaled a frustrated sigh, stepping into the long line to enter the club. The girls checked their watches and looked at Datu and Erez.

"We won't have time to hang here if we have to wait in this ridiculous line," Aria declared to the group.

Datu glanced around the long line of bored patrons. "I know the bouncer. I'll be right back."

He strode up to the behemoth of a human and shook his hand while grabbing his shoulder and whispering in his ear. The bouncer looked a bit lost, then nodded vigorously and unhooked the rope. Datu signaled for the three of them to come over.

Walking past the groans and curses of the ones waiting in line, Aria looked impressed while Dylan felt like he did something; something she couldn't quite put her finger on. Dylan glanced at Erez for some kind of answer, but he only shrugged with a smile. His go to answer, she guessed.

They walked into a dimly lit room that smelled of incense underlined with something sour. The walls were decorated with different shades of blue silk, that all seemed to gather together in the middle around a beautiful piece of cascading glass art. Underneath the chandelier was a crowded dance floor with a caged DJ booth off to the side mixing beats of techno and the latest hits. Aria immediately started to bounce up and down.

"This place is *nice*!" She grabbed Dylan's hand and the girls skipped to the bar.

Erez and Datu followed still whispering, which made Dylan wonder what vampires whispered about. The buffet of humans? Or perhaps the thoughts of the almost naked girls grinding on the dance floor? She probably shouldn't think about it. Focusing back on the bar, a line of shots was placed in front of them.

"What's this?" Dylan raised a questioning eyebrow at Aria.

"Screw the movie. Let's stay here!" Aria yelled over the music.

"Sounds good to me," Datu said, appearing at Aria's side caressing her shoulder as Erez moved next to Dylan.

Hmm, clubbing round two. Hopefully, tonight will be less eventful.

Erez leaned into Dylan bumping her shoulder with his.

"We can still go catch the movie if that's what you want."

She smiled, grabbing two shots and handing one to Erez.

"Let's stay." She clinked his glass. "Salud!"

"Round two," he winked.

They all downed the astringent, clear liquid and coughed.

Dylan's eyes began to water. "Aria! What the hell did you order!" she scolded while swallowing against the burn in her throat and kneading her neck. Dylan felt as if the acid might actually leak through.

"I have no idea!" Aria gagged fanning her tongue. "That was like gasoline." She coughed and leaned into Dylan to whisper, "I told the bartender to mend your broken heart." Aria started laughing and wiped at the tears that sprang up. "Oops."

"Well, I'm moving to something less potent. I'll let you guys stick to the Everclear," Dylan said boasting a sour face before waving down the bartender. She leaned over the polished concrete slab, "Vodka, water with lime!" Looking back at the others while still partly hoisted on the bar. "You guys want anything?"

After they received their drinks and a little bowl of olives that Aria demanded for her dirty martini, they headed to a newly vacated table that Datu had conveniently found; if you could call it a table. It consisted of a low piece of glossy wood surrounded by plush suede-like pillows. The four of them sat and talked about school, jobs, and the boring details of their lives before Aria stood and announced it was time to dance.

Dylan felt the alcohol swimming hot through her veins, giving her a delicious wave of false confidence. The girls started dancing, singing along to Birthday Cake by Rihanna and laughing, even Erez and Datu joined in on the fun. Dylan was enjoying the numbing feeling of alcohol and blaring music more than she cared to admit. Too much had been going on in her life to look at anything with excessive thought. She just wanted to let loose and forget about everything.

She moved against Erez in what she hoped was a seductive roll. His hands gripped her roughly as she popped her hips to the music. Squeezing her eyes shut, she wondered if she could forgive Tristian. What was to hold him back from hurting her again? Did she really want to take the risk?

"Don't think about him tonight, *Tesoro*," he breathed, his cold breath licking her neck. "If he isn't following you like a sick puppy, he isn't worth your time." She nodded slightly incredulously against the side of his face.

So much for secrecy of one's own thoughts.

"Damn, you move good," he groaned, pulling her even closer, maybe too close.

After several songs, Aria and Datu ran off to the table, leaving Erez and Dylan still dancing within the sweaty crowd. They laughed as he twirled her around, keeping the mood light after the first song, which she appreciated.

Dylan was panting and a completely composed Erez offered to go get some water. She waved him off feeling out of shape next to the breathless vampire and mouthed she'd be right back.

She made her way through the pack of people standing near the bar to the shimmery, dark-pink ladies room around the back of the club. A group of girls congregated around the mirrors laughing and talking about how drunk they were until they spotted Dylan. They finished their makeup and quickly exited, leaving her strangely alone and feeling a bit uneasy all of a sudden. After glancing in the mirror to make sure nothing was wrong with her face, she shrugged and started walking to a stall.

A cold breeze tossed her hair, standing the fine hairs of her neck on end. She turned taking in the towering vampire that she was just dancing with.

"Erez," she exhaled in relief. "What are you doing in here?" She hooked her hands on her hips and tapped her foot. "You do know this is the little girls room?" she said mockingly.

He responded with a wicked grin and snatched the back of her head landing a startling kiss. Dylan gasped at the surprise and his icy embrace. Her arms flailed as he pushed her into the adjacent stall where she scratched her nails along the walls of the slick plastic stall, struggling for balance. Hitting the toilet, she fell against the wall and winced at the impact. She felt his knee push between her legs and his tongue dive into her mouth. His lips were cold, dead, and unwelcome. His tongue was even worse. It darted in and around her mouth like a cold, wet, slithering slug. *Eck*!

"Erez-" Dylan whined while he moved his mouth to her neck, licking and flicking his tongue. "I think," she pushed at him grimacing, "You have the wrong idea."

...*Get the hell off me!* She screamed within her mind.

Erez immediately stopped, snapping his head up and stared into her eyes. Dylan locked her glare with his wild blues as her chest heaved, brushing against his pecks. With her buzz gone, she knew she needed to find Aria and get the hell out of there. Erez obviously had the wrong idea and the thought of kissing anyone other than Tristian brought a downpour of guilt into her stomach.

When Erez didn't move, Dylan started to feel a tad awkward and on the verge of falling onto the toilet seat. However, that only lasted a moment before his pupils dilated, bleeding to a dark red. He released his frightening curved fangs and lunged to the spot he had been caressing on her neck. Dylan's eyes bulged, except where she thought horrible pain would erupt—an intense flutter like butterflies did instead, filling her veins with pleasure.

"Oh God," she groaned. Suddenly unaware of which way she was pushing... or pulling him. Her stomach flipped flopped as bliss gripped her insides. She grew hot and her knees threatened to give out. One of his hands slid down her body and gripped her rear with bruising force that surprisingly felt good. *Everything felt really good.* Now she understood why someone might want to be bitten.

With her fingers tangled tightly in the fabric of his shirt, he pulled her closer against his hips, locking her body within the expanse of his broad form. Somewhere deep in her mind she was screaming for help, but her body cried for him not to stop.

She suddenly felt the muscles at the pit of her stomach clench into a tight ball as her eyes rolled into the back of her head. Her struggles, her burn of guilt, her revulsion—everything seemed insignificant and ridiculous as her body climbed, higher and higher; her fingers gripping the edge of a cliff—dangling on the precipice. Then something inside her burst, flinging her off and into the oblivion.

Closing her eyes, she let Erez pull her along the waves of pure, unadulterated bliss.

She focused on his thumb grazing over her chin in slow, tantalizing circles where he held her head at an angle. She listened to his gulps, feeling extremely drugged and heavy.

The blissful haze began to lift and she was instantly embarrassed for enjoying Erez for that brief moment. The need for him to stop rose back to the forefront of her mind, but she couldn't seem to command her body to move.

Tristian... Help.

A growing numbness spread up her legs, slowly taking over her body. It felt like death pulling her under—scratching and clawing at her legs, yanking her into the cement void, never to return again. The awareness of her imminent demise flooded wetness to her eyes. She didn't want to die! A lone tear escaped out of the corner of her right eye as she silently pleaded over and over again for Tristian to save her.

As the numbness rose to her neck, a familiar but distant voice told her, "It will all feel better once you just let go." Heeding the voice, her extremities abruptly fell limp, blinking out the world like a burned light bulb.

CHAPTER 12

"There is no place like home."
L. Frank Baum

TRISTIAN opened his eyes and focused on the quaint room around him. He gave a tight smile. It was sunrise in Elon. Pinks, blood-oranges, and yellows layered the dusty dilapidated furnishings and graying walls; mimicking color in the monotone space. A faint memory of his mother's smile and his father's voice echoed in his mind, but soon followed their unjustified deaths by the Shadow Horde.

Hardening his face, he thought of the Omnipotence choice to ambush his childhood home while he was sent out on a *mandatory collection*. Yes, he hated going to the Soul Society for help, because it meant he *needed* their help. The Omnipotence was all too generous in lending a hand while slathering condescending smiles across their eager faces.

Tristian exhaled, put his sunglasses back on, and walked out the door towards one of the very things he despised most of all.

The suns were beginning to overlap each other indicating mid-day. A dome of deep azure wrapped the small world, dotted with thick clouds like cotton balls strewn across the sky. He felt an overwhelming need to bring Dylan there. To show her how beautiful it was. Her dream couldn't have done it justice, but the place held too many good, and horrible, memories for him. He just couldn't decide how to feel about the world he called home.

222

After the extensively long hike, he arrived at the main city of Elon: Asau. He could have portaled closer, saving himself the five-hour walk, but he liked seeing his childhood home; confirming it was still intact grounded him; as well as gave him some much needed time to compose himself.

The small city was bustling with activity. Tristian kept his head down as demons of all kinds brushed past him. No one giving him a second glance. Despite the air of freedom, he couldn't help but feel caged and conspicuous; as if any creature could sense his detailed vendetta.

Reaching the marble steps of the glass Tower of Souls, Tristian looked up at the Omnipotence crest—a crackled black shield with three crowns connected in the center like thorns reaching for the corners; a painted orange flame seared through the middle, licking the tip of the emblem—He felt his passive face harden again and anger flare in his veins. The fact that he ever wanted to be one of *them* boiled his blood. Taking a deep breath, he pushed emotion aside, slipped off his sunglasses, and stepped into the Tower of Souls.

"Mr. Effingo!" sang a shrill voice.

Cringing, Tristian rubbed the back of his neck and ran his nails along his jaw, trying to summon the energy he so desperately needed to placate these creatures. He exhaled, smiled and finally turned around to greet Lord Edward Struo.

Lord Struo had a knack for knowing everyone's business and, besides being a general gossip, was the new head of the Soul Society. Always a level below Tristian, he knew Edward was more than willing to step in the day Tristian threw it all away. It was only natural he would be here, but that didn't make his presence any less annoying.

"Lord Struo." Tristian bowed his head slightly, never releasing his intense stare.

The large round man in red robes, who resembled a Buddha idol, laughed obviously basking in Tristian's prostration.

"Oh, Effingo! Please call me Edward." He shook his head and clicked his tongue. "You know, that title has always been too heavy for my liking." *Right.*

"Well, Edward..." Tristian narrowed his eyes slightly and clasped his hands behind his back. "I think you like it. I think you only want to make me feel better for losing my title."

The bald man giggled. "Oh you've got me caught! Lord, I mean, *Mr.* Effingo." Tristian couldn't help but grit his teeth at the statement. "Please, I can only imagine your presence is strictly business." He mimicked Tristian's stance. "Am I right? Or is this a leisurely visit? Your reputation precedes you and well... your lack of *fun*." Struo smiled baring his needlepoint teeth.

Tristian let his smile slip. "Strictly business, Edward."

Motioning for Tristian to follow, "Come on."

The two demons walked towards Rose Hall—the section in the Tower of Souls where demons came to collect and release their legal contracts. It was neither red or pink, nor filled with roses, but a play on the shape and swirl of the attendant booths.

"Mr. Effingo, can I call one of the boys to bring you a vial of Essence? I hate to say, but you look dreadfully pale."

"Please," said Tristian impassively.

Struo snapped his fingers at one of the boy servants who scurried away fetching the much needed energy. The place was exceedingly quiet for his general comfort. The only sound was the clicking of Struo's wooden shoes echoing in the large foyer. He had been so careful to avoid this place until now. Yet, everything looked exactly the same as it had twenty years ago.

Light filtered through the cloudy glass walls bringing out the blue veins along the marble floor. Benches covered in black velvet and gold, ran the sides of the atrium surrounding a glass tube, as wide as a small house, filled with swirling blue Essence that reached the top of the tower. He thought about how much power that vat of Essence would give... he looked forward and noticed Struo giving him a skeptical glare.

"From time to time," Struo whispered, shifting his gaze away from Tristian. "I think about what that much Essence would do to a small demon as myself."

He's fishing, thought Tristian.

"Do you now?" he mocked keeping his voice at its normal pitch. "I wouldn't brag about that if I were you. You might give off the wrong impression... or the right one... I have no idea what that tainted mind of yours holds.

"Haven't you?" Struo raised an eyebrow never missing a step.

"Actually, I was just thinking about how much I need some energy," Tristian sighed. "Obviously, that amount is unnecessary."

"Yes, but surely obtaining that amount has swum through your mind once?"

Pick your words wisely, but Tristian couldn't help it.

"Just spill it, Struo. What do you want to know?"

He hated the mind games they played. The Omnipotence calculated their moves based on perfectly constructed double-dealing, scheming, and deceit. Turning those who saw differently in infinite circles until they grew so dizzy they turned the sword on themselves, unable to differentiate their own heart from the blackness of their enemy.

The round man stopped. "I've heard the rumor, you know."

"And what rumor are you referring to?" Tristian sighed again, feeling the burn behind his eyes, an allusion to the vacancy of energy needed in his stomach. "There are many rumors about me. Some scandalous and even entertaining. Please enlighten me on the particular one you're thinking of."

"Surely, you know." Struo clicked his tongue and shook his head. "I have a hard time believing you don't. In fact, I doubt it's a rumor but truth."

Tristian itched his jaw vigorously. "Spit it out, Struo."

Coming here was such a bad idea.

"You're working for the Elementas." Struo moved in front of Tristian blocking the entrance to Rose Hall.

Narrowing his eyes, Tristian hissed, "I haven't done anything illegal, and you should know we don't discuss our contracts-"

"We don't discuss our *Legal* contracts," retorted Struo. "Anyone associated with the Elementas is considered rogue. Tell me where they are Mr. Effingo, or should I say *Stewart*?"

Keeping a straight face. "I have absolutely no idea where they are."

"What about Temperance Elementa?"

Tristian's eye twitched slightly at her name. "What about her?"

"Hand her over to the Soul Society, Mr. Effingo. She is promised to the Shadow Horde for the Three Kings use."

"I don't know where she is either." Tristian never broke eye contact, knowing lying was always something he was good at. "Isn't she supposed to be dead?"

"Perhaps, Mr. Effingo. But if we find out that you even know the vicinity of her location and you didn't report it, expect the same fate as your parents."

Tristian growled low in his throat as he tried not to show any emotion to feed Struo's insinuation.

A boy's voice broke the tension, "Essence, sir?" He held a vial of blue swirling mist. Tristian took it and inhaled the energy. "Thank you, boy." The young demon took the vial and bowed before sprinting out of sight.

"Edward." Tristian felt rejuvenated and looked back at the tainted demon. "Get out of my way. I need new contracts and to release the amassed. If you have any evidence supporting your implications, then by all means, interrogate me, but if you don't, *step aside*."

Struo stroked his chin, squinting his eyes as if to look for the answers on Tristian's face. "Fine, but we'll have our eyes on you."

"Sure, you do that," he said as he side stepped the round man and walked into the large room of Rose Hall.

◇◇◇

The air was frigid and smelled of something burning. Dylan watched the white puff of her breath drift away with the cold wind. It was night but the streets were nowhere she recognized. She squinted around at the English tutor style homes lining the path she was walking on. The windows were dark and lifeless causing a deeper chill to course through her.

Wrapping her arms around herself, she continued to walk cautiously, the gravel crunching under her boots. She stopped, feeling something cold and wet against her stomach and palms. Lifting her palms in front of her, under the glow of lamplight, she took in hands that were wet and stained red with blood. She gasped and snapped her head up. A towering building abruptly appeared to her right. The sudden urge to touch the translucent structure overtook her. Placing a single finger to the building's frosty exterior, Dylan watched as a crimson ripple rang out from her touch.

Keeping her wet finger steadily fixed in place, she watched the tower drink up her blood and dance like water. Cocking her head to the side, she looked back at her clean hand. Her finger now stuck inside the strange liquid siding.

Confused, she looked back up hearing a distinct cracking sound. Fissures began to run speedily from the top. She panicked and tried freeing herself with her other hand and foot. The liquid was sticky, tacking to her body like glue. The fissures split off into tiny, red splintering webs, crawling like eerie

227

fingers reaching for her hand—to pull her in forever.

It reached her hand as she felt the surface harden. Wide-eyed, she heard an explosion. She jerked and threw her free arm above her head in protection. Another explosion, and another. She cautiously looked towards the source of the deafening noise. The building was exploding in chunks, but gravity seemed to be nonexistent. Another explosion burst just above her and glittering shards danced around her head. Staring at the floating debris, she noticed something blue reflecting off of it.

Craning her head back, she beheld a brilliant swirling blue mist dancing across the sky. Seeping into a radiant oblivion like the spiraling Milky Way Galaxy. It was beautiful and haunting at the same time. She felt an ache of bewilderment, like she'd lost something valuable. A cracking sound broke her muse followed by the last explosion jolting her awake.

Her body spasmed and she tried blinking the darkness away. No matter how many times she blinked the black wouldn't dissipate. Wherever she was it was pitch black. It wasn't even the black of night or underground, but so black Dylan felt like she could taste it, touch it, *hear* it. Like a hot, live mist, hissing as it hovered around her.

Was this death?

Her heart constricted and immediately began to pound so hard she thought it might crash straight through her chest. Her nose itched as a sweet smell of rot filled her nostrils. She lifted her hand to her face and felt the cool bracelet of metal around her ankles and wrists. Moving her hands along the thick, loose chains attached, she knew this wasn't an afterlife at all. Someone or some*thing* had brought her here.

Dylan suddenly wished she had listened to Tristian, or even stayed at his place, skipping the date that led her here.

Wherever here was.

Aria suddenly came to mind, but Dylan was too afraid to call out.

What was the last thing I remember? She curled her lip, *Erez.*

Way too scared to be mad, Dylan sat up carefully, feeling the unusually warm, cobblestone-like floor. Her fight or flight response sounded leading her to hesitantly push her way forward. Fingering the lumpy floor, Dylan brushed against something cold and damp. Without thinking, she seized it and screamed against the bolt of electricity that shocked and rippled through her body, throwing her back-first to the hard floor. Gasping at the sudden loss of air from her lungs, she clutched her right hand, which radiated a nauseating red-hot pain, to her chest.

Dylan felt hot tears spill down her cheeks. Her stomach abruptly lurched and the contents of her belly disappeared into the blackness with a sickening splash. After several heaves, she finally caught her breath. She began to cough and sob uncontrollably moving into the fetal position for what felt like hours crying until she passed out from exhaustion, never seeing an end to the darkness.

Dylan shot upright from her blackout, peeling open her crusty, swollen lids. The black mist was gone and somehow the room was illuminated, but Dylan couldn't seem to pinpoint the source of the light. No fixtures, torches, or even windows. It was just lit. Frowning, she looked at the floor and ran her fingers along the bumps. It was cobblestone like she had thought, but it was stained by a dark reddish/brown substance.

Old Blood.

Yanking her hand up and wiping it against her sweat soaked shirt, she felt her heart pick up where it left off the night before.

She licked her parched, cracked lips and rubbed her bruised wrists, noticing her manacles had been released. Looking closer at her surroundings, she noticed something off about the walls. They were broken with something red, oozing, and throbbing inside, like peeking through dry skin at someone's exposed heart pulsating to life. Except it felt the other way around, almost like she was inside the heart, trapped.

Inspecting her throbbing and trembling hand, tears welled up and streamed down her face. It was swollen from the severe burn, crusted with blood and pieces of dirt. Her stomach contracted and she thought she might hurl, again. Doubling over, she heaved a dry sob.

Why am I here? What had I done to deserve this? What do they want? Who are they?

As if on cue, a shuffle of feet and sharp clicks of heels halted her tears. Fear swallowed anything else she might have been feeling. She darted her eyes around the small room for anything that could be a weapon, but the room was completely bare.

She kept telling herself, *move! Damn it, Dylan, move! ...please!* But she was absolutely frozen, not even a tremble. Staring at her unresponsive legs, she realized the footsteps had grown closer and with each step the walls throbbed to the beat.

As if slapped across the face, she scrambled into a half scoot, half crab crawl, furthering herself from the ominous fence of her prison doors. Pressing herself as far away from the only entrance without touching the disgusting wall, she crouched hugging her knees. The pounding footsteps silenced as a woman's voice drifted to her.

"Temperance Elementa?"

Peeking above her knees, Dylan saw a woman with long black hair, wearing a red shift dress. She had frightening deep-set, green-eyes with a starburst of gold from her star-shaped pupil.

Demon.

Sucking in a ragged breath. "How do you know that name?" Her voice came out shaky and worn.

The woman sighed a smile. "I knew it was you. I would like

you to come with me-" She glanced down at Dylan's body with a flicker of disgust. "-and get cleaned up."

Hurrying to an uneven stand, Dylan crossed her arms now fueled by fury. "I'm not going anywhere with you! Why the hell am I here!" she screamed and stomped her foot.

"Due time, dear. I will explain in due time."

Dylan was so frustrated tears prickled the backs of her eyes threatening to fall again. "I want to go home," she cried.

"This is your home," she smirked. "Now."

The woman snapped her fingers and two of the most hideous beings Dylan had ever set her eyes on, marched over in a snarl. Dylan shoved a trembling hand to her mouth to stifle a scream. Blood and the grittiness of dirt touched her tongue as the two muscular, golden *things* towered over the small woman with long knife-like fingers and shark-like teeth. Their eyes were blank, white balls that seemed to follow Dylan closely. A sob bubbled up in Dylan's throat when the woman commanded the creatures to fetch her. They grabbed her, cutting the delicate flesh of her upper arms with their razor claws.

"Stop! Please! Stop!" she cried over and over again. Tears streamed down her cheeks and into her nose and mouth as the creatures dragged Dylan away from her cell of Hell.

"This way," the woman directed.

Dylan continued to sob and wince. Their talons digging into the cuts deeper and deeper with each step and erratic movement. Above the pain, all she could think about was her broken promise to Tristian, getting away, and why Erez had done this to her. Did Datu know? Was he in on this too?

They started up some stone steps that were lit by metal candelabras and housed by walls similar to her cell. Oozing red globs dropped on her head as they pushed her forward.

Dylan's crying had slowed to a stop and became exhausted dry hiccups. At the top of the stairs, the rock and worn style of the basement ended and a picturesque mansion began. Dark hardwood floors were covered by a red carpet runner, like a river of blood, muffling the demon's heels. Normal walls boasted a series of traditional, floral, oil paintings and delicate glass sconces. Room after room of large, dark, vacant bedrooms lined the right side of the hall. Towards the end of the corridor the woman stopped and gracefully pivoted around *smiling*.

"These are your new quarters," said the woman flatly. Dylan peered inside. It didn't look like a prison, but a bedroom, a really nice bedroom. This made Dylan even more worried, none of this made any sense.

"What's your name?"

"Lucia." The woman narrowed her eyes slightly. "Get cleaned up and rest if you need. Don't try to escape. We aren't in your pathetic world any longer." Lucia cleared her throat and with a twitch of her head, the two creatures dragged Dylan into the vacant suite. "We'll talk more at dinner." And with that, the creatures dropped Dylan in the middle of the floor and all three left the room leaving the door wide open. Dylan thought for a moment about the possibility of escaping. Staring at the open door, she stood tentatively, sucking air from the stinging cuts on her arms, and lurched to the door. Peering out into the hallway, she came face to face with one of the creatures causing her to release a scream as the thing snarled. Dylan ran back into her room and slammed the door. Throwing the lock home, she pressed her back to it, feeling her heart slam itself against her rib cage.

"Why," she cried over and over again. "Why... why."

She sat in the middle of the room for what could have been hours, crying and pleading to a God she wasn't so sure she believed in. When a blaring loud noise rang, Dylan threw her hands up to her ears. She stopped crying and looked around anxiously, worried something would come bursting through the door at any given moment. Scooting backward towards the large four-poster bed, she continued to stare hauntingly at the arched wooden door. An eerie quiet took over and the only thing that sounded was the rapid 'thump, thump, thump' of her beating heart.

CHAPTER 13

"They've promised that dreams can come true - but

forgot to mention that nightmares are dreams, too."

Oscar Wilde

THAT morning, Tristian returned from Elon with a slew of new contracts liable to last him fifty years. He turned his phone back on noticing no reply text from Dylan. Panic flashed, but then he remembered her mentioning the loss of her phone. His shoulders relaxed and he smiled at the anxiety she brought on him. He just wasn't sure how to proceed with her. Definitely with caution. The woman owned him and he didn't think he could breathe if she hated him.

Stepping out into the dark LA morning, Tristian walked to his Audi feeling much stronger than he did the night before. The sun hadn't shown itself over the crest of the horizon yet; giving him enough time to rest a bit and get ready for the inevitable melt down this completely unpredictable and enamoring woman was sure to exhibit before class.

Positioning his Ray-Ban's back on, Tristian's phone chirped. Swiping the screen open, he noticed a voicemail from Asher. Thoughts of Asher using his *Unda* on Dylan seeped anger into his being, causing him to clutch his phone so tightly his knuckles turned white and cracked the plastic case. His phone beeped again, but this time it was a text from Asher.

ASHER: She's gone.

Was all it said.

Tristian stood frozen, staring at the message. Struggling to fathom the weight of the situation. Confusion and worry vied for domination of his emotions, when panic finally set in. Finding his legs, Tristian ran to his car, burning rubber into a thick demonic smoke as he peeled away from the church.

"What the hell do you mean, *'She's gone'*!" he roared on the phone to Asher.

"I don't know how it happened... but her roommate is flipping out and Dylan is gone." He heard a rustling and a woman yelling.

"Someone came into her apartment?"

"No, her roommate-" Tristian heard Aria scream her name in the background. "Aria, told me they went out with my friend Datu and his friend Erez. Aria and Datu left Dylan and Erez on the dance floor and the next thing she remembers is being home alone."

Tristian hissed, "She left the apartment?"

Asher's voice dropped to whisper, "Yeah. I can't believe I'm going to say this, but I'm pretty sure this was Datu's plan. Erez was sired by Datu and would pretty much do anything he would ask. I have no idea what for or should I say *who* for." Aria started yelling profanities at Asher as a crash sounded. "Geez, woman, chill the fuck out!" he heard Asher yell away from the phone. "Tristian, you need to get your ass over here and help me talk this girl into not calling the cops. We may have to tell her what's going on."

Tristian snarled, "Don't tell her anything! I'll be there soon." He ended the call chucking his cell phone onto the dashboard. "Argh!" he grunted, ire burned through him as he gripped the steering wheel tightly. Trying to calm his nerves, he concentrated on possible suspects.

Who other than the OP would want her? Think, Effingo. Think!

Asher had been rumored to be working for the Omnipotence and if he didn't really know where she was then it couldn't be them. Not to mention, he was just in Elon. If she had been there, surely the court would be in session and bragging about their new find. His mind raced through the self-ruling demons, those who hated the Elementas and cancelled out those who were with the OP.

His mind stopped at the thoughts of Gerion, Anna, and Daniel. They were on the same level as Constance and Atticus. Anna was an active supporter of the schools in Elon and something like this could really ruin her pristine reputation. Gerion on the other hand was bound to benefit from Dylan's powers, but had been missing for a couple hundred years and rumored to have been slaughtered along with his family, so it was unlikely him. Daniel… Well, he was a hermit in full view of the Law, living off his parents and refusing to collect or do anything proactive with his existence.

Pressing his foot against the gas pedal, he floored it down the 10. Wondering if he would have to get in touch with a few contacts for their help. *If* he needed their help. For all he knew the vampires could have taken her for their sick form of fun. Plus, talking to them would raise questions he wouldn't be able to answer without severe repercussions. He needed to keep the situation contained. The more of those who knew about Dylan and the disappearance, the more damage control he would have to carry out after the fact.

Thirty minutes had passed by the time Tristian pulled in front of Dylan's apartment near campus. The anger in his eyes had died down to embers and he only felt a sickening sensation like he'd lost her forever. Worry permeated each and every cell of his being as he took to the stairs, three at a time, until he came to the third floor door that emanated all the yelling and banging.

He looked to see multiple neighbors peeking out their apartments to witness what was surely some kind of altercation. A loud crash sounded against the door, causing him to jump slightly. Curling his lip, he pushed open the door just in time to duck below the flying mug aimed, most definitely, at Asher.

Asher had his arms up, pleading with Aria to "chill out" when he looked at the wrathful redhead with raccoon eyes and wrinkled—obviously last night's—clothes aiming a coffee mug in his direction.

"Where is she!" squalled Aria.

"Hell if I know! Just let me help you figure it out," pleaded Asher.

She jerked her armed hand back as Tristian spoke, "Aria, this was Datu's doing. Let's figure out where our girl is."

Her eyes flew in his direction, accidentally chucking the mug at him. He effortlessly dodged the porcelain. Looking where it landed, he raised his eyebrows at her.

"Sorry!" She slapped her hands to her mouth. "Tristian, I didn't see you."

"It's fine but stop-'

"Tell your friend to stop trying to touch me!"

He looked at Asher still crouched to his right.

"What?" Asher shrugged throwing a wide gesture towards Aria. "I was trying to get the crazy bitch to calm down."

"By trying to touch me, you freak!" She grabbed a plate when Tristian appeared at her side using his inhuman speed. He grabbed her wrist where she held the dish and watched her shaken expression. Before she could scream, he sent a steady stream of *Unda*, not too much to immobilize her, but just enough to calm her down.

Her face fell with heavy lidded eyes. "W-what are you?"

"Let go of the plate and sit on the couch." She nodded and did as directed.

"Well," huffed Asher. "I could have done that."

Tristian glanced at Asher as he stood, brushing off porcelain shards and dust.

"I can tell. That's why she was under control when I got here, right?" Tristian sneered, still wanting to rip his face off, but instead he strode over to a dazed Aria, sitting numbly on the overstuffed couch.

Looking around at the mismatched furnishings and eclectic chevron and floral décor, he realized this was the first time he stood in Dylan's apartment. It wasn't exactly how he had imagined it would play out.

"Aria," Tristian said calmly as he crouched in front of her, "tell me what happened. Why were you both out with Datu and Erez?"

Asher walked over, leaning against the large window framed by white curtains and metal blinds. Aria glared at him then shifted her attention to Tristian.

"While you and Dylan were out, Asher had stopped by looking for Dylan, then Datu, then Garret-"

Asher cut in, "I didn't know where she had disappeared to and you never got back to me if you found her or not, so-"

"Datu brought her jacket with her phone inside. I panicked," Aria continued ignoring Asher. "He calmed me down, flirted with me, and asked me out." She frowned like she was trying to make sense of it herself. "Well, he asked us both out on a double date in a couple hours. I told him sure, if you know, Dylan came back in time. She did and I convinced her to go." Aria threw her head in her hands, a veil of crimson covered her ashen face. "Omigod," she mumbled before looking at Tristian with glassy eyes, "It's my fault. We need to call the police. What if he's doing stuff to her, or who knows!"

"How do you know she's not just out with this vam- Erez?"

"Because, one moment I was walking back to the table and the next I was in my bed alone. The door was unlocked... It just doesn't make sense. Dylan would never leave our apartment open like that... and if they had come to drop me off, after I miraculously passed out mid-stride, she would've definitely left a note or taken her phone, because... I tend to worry." She shook her head, letting her face fall back into her hands.

Tristian looked to Asher, who only shrugged, then put an awkward hand on Aria's shoulder. She jumped. "Now tell me Tristian Stewart. How the hell did you move that fast?" Aria glared at him waiting for an answer.

Sighing Tristian said, "It's not important, but the police can't help us." He crinkled his face waiting for her retort.

"Not good enough," Aria snapped. "Without the police how do you plan to get her back?"

He didn't want to tell her that adding a complication, such as the police, would only result in more casualties than necessary. He had a feeling the revelation would scare her into silence.

Asher started laughing to himself. "We?" Tristian and Aria both looked in his direction with glaring eyes. "No, no, no." He motioned between Tristian and himself. "*We,* will be looking for her, not you." He then pointed to Aria. "No calling the cops, tell us the last things you remember, and just sit tight, *doll*." He gave her a seductive smile and wink as he spoke the last word.

Tristian watched Aria slowly clench her fists, as her face flamed red with rage, almost matching her hair color.

"My name is ARIA, not *doll!*" she screamed, jumping up so fast, Tristian quickly backed up. "And there's no way in hell I'm sitting around while my best friend is being tortured, raped, or God knows what!"

Before Asher could speak Tristian cut in, "Very well. Then

there are a few things you should know."

◇◇◇

Dylan sat with her back pressed firmly against the large wooden bed, blinking with the erratic beat of her heart. She shook with overwhelming terror as she continued to stare hauntingly at the arched door. Spots clouded her eyes as she felt her anxiety climbing to a crescendo just waiting for something, anything, to happen after the loud alarm. Time was non-existent as every second felt like an eternity ticking towards her death.

Suddenly the TV mounted on the far wall to her right flicked on. Dylan jerked almost wetting her pants… again. She was slightly relieved an abandoned well with a girl crawling out of it didn't appear, but the woman in the picture wasn't any better.

Lucia.

She was wearing the same color red, but a different dress. It was almost over exaggerated in every way. The edgy collar was too high, it seemed, for comfort and the tight neckline excessively low. And what topped the menacing dress off was Lucia's annoyed expression.

"Temperance, get up and get dressed." Dylan froze, trying to hide behind the ginormous bed. "I can still see you. I can see this entire plot of land, not an inch hidden."

Dylan clamped her hands over her eyes and whispered to herself over and over again, "This isn't real. This isn't real…"

"Why of course it's real. Now get cleaned up and get dressed in the clothes set for you in the armoire."

"No." Dylan's eyes flew open shocked at the confident voice that flew from her lips.

"Very well. I can send in the worm guard standing outside your door to make you. If I were you, I would do as I was told. It won't be gentle."

The television flicked off and Dylan heard the door rattle.

She scrambled upright and ran to the en-suite bathroom, locking the door behind her. Her breath was so quick, she thought she might hyperventilate and pass out. Grasping the marble vanity, she squeezed her eyes shut, willing herself to calm.

Continue to breathe in and out... a friendly voice spoke in her mind. Garret's words of meditation calmed her breathing and brought her pulse down to a manageable level.

Slowly peeling open her lids, she gasped at her reflection in the mirror. Her hair was a tangled mess and she was covered in smeared dirt and blood. Her face was puffy and stained with dripping mascara—no doubt from the endless hours of crying. She looked like a crazy person from the streets that had been dragged along the road like garbage. What could they have possibly done to make her look like this?

Looking around the ornate white and gold bathroom, Dylan shook in terror, afraid to clean herself, but, even more afraid of the creatures outside her door if she didn't.

She moved to the antique, claw foot tub and turned on the bath water to scolding before gaining the confidence to strip. Pulling off her jeans, a strange feeling of being numb overcame her. A part of her wondered if she would even feel the heat of the water, or if she had simply lost touch with reality.

She stepped into the scorching water after the tub had filled. As soon as she hit the hot water her body woke, screaming with pain—but it was welcomed. She needed to feel something to remind herself that this was all very real.

As if her body sucked the moisture in—tears began to fall. Dylan sobbed and washed her sore body, scrubbing off the blood and grime.

After she was clean, she quickly stepped out of the red, cloudy water, toweled off, and dressed in her underwear. Holding the plush, vanilla scented towel against her nakedness, she padded to the door leading to the bedroom.

Unlocking the door, she gingerly peered into the empty

bedroom. Confirming she was in fact alone, she stepped toward the armoire. A single dress hung before her, an emerald satin dress. Pulling it on, Dylan looked at herself. It was floor length and long sleeved. The front grazed across her collarbone while the back dropped all the way just above her bottom, where a brooch of diamonds in the shape of a snake accented. It was a strange but gorgeous dress and it only made her nerves more twisted.

Why do they want you dressed this way? she brooded inwardly.

The door opening snapped her out of her thoughts. Just as she was about to scream, a young girl with long chestnut locks and faded teal eyes, who couldn't have been any older than twelve, walked in with a bucket of... hair styling tools?

"Hello, Miss" said the girl curtsying in a black cotton dress. "I'm here to fix your hair."

Dylan stood shocked, unable to form words.

The young girl only smiled politely with her eyes downcast and pocketed a set of keys.

"Come on, Miss. We mustn't anger the Mistress."

Completely caught off guard, Dylan ended up just nodding listlessly and following her slowly to the makeup vanity in the bathroom. She plopped down on the delicate stool as the young girl went to work silently.

After a few moments Dylan found her voice, "Why am I here?"

The girl paused and hesitantly made eye contact through the mirror. "I don't know the dealings of the Mistress, Miss Elementa." She looked back down.

Dylan took a deep breath. *That name...*

"Do you know why I'm dressed this way?"

The girl gave a weak smile. "The dinner, Miss. Mistress Planto has formal dinners every day. You are our guest of honor."

Dylan's face was quizzical. *Guest of honor? No, that didn't make sense.* Dylan turned, stopping the girl's work.

"What's your name?"

"My name, Miss?" The girl looked shocked that she was asked; as if she were never asked such things.

"Yes."

"Peppi. Peppi Calibri."

"Thank you for the information and my hair, Peppi."

The young girl beamed at the mention of her name.

"Miss?"

"Call me Dylan."

The girl raised an eyebrow. "Very well, but with all due respect, I thought your name was Temperance, Miss."

"I go by Dylan."

"Dylan, are you…" The girl fumbled over her words. Dylan thought she was going to say something about her being held prisoner, but she didn't. "Are you okay, Miss? You look pale."

Dylan let out a rush of air, strangely on the verge of hysterics.

"No, Peppi. I'm not okay."

She looked at herself numbly after Peppi had worked her magic. Her hair was strewn in an array of fat curls, half up and half down. Peppi curtsied and left a large box of make-up and exited the room. But Dylan felt ill. None of this was okay. She could care even less if she looked pretty.

She stood from the stool and faltered to the bedroom where one of the creatures waited. Dylan gasped, but the thing stood there vacantly. A beat later the television flicked on.

"Temperance, follow it to dinner," snapped Lucia. Then, it flicked off.

She looked at the creature feeling her frantically beating heart. There was *no* way she was going anywhere with that thing. Whatever that thing was. She stood, wild-eyed, staring at it, completely stuck by panic. A few minutes went by and Dylan couldn't seem to command her legs to move. The television flicked on again.

"Bring her to dinner." The creature seemed to snap awake, flicking its blank white eyes in her direction. It strode toward her, reaching out its talons and snarling through sickly decaying fangs. Dylan screamed, finding her legs could move after all.

"Fine!" she screamed crouching in the corner of the room with her hands over her head. "I'll go, I'll go! Just don't touch me!" she pleaded.

"Stop," was all Lucia said and the creature obeyed. "Temperance, follow it to dinner, *now*," she growled and the television flicked off again. Dylan wanted to scream at the top of her lungs, fling herself on the bed, rip her hair out, and tear the dress into tiny little pieces.

Why was this happening?

Against her better judgment, she followed the creature out of her prison to her attacker.

Walking through the maze of duplicate ornate corridors, Dylan felt trepidation increase with each turn. Her fists were clenched so tightly; her fingernails were surely drawing blood. At the thought of blood, Dylan looked where her wounds existed from the creatures grabbing her. They must have just reopened because red seeped through her satin dress. She felt like a gruesome Christmas ornament.

At the end of the long corridor were two aged, wooden doors similar to the ones in her twisted bedroom. The creature halted, bringing Dylan to an almost collision with the large beast. Holding back a squeal, she swiftly backed up as her breath started to quicken and her legs quaked. The doors opened as if automated, revealing an equally elaborate room. The creature didn't move, but merely stood like a haunting statue. Dylan instinctively hid behind the creature, more afraid of what was just around it.

"Enter," said a woman's voice.

The creature started to move forward and Dylan reluctantly followed. The creature stepped to the side of the room, leaving Dylan suddenly exposed in the large... dining room?

Taking in her surroundings, the place was so far away from her taste it was alien. Intricate glass sconces and matching dainty chandeliers lit the royal dining room pensively set for an elaborate meal. Decorative porcelain and gold-rimmed crystal stems were placed at the far end where two demons resided. Lucia and a man she had never seen before, an exceptionally stunning one as much as she hated to admit it.

"Temperance, please sit here in front of me." She motioned to the spot across the table from her and to the right of the curious man. He sat at the head of the table. With his elbows neatly resting on the arms of the chairs, he observed her. His pointer and middle fingers feeling the slight crease on his chin. Dylan kept her eyes cast down at the intricate green, black, and gold rug that lay under the ostentatious table as she moved to her designated seat.

She sat down feeling the piercing gaze of the man next to her. Impulsively, she flicked her eyes in his direction, immediately regretting it. She took in his features, dark blonde hair, slightly long and curling over his ears. Dark stubble dotted his cheeks, rounding his full lips and set jaw. Moving up, her eyes locked with his startling blood-orange orbs. He lifted a corner of his mouth and shifted his speculating eyes down her body, drinking her in, and returned eye contact.

Lucia cleared her throat, making Dylan jump and elbow the fine plates. Her face exploded into crimson and she instantly looked down to her lap, gripping her hands until they were tightly wound—splotchy, white, and red with tension.

"Temperance." Dylan kept her head down, but looked at the woman through her lashes, who gestured to the man next to her.

"This is my son, Silas Planto."

Dylan nodded in his direction, keeping her attention numbly fixed on her splotchy hands.

"Temperance, don't be rude. Acknowledge my son, *now*"

Tears burned her eyes and pooled in the corners. She looked in his direction and gave the best smile she could muster at the moment then looked back down. He's smug expression fell at her misery.

She heard him grunt, "Mother, let her be."

"Very well," Lucia snapped as a set of double doors flapped open, revealing Peppi and a group of servants all dressed in similar black dresses, carrying plates of steaming food.

At the thick smell of savory beef and onions, Dylan's stomach spoke, reminding her of the last time she had nourishment. An old woman set a steaming plate of beef, mashed potatoes, and asparagus in front of her—wafting to her nose. Another woman set a large bowl of piping hot buttered rolls down and another moved to pour each stem with red wine. Even at her slightly devastating hunger, Dylan was too terrified to eat anything set before her by her captors.

Lucia and Silas started cutting into their feast as Dylan bore imaginary holes into her plate with her eyes.

"Eat, Temperance. You haven't had food in over twenty-four hours. You must be hungry."

Dylan brought her somber gaze to Lucia's ferocious eyes. "I'm vegetarian," she lied.

"Then eat the potatoes or rolls. I can't have you passing out from starvation."

"I'm fine," snapped Dylan.

"Do I need to have one of the worms feed you?" Lucia threatened with a raised eyebrow.

Dylan shot her eyes in their direction. She watched as a glob of drool dripped out of the worm's sharp, rotting mouth, hitting the floor with a muffled thud. She shook her head viciously.

Silas interjected, "Mother. If she doesn't want to eat, let her be!" He slammed his fist on the table making even the terrifying Lucia jump. Dylan had her eyes wide and her entire body tensed. She prayed silently for the opportunity to flee.

"Fine, but you're taking care of her when she starves to death. It's not like we have an abundant supply of Essence to keep her alive without food." Lucia spit.

"Even if we did, she's obviously still a youth with those gray eyes. Essence wouldn't do her any good until she collects," Silas added.

Dylan didn't know how she felt about them 'discussing' her while she sat at the same table. A single tear escaped her right eye when she felt a warm hand graze her shoulder. Dylan jerked, slamming her knees into the table. Silas instantly backed his hand away.

"Don't eat if you don't want to," he said in a gentle whisper.

All she could summon was a half nod, not really convincing anyone.

"Temperance, as my son has so aptly shared with you, don't eat if you don't want to. This place you're in is your new home. This castle is on a desolate world, so I don't worry about the possibility of escape. The worm slave is here for your protection or if you don't do as I please; otherwise it is yours to command. I want you to feel comfortable here. I understand the initial introduction was unpleasant, but I will attempt to be more hospitable." Lucia continued as Dylan stared at her gravely. "You may use all the facilities, library, salon, fitness, music, and art rooms. Almost anything you can think of, we have here for your convenience."

"I just want to go home. This is not my home," Dylan whispered.

Lucia let out a rush of frustrated air. "Like I said before, and

247

please note, I do not like to repeat myself, this is your home now, *get used to it*. If you wish, you may leave the table, but only if you let Silas accompany you."

Dylan's face scorched.

What the hell was wrong with me! She thought widening her eyes and looking back at her strained hands. *I've been abducted, held prisoner, cut by those things she calls Worms, and I'm blushing from a boy?* Dylan quickly stood making Silas scramble upright.

"I don't need a chaperone," she snapped, heaving all her hate in his direction and back at Lucia. "If you say there's no way for me to escape, then you won't mind if I leave by myself." Her voice was confident but her trembling body betrayed her.

"Very well," Lucia said, swirling the wine in the cut crystal.

Dylan's eyes flashed surprise, but she immediately fixed her features. Turning slowly away from the dining room, she lifted her head defiantly and followed her Worm slave through the double doors and back to her prison chambers.

CHAPTER 14

"The truth is rarely pure and never simple."
Oscar Wilde

"SO you're a demon... And Dylan is a demon too... but she didn't know 'till recently," Aria spoke summarizing Tristian's words. "Her real name is Temperance?"

She sat on her living room couch frowning quietly while Tristian rehashed everything that Dylan had been going through.

"This Datu guy..." She looked up darting her eyes between the two demons. "He's a vampire? ...Werewolves, faeries, angels, those really exist?" She shook her head smiling. "You guys are fucking with me. We just need to call the police."

She started to get up when Tristian grabbed her wrist again. But this time he took off his sunglasses, revealing his unusual eyes. He watched her take him in, then switched her stare to Asher, who winked his pupils flashing a wicked smile. Aria gasped and pulled her legs up and away from the two demon boys.

"H-how the *hell* did you do that?" Aria hissed.

Placing his sunglasses back on, Tristian asked, "So, do you believe us yet? We cannot call the police. It will only make the situation more complicated."

He watched Aria sit wide-eyed for a moment before she nodded vigorously, letting her bright red hair dance on the sides of her face.

249

"All right. But both of you need to keep your freaky fingers to yourself," she said wiggling her fingers at Asher with a glare.

"No problem," said Tristian.

"Fine," muttered Asher, letting out a rush of air.

Now that the situation seemed to be under control, Tristian stood. "Sit tight, I have some calls to make."

"Who are you calling?" voiced Asher as he pushed off from the window. "We need to find the location of the LA Vampire Lair."

Tristian rolled his eyes and scowled at the other demon. "Sometimes I wonder about your intelligence… just watch the human." Without waiting for Asher's counter, Tristian turned and walked down the small hallway lined with white frames of Aria and Dylan smiling and laughing at different locations. Or more like Aria smiling and Dylan looking strained.

He scanned his phone and found an old acquaintance that still owed him a favor. While it rang, he set his eyes on a photograph towards the end of the hall. Aria was leaning on Dylan as both girls laughed heartily, lounging in their pink and teal bikinis, surrounded by white sand, sun, and chevron printed blue towels. He felt anger swell in his chest. Even if it wasn't in his contract to bring her to the Elementas, he held no shadow of a doubt that he would try just as hard to find her. After all, it was his fault she had been stolen. If he hadn't been so childish with his feelings, none of this would have happened. They would be sharing coffee and tacos again like the first morning they spent together. She'd insist on removing his shades while he'd insist on touching her any place he could.

Clenching his jaw against the deep ache of regret, he knew nothing good came from wondering what would have or could have been. It happened and he needed to fix it. He needed to find Datu and make him pay for taking his contract away. Now *that* thought brought a sinister smile to his lips.

Oh yes, Datu would pay.

"Hello?" yawned a tired male voice on the line.

"Hey, Ulysses, it's Effingo."

"What's up, brother? Haven't heard from you in a while." Ulysses yawned again. "What the hell time is it?"

"Early. Look, I need to call in that favor you owe me."

"Sure, man. What's up?"

"I need to find Datu, the vampire."

"He'll be at their lair for sure. You need me to take you?"

"No, just the address. It's not exactly going to be a friendly visit."

"Those vamps will be trouble if you just go busting in by yourself. You'll need some help, my friend."

"I guess you make a good point. Where should we meet you?"

"We?"

"Asher and a human."

"Wait, wait, wait," chuckled Ulysses sounding more alert. "Let me get this straight. You were planning on breaking into one of the largest vampire lairs and taking a *human* with you? Why?" He continued to laugh, "For bait?"

"No," sighed Tristian. "I'll explain later. Where should we meet you."

After they agreed on a meeting place, Tristian smelled the familiar, delicious scent waft from the adjacent room. Pushing open the door, Tristian looked around Dylan's extremely messy room. Dirty clothes and towels were everywhere and her desk was packed with textbooks and loose papers. The walls were painted a dark purple and her sleek, iron-canopy bed was draped with a gray silk and chiffon duvet. He didn't understand how anyone lived this way. Stumbling to her desk, he leafed through a couple pages, stopping on one that caught his eye.

"My partner, Tristian Stewart, is nothing like I expected. At

first glance he's closed off, guarded, and frankly an asshole. But after spending time with him, I've realized how sweet, careful, and kind he is. He holds a great weight of sorrow and emotional scars that I can't even begin to fathom. What he hides from the world are the very essentials to understanding him. I cannot explain more about him without revealing secrets that are not my own to voice. So I am leaving it at that. Tristian Stewart- the sweet, kind, enigma. I feel privileged to have met such a person."

He slowly set the paper back down. Where was the Transylvania story? Or the sarcasm and hate? Had she wrote this and changed her mind? Or had she lied about the former altogether?

Shaking his head, he scanned the room and noticed the black nightstand cradling her fully charged cell phone. He snatched it and inspected the several missed calls and texts. Nothing seemed to really stand out only a 'Garret' called five times. Tristian unleashed a jealous growl deep in his throat before calling out to Aria.

"Who the hell is *Garret*?"

He heard quick steps stomping down the hall and her angry muffled voice, "Get away from me!"

"What?" said Aria pushing open Dylan's door.

Tristian waved her phone. "I was looking for clues and found her phone. Who's Garret?"

"Oh." Aria raised an eyebrow then smiled with amused, narrowed eyes. "He's her Yoga/gym-whatever instructor. A real hottie. She goes to all his classes and he sometimes gives her *private* lessons."

He narrowed his eyes; the annoying human was becoming more annoying and obviously enjoyed his jealousy.

Aria smirked, "Hmm, did you really think someone as

pretty as Dylan wouldn't have multiple guys lined up?" She posed with her hands on her hips and pouted. "Aww… you did."

"Leave him alone," interjected Asher making Aria jump.

"Stop sneaking up on me!" she huffed at Asher before turning back to Tristian. "Tristian. She told me what you said. I understand that in order to get Dylan back, we need to work together. But I just want you to know, Dylan's my friend, you are not. You flipped my bitch switch and I don't plan on being nice to you."

Was she even nice before?

He nodded understandingly, because he'd hate himself, too, if the roles were reversed. She gave a curt nod and turned around facing Asher, who was in the middle of rolling his eyes.

"Yeah, keep rolling asshat. Maybe you'll find a brain in there," she hissed storming off to the living room.

Tristian pressed his lips together, trying not to smile at Asher's dumbstruck face and continued to scan Dylan's phone. He went to their text conversation to see if she read his message. She did, and wrote one too, but never sent it.

DYLAN: I'm sorry too. Some of the things that you said were true. I get that I'm inexperienced with this new life, but what we have isn't a mistake. I'm willing to give it a try, if you are. I'll see you tomorrow. X

He felt like a complete mess, worried he'd lost the one creature that seemed able to bust down all the ironclad walls and make camp within his heart.

Happy for his sunglasses once again, he slid Dylan's cell into his pocket.

"C'mon, we need to go find this vampire and make him wish he were never reborn."

Asher grinned rubbing his hands together. "I never did like him all that much. This should be fun."

◇◇◇

Storming back to her bedroom, Dylan feigned confidence where none existed. She stepped inside and carefully closed and locked her door. Sucking in trembling, slow breaths, she strode to the bed and grabbed a pillow. Smashing it against her face, she let out an ear-piercing scream. Her whole body rippled with rage and the pillow burst into thousands of little feathers raining around her clenched fists still grasping pieces of fabric. Dylan's eyes bugged when she comprehended what she had just done.

Frustration at her lack of control coursed through her body. Large drops streamed from her eyes. With clenched, trembling hands, she tried to take off the creepy dress. Frustrated, she began ripping the delicate fabric to shreds. Tears continued to fall mixing with the rivulets of blood from the reopened wounds on her arms.

Falling into the pile of green silk and feathers, Dylan dug her trembling palms into her eyes looking for pain, anything to give her the feeling of control over something. A light knock sounded at the door, silencing her tears and erupting dread back to the surface.

"W-who is it?" she trembled, fumbling over her words.

"Peppi, Miss," a small voice called. "I have a change of clothes for you."

Dylan began to sob from relief and crawled to the door on all fours. Throwing her hand up to free the bolt, she fell against the wall. Peppi gingerly opened the door. Seeing Dylan, her innocent blue eyes widened with shock.

"Oh, Miss!" She quickly and quietly, shut the door, locking the bolt and kneeling next to Dylan's naked, trembling, bleeding body. "Miss, please, I have clothes." The little girl was bound to have seen her fair share of crazy, but she acted like this was the last thing she expected to find.

"Please, Temperance, Dylan—Miss, let me draw you a bath. The Mistress can be mean, but she means well. You're bleeding again. Oh Miss!" Peppi pleaded bringing her apron to the thick slashes gouged on Dylan's shoulders.

Dylan suddenly threw her arms around the small girl who smelled of butter rolls and honey. The young girl flinched, surprised at her forwardness.

"They kidnapped me, Peppi! I have a home, a family, someone special. This wasn't supposed to happen!" she sobbed into Peppi's tiny neck. The girl finally returned Dylan's hold, gently stroking the honey-blonde curls stuck to her sweaty back.

"I was born here. I don't know much about the Mistress or her business. She's mostly very private, you see." Dylan's sobs mellowed to hiccups as she listened. "But you're the first person to acknowledge me or even ask my name; that tells me you are a good person. You are nothing like the Mistress, and I'm sorry she's doing this to you." Dylan sat back and wiped at her dripping nose with the heel of her palm.

Peppi continued, "If I knew how to get you out, I wouldn't think twice before doing so. Maybe, I can ask the other servants… but I have a sneaking suspicion, no one really knows how to leave or if it's even possible. You are our first guest who's stayed overnight in a very long time. You're the first guest I've ever seen or spoken to."

Dylan felt a pang in her chest for Peppi. This girl had never known freedom and was risking everything by talking to her in this manner.

"Why are you telling me this? Aren't you afraid she'll hear you?" Dylan sniffed as the little girl thought a moment.

"This has been my whole life and a rough one at that. If she were to end me, I guess," the girl paused pursing her lips. "I guess, I don't have much to lose, Miss."

Dylan hugged the little girl again and pulled away giving a tight smile that didn't reach her eyes.

"Miss, I thought you might be hungry." She dug into her apron pockets and pulled out two large, buttered dinner rolls.

Dylan's mouth salivated and her stomach audibly grumbled.

"Thank you, Peppi," she said around the saliva pooling in her mouth.

She snatched a roll and tore off a piece of the steamy white dough, shoving it into her mouth.

"Mmpf, mis is smo good," she mumbled as Peppi set the other roll and a pair of pajamas down next to her feet.

"Thank you, Miss. I made them," she beamed.

Pushing the rest of the roll in her mouth, Dylan knelt down while sliding on the buttery silk button up and matching shorts. She heard the shuffle of objects in the bathroom before Peppi reappeared in the bedroom, holding a small red box.

"Miss, please sit." She motioned to the bed. "I need to fix your wounds." Dylan sat freeing an arm from her pajamas and wrapping the fabric around her nakedness.

"I can't believe she allowed the Worm to touch you." The little girl sighed and shook her head. "They aren't allowed to touch anyone." She shook her head again and dabbed alcohol to the cuts. Dylan whimpered from the sting.

"Do you know what they are, Peppi?" Dylan spoke hoarsely through bites of the second roll. "Lucia and Silas."

"Hell's children. Demons." Peppi replied automatically, then looked at Dylan's wide, glassy eyes and threw her hands over her mouth, still pinching the wet cotton ball.

"Oh, Miss, I'm sorry-"

Dylan held up a weak hand before letting it fall to her lap. "Don't. You're exactly right. I am a child of Hell," she spoke gravely. "Have they taken your soul, yet?"

Peppi finished taping down the gauze bandage and twirled

her finger for Dylan to shift and free her other arm.

"No, they don't touch the servants so as not to alert your government to our location."

"Yeah, I wouldn't want to be found by the Omnipotence either," she mumbled, wincing from the astringent burn of the alcohol seeping into her cuts. Tristian's words about the corruption of the government floated to her mind—then to him. He better be looking for her. She sent a silent prayer that Aria was safe from the vampires and that she'd be found before these two demons got whatever twisted thing they wanted from her. Dylan's eyes began to droop with the exhaustion that was tugging at her aching body. Peppi finished, curtsied, and left Dylan for the night.

Dylan collapsed on the bed. Staring at the door, she was unable to fall asleep despite her extreme fatigue. Thoughts encased her mind with sick scenarios of Lucia, Silas, or even her worm torturing her, pining her down in her sleep.

She jumped out of bed and quickly secured the door. Taking a tattered breath, she looked around for something to move in front of the door. She tried the armoire, but it wouldn't budge. Moving to a small nightstand, she frowned—it wouldn't budge either. She was curious and tried to pick up the lamp, looking closer to see it was obviously bolted down. Everything was fixed permanently like a hotel room. She shivered at the fake coziness of the room and cursed herself for watching so many horror films. Wrapping her sore arms around her waist, Dylan slid under the sheets, wafting a puff of vanilla to her nose. She would never like the scent again.

◇◇◇

The blinding sunlight overhead reflected off the broken pavement like thousands of glistening stones set to give him a headache. Tristian squeezed his eyes shut, willing away the light that burned into his retinas.

"Where *is* he," Aria whined. "We've been here for like thirty minutes."

She crossed her arms over her chest leaning against the hood of Tristian's car. She was wearing Dylan's Ray-Ban's and that slightly edged his mood even more. Asher smirked at her comment and continued playing with his phone as he sat straddling his parked Duc. Tristian was too tightly wound to sit like the others. He paced in front of his car intermittently checking his phone for Ulysses' call. They were stationed at a vacant parking lot behind a large abandoned warehouse on the outskirts of LA.

"Did we even come to the right place?" Aria continued to whine.

Tristian was becoming increasingly agitated with Aria, the growing scorching air, Ulysses' tardiness, and especially with Datu. He imagined ripping his extremities off one by one. Starting with his fingers and toes, snapping each one slowly as he begged to end his existence. Tristian would then heed him his request by tearing off his arrogant head in one swift yank. The thought of watching his clotted blood spill into a wide pool of death, his cries waning until silent, filled him with more joy than he cared to admit.

Tristian continued to fume, his jaw hurting from the constant pressure of his teeth. A dim rumbling of an engine broke his sadistic reverie. He and Asher looked up as Aria continued to lay on the hood unaware of the faint sound of the car approaching. Seconds later the rumbling grew loud enough to alert Aria. She quickly sat up as an old gunmetal gray '67 Mustang pulled into the parking lot.

"Finally," Tristian muttered, walking towards the mint condition muscle car.

Ulysses' orange head popped out of the driver's side boasting a large smile.

"Tristian!" he yelled, cutting the loud engine.

Tristian immediately noticed many changes in the new demon since the last time he saw him. He had pierced many holes in his hawk-like features, a few hoops in his eyebrows, a lip ring, and two large, black gauges; tattoos blanketed the exposed skin on his arms. Tristian wondered why anyone would willingly deface their immortal body as he had. Ulysses swaggered over, pulling up his way-too-baggy ripped jeans.

"Hey, man. Ready to bust this place?"

Tristian looked at the warehouse less than five hundred yards from where they had been waiting. It was a three-story, white building that used to be an old candle factory. Every window was boarded up and a faded logo of a drop of fire hovering over *'Unmatched Candles'* was plastered near the top.

"That," he nodded to the warehouse and raised an eyebrow, "is the LA Vampire Lair?" Ulysses sucked in his lip ring and nodded affirmatively.

Somehow Tristian had pictured it as a large edifice in the side of a mountain. Something more creepy and well, more vampire, than a boarded up warehouse.

"Yeah, what'd you think?" Ulysses asked genuinely curious.

Tristian only shook his head and headed over to Asher and Aria. Aria jumped off the hood as they approached and smoothed her shorts. Ulysses sauntered straight up to her and took her by the hand.

"You must be the infamous human." He kissed her hand and looked up. "I've heard so much about you."

Aria giggled and Tristian thought he was going to puke. "So, are you a demon too?" She flirted.

Is she serious? Tristian narrowed his eyes.

"Not exactly-" Ulysses started, but before Tristian could interject and get them back on course, Asher surprisingly stepped in.

"He's a new demon or a fallen seraph." Asher glared at Ulysses then motioned to Tristian. "Now before Tristian pops a vein, we need to discuss business-"

Aria held up a firm hand straight up in Asher's face ignoring him. "Fallen seraph? So, you were like... up there?" She motioned upward and Ulysses nodded. "What made you fall?"

"A girl, of course." Ulysses gave an impish half smile.

Tristian sighed loudly. "As entertaining as this whole episode of two demons fighting for the human girl is..." Tristian trailed off when all three snapped their heads in his direction, making him smirk. Asher cleared his throat and instinctively backed away from Aria.

"Ulysses, how do we get in there?" Tristian asked bluntly.

"Can you tell me first why we're busting into their lair? Or is it just for fun?"

"My contract..." Somehow that word didn't feel right anymore as Tristian described Dylan. "Has been kidnapped by Datu and his fledgling Erez."

"So... We find them, we'll find your girl too."

Tristian immediately narrowed his eyes and hissed, "How'd you know my contract's a woman?"

"You've got it written all over your face, bro." Ulysses patted Tristian on the shoulder, causing him to growl automatically. "She's definitely more than just a contract. I also took a guess because I didn't think you swung the other way." He chuckled and slapped his hands together, rubbing them mischievously.

Tristian didn't say anything, only nodded and pulled a knife out of his back pocket. It was his fathers and he called it *Argyre*. Tristian owned many knives but this one fit perfectly, it always had. The weight, the grip of the granite hilt, and not to mention, it was sharp as hell. It had a Tanto style point with a half-length blade swage, a thumb rise, and a fishtail bolster.

Aria's eyes widened in shock. "Were you holding that this whole time?" she asked, staring at the six-inch blade. "Where?"

Tristian smiled and flipped it waving the hilt in front of her face. "Take it, you'll need protection out here."

Aria grabbed the knife. "I'm going with you," she said, examining the sharp blade. "You can't stop me. It is *my* best friend that's in there."

Asher started laughing and shaking his head. Aria snapped her gaze in his direction.

"What's so funny, *demon*?" she hissed.

"What's funny?" Asher asked condescendingly. "What's funny is, *you* are the reason Temp- Dylan is in there having, who knows what done to her. *If* she's even in there." He started clapping slowly. "Way to go *best friend*." Aria's smirk fell from her face as she nodded solemnly.

Tristian cleared his throat. "Actually, Asher, you introduced the vile thing to her. Therefore technically, it's your fault," he sneered, still bitter.

Aria looked more relieved as Asher surprisingly looked sick.

"Uh, why a knife not a gun?" Aria said, darting her eyes between the three demons. "Do you have to stick it in their heart or something?" She made a quick stabbing motion in the air right in front of her and twisted the blade with a look of distaste.

"Guns will only slow down a vampire," Asher stated with less confidence, while simultaneously pushing the dagger down and away from Aria's invisible victim. "You need to cut off their heads to kill 'em."

"Then it's settled," Tristian said. "Aria, you stay out here with Asher, while Ulysses and I go in." Asher growled and Aria's face snapped up to Tristian's.

"What the hell?" Asher snarled.

"Well, she certainly can't stay out here by herself and we'll need you to bring the car up when we grab Erez. I'll also need the keys for the Duc."

"Why can't she stay out here by herself?" Asher retorted handing him the Ducati key.

"Yeah, why can't I stay by myself?" Aria agreed looking equally horrified. "I can drive and vampires can't go in the daylight... right?"

"Yeah, but we'll need back up if something happens to us." His smile didn't reach his eyes. "So you two, make nice and listen for us."

Tristian watched as Asher and Aria glared at each other then turned with Ulysses towards the LA Vampire Lair.

"Oh, Aria," he called over his shoulder and she looked up. "That blade is special, try not to lose it."

"I see what you did there," murmured Ulysses.

"And that is?" Tristian said tight-lipped.

"They're completely into each other. It was so easy to make him jealous."

He scowled forward. He didn't give two shits about Asher and Aria, and whether they liked each other. He cared about finding Dylan and he needed someone trustworthy on the outside, even if Asher did kiss her.

Tristian stared vacantly at the cracked, white paint on the metal, double doors that stood between him and the largest vampire lair in the country. He hoped with everything he had that Dylan was just beyond the metal in front of him. That this was just some sick, deranged game and she was hanging with them, playing cards, laughing that beautiful tinkling laugh. But he knew deep down that wasn't the case. This was beyond vampire fun and had to do with her identity as Temperance Elementa. She was the most powerful and desirable demon in all the worlds. It would be foolish to believe she wasn't taken into some world far away from here.

Releasing a thick breath, he hadn't realized he'd been holding, Tristian lightly tried the door handle finding it unlocked. *Hmm, they really should invest in better security.*

He looked at Ulysses and mouthed, "Ready?"

Ulysses pulled out three knives, handing a ten-inch blade to Tristian and nodded.

Tristian examined the long dagger and tightened his grip on the black, plastic hilt. This wasn't like him. He didn't go searching for trouble. He liked playing his dealt hand on the outskirts of unnecessary conflict. It wasn't that he was scared. He would only rather not suffer the repercussions of avoidable scrutiny.

Tristian's muscles tensed and he shoved his foot against the metal, kicking open the two doors. Direct sunlight poured into the space immediately burning to a crisp those vampires that were asleep. A humid breeze blew in kicking up the ash and swirling it in the air. Tristian and Ulysses strained their eyes, trying to focus through the dust and shadows. When the ash dissipated and their pupil's fixed to the change in light, they set their eyes on hundreds, no thousands, of red glowing eyes like feral cats caught in the dark, poised and ready to strike, just outside the reach of sunlight.

One of the vampires hissed and Tristian heard a distinct swoosh and watched as Ulysses threw one of his blades; curving it at an angle, swiftly cutting off the hissing vampire's head. Tristian, only slightly shocked, craned his head slowly towards him and raised an eyebrow.

"What?" Ulysses shrugged. "I didn't like the way he hissed at me."

Tristian pressed his lips together, trying not to smile and shook his head. "So much for attempting a polite approach."

"Like you didn't ruin that already, baking their friends?"

Tristian pulled his lips to the side and nodded at Ulysses' valid point, then addressed the crowd.

"I'm looking for Datu!"

No one came forward and Tristian spoke again.

"We can pick you off one by one if you so choose, and I," he chuckled picking his fingernail on the blade, "will look forward to taking each and every one of your delicious souls." He grinned wickedly.

"Datu isn't here," boomed a woman's voice. Ulysses raised his other knife and Tristian snatched his arm to halt his throw.

"How do I know you're telling me the truth?" Tristian inquired.

A pale woman with short white hair and cloudy blue eyes, dressed head to toe in black leather stepped forward. "I have no reason to lie. Most of these vampires have no meaning to me personally," she said with lack of emotion. "Datu doesn't stay here, but his many fledglings do."

"Then you won't mind if we look around, sweetheart?" Ulysses cooed, but Tristian knew better than to think he would just turn away if she said no.

"I believe it unwise, Collector." She smiled. "You do have certain abilities over us, but we have many over you, and I cannot guarantee your safety."

Tristian's heart hammered in his chest. The vampires should be afraid of him. They may have many powers exceeding a normal demon, but one of his unique abilities was superior to all vampires and many creatures of the underworlds.

Tristian mimicked her easy smile. "I think we'll take our chances."

Her smile fell, revealing the ice he knew lay underneath.

"As you wish."

He glanced at Ulysses, who was sweating and panting with bloody excitement lacing his eyes. Tightening his grip on the hilt, he eyed the vampires in his immediate vicinity. They all posed in defending stances. Tristian began to raise his arms and dropped the knife.

Ulysses snapped his head at Tristian. "What you doin', bro?" he whispered, keeping his eyes on the vampires.

Tristian ignored him, holding his arms up as he called out to the vampires, "I don't want trouble, only Datu, or Erez."

Whispers and hisses befell the crowd of dimming red eyes. Tristian slowly lowered his arms and began walking forward. Ulysses scooped up the dropped blade and followed in step with Tristian. The vampires hushed and all that sounded were the scuffs of his and Ulysses sneakers against the ashy concrete floor. He reached the crest of sunlight and watchfully stepped into the shadow. All the vampires glared at him as he strode up to the ice queen.

"Erez?" she inquired quickly flicking her gaze to her right and back. "What do you want with him?"

"He took something of mine. I demand him to come with us."

"I'm sorry, little Collector. Although I don't have an emotional connection with any of the children, I still can't let you take anyone away from my home."

"That's all I needed to know." Tristian needed to know that either Datu or Erez was there and she unknowingly revealed the fledgling's location with the swift flick of her eyes. Confusion contorted her features and he quickly grabbed her by her cold neck, lifting her above his head. She wiggled in his grasp, clawing at his flesh, drawing deep gashes that oozed his precious blood.

"Did I forget to mention," Tristian said maybe a bit too blithely, "that I have this little thing that lets me soak the powers of others?" He chuckled. "What's that children's rhyme?" He looked around at the wide-eyed vampires and pointed his finger. "Anyone?" He heard the ice queen squeak as a torrent of blood began to stream down his arm. "I'm rubber and you're glue. Whatever you throw at me, comes right back to *you*."

He tossed the vampire easily across the room, knocking down the pallid faces behind her like bowling pins. Ulysses tossed him a knife when he heard a rustling to his left. He shot his eyes there. A tall vampire with curling brown hair was struggling to elbow his way through the mob.

"Found you," he seethed to himself with a vicious smile.

A black and white blur shot up and hurled itself at him. He quickly evaded the queen and heard a sickening *slick* and *thud*. He darted his eyes to his fists slathered in black blood gripping an equally painted knife; then down to her severed head. He felt a delicious pride bloom in his chest.

Stupid bitch.

Tristian sprinted in the direction of the fleeing fledgling. Courageous vampires sporadically stepped forward as he easily overpowered each one using their very powers back on themselves. The harder they worked, the more powerful he became.

His vision tunneled as he fixed his eyes on the disgusting creature scrambling away from him. He made it to the side of the warehouse when another shadow shot up to his right, slamming a good hit to his eye. Bone crunched, knocking him over. Surprised, he grunted and slapped his hand up, applying pressure to the painful throb. Before he had time to react, the vampire connected another punch to his nose and a swift kick to his side. He hunched over, holding his now oozing face and cracked ribs.

A gleaming shape shined and he knew the vampire had found Ulysses' thrown knife. Clambering to stand, ready to fight whatever was coming for him next, the vampire's severed-head and blade fell before him. Tristian looked up as blood seeped in and around his eye, slipping into the creases of his mouth with a salty, metallic taste.

Ulysses smiled. "What?" he yelled as another vampire charged at him easily getting sliced in two. "I'm watching your back, man! Grab the bloodsucker before he gets away!"

Tristian nodded and dialed Asher.

"The trunk, left side door," he panted, shoving his cell back in his pocket.

As he pressed forward, many of the smarter vampires moved out of the way and some even nodded in Erez's direction. But a stubborn vampire with black dreads jumped in his way, hissing through his sharp fangs while swiping his pointed nails at him. Tristian evaded the first couple swipes when another vampire joined in just as the nails collided with his shoulder. Four gashes marked his arm. He dropped, rolling out of the way before bringing his blade across the Dread's ankles, severing his Achilles tendon.

The vampire's legs crumpled as he screeched in agony. Tristian jumped up, slicing off the vampire's head and twisted to throw his dagger at the intervening bloodsucker, nailing her straight in the chest. She threw her hands to the blade releasing an excruciating howl. Darting to her side, Tristian yanked out the knife and immediately hacked off her beautiful, blonde head.

Worried he had lost Erez, he scanned the back wall and spotted his form beginning to scale the wall like fucking Spiderman. Racing, Tristian made it across the warehouse in a matter of seconds and grabbed the vampire's calf. Erez kicked and snapped his head at Tristian, snarling through dropped fangs. With one hastened yank, Tristian used all that was left of his strength and Erez came tumbling down. A rumbling sounded and Erez naturally jerked his head in the direction of the noise.

The back of Ulysses' Mustang came crashing through the side of the building. Sunlight poured in, scorching Erez's hand to a crisp. Tristian chuckled at the whimpering vampire clutching his sizzling stump of an arm, then walked toward the Mustang and flipped open the trunk. He strode over to Erez and tugged the collar of his shirt, careful to drag him around the pool of sunlight. For now, he needed him alive; then maybe he'd let him burn.

Lifting him up and over the bumper, Erez shook the muscle car as his body collided with the green lining. Tristian shut the trunk and patted the top, cueing Asher and Aria to take off, leaving a cloud of ash dancing in the sun's rays.

He turned noticing Ulysses sprinting toward him, a look of panic evident on his face. Tristian raised an eyebrow, wondering what could frighten the cocky and bloodthirsty angel, when a snarl broke the howls and cries of battle. Tristian's eyes widened as he took in the pack of red-eyed dogs charging his friend. Tristian turned on his heel and dashed through the hole the Mustang had made. Ulysses just behind him. Thankfully their speed was no match to the demons, even if they were the fastest dogs in the worlds.

Tristian tossed his keys to his friend and jumped onto Asher's Ducati. Peeling out, Tristian burned rubber in a smoky circle just missing a remarkably muscular Rottweiler. He released a harsh breath as he exited the parking lot feeling one step closer to finding Dylan.

Zipping down the vacant wide streets, he noticed the painful pops and crackles that his bones made as they mended underneath his flesh; causing the distant, nauseating whirl of his waning strength to become more apparent.

The wind slapped his face and the blazing sun beat down on his head. He squinted down the winding streets already half way to his apartment. But the adrenaline had already begun to subside and he started to feel his weakened and shaky state. He knew he needed to grab Essence before interrogating Erez. He could feel his shirt sticking to his clammy skin and his vision double. The urge to vomit flirted his mind then overcame his senses. He slowed to a wobbly stop, laying down the cycle and tumbled off the bike into the grass. Tristian began heaving as he crouched and held his stomach.

Ulysses appeared at his side. "You okay, man?" he asked.

When Tristian didn't respond, he laid a hand on his shoulder. Tristian jerked and growled before collapsing on the grass.

No… not now.

His head pounded, body trembled, and his heart hammered. Yet, he could feel his body still working—healing his wounds. He needed Essence quick before he passed out for however long. Ulysses helped him up to a half stand. The world twisted and doubled as he stumbled to the back seat of his Audi.

Laying his head on the seat, he inhaled the sweet scent of the flowers and coconut. For a very brief second, he'd thought he'd found her; *in his back seat all along.* Willing his eyes open, he realized he was face first into Dylan's old jeans. His delirious mind was playing the cruelest of jokes. Pinning them to his chest, he felt the car take off as he shut his eyes willing the earth to still.

He felt defeated despite the feat of busting into the largest vampire lair and leaving with only considerably minor injuries. But the lack of energy wasn't even the reason for his disturbed thoughts. It was that Dylan had been taken by another demon. He wanted her to be in there; even if it meant Datu had taken advantage of her. Because that would have, unfortunately, been far better than the horror awaiting her by the demon Collectors who wanted her. She was so powerful, there wasn't a single family in all the worlds that would turn down the opportunity to rule her.

He felt his pulse and breathing slow. It was inevitable now. His body was falling; drifting into a comatose slumber. He didn't know how long it would last this time before he awoke; how much time he'd lose. He just hoped it wouldn't be too late.

CHAPTER 15

"I think we dream so we don't have to be apart for so

long. If we're in each other's dreams, we can be together

all the time."

A.A. Milne

SITTING on the grassy patch in Santa Monica, Dylan *watched the morning tide slide in and out; slowly pulling back with the moon. With her arms draped around her knees, she closed her eyes, basking in the soothing crash of the waves and feel of the cool, salty breeze kissing her cheeks; her golden locks tossing around her face. She smiled as she sensed someone's presence—but not just anyone: her forever someone.*

Opening her eyes, she locked her eyes with Tristian's seductive emerald gems. His sable locks tousled across his forehead in lazy ripples reflecting the morning sun like sun-kissed golden brown waves. He was wearing that soft, gray tee and dark jeans that he wore the last time they were together. Looking down, she realized she was wearing the same outfit as well without the button up.

Her heart sped up as he closed the distance between them. She missed him so damn much that she had to physically hold herself back from flying into his arms.

"Dylan," he breathed pulling her upright. "I've missed you."

She wrapped her arms around him tightly and whispered in his ear, "I, you." She pulled back leaving only a breath between them.

"How is it I fell so hard, so fast?" he asked searching her eyes.

A broad smile broke across her face. It never got old each time she heard him say it. He wasn't holding anything back, completely open, no sunglasses or silly pretensions to mask his true self. But it wasn't just him. Her heart was exposed and raw, bleeding out emotion unlike ever before. And it was beautiful. She didn't know how she'd become so lucky to have him.

"I don't know. I've never felt this way about anyone. You've got me enamored, Tristian."

"I do?" His fingers found her shoulder, running his thumb along the thick scars from the worm.

They were lying in the grass, feet interlocked, facing each other. She smiled, cupping his face. "Can't you tell?"

"When I'm away from you... I doubt myself."

"I do as well."

"Do you forgive me? I never meant for any of this to happen." He worked his fingers through hers and brought her wrist to his nose. "You became everything to me. Losing you was the mistake, not us," he breathed, inhaling her scent.

The sincerity of his words yanked at her heart and she felt like it was going to burst.

"Of course, I forgive you... but only if you forgive me."

"I'm going to find you, Dylan," he said moving a lock of hair blown by the wind. "Even if it kills me. I'll find you. Don't give up on me."

"I can't give up. I'm yours completely."

"Mine," he growled a smile.

"Yours."

He pulled her possessively to his mouth by the back of her neck possessively. His tongue pushed past her lips with hunger as she relished the Essence that was him. Everything about him *was as familiar as home.*

She breathed him in, rolling over, and pulling him on top of her. She loved the way his mouth fell on hers, how his hands moved down her body greedily, worshiping her curves. She held onto his neck, wallowing in the feel of her fingers gliding through his velvety locks. She was insatiable for his touch and realized it wasn't a secret at all that her innermost self needed to be a part of him for the rest of her existence. As if he had simply stolen a piece of her heart, and without him it refused to beat.

He trailed his tongue down her neck while nipping starved kisses. Shivers raked her body from the sheer force he evoked in her. She pressed her palms against his shoulder blades and inched them down to the bottom of his shirt. Thick muscle greeted her fingertips. She shifted her touch around his hips and through the valley of the V dipping into his jeans.

Tristian's body was perfect. She traced the unmistakable rise and dips of his abs. He yanked off his T-shirt, giving her an unobstructed view of a landscape sculpted with smooth skin and sinew, soft and hard.

Her heart raced as she swiftly tugged off her own shirt, tossing it on his. His immediate intake of breath and dimpled grin melted away any negative notions she had about her body.

Dylan felt an abrupt sense of urgency, a need to pick up where they had left off before; she knew they didn't have a lot of time. She just wanted to feel him, to taste him, to see the burn in his eyes as she pushed him over the edge, just as he had with her.

Her wandering fingers latched onto the waistband of his jeans. She tilted her head to the side to look for the button. But his hands jumped onto hers. He grabbed the hand that rested on his jeans and shook his head. Her stomach felt heavy with embarrassment, driving her confidence straight into the ground with a thud. But then he brought her fingers to his mouth, kissing them sweetly and securing them above her head.

"You're so incredible, Dee," he groaned, trailing a finger over the edges of her white cotton bra and down her stomach to her jeans. He flicked open the button causing her muscles to clench. "But this is my dream. And I have better plans for you."

She didn't know what to make of this, because it was her dream. But she wasn't going to argue with this Tristian.

Finding his luscious eyes, Dylan watched as he seemed to be analyzing the moment. Memorizing her reaction to each claiming caress. The way her breath raised and lowered her chest, the staccato of her whimpers. He suddenly pushed his fingers lower and she felt her eyes slip shut. There wasn't anything hesitant about him. He knew what he wanted and she was there to give it to him. She imagined his touch was like a glorious fire, searing his print into her heart and mind.

He dipped to her mouth in a painfully slow kiss, mimicking his movements below. She couldn't stand it. It was aggravating, frustrating, hot. Her hips pushed up to meet him and he, to her horror, retreated.

Her eyes flipped open and her mouth fell into a pleading O. He began to smile with his lips still touching hers.

"My dream," he reminded before claiming her mouth once more and pressing their interlocked hands above her head. She couldn't help the pout in her expression but his needful lips easily melted that away.

Leaving her mouth, he slowly worked his way further down her neck, through the valley of her breasts—when the familiar vanilla scented, cotton sheets began to form under her. She held onto him with more might, willing herself to stay in the dream, but it was inevitable now.

With desperation lacing her words, she implored, "Please find me, Tristian."

His head popped up from her stomach as anger and

devastation flashed across his face.

"Not yet!" He threw his fist into the sandy grass while griping her hand tighter. "Dammit, Dylan! Where are you!"

"I don't know. God, please just find me, Tristian." She grazed his cheek with their interlocked fingers as he, and everything around him, puffed into nothingness.

Blinking her dream away, Dylan woke to her living nightmare. Grimacing at her surroundings and the nauseating scent of vanilla, she closed her eyes forcing herself to fall back into the tangle of bodies by the beach. It was the same dream every night. That had to be a new world record for recurring, frustrating dreams. If Guinness could see into minds, she felt without a shadow of a doubt, she'd be featured on the cover.

Why was she still having this dream? Was it God's way of punishing her for being a demon? Or killing Dylan Prescott? If it was, He was doing a stupendous job. That combined with this hellhole had her more depressed with each passing day.

On top of that, each time she had the dream it felt so real. Her lips were always swollen and wet like she had actually been kissing. A few times she could've sworn she even smelled like him and the ocean, but that was just crazy. It was only a dream and a bit of an embarrassing one at that. There was no way Tristian was in love with her. So, maybe she had fallen for him, but that didn't matter if she never saw him again.

She wondered constantly if anyone cared she was gone. Of course, Isabel and Aria would. They would have called the police, filed a 'missing person's' and found her abandoned car, but that would be all they would do. They wouldn't know to look for a vampire or to search distant worlds because she had never told them about her true self.

Several weeks passed by and Dylan refused to leave her room except for the awkward mandatory dinners, hosted by the infamous Lucia Planto. Each night she was given a delicate dress, sent Peppi to do her hair and provided the worm freak outside her door to escort her to the dining room. She would never eat. She would quietly listen as Lucia, time and time again, tell her how she was free to roam as she pleased. She never spoke, except for the few times she started screaming and crying to go home. That only resulted in a worm carrying her, kicking like a mad woman, back to her bedroom followed by her door being locked for two days. She actually didn't mind being locked in. It meant no hideously fake dinners like they were some kind of twisted family. Dylan had no idea what their agenda was for her, but today she felt like trying to figure it out.

She let out a loud groan at her inability to fall back to sleep and finally wiped the tears off her cheeks. Throwing herself out of bed, she moseyed over to her armoire and pulled on a pair of jeans and a white T-shirt. Throwing her hair into a lopsided ponytail, she looked in the mirror and grimaced at the weight loss and dark circles that now seemed permanently formed under her eyes from restless nights and stressful days. But the flush from her dream brought a small smile to her lips.

She peered outside her door, catching the gaze of her worm slave. His white eyes, like two blank marbles, looked at her impassively until she spoke.

"Worm, take me to the front door."

The beast straightened and started to walk down the hall. Dylan quietly shut her door and scurried after it. It led her through a maze of corridors; the red carpet like a never-ending river of blood. She followed her worm to a vast, dark room illuminated with sizzling torches.

Taking a deep breath, she looked at the expansive foyer. The carpet bled from each hallway, meeting like an artery in the center; creating a long and wide pathway lined by soaring marble columns. The pillars paved the middle of the room ending at a massive, empty, metal throne squatting atop thick marble steps. It was organic. The metal twisted like creepy, black, iron fingers. It spoke of power, authority and, mostly, an all-encompassing evil. As if there were a twin, white and polished, lost on the other side of the world and dominated by goodness.

Looking to her left, she spotted the worm half way to the double wooden doors big enough for a giant. She raced after it darting her eyes all over making sure no one was around. The worm moved to the side of one of the doors, where a large metal lever was positioned. It pulled and the door creaked and groaned from its antique hinges. The noise made her jump and look behind, again, confirming they were in fact alone. Dylan felt a numbing cold wind. It cut through the room like a determined blade.

Sucking in a sharp breath, she looked forward at the hazy blizzard in front of her. A white sheet of ice veiled over a steep hill of black rocks laid out across the horizon. Her heart sank, like it did every day for the past week. Did she really think it would be any different today? That she would just walk out of here?

Feeling pain start to erupt on her exposed skin, she told her worm to close the door and leave her alone. Surprisingly, the thing obeyed and she found herself wandering through the boundless corridors alone. Part of her knew there was no escaping, and that small bit of hope she held on to for the past six weeks was crushed, burned, and stomped on. Tears pooled in the corners of her eyes, blurring her vision. Dylan roamed the halls for several minutes as if in a defeatist daze, before coming upon a large, bright room.

Rubbing her eyes, she peered into the space. It was what she could only describe as some kind of art room. Easels, paints, stacks of canvas, paper, and bushes filled the area. The room looked out onto the same expanse of snow through floor to ceiling windows, creating a dizzying effect. She walked towards the stunning view, feeling the urge to press her nose up to the glass, when she heard someone clear his throat. Dylan gasped and jumped around throwing her hand over her heart.

"My apologies," said Silas, a bit disheveled. "I didn't mean to startle you."

Dylan froze. She wasn't sure if she should run away or start throwing art supplies at him. What felt like an eternity passed when Silas finally raised an eyebrow. Shaking his head, he went back to his canvas.

Feeling slightly like the freak in the room, Dylan grasped at her last strings of confidence from deep inside and walked over to him. She wasn't sure what she was planning to do. As she approached, Silas never looked up. Rounding the easel, she clenched her fists and her muscles readied for fight. Then, she saw his painting.

She raked her eyes over the thick layers of blues falling down the canvas like a waterfall, with touches of oranges, reds, and golds. Her body relaxed as she watched Silas work the palette knife, slicing through the paint creating beautiful texture.

She was slightly surprised to see her keeper have such a humane side. Her limited knowledge of villains had her convinced that Silas and Lucia were evil demons that only plotted with their legions of terror and laughed maliciously together after their insanely boring meals. She pressed her lips together at the thought of Lucia holding her wine glass and roaring, "MUAHAHAHA."

Dylan glanced at Silas through the corner of her eye; his dark blonde hair had grown some and rained around his unusual eyes. He wore a thin, paint splattered, blue tee hugging his fit body and torn jeans. He looked nothing like the proper man she was forced to dine with each night.

"So," he mumbled, making Dylan start and quickly step back. "You like what you see?" Silas said exasperatedly, never looking away from his creation.

She swallowed against the burn in her throat. "Um, no." He scowled as he tightly clenched the muscles in his jaw. "I mean, you're, uh... fine, just your painting is so beautiful, I guess, I was just... surprised?" She rounded her eyes and mouthed 'wow' at the lame jumbled explanation. "Er... I'll leave you to it," she blurted immediately turning away and silently cursing herself for behaving so strangely. Dylan hastily walked out of the room, only glancing back once to see him staring at her intently.

The next day, Dylan rose early. The sun hadn't welcomed the harsh weather outside her tiny skylight yet. Holding onto the mental image of Tristian for just a beat, she finally jumped out of bed. Wiggling into some black yoga pants and a purple tank, she left her chambers telling her worm to stay put. Except this time she didn't go to the front door. She wandered the hallways quietly passing the slew of empty bedrooms, the dark music and art rooms, and miscellaneous spaces.

The thought of the night before echoed in her mind. She was surprisingly embarrassed at her actions earlier in the day. She found herself fidgeting more than usual throughout the awkward meal. Silas had ignored her, as always, but last night she actually felt somewhat disappointed.

What's wrong with you! That's your attacker you're crushing over! Seriously, Dylan, snap out of it!

She'd tossed and turned all night. Unable to rest, she knew she needed a release. She had been in that room way too long and obviously was losing it. Yes, sunrise yoga was just what she needed.

At the end of the hall was a set of stone steps. Without a thought she climbed each one. Nearing the top, she slowed her stride realizing she was meeting total darkness. Stepping gingerly on the top step, she pushed open the heavy door as the space was automatically lit with more candelabras.

The area was what only could be described as a fitness floor. To her left flanked numerous machines and weights;

followed by basketball, racquetball and indoor tennis courts. There was even a ping-pong table! In front of her was an area of padding for wrestling or gymnastics; then an elevated decked area tucked in the corner surrounded by floor to ceiling glass, overlooking the snowcapped mountains and slightly highlighted morning sky. This was the first time her eyes were able to see beyond the blizzard revealing the desolate earth. It was breathtaking, but gone before she could study it further.

Sighing, she padded to the perfect spot for her yoga, passing a wall stuffed to the brim with an assortment of gym equipment. She spotted a lime green yoga mat and snatched it before taking to the wooden steps.

Closing her eyes and inhaling the sweet scent of morning, Dylan moved into her normal routine. She felt a bit rusty, but quickly dusted the cobwebs. Several minutes passed and tiny beads of sweat collected along her hairline, intermittently sliding down her nose. Feeling the sweet burn of her muscles, she moved into a more difficult pose. Kicking up to a handstand on her forearms, she balanced her feet atop her head in the Scorpion pose.

Continue to breathe in and out... she thought, slightly trembling from her tensed and sore muscles. A strange peace enveloped her and for the first time in six weeks she felt herself on the verge of a smile.

"That's nuts," husked a man's voice, making Dylan start and lose her balance. Trying to regain her composure, she failed as she let out something like a yelp and fell backwards. Squeezing her eyes shut, she braced against the inevitable, except the hard floor never met her body. Keeping the large breath of panic still fixed in her chest, she reluctantly peeked open one eye. She opened the other only to find herself face to face with the blonde demigod holding her inches away from the firm ground. Her stomach dropped as his hot breath grazed her lips. He fixated on her lips, holding her just a beat too long before clearing his throat and sitting her upright.

Giving her an awkward pat on the shoulder, Silas asked, "Are you all right?"

Dylan blinked a few times, still not quite able to release her held breath. "Yeah." She frowned avoiding eye contact. "Still not used to the speed thing," she grunted, "but thanks for catching me." *I think.*

"I didn't mean to startle you. That looked difficult."

She swallowed and met his fierce penetrating gaze. "It's all right, uh," she fumbled, squirming under his piercing stare. "What are you doing here so early?"

"I like to come swim and watch the sunrise," he said, sitting back and dragging his fingers through his perfectly messy hair. She found herself strangely drawn to this demon; but why? Suddenly, like switching on a light, she realized he was the epitome of the perfect guy she would have dreamed up before Tristian. No, not what she would have dreamed up, but had dreamed of. She had even seen those eyes before. How was that even possible? She must have been staring or making him uncomfortable with her silence because he quickly changed the subject.

"Do you usually do crazy spider poses this early in the morning?" His words broke her reverie. "Although, I have a hard time believing I could miss that if you did-"

"Crazy spider poses?" she interjected, feeling slightly lost on the subject.

"That's what it looked like to me." *Oh, the yoga.* "You'll have to show me how to do that sometime." His easy smile brought a flush of red across her face.

Quickly looking away, Dylan tried to divert his attention. "So, where's the pool at?" she said looking anywhere and everywhere else.

Butterflies licked the insides of her belly as she took uneven breaths. Silas made her uneasy in so many ways and her new revelation didn't make it easier. He jabbed his thumb behind himself at the large Olympic sized pool never averting his eyes from hers. Dylan must have been in shock with her surroundings not to notice the massive natatorium.

"Have you ever seen the sunrise in Zadar?"

She looked back at him and blinked, her confusion surely written on her face. When Dylan didn't answer, Silas placed his fingers gently on her chin, shifting her gaze to the brilliant rays crawling over the snow packed peaks cutting through the frosty haze. The sky began to clear again as it celebrated the arrival of its source of life. Various shades of violet and crimson splashed across the horizon, drawing a gasp out of her breathless lungs. She was vaguely aware that Silas hadn't moved his hand from her chin.

"I like to lose myself in here," Silas started to speak hauntingly, as if his mind had drifted far away from the horrors of the palace. She listened, unable to tear her eyes away from the incredible view. "Pretending to be someone else, to be somewhere else."

She frowned at his statement as he finally dropped his hand. It was like he had plucked the precise words drifting aimlessly throughout her mind. Silence spanned for several moments as the sky began to settle back into its fitful flurry.

She sighed and turned to him. "Well," *as weird as this was,* "I'm going to finish my routine." She hinted for him to leave her alone. But he seemed completely lost in thought still gazing at the thick blizzard. Dylan cocked her head to the side and, before she was able to process her actions, brushed her fingertips against his shoulder.

"Silas?" she spoke just above a whisper. He quickly grabbed her hand, holding it in place. Dylan screwed up her face.

EH! Get away! Your attacker! Voiced the logical girl over

and over again inside her mind.

Adrenaline flooded her veins and she thought she might vomit from panic. Keeping the nervous bile down, she opened her mouth to say something, anything, to appease the situation when Silas finally looked over at her tensed hand on his shoulder then up at her shaken expression.

He simply said, "Sorry," and let go.

Still with that lost look on his face, he stood and sauntered over to the pool and stripped down from his white t-shirt and gym shorts to a black Speedo and dove in. Dylan let out the air of fear that was jammed tight into her lungs and watched him for a moment. The ripples of liquid slid over his perfect body, catching light like thousands of tiny crystals as he moved into the butterfly stroke. Looking closer, she noticed white scars laced all over his back.

What's your story, Silas? Why are you keeping me here?

Dylan turned while shaking her head. Thinking anything other than fear around her kidnapper was utterly futile. Dream man or not, he didn't deserve her pity or sympathy. He was holding her against her will for goodness sake. Letting out a long exhale, she moved back into her routine.

Unable to maintain good focus, Dylan fell out of the Dragonfly Pose, nearly smashing her face into the lime green mat. Releasing a loud groan, she rolled over to stare at the vaulted ceiling supported by long, distressed, wooden beams. She could still hear Silas splashing about in the distance.

Dylan closed her eyes, trying to meditate. She tried to imagine his splashes as the crash of waves against the soft sand of the California beach, feeling the warm sun lightly toast her skin and the rush of the briny air. Home. Dylan felt a strong pull of nostalgia for the familiar, to see her friends and family, to smell the ocean, and to feel the warmth of her bed. If only she could talk to her family to tell them where to look or for simple words of encouragement. Retreating further into her mind, she let herself imagine the words of encouragement. What would Aria tell her to do? Most likely, her obsession with spy movies would surface.

"Snoop on the kidnappers. Act like Nyah Nordoff-Hall from Mission Impossible. Don't be a wuss!" Dylan smiled. It was possible her friend would have made the statement a bit more colorful. Isabel would say otherwise. She would tell her to buy time and look for an escape—to just get out alive, that'd be her main goal. Dylan couldn't imagine Isabel dealing with her disappearance well. They were all they had left, just each other.

Tristian. She gave a mental sigh. He'd tell her to concentrate on her powers and definitely kill the hot kidnapper first. That is, if he even cared. Part of her mind still held out for a miracle that he would come busting in like her own personal knight in shining armor, taking her far away, rescuing her from this deranged castle. Tristian held a special place in her heart that she had never given to anyone, and the time away from him seemed to only intensify her feelings. She just couldn't get him out of her head. It was as if her being was made for him. His sinful taste and the deep timbre of his voice made her body respond in ways it never had before.

If she got out of here, no, when she got out of here she promised herself to tell him how she felt, even if he didn't reciprocate the feelings. *"I feel it too..."*

But as time moved on, it had been almost two months and no one had come to save her. She knew it was possible he didn't feel the same way, even if he did say it wasn't a mistake. Besides the heated kisses, the constant careful touching, and that text message, she had inferred most of his feelings.

The words he shot at her that horrendous night still stung deep inside—like trying to swallow shards of glass—every time she thought about it, it only cut her deeper. Maybe it was time to let go, because what if she never even saw him again? Or her grandma, or Aria, and never even got to meet her parents? A tear escaped her closed eyes. She had only felt this feeling once before and the atrocious memory still haunted her.

She saw the light shift in front of her closed lids and a chilling male voice fill her ears.

"Enough with the pity party."

She frowned and opened her eyes to glare at a soaked Silas. Droplets of water still cascaded down the ripples of his toned chest.

Damn he's hot. Why does he have to be so hot?

"I'm not having a pity party, per se," she grunted.

"Well, it looks to me," he smirked, "like your sitting in the corner crying."

"Exactly, definitely not a party," she snapped and closed her eyes to resume her desolate thoughts.

"Oh no." He reached down and picked her up with ease.

Dylan's eyes flew open. "W-what the hell!" she screamed, stunned by his audacity. "Put me down!" She flung her arms against his slick, wet muscles, but he didn't appear to be bothered by her strikes. Ignoring her pleas, he continued to walk away from the decked space.

"Where are you taking me?" Dylan yelped about to start really crying.

She felt his body shake with silent laughter before he flung her into the deep end of the pool. Thrashing her arms and legs about under the heated water, Dylan gasped as she raised her trembling head above the surface. Sucking in air and wiping the water from her eyes, she looked up seeing Silas with a huge smile on his face.

"Seriously!" she yelled. "What if I couldn't swim?" She tried to sound angry, but failed terribly unable to hide the smile lurking at the side of her mouth.

For a brief moment, his radiating grin made her feel weirdly normal. As if Silas was just a cute boy trying to make a sad girl laugh.

"You need to stop thinking so much. You know that's the first time I've seen you smile."

She frowned petulantly and tried to cross her arms while treading water. It was harder than she thought it'd be.

"I'm not smiling," she panted, returning from her alternate universe because unfortunately that world was fake, and Silas, the demon kidnapper, was real.

"Whatever," he chuckled as Dylan started to swim towards the edge to get out. "Oh, we're not done swimming yet," he warned as he dove into the pool.

Dylan's eyes rounded and she started swimming as fast as she could to get away from the perfect, but demented, man.

Slapping her hand on the stone edge surrounding the pool, she felt Silas' thick arms wrap around her waist pulling her back.

"Stop," she grunted while attempting to pry his hands off of her. She began to tremble as her heart hammered wildly in her chest, and tears threatened to surface again.

Oh, God! What does he want? Is this where he's finally going to kill me?

Unable to fight any longer, her body went limp as he dragged her to the center of the Olympic sized pool. Maybe she should just let him. What was there really left for her if she never escaped?

"Just get it over with," she whimpered with a shaky defeated voice. Silas immediately stopped and let go of her waist, turning to look in her eyes.

"Temperance, I…" he trailed off looking genuinely hurt but then hardened his face. "Get what over with?"

Her breath came out in quick puffs as she started treading water. He was able to stand, but she was still too short.

"You're going to kill me…" She raised an eyebrow. "Right?"

He drifted away from her.

"No." Silas looked like she had just punched him in the gut. "That's what you think?"

"Uh, yeah?" she said feeling the weight of her accusation. "What am I doing here, Silas, if you're not going to kill me?"

"My mother wants you to be a part of our family," he blurted out while a fat drop of water rolled down his face from his wet hair.

"To be what…" A smile flirted her lips. "Your sister?"

His face went a bit pale. "N-no, Hell no. Sister, not… No."

She started to titter at his incoherent set of words.

"Glad something makes you laugh." He shook his head. "What I mean is…" He frowned. "Don't you know how demon families work?"

She shook her head, remembering Tristian explain something about families, but couldn't recall what he had said through all the rushed information clouded by a sense of paranoia.

"Well, few of us are actually related, but 'families' are groups of demons that live and work for each other or a common purpose."

"Okay…" she said slowly, feeling a pinch in her side. "What if I said no and wanted to go home and forget about this whole demon, life, thing, and live like a human?"

"My mother won't have it," he said matter-of-factly. "But I can tell you this." He reached out noticing her labored swimming. "She's trying really hard to make this place a home for you." He smiled sympathetically.

She grabbed his arm, resting her weight on him as he curled her into him. Her heart started to pick up again, but she was too tired to care about the close proximity to her captor. The severe yoga session, stress, and sudden swimming had all taken their toll on her energy.

So… it was either this or drown, she convinced herself.

She couldn't stop her hands from sliding over the thick scars on his ripped upper back—feeling each sinew toned and defined but not overdone.

He continued in a lower tone as he gripped her waist. "Why not just enjoy it and let go of what's not meant to be?"

Narrowing her stare, Dylan wanted to scream in his face, how dare he try and dictate her life! That none of this was really meant to be but completely forced. Except as those severe blood-orange eyes examined her, she decided against it, too afraid of what he might do with her vulnerable body in his arms.

"What's your family's common purpose?" she asked.

Silas looked slightly surprised by her question.

He clenched his jaw as if he were assessing whether or not she was worthy enough to know.

Noting his hesitation, she continued, "I'm apparently here for good." She laughed sadly. "I mean, it's not like I have a choice, right? So, you might as well tell me what your plan is."

"Soon," he breathed. "We just need to know we can trust you first."

She felt like a popped balloon. "All right," she worried her bottom, chapped lip—a habit that unintentionally brought his gaze there. She suddenly felt way too close.

Sucking in a sharp breath, she wished her side cramp would dissipate so she could jump out of his arms, but knew if he let go she'd sink from exhaustion. Everything about this screamed danger!

But what if you liked it? You like his touch… what about a kiss? A strange voice called from the deep recesses of her mind. He leaned in making her body tense and her eyes widen.

Silas got within a breath of her lips before backing away.

"I should probably get you some water," he husked, still looking at her mouth then meeting her skeptical gaze. "You know, for your cramp." She nodded slowly, letting out a rush of air as he helped her to the edge of the pool.

Flopping onto the slick stone like a fish out of water, Dylan finally sat up and glanced down at her shirt. She gasped silently and threw her arms across her chest. She thought she might as well be naked; her soaked shirt was doing nothing to conceal her body.

Seeing her actions Silas chuckled to himself as he effortlessly climbed up next to her. His virtually naked body caused a blush across her face and she immediately looked away to the water.

A hand moved into her line of sight and she took it, still averting her eyes. Silas helped her stand and tossed her a towel before walking away.

"Hey," Dylan said, wrapping the thick towel around her shoulders. Silas looked at her already half dressed in his gym shorts and clutching his shirt. "I-I'll see you at dinner," she fumbled. "I'm going to go lay down."

"At least come drink some water-" he started, but Dylan quickly rejected his invitation.

"I will. I'll have Peppi bring it." He seemed a little disappointed before shrugging his shoulders and disappearing down the stairs.

What the hell was that? she thought, gripping the towel tighter and heading back to her room.

CHAPTER 16

"Before you embark on a journey of revenge,

dig two graves."
Confucius

A distinct whoop, whoop, whoop seemed to run laps around Tristian's head connecting to the intense throbs of a headache. He crinkled his forehead and slapped his tingling fatigued hand to his right temple. He shifted his body into the fetal position, grumbling at the pain and stiffness. Tristian squinted open his eyes as blurred shapes moved in a synchronized circular movement. His eyes began to focus and he realized the shapes were the blades of his bedroom fan.

Licking his dry lips and looking around the sparse space, it suddenly came to him: vampires, blood, stumbling, Dylan.

The tumbling events from his memory brought him up to a rigid sitting position despite his underworked body. The intense rush of blood from his head brought fuzzy, black spots clouding his vision; urging him to take it easy. Gingerly sliding from the comfort of his bed, he stretched as the wave of vertigo subsided and headed to the bathroom. He felt the distinct grittiness of dirty teeth and layer of grease on both his body and his hair. He had been out for too long, that was for sure.

That was one of the cons of being a healer. The majority of demons were able to stop after feeling the slice of fatigue from the overuse of their powers, but healers were cursed. Their bodies didn't know when to stop. Even if the demon stopped his actions with enough time to collect or go to the Tower of Souls for Essence, a healer's body would inadvertently heal the remaining wounds, continuing to work and exhausting itself to the point of blackout.

Squinting, Tristian glanced in the bathroom mirror; doing a double take, he cocked his head. Someone had changed his clothes and cleaned the blood off his body. It must have been Aria. He couldn't imagine Asher or Ulysses doing anything remotely like that; nor would he want them to. He shook his head and jumped in the shower.

Letting the water rain down on his throbbing head, he thought about the recurrent dream of Dylan. It always ended right before it got good. He spoke to her in a way he wished he had when she was here. It was quite strange though, he never dreamt during a blackout before, but then again, maybe he was just remembering for the first time.

"Please, just find me, Tristian" were the last words she had spoken. He would, even if it killed him. He would black out for a thousand years if, in the end, it meant he'd have her in his arms. But for the time being, he was happy to at least have her when he closed his eyes—even if it was the same torturous dream set on rerun.

Twenty minutes later, he was clean and dressed in his favorite jeans and black tee. He headed to the kitchen, hoping unspoiled food sat in the fridge. He opened the refrigerator and scanned its contents: a clear bag encased green live fuzz, no doubt what used to be tortillas; a head of lettuce which had turned a full shade of dark, slimy, green ooze inside its shrink-wrap, and some white mystery food in a glass Tupperware. *Yuck.*

His stomach grumbled begging for anything. Mortal nourishment wasn't necessary for a demon's vitality. As long as a demon consumed Essence, it would be everything they needed—calories, energy, and fulfillment. But once one started eating, a demon's body grew accustomed to the feeling and would plead for it just as their bodies pleaded for Essence. At least food was a slight substitute for everyday nourishment.

On the verge of abandoning the task to check out the barren pantry, he finally set his eyes on a foil bowl with a white paper lid. He immediately snatched it. With his head still in the fridge, he peered into what looked like someone's leftovers. He sniffed it and shrugged, it seemed fairly new. He tossed the take-out box onto the island countertop and pulled a fork from the drawer below. Just as he was about to stuff the cold pasta into his starving stomach, he looked up and realized he had completely missed the two sleeping figures spooning on his couch.

Shoveling the food into his mouth, he raised an eyebrow and laughed silently to himself. Aria was laying mouth agape with her fiery hair and arm sprawled over Asher's gleeful face. Apparently, they had made nice.

Seeing them together unfortunately brought Dylan to his mind's eye. He thought about the night they spent sleeping together at the old motel. Her delicious, buttery hair smelled of flowers but with a tinge of salt and blood as she cuddled into his chest. He listened to her soft rhythmic breathing for hours before falling asleep himself.

Damn, he needed to find her, to save her, because he needed to be with her again. It had only been a few days and his heart was withering inside—begging for hers to beat in sync. For her intoxicating warmth, for the soft cadence of her voice. Heaving a deep breath, he spotted his cell on the countertop plugged into the black docking station.

Dropping his fork, he snatched it up and swiped open the screen. His eyes grew wide as he dropped the phone straight into the pasta. He brought both of his hands up to his face rubbing large circles and shaking his head through a long groaning sigh.

Six weeks.

He had been out for *six* weeks, forty-two damn days to be exact. He hoped she hadn't given up on him, succumbing to her new life, wherever she was, *if she still existed*- his brain snapped, halting his thoughts. He couldn't go there. She had to be okay. He'd already promised himself he'd search until death. Without her, life wasn't much worth living. He didn't want to think about the demon he would be forced to become if he had lost her. As much as he wanted to finish his makeshift breakfast, he had lost his appetite. The bitter taste of dread was too much. Nothing would be satisfying until he knew she was okay.

Tossing the half eaten pasta into the trash and wiping off his phone, he marched over to his friends. He flicked Asher in the nose, making the demon jerk upright and send Aria straight to the floor. Tristian stifled a chuckle, pursing his lips together. Asher blinked as Aria groaned on the hardwood.

"The fuck?" Asher grunted rubbing his eyes before pushing his fingers through his curly mane.

"I should be asking you that!" snapped his fierce counterpart, righting herself and rubbing her eyes as well.

"Yeah, throwing your girlfriend to the floor isn't cool. Definitely not while sleeping," Tristian stated dryly.

"I'm going to ignore that. So, sleeping beauty," Asher yawned as he sat up and yanked Aria back to the couch as she tried to walk away. He wrapped his arms around her and nuzzled his nose on her shoulder. "Who kissed you awake?"

Aria was holding back a content smile when she slapped him in the stomach and jumped off the couch.

"Asher filled us in on the coma thing while you were out."

"Yeah," he said slowly, while kneading the back of his neck. "Well. Every superhero has his Kryptonite, right?"

She smiled sadly at Tristian then pulled him into a

startlingly intense hug and brushed a peck on his cheek. "Well, I'm glad you're awake." He smiled awkwardly knowing he wasn't good with emotions of any kind. "And he's not my boyfriend," she said, thrusting her thumb over her shoulder at Asher then lumbering into the guest bathroom.

Asher grinned. "She's not exactly a morning person."

"I heard that!" she yelled as the door slammed shut.

Tristian pushed his hands into his pockets and shook his head. "So, please tell me you made progress while I was out, and weren't just cuddling and taking advantage of the amenities?"

"We did both." He stretched like a cat. "We took care of the Erez situation. All he was really able to give us was a name of Datu's muse. I don't think he really knew anything other than what Datu wanted him to know for this specific situation. Then we fried him."

They both seemed to leer at that.

"Wait… That's all you got?" He narrowed his eyes. "A *name*?"

"Relax," Asher said, suddenly serious. "We tracked down the name and she's Nadia Burke, the leader of the wolf pack here in the city."

"So, what did she have to say?"

"We don't know-"

"What are you waiting for?" Tristian hissed.

"You."

Tristian's head was spinning. Six weeks had flown by and that was all they were able to accomplish?

"What do you need *me* for?" Tristian all but yelled, not understanding why they couldn't just obtain all the information to her location while he was incapacitated.

"Well, for one, this is your woman we are searching for. Two, Nadia will only see you, for whatever reason. Three, we have no other leads."

"That doesn't make any sense. She doesn't know me. Why would she only see me?"

Asher shrugged. Tristian felt his headache grow in intensity, he needed coffee, Essence, and to find this Nadia Burke soon.

Ulysses stepped out of the guest bedroom that had been renovated into a library and froze. Tristian nodded his head at him and Ulysses nodded back with a blank expression, then pivoted back into the library. He wasn't sure what that was about, but the truth was, he didn't really care.

A shrill ringing jostled Tristian out of his thoughts as Aria popped her head out of the bathroom.

Holding the phone, Asher looked around Tristian and called to her, "She's calling again."

"Ugh," Aria grunted. "I can't take another crying phone call. Don't answer. I'll call her back later, I guess." She shook her head, retreating back into the bathroom and softly closed the door.

"Who?" Tristian inquired.

Asher pressed his lips to the side, silencing the incessant shrieking. "Dylan's grandmother. She's not taking the disappearance very well. But because the police found her abandoned car full of clothes, they figured she just skipped town." He shrugged. "She's going crazy with flyers... Aria gets insanely stressed talking to her—lying to her. I don't blame her for dodging the call. I don't think I could watch her break down again either."

Tristian had forgotten Dylan had a human family and friends. He couldn't imagine what they were going through. At least when a demon went missing or died, there was this known element that passed a small bit of peace into your heart that you had, in a way, prepared for it. The human world was encased in this bubble of protection and ignorance, making the unknown of loss distressing.

As Tristian stood there waiting for his friends, he felt each valuable, passing second like a grain of sand in a bottomless hourglass. They were losing precious time and he couldn't contain the pain in his chest from rising to an all-new excruciating hell with each lost moment.

The four of them finally piled into Tristian's Audi. Pushing over an empty bag of potato chips and a couple of random wrappers, he found himself in a constant frown.

"Hope you don't mind I've been using your car," Asher said from the back seat. "I mean, you did kind of wreck my bike."

Grunting "sure" under his breath, Tristian depressed the button for the car's engine, bringing it back to sweet life. For a brief moment, the sound instantly soothed him.

"So, what do we know about Nadia?"

He was surprised to hear Aria to be the one to answer.

"She's a werewolf and the leader of the wolf pack. She's Datu's girlfriend and every time we tried talking to her pack, which was several times by the way, about meeting with her, she requested *the woman's Collector with the green-eyes,*" Aria said, air quoting the last statement in a dramatic voice. "Otherwise, we have nothing. She's extremely private and wouldn't even let us in the door without you."

"Asher and I have called everyone we could think of and even raided your contacts," Ulysses added staring straight forward at the road ahead. "But we got nothin'. This Nadia Burke seems to be our best bet."

Navigating his way through the downtown streets, Tristian squinted suddenly realizing he'd forgotten his sunglasses. He shot his eyes around the trash filled car, intermittently glancing at the road. Suppressed anxiety seemed to bubble up to the surface of his skin, causing his muscles to bunch and sweat collect along his upper lip.

"Are my sunglasses back there?" Tristian fumbled feeling naked and vulnerable without them.

Aria looked around then finally squealed, "Oh! Lucky ducky!" He flinched at her boisterous voice. "Must've fallen off you that day Ulysses brought you back." She beamed, rubbing the dust and grime off the lenses with the end of the shorts connected to her light blue romper. Inspecting them to make sure they were clean, she then set them on his shoulder, letting them drop to his lap.

He sighed a small piece of stress away. "Thanks."

It was probably silly to invest so much faith in a piece of plastic to conceal his inner demons. But without his sunglasses, he felt like all the worlds could observe everything eating at him. That his eyes were the windows to his deepest, darkest secrets, and so far the only person that made him feel at ease without them was Dylan. He didn't mind her catching a glimpse of all the dark as long as he could be a part of her light.

"Hey, man, you need to collect?" Asher asked.

"Yeah, you look like a ghost," Aria added.

"Yes, but after we see this chick."

"Stop up there," Ulysses cut in after being unusually quiet. Tristian slowed to a stop in front of a ratty diner in the shape of a large aluminum trailer.

"Hungry, Angel?" Tristian asked, knowing the name boiled Ulysses' blood. "Because I'm sure there's something better around here. Personally this place looks like it serves feet." Ulysses only pursed his lips and shook his head.

"This is kind of like their front," Asher said. "Behind the restaurant is an old public storage, where they live and what not."

"What not?" Tristian smiled, but everyone kept their poker face. "Why is everyone acting so weird?" He focused on each individual with his eyebrows raised. "This happens all the time.

It's nothing to freak out about."

"I thought you were dead, man," Ulysses spoke maintaining his cold stare forward. "It's just weird. I'll get over it." He cleared his throat and pulled on the handle immediately jumping out of the car, followed by the others.

They left Tristian alone with his thoughts for a moment. He had never thought of the blackouts affecting anyone but himself. Then again, he had never had any friends hang around after one of his episodes. Not that he had ever had any actual "friends" to begin with, only acquaintances or fellow members in his family. He didn't even really consider Sansvi as a friend. She was... something else.

He slid out of the leather seat and into the cloudy, damp heat swallowing up his body. He skulked over to his friends, feeling sweat moisten his neck. He shoved his hands into his pockets and bunched his shoulders, apologizing a bit awkwardly. He had been ordering them around since the moment he awoke and had forgotten to thank them for taking care of him. Tristian had awakened in many odd circumstances after his innumerable black outs, and this had been, fortunately, the most pleasant despite the extensiveness.

"All right, hug it out you three," Aria said, twirling her finger and throwing her other hand on her hip to move things along. "And hurry so we can figure out what this dog knows." Asher shook his head, chuckling, and led the way into the vintage diner.

A large, pink neon sign's letter C flickered on and off of the illuminated *'Cindy's Diner'*. The place looked run down and Tristian wondered about the restaurant's sanitation. Through the beaten screen door was a line of empty booths fixed to the exterior side of the trailer. The entire place seemed to be dipped in Pepto Bismol. Sickeningly pale-pink leather and pink paint covered eighty percent of the decor. A matching white Formica bar with aluminum and pink leather swivel stools took up the opposite side.

An older waitress with wavy, short, white hair and dark roots smiled, motioning for them to sit wherever they wanted, as if she were so busy she couldn't walk the five measly steps to the group. The four of them sat at a booth; Asher moved next to Aria and Tristian next to Ulysses. The woman sauntered over in a stained blue uniform with white cuffs. She smiled, revealing bright red lipstick smeared on her upper teeth. Tristian couldn't help but cringe. Aria kicked him under the table and Tristian jerked his plastic menu up hiding his face.

"I'm Beth. What'll ya have, sweet'ems?" The waitress smiled, smacking her gum while pulling a worn pencil and pad out of her black apron. Now Tristian understood the front. Who in their right mind would come here to eat?

"We'll all have some coffee," Aria said, beaming her innocent act.

He peeked at her over the menu in question. *We will?*

"Only coffee?" Beth asked, eyeing the boys with a raised eyebrow.

"Only coffee," Ulysses cut in. "Thanks, Beth."

"Sure, sweets." She smiled, smacking her gum again and sashayed back to the bar to prepare the coffee grounds.

"So, what now?" Tristian whispered to the group while standing his menu up for a false sense of privacy.

"We wait," Ulysses said.

"Wait for what?"

"For me," said a deep male voice on the other side of a plastic partition. Tristian slapped down the menu and stared at the tall, lanky man in ratty jeans and a red tee. The obvious werewolf glared at Tristian through large brown eyes. Tristian returned the stare, not relenting, to show he was serious.

"Come with me, Mr. Effingo," the wolf stated. He had obviously excluded his friends. Tristian found himself glancing at Asher, who nodded with a stern look in his eye and silently confirmed they had his back.

"Sure," Tristian said spiritless. "After you."

He followed the wolf, realizing the creature wasn't as tall as he had originally thought, maybe an inch, or two, below him. The wolf led him through the empty kitchen where large commercial ovens and cookware screamed to be cleaned and used. Passing the murky water of the dish filled sink, Tristian was led to what anyone would believe to be the locked back office. It was, in fact, the entryway to the public storage.

They walked into a small concrete room lit by a single exposed light bulb. The door clicked shut and the wolf quickly spun, pinning a surprised Tristian to the wall by a forearm against his throat.

Tristian grunted and held up his hands. "I'm not here for trouble. Only to meet with your leader," he said through a strangled voice. Tristian didn't feel like getting into any fights, and this wolf probably just needed to make his authority over the situation known.

The wolf growled, "Give me all your weapons, *Collector*."

Tristian deftly moved his hands along his waist retrieving his two daggers.

"There," he stated as his blades fell to the floor with a distinct *ping*. The wolf eyed the weapons and released the demon. He picked up Tristian's knives and motioned for him to move through to the opposite door. Tristian massaged his neck and shook his head disapprovingly at the wolf. "I expect those back when I leave... They have sentimental value."

The werewolf responded with a grunt as he yanked the door open. Tristian found himself in a room full of, what looked to the regular eye, to be a bunch of teens just hanging out. The place was musky with a fine layer of dust blanketing, well, everything. Random naked bulbs lit the space, casting unfriendly shadows across their faces. Some were playing video games while others were lounging or laughing loudly in groups on ratty lawn chairs or beat-up couches. The creature behind him cleared his throat and all the wolves stopped what they were doing and stared at Tristian. He knew he really didn't need the knives, but he now felt quite naked and weak in a room full of antagonistic werewolves. A sharp point pressed against the small of his back urging him forward.

He really shouldn't push me...

Tristian sighed over his shoulder, "Look, you can act like you're going to stab me with those daggers all you want," he smirked. "But that still won't change the fact that I have no idea where I'm supposed to go."

He heard the wolf grunt again accompanied by a couple snickers from their audience. The wolf stepped in front of Tristian then, suddenly, turned whipping his *Argyre* blade in Tristian's face, causing his eye to twitch.

"Don't think about trying anything," the wolf warned.

Tristian smiled derisively. "Wouldn't dream of it."

"Good," the wolf spat and turned around, leading the way to Nadia Burke.

Passing the speculating eyes of the wolf pack, Tristian recognized a few from classes at UCLA and other various places around town. He nodded at them and continued forward. They walked down a dark, wide hallway, where the storage units were converted into bedrooms. Bed sheets closed off some of the occupied units, while the strobe of the silenced televisions danced the shadows of its inhabitants. It seemed eerily quiet as they made their way towards the back of the building.

This doesn't feel right... Tristian began in his mind as the wolf halted in front of him. He knocked three times slowly and the metal door creaked open. Tristian was led into an aphotic-like room that only made him feel even more uncomfortable. Stepping through the threshold, the distinct scent of wet dog invaded his nostrils causing him to grimace. As he adjusted to the dark, he set his eyes on dozens of dark haired humans, werewolves, scattered around like lumps of shadows.

The room reminded him of an actual den, where wolves slept around the elevated grounds of their leader. But instead of a large, ferocious wolf on top of the slate stage, Tristian gazed at the beauty lounging gracefully atop a cracked, black leather couch with her legs tucked neatly at an angle beside her. As the door shut, a faint light switched on illuminating the concrete facility in a soft neon green glow. She had large brown eyes, and sharp angles to her face. Long, silky, russet hair cascaded down her voluptuous, bronze, naked body.

The sight of the stunning bare woman surprisingly woke nothing within his body. But he knew why, because he only wanted to be with Dylan, and that was becoming blazingly apparent with each passing second. She was made for him and he for her; she was the breath in his lungs and the Essence for his being. After all, that was the reason why he was here, for Dylan Prescott. He swallowed his bleeding heart and let his five hundred-megawatt smile flicker on.

"Nadia, how lovely to finally meet you," he beamed, hoping the woman could be charmed.

Nadia had two werewolves in wolf form sitting alert in front of her. They snarled as Tristian and his unfortunate companion approached stepping over random nude women sprawled out on the ground. Several hands reached for him, caressing his calves or anything they could get their paws on. Nadia held up a firm hand and placed it on one of the wolves' head, raking her fingers through its dark mane and over its ears. The wolves immediately silenced.

Nadia cocked her head to the side, letting her shiny hair shift from her breast over her brown shoulder. Tristian instinctively guarded his eyes by looking to the side of the concrete cell. He cringed, immediately regretting it, knowing there was no way she missed that. Quickly looking back, he found her with narrowed eyes in bemusement.

"You do not like what you see, Collector?" *That couldn't be why she only wanted to see me, would it?* She continued before he was able to open his mouth. "Finding a love that strong is a curious thing. Is it not?"

"Excuse me?" He wasn't sure what she was getting at.

"The can't eat, can't sleep without her love. It happens once in a lifetime. You are a lucky demon to have found it."

Love? Did he love her? Dylan was a remarkable creature and he knew he cared for her deeply. *'How is it I fell so hard so fast…'* No that couldn't be. He didn't believe in that. Not since his mother told him love was a lie, something for the young and weak.

Ignoring the useless banter. "I need to find your lover, Datu."

"Datu," she quickly retorted in a snarl. "Is *not* my lover-" both wolves seemed to be standing more alert as Nadia's nails bit into the sofa.

Damn, Tristian gave a mental sigh, *fucking Erez.* He drew his arm up, rubbing the back of his neck and scratched the fresh shave down his jaw, worried he had been set on an organized goose chase.

"-But," she continued in a low, almost hurt voice, "we used to be until recently. I know where you can find him."

Tristian's head shot up. "Where?"

"Our villa in Lamu, Kenya,"

"I need an address-" Tristian started, but was swiftly cut off by a vicious snarl. Nadia held up another firm hand and pet the malicious beast.

"I cannot give it to you, but I will have my first in command, Mr. Cottom, lead you." As soon as the words escaped her plump lips, the snarling wolf shifted into a stark naked hulk of a man. He stood erect ready for direction from his commander. Tristian screwed up his face. He didn't understand what was up with all the nudity. Couldn't they figure out how to wear stretchy pants that fit on their wolf and human forms? The remaining wolf leapt onto the couch and Nadia pet it as it lay across her lap.

"Collector?" she asked, grinning impishly with a quick glance at the wolves clutching his legs. "Feel free to make yourself at home. Your particular seed would make for an interesting breed."

A deadly breed, he thought, peering down at the two dark beauties hugging his legs and caressing his stomach and rear. Only a short time ago, he knew he would have accepted the offer without a moment's hesitation; but all he could do now was compare the creatures to Dylan. He immediately shook his head at the women and pried their happy hands off of him. The women whined and swiftly slunk back to the floor.

"As you wish, but please, make him weep from pain for me," she added casually, pouting and making kissy faces at the wolf in her lap.

"Yes, ma'am. I plan to do many unpleasant things to him. You have my word." He started to turn and stopped. "Nadia."

"Yes, Collector?"

"Why wouldn't you see my friends? If you knew we were looking for Datu."

"Well," she spoke pushing the wolf aside harshly. "I wanted him to feel a great deal of pain, and since I do not do these things, I knew I needed to send you. Because vengeance is sweeter when it comes from the lover scorned."

Tristian only nodded, knowing in a way she was right before he spun on his heels as the once naked werewolf, now clothed, simultaneously opened the door and led the way back to the pale-pink diner.

The den seemed more alive as they made their way through

the public storage. TV's chattered, wolves laughed, and dishes clanked. The wolf leading the way was tall with buzzed blonde hair and built like he spent his days at the gym.

Tristian picked up his step. "Hey, man. What's your name?" he inquired not feeling ecstatic about calling him *Mr. Cottom*. The wolf kept his frown, not bothering to glance at Tristian.

"Garret Cottom."

CHAPTER 17

"Perhaps everything that frightens us is, in its deepest essence, something helpless that wants our love."
Rainer Maria Rilke

THE day had moved excruciatingly slowly. Dylan was embarrassed to admit she was slightly excited to see Silas at the mandatory dinner that evening. Her logical self was screaming at the new feelings she had apparently developed. She knew everything about this was off; she was kidnapped and developing an affection towards one of her keepers. She had seen documentaries about victims becoming brainwashed and living 'happily' with their abductors.

Stockholm Syndrome, she remembered. She was starting to see why, besides the isolation, it wasn't so bad- *Whoa. Snap out of it, Dylan!*

Shaking her head, she pushed the idiotic thoughts aside. A knock sounded at the door alerting Dylan of Peppi's arrival and the thirty-minute window before dinner. The little girl held a violet, chiffon dress and her bucket of supplies. Once, she had asked Peppi why she didn't just leave the supplies so as not to lug them back and forth each day. She explained that 'the Mistress told her to'. Dylan had the sneaking suspicion it was to keep her from trying to take her life or the life of those around her. Not that those were the only instruments that could do harm. She could always drown in the pool or bathtub, or hang herself.

Break the mirror and slide the glass slowly up your forearm...

She couldn't deny it hadn't come to mind a few times recently, but she was very much against suicide no matter the situation since unsuccessfully trying it six years ago. Yet, the thought was always there, lurking like an ugly scar, whispering in her ear about how easy it'd be to end it all here and now. Before falling into this hellhole, she'd thought she had put it all behind herself with years of counseling, group therapy, and Prozac. She subconsciously ran her fingertips across the surface of her pajama bottoms, tracing the thick scar on the middle of her upper thigh.

"What'll it be today, Miss?" asked Peppi, through the vanity mirror as she tossed Dylan's hair interrupting her bleak thoughts. Dylan chuckled at the little girl's whimsy.

"Just straight today," sighed Dylan. Peppi frowned, then nodded, obviously hoping for something a bit more extravagant.

"I can do my own hair, you know," she spoke to Peppi knowing exactly what she'd say.

"And like every day, Miss, it's my pleasure. The highlight of my day, mind you."

Dylan laughed and shook her head. "Just reminding you."

"Did you do anything today, Miss?"

A coy smile touched Dylan's lips. "I found the gym this morning, practiced some yoga, went swimming-"

"Yoga?" Peppi asked, looking confused.

"Oh, you've never heard of it before?" The girl shook the two pig tails on either side of her wavy brown head. "Yoga is a way to control and combine all levels of the mind. It strengthens your muscles and relaxes through a series of poses. It's very calming."

"Sounds beautiful." Peppi smiled. "I'm glad you decided to

make use of the facilities today. Mister Silas swims, too, every morning… did you see him?"

The near kiss surfaced in her mind's eye prompting her face to heat up. Dylan cleared her throat.

"Yes. Yes, I did."

The girl frowned picking up on Dylan's mood and averted the conversation to a lighter subject.

On her way out, Peppi turned. "Do you want me to bring your meal after dinner like always?"

Dylan thought a moment. "No," she said slowly. "I think… I'll eat at the table today."

Peppi nodded with an unreadable expression, then curtsied before slipping out of the room.

Dylan decided in that moment she needed to convince her keepers she was trustworthy. She *had* to find their weakness or buy time until they took her somewhere she could easily escape. The only thing she had at the moment was to play along, act like she was settling in and *enjoying* herself.

She curled her lip.

She could never enjoy herself here. However, they would believe it because they wanted her. Wanted her for something much bigger. Something she planned to find out.

Studying herself in the mirror, Dylan felt pretty in the fitted, sleeveless, plum dress. It hugged her body in all the right places. It was shorter than usual, but still concealed her scar and was really cute with its sweetheart neckline and ruching.

Glancing at the silver clock on her wall she had recently requested, Dylan chewed her bottom lip and looked around for a way to utilize the last ten minutes.

She stepped into the bathroom where the large, black leather box of makeup lay. Flicking open the small silver hook, she peered inside cautiously. The case was full of delicate shadows, mascaras, pencils, brushes, and lipsticks. Anything and everything she could possibly need. If she had owned this a few months ago, Aria would have guarded it with her life.

She felt slightly torn between her stubborn side that wanted to cross her arms and pout in the corner until someone saved her, and the girl in the mirror who was just plain tired. Tired of fighting and losing. Tired of waiting for someone who was never coming. She pushed her stubborn self away for the night and picked up the liner, getting to work.

By the time the loud alarm sounded throughout the castle Dylan had made herself stunning.

Eat your heart out, Plantos.

The worm slave waited in her bedroom as she slipped on her Louboutin suede pumps. Heels had unfortunately become a staple in her new closet. The damn things took so long to get used to. Six weeks and she was finally walking semi-gracefully instead of hobbling with rubber ankles. Other than the dinners, Dylan kept it barefoot.

Part of her wished Tristian could see her right now.

Tristian.

She expelled a wistful sigh. Looking in the mirror one last time, she plucked his silver chain from her chest, twirling it around her finger. This wasn't her. She felt like a complete fraud.

Eyeing her Elementa ring on her right hand finger, she clenched her fist.

Now or never.

Stepping away from her depressing thoughts, she departed to the twisted dinner.

Walking through the double doors, Silas looked up at Dylan. Actually doing a double take, his eyebrows arched and his mouth fell slightly agape, simultaneously. Lucia cleared her throat and Silas scrambled to stand as he always did when she arrived or departed the table. But this time he didn't ignore her—his eyes were glued to her every move. Dylan suppressed the urge to giggle and acknowledged him with a slightly intense, small smile and Lucia with a sincere bow of her head.

The woman seemed enthusiastic at Dylan's appearance and poise, while Silas just continued to stare, making her heart fling itself wildly about in her chest.

Focus. Focus on the plan, she thought, willing her pulse to slow.

"Temperance, you look more comfortable this evening," Lucia crooned, swirling the red liquid in her crystal stem before taking a sip. "Finding this place isn't as bad as you thought?"

Dylan mimicked her sinister smile. "I guess you could say I've decided to make the most of it. *Why fight what's meant to be*?" she asked, glancing at Silas while taking a slow sip and savoring the peppery bouquet of the Cabernet Sauvignon.

"Good to hear," Lucia said flatly, then looked to Silas. "How was your day, dear?"

"Pleasant," Silas said still staring skeptically at Dylan. "The sunrise was… enlightening."

Dylan glanced in his direction daring eye contact. Seeing his hungry eyes made flutters ignite in her belly.

Bad move.

She swiftly looked back at her wine as a blunt heat clutched her face.

"How?" Lucia asked.

The question seemed to snap Silas' attention away from Dylan.

"Huh?"

Dylan had to admit seeing him squirm made her smile deep inside. *Got you.*

"The sunrise." She darted her eyes between Silas and Dylan. "How was it enlightening?"

"Oh, just a good time to think is all," Silas murmured

vaguely.

Lucia narrowed her eyes then sighed a smile like she suspected more but really didn't care.

Dylan looked down and bit her lip. She wondered why he wasn't telling his mother about their swim. She would think Lucia would be ecstatic.

Zoning in and out, Dylan sat quietly twirling the silver chain around her neck as Lucia and Silas discussed the ever-constant dreary weather, a missing servant—who apparently turned up at the end of the day, dead of old age, and Lucia's boring day.

Blah, blah, blah, blahh...

"Temperance Elementa."

Huh? Dylan snapped her eyes to Lucia. "Sorry?"

"I asked, have you a chance to check out the rest of the east wing yet?" Lucia spoke with an irritable edge. Dylan suspected the demon didn't take kindly to being ignored.

"The east wing?" She raised an eyebrow.

"Yes, this is the east wing of the manor. It holds many of the guest and entertainment facilities."

Dylan's eye's widened with amazement. "This side is only a quarter of the whole house?" She sat up straighter and looked around as if she could see the whole castle from her spot.

"Yes," Lucia reiterated.

Silas cut in, "I can show you around tomorrow, if you'd like."

Before she could answer the kitchen doors flapped open wafting the savory aroma of Fillet Mignon. Her stomach grumbled, twisting itself in favor of the anticipated meal. Dylan was delighted she had decided to eat this time, because sitting through two long hours starving was pure agony.

A woman set down Silas' plate, then Dylan's, then Lucia's. The fact that the head of the house got her plate last made Dylan wonder, but then again this was a completely different culture and race than she was used to.

Looking down at the variety of forks, spoons, and knives, Dylan chose the larger fork in the middle. She could feel Lucia's piercing eyes studying her. Like she couldn't believe she was going to eat or maybe she was using the wrong utensil. Not that she cared. Dylan brought the bite up to her lips and gave Lucia a challenging smile, then shoved the delicate meat into her mouth. A flicker of a smile touched Lucia's lips so quickly Dylan wasn't sure if she saw the approval.

"Temperance, you never answered my question. Have you been able to enjoy the facilities?" Lucia said between sips of wine.

"Yes," Dylan swallowed. "I've seen the music and art rooms." She brought the wine glass up to her mouth and mumbled quickly, "And utilized the gym this morning."

A look of recognition flashed Lucia's face as she flicked her eyes to Silas.

"You must see the library; it's quite magnificent. Silas, take her there tomorrow."

"Yes, mother."

The rest of dinner ran without incident. As the dessert was being set, Lucia excused herself from the table feigning exhaustion. Dylan didn't care what the demon was up to. Once she left, Dylan felt weight release off her chest and the air clear. Lucia down right gave her the heebie jeebies.

Unable to shovel any more food down her throat, Dylan sighed and leaned back with her wine glass.

"So… You ate this time," Silas pointed out, studying her lazily slouched to the side—his pointer and middle finger tapping his chin thoughtfully.

He looked straight out of a GQ magazine in his standard black suit that she guessed was a Hugo Boss designer. After the seventh Dior dress, she stopped wondering where they obtained the contents of their closets.

Dragging her alcohol-induced lazy eyes back to his, she noticed his frightening eyes smoldering with intent. She nodded with a suppressed smile hovering her lips, fighting the urge to say "Duh."

"So… You spoke to me this time," she returned, matching his tone. "Lots of things are apparently different tonight."

He sat back and waved the hovering servants away.

"Well, I couldn't help it. Not when you look like you do tonight."

She bit her lip to stifle a ridiculous smile.

Crap, she immediately frowned at her innate reaction to him. *Say something. Regain control!*

"Er… tell me about your family's common purpose."

Shit. Way to be covert, Dylan.

A flicker of something flashed in his eyes before he looked away working his jaw.

"Temperance, I'll tell you soon, I promise. Just enjoy your time here for now. The specifics aren't important, yet."

She narrowed her eyes, mentally willing him to look back up. "How are they not important?" Dylan protested. "If you want me to be a part of this *family*," she threw some air quotations around family, "then why aren't you trying to persuade me? Or clue me in?"

In a blink, Silas tipped back her chair holding his face a whisper away from hers. Dylan, wide-eyed, sucked in a startled breath.

"How would you like me to persuade you, Miss Elementa?" he hissed in a husky voice as his eyes scaled her body.

Dylan's heart picked up to a dangerous pace as she felt the impulsive need to shield her body as if she were suddenly exposed.

"By telling me why you want me," she swallowed, "in this family."

Silas turned his head away then gingerly returned her chair upright.

"Come with me." He stood and held out a hand. The look on his face was that of a challenge, like he was daring her to trust him; with what she had no idea. However, no matter how much he unnerved her, Dylan needed to figure out what they wanted with her.

Besides this is why she dressed up and ate at the table… right?

Returning his fierce look, Dylan stood swatting away his hand. *Challenge accepted, Planto.*

"Where to?" she asked.

He started to walk a bit in front of her with his hands in his pockets. "The Library."

Dylan stopped. "Silas, I don't feel like a tour right now, just talk to me."

He turned around walking backwards. "Suit yourself," he shrugged before pivoting forward again.

She weighed her options for a moment, bouncing on the balls of her feet then, "Wait! Fine. Tour it is." She scurried after him.

Catching up, she matched the speed of his gait and walked next to him. "So, where's it located?"

"In the east tower," he said without looking at her or offering more explanation. If it wasn't for his easygoing stature, she might think he was irritated.

"Yes, because that tells me a lot," Dylan mumbled more to herself.

Silas stopped and stepped disarmingly towards her making Dylan halt and fall back flush against the wall. She tried to exude confidence, but her knees quaked with dread. Her trepidation wasn't from terror but from his reign over her body.

He narrowed his eyes. "You've got quite the clever mouth tonight," he whispered tracing a finger along her jaw and running it across her quivering bottom lip. "Or are you always this devious and I've just never noticed."

If it were possible to move further back into the wall, she did, as he stared at her lips. Needing to mollify the situation, she only shrugged playfully.

"I guess you just bring it out in me."

He stepped back and smirked, "Apparently."

She snatched hold of his sleeve stopping him just as he started to walk again. He parted his mouth and frowned as she braced herself against him, taking off the blister causing heels.

"Sorry, these things are just killing my feet," she said all breathy, aiming to show he didn't get to her.

She sighed, brushing her chest against him as she continued in the direction he was headed. She heard him clear his throat, then move quickly, appearing back at her side.

Silas:1: Dylan:5

They arrived at a large, arched, wooden opening. Her fingers traced the rich walnut, which featured intricate carvings depicting fairytales. Dark fairytales.

Where her hand rested, Dylan noticed a boiling pot with two small children screaming in a witch's stew; a gorgeous woman in fitted robes held a stick, churning the liquid with a ravenous smirk. However, the haunting designs were immediately pushed to the back of her mind when she saw what was just beyond the threshold.

Dylan let out a gasp.

Magnificent wasn't enough to describe the incredible scene before her. The tower was that—a four or five story expansive circular room. A narrow staircase ran along the edges, where thousands of books were housed against the cool stone. Narrow balconies ran each story with various ladders on rolling casters. The distinct smell of leather and almond hung in the air, no doubt dating the numerous novels.

Craning her neck back, she stared at the top of the tower, which ran to a point with dozens of glazed skylights used to illuminate the space during the day. Now blazing torches lit the area. Tables and chairs were neatly oriented around an extravagant fireplace, which was alive with hot licking flames.

Still with her mouth agape, Dylan moved toward the warmth, unable to decide where to start. She wanted to examine all the books, touch the delicate yellowing paper and antique hand-bound leather, and maybe even glide on a rolling caster. Running her fingers along the edges on the engraved spines, she found herself in complete awe.

"A room without books is-" Silas started.

"Like a body without a soul…"

Dylan abruptly turned around and sucked in her surprise. She hadn't felt Silas that close behind her.

"You know Cicero?" he spoke softly moving a lock of hair behind her ear—a move she had only been comfortable with Tristian.

Standing her ground quite awkwardly, Dylan took a deep breath through her nose and murmured, "I, uh, studied him in a Philosophy class."

A class I would be finishing now if it wasn't for you, she hissed in her mind.

"Philosophy class, huh…"

Inwardly shaking her head at the perplexing demon, she averted her eyes to the wall of books next to her and ran a finger along the spine of a book written in Latin.

"It's too bad, the quote doesn't even apply to us."

"Why do you say that?" he asked, drawing her gaze back to him leaning casually against the shelves with his arms crossed.

She thought that was quite obvious. "Because, well… we're soulless."

He examined her for a moment. "I disagree. Out of the two of us, you're the one that's soulless."

She curled her lip at this. What the hell was that supposed to mean? Just as she was going to cue that very question he pushed off from the shelves and casually grabbed her hand, interlocking their fingers and pulling her towards the roaring flames.

"Silas…"

"This is my second favorite place in the east wing," he said apparently changing the subject.

"What's the first?" she sighed, tripping over herself to keep up with him.

He sat on the lush rug in front of the elaborate hearth and yanked her down to sit next to him.

"The pool."

"When did you start swimming?"

"When I was four. I never listened to anyone and absolutely not when my parents told me to stay away from the gym unsupervised." A strange expression made its way across his face; it was mixed with pain and satisfied defiance. "One day, I wandered up there and found the pool. I didn't plan to go to it, but I felt a strange pull. Standing at the edge, I slipped and fell into the deep end. No one was around. I really thought I was going to die."

He looked her in the eye. "But I didn't. In a moment of clarity, I began to swim and realized that pull I felt was due to the fact that I can manipulate water. I rose to the top of the pool and never wanted to leave." He smiled distantly. "My parents actually had to pry me away later that evening. Soon after though, they had to find more unusual forms of punishment for my many outbursts." His eyes returned from their clouded memory. "Now I satisfy that pull by swimming every morning."

316

'Unusual forms of punishment', this made her smile disappear as she remembered the many scars lacing his body. *Oh Silas, what did they do to you?*

"Temperance, don't pity me. I deserved everything I got."

She nodded knowing full well no child deserved to be hit, no matter how rotten the actions.

"So, you can manipulate water?" she asked as a look of relief washed over him. "I'm supposed to be able to do that too, but I didn't feel a pull to the water this morning or… ever."

"Have you had a chance to use your powers, yet?" Silas asked, loosening his tie and removing his jacket. His light blue dress shirt stretched against the perfect but scarred muscles she knew lie underneath.

"Yes, but I have no idea how to control them." She studied the reflection of the crackling flames in his eyes. They resembled the cinder burning on a lit cigarette. "They only seem to emerge when I'm flipping out."

"That's probably all the time, right?" he joked twisting the cut pile of the carpet. Her mouth pinched as she tried to look pissed.

"No!" she narrowed her eyes in mock irritation. "It's only happened, like, maybe three times that I remember."

"Dang, I'm kidding!" He held up his palms. "I'm sure your crazy spider poses keep you from lashing out on the worlds."

"Yeah, I guess," she said shaking her head and falling back on the rug. She traced her eyes along the iron details of the soaring ceiling, her golden hair fanned out around her. "I still managed to kill the real Dylan Prescott and my, I mean, *her* parents."

Silas looked down at her. The flickers and flashes from the fireplace contorted his features and for a very brief moment he resembled Tristian. She blinked rapidly dousing the painful hallucination.

"The Omnipotence killed Dylan. Her parents, well, a truck killed them." Hearing about her parents' deaths, no matter how long it had been, still stung, bringing a faint wetness to her eyes. "So, you didn't kill them, Temperance. Unless…" he said as she met his sweltering eyes. "You're a cement-truck shifting, evil, demon king," he said as seriously as he could. "Because that could be quite the turn off." Dylan burst out into a loud laugh that she couldn't seem to stop. "Oh hell, I broke her. You're not going to start flinging the fire on me… are you?"

Dylan laughed even harder at that. After a moment, still chuckling, she wiped at the tears that escaped her eyes. "Sorry. For the past six weeks, I feel like I've been on an emotional roller coaster and the first joke I hear nearly makes me fall over, well you know, if I was standing." She began to laugh again at her own pun. "Oh, now *that* was from the alcohol," she giggled with a lazy hand over her mouth.

"Apologies are for the weak. I like hearing you laugh."

He twirled some of her hair on the rug.

"So, you don't like the Omnipotence either?"

"No," he snapped with a sour look.

"Hmm…" She frowned. "It doesn't sound like anyone likes them. How are they still in power? Or does it just come with the territory of being a king?"

"I'm sure part of it is, no demon really likes to answer to anyone. Especially those who rank at or below your strength."

"I guess that makes sense." Dylan's eyes began to droop and suddenly the floor felt very comfortable.

Damn that delicious wine.

"How did you know about my parents?"

"The Elementas?" he said with an eyebrow quirked.

"No, the Prescotts."

"I did my research," he muttered as she nodded, letting her eyes fall shut.

Silas was surprisingly easy to talk to. Almost as if they shared the same humor or thoughts. She felt comfortable in his reach—which slightly bugged her, because less than twenty-four hours ago his presence evoked creepy crawlers under her skin.

"Temperance."

"Hmm?" she hummed through a smile with her eyes closed.

He didn't immediately respond, and when Dylan was about to open her eyes she felt his full lips graze hers. Her shoulders tensed in panic, but the slow tracing of his tongue melted away her alarm.

He continued to lick the seam of her lips with his warm tongue, just waiting to be let in. Before she knew it, her muscles released as her body responded to his touch.

Oh.

She mindlessly opened her mouth and returned the soft kiss, bringing a hand against the grain of his heavenly stubble. He tasted of chocolate and wine as their tongues danced. She found it hard to think of anything other than him and their bodies colliding. If she tried to concentrate on anything beyond, it was like her mind would snap—halting her from turning away and yanking her back to his mouth on hers.

He brushed the tips of his fingers lightly along the side of her face and down the sweep of her neck, over the peaks of her breasts before reaching the end of her stomach, gripping her hard. She shivered as his hand traveled back up to her neck.

He captured her nape, keeping her steady as his tongue twisted with hers. She moaned, low in her throat, setting off a bomb of greedy passion.

Thrusting her fingers into his hair, she tangled them in the soft satin and yanked him harder against her.

She sensed elation within his kiss as he gripped her forearms tightly, pulling her up into a kneeling position.

Trailing his nails down her spine, he reached the zipper on her dress. He began to pull it down, dragging a nail through the opening.

Dylan's mind raced at what was about to happen. It felt so right. Why hadn't she wanted this before?

He shoved her dress down.

She gasped as his hands found her bare hips, yanking her against him sharply. Butterflies thrashed around in her stomach as he moved his mouth down her neck; she arched against him beckoning him further.

"Temperance," he groaned as he began to nip kisses across her collarbone sending earth-shattering waves of his *Unda*.

She felt completely at his mercy as his hands moved even further down finding the hem of her dress.

"Yes," she breathed letting her head fall back as her mind fogged with lust. She wanted him so badly that her body actually ached with need.

"I'm so happy you're here."

Her eyes flew open and enlightenment of where she was and who she was with cleared her desire filled mind.

He continued kissing along her chest oblivious to her cooled libido. His other hand inched up her thigh, surpassing her scar and traced his fingers along the hem of her underwear. She jumped at the intimate contact and grabbed his shoulders, immediately pushing him back as confusion befell his face.

"Temperance?"

Still panting heavily, Dylan's mind worked overtime to come up with a reason for the abrupt stop. She didn't want to undo the trust she'd earned but couldn't do this, not with him.

"I'm a virgin," she blurted out throwing her hands up to her face then peeking through her fingers as if she were ashamed.

He sat back and started to chuckle. "That's it? A virgin? I thought twenty-one year-old virgins were a myth."

"It's not funny," she winced sheepishly. "I'm, uh, waiting 'til marriage." She lied dropping her hands to her lap, trying to be playful and mask her agitation.

"You don't kiss like a virgin."

His eyes slipped down her body greedily and Dylan's followed. Her dress was still pushed down around her waist with absolutely nothing concealing her.

As she quickly crossed her arms over her chest, he raised his eyebrows. "What? Suddenly shy, Tempy?"

"*Tempy*?" She fumbled pulling up her dress.

"No good?"

"It makes me sound like a thermometer." She crinkled her nose, glancing up at him briefly while searching blindly for the top clasp.

Silas inched forward and reached around to pull up her zipper.

Her face flushed; she hated the way her body reacted to him. No matter his stunning, delectable looks and charming persona he was still on Team Bad.

He halted, inches from her face, his intense eyes burning into her, paralyzing her. She breathed tremulously as his fingers trailed up from her back and over her bare shoulder, brushing over her scar inflicted by the worm. He continued down her arm to her palm and lifted her right hand.

A shiver struck and goose bumps pricked her skin as he examined her family's ring. A callous had formed from the constant wear of the damaged ring.

"We'll need to get you a new ring," Silas said, twisting the current one and causing her to wince.

A pain shot through her chest. Lately, she had kept forgetting her situation was of the permanent kind.

She let out a drained breath. "Silas-" she started to say she didn't want a new ring, she wanted her parents, she wanted her friends, she *wanted* to go home.

He placed her hand back in her lap. "Yeah?"

But she decided that wasn't the course to follow. She needed him to trust her, to tell her his plans, to let down his guard long enough for her to escape.

She needed him to love her.

"I wish we'd met a different way," she said instead.

◇◇◇

"Garret?" Aria shot upright from the small diner booth, knocking Asher's shoulder and sending his coffee into his lap.

Asher yelped at the scalding liquid blistering his skin. "What the hell?" Asher glared at her, but she didn't waver from staring at Garret.

"Y-you're a werewolf?" she hissed her eyes wide, darting around. "Did Dylan know?"

"Shit," Garret mumbled.

Tristian jumped in as he placed the pieces together, "Garret…" He cocked his head to the side. "The yoga instructor?" Tristian immediately had images of him giving Dylan intimate sweaty lessons. His fists involuntarily balled as his jaw clenched and unclenched.

Garret turned with a narrow stare at Tristian. "Dylan didn't know." He looked back at Aria. "I tried to keep her from the demons, to keep her *safe.*"

Tristian was furious that this *dog* thought he could do a better job than him.

"What do you think we were doing!" Tristian growled in his face, fighting the unmistakable urge to tear his head off.

"Well, it looks as if she isn't safe, is she?" Garret baited. Tristian's vision blurred with rage as Garret continued with a mocking smile, "At least, when she was with me, I never let her out of my arms."

That was it. He couldn't hold back any longer. Tristian lunged at the bulky wolf slamming his head into the booth's table surrounded by his friends. The table cracked as everyone started and Aria yelped. Garret rolled over and *turned* jumping out of the way and rounding the diner. He leapt onto the bar, shoving the miniature Lazy-Susan's filled with menus, syrups, and salt/pepper shakers to the ground with a crash. Garret's claws scraped at the cheap bar, drawing deep gashes, and drool sloshed onto the white and black checkered linoleum floor. Tristian stood his ground, egging the wolf to fight him. Werewolf bites were nasty, but nothing he couldn't handle.

"Heel, *Bitch*," Tristian hissed. The wolf had made the grave mistake of messing with him, and talking about his woman. *His woman.* Yeah, he liked the sound of that. Just as he was about to lunge, Asher and Ulysses stepped in the middle of his feral tunnel vision.

"Relax, Effingo," Asher glowered. "He's on our side, remember?"

Tristian's eye twitched as he worked to restrain the fire blazing under his skin.

"Fine," he snarled forcefully through gritted teeth. Ulysses shoved him into the broken booth as a naked Garret climbed off the bar.

"She's mine!" Tristian declared over Ulysses' shoulder.

Suddenly it was Aria that rushed at Garret. "You need to get yourself in check, Garret." She pointed a firm finger in his face making the werewolf flinch back with wide eyes. "You were nothing to Dylan in that way. She told me herself she liked you only as a friend. So, don't you try and act like it was more. Tristian is her boyfriend, not you."

Boyfriend?

Tristian's eyebrows briefly shot up. Somehow being labeled anything exclusive with Dylan sent a primal sense of emotion tingling within his chest. He couldn't conceal the satisfied smile that threatened to break through at the wolf's obvious shock from the news. Not to mention, watching a human girl frighten a large werewolf was extremely entertaining. Except she was right. They all needed to get themselves in check. Dylan, girlfriend or not, was still missing and it had already been six weeks going on seven.

"Look," Tristian spoke, bringing everyone's eyes to him. "Garret, get some damn clothes on, grab my weapons from Tiny Tim, who escorted me in, and let's find Datu. It's been six weeks. We need to find Dylan."

The wolf narrowed his eyes then nodded curtly.

"I'll be right back," Garret said in a husky voice.

"Oh, maybe you should grab a change of clothes as well," Tristian called smirking. Garret grunted punching the kitchen door open.

With the four of them alone, they all seemed to sigh stress.

"I was not expecting that," Aria stated throwing herself onto one of the still standing bar stools. "I still find it hard to believe all of this is real." She lowered her head onto the bar and gripped her head with her hands. "Then I see *that*," she spoke her voice muffled. Asher walked up to her and started massaging her shoulders.

"Think how Dylan probably felt," Asher said, perhaps trying to comfort her. "And she was one of us. At least you're still human. Your life is still the same, only your eyes are open to the truth."

Tristian cut in, "Yeah, she had to adapt to the fact nothing in her life was going to stay the same, other than having you as her friend."

Aria's head popped up, her hair flipping over her shoulder straight into Asher's face. The way he seemed so unfazed made Tristian curious about their relationship. He'd never seen the demon so content, not even with Livia.

"Of course, I wouldn't have lost her as a friend, but it felt like she couldn't even tell me. She never told me anything going on in her life. It makes me wonder, how much of a friend I really was to her."

"She probably just wanted to keep you safe," Tristian spoke rubbing the back of his neck. "To save you from this." He didn't like talking about Dylan in the past tense, but it seemed to fall into that direction in every conversation.

The kitchen doors swung open as Garret entered wearing khakis and a blue tee. He tossed a wrinkled, brown paper bag at Tristian. Tristian peered inside and fished out his daggers, securing them into place.

"I think you forgot your extra clothes, wolf." Tristian smirked making a display of the bag being empty. "Must be embarrassing, turning in public." He couldn't help himself. Every time he saw the poodle he felt the urge to hurt him—to hurt him for ever thinking he had anything with Dylan. Which was probably crazy. Of course she had had previous relationships. But still, that primal need gripped him. He needed the worlds to know she was his, crazy or not.

Garret only shook his head incredulously as he pushed open the screen door. Aria walked up behind Tristian and slapped him in the back of the head, then pointed a finger in his face. The action made him think of Dylan—their first night at the club.

"Get it in check, Effingo."

Ulysses and Asher chuckled as they all followed the annoying wolf out into the stunningly hot, misting air.

Garret led them down the street as Tristian filled everyone in on the details. They arrived at a large building with two soaring columns and a grand cornice where 'Los Angeles First Bank' was spelled in thick, gray letters.

"I'll be right back," Garret said, bouncing up the concrete steps.

Aria looked at the bank and then at Garret. "What? Why? Do you need to make a de-paw-sit or something?" She laughed at her horrible joke, which in turn made the rest of them laugh *at* her, except for Garret.

"Get it?" She continued to laugh. "Sorry, I must be really tired." She cringed, looking to Asher who shook his head as to say you're on your own with this one. Garret grunted and muttered something under his breath that sounded like... sandwiches? Then disappeared into the bank.

Tristian looked at an embarrassed Aria. "Way to keep it in check," Tristian chuckled.

"I tend to say stupid shit when I'm nervous." She bounced her shoulders.

"Don't worry about Garret," Tristian said, hiding a smile. "I'm sure he can survive the wrath of your horrible jokes."

To his surprise Aria only nodded with a frown. "Do you think she'll be there? In Lamu?" Tristian had pondered it himself, but highly doubted Datu had her. He shook his head solemnly.

"But Datu will know where she is. I'm sure of it." He had to be sure of it, because it was the only thing he had to hold on to.

She nodded again, apparently feeling the same way. Ulysses sat on the steps looking up at the sky and blinking through the warm mist.

Aria sat next to him. "Do you ever miss it?" She asked, looking to the sky. Tristian took a cautious step forward, knowing the fallen never liked talking about their fall.

Ulysses face turned rancid. "Sometimes, but mostly not."

"Was it not nice? I can't imagine wanting to leave heaven."

"It's not what it's cracked up to be." He sighed and looked at her. "You have freedom here, free will. You get to choose the direction to walk, what to say. There," he looked back up to the menacing, gunmetal gray sky, "everything is programmed like you're a damn robot."

Aria nodded with an even deeper frown. Tristian could tell too many hard truths were sinking into her mind.

"Day after day, I was sent for single missions down into this world. I couldn't talk to anyone, or do anything else but what I was commanded. I was allowed to watch, and I made sure to soak in as much as I could during each visit. It was so cruel to give us these minds, but to limit our actions."

He shook his head looking at the ground. Except Tristian knew he wasn't focused on the pavement, but on the images seared into his mind's eye that forced his fall.

"So many of us fell. But I never felt the need to until I witnessed a couple kissing on the street. Stupid, I know… but they looked so happy together, laughing and flirting. I wanted those things." He raised his eyebrows with a sad smile. "Well…that was the end of Zophiel and the birth of Ulysses."

Tristian was slightly shocked at his confession. He'd never heard a fallen seraph talk about the fall or about their past life with the human deity.

"You chose your name?" Aria asked.

"Yes."

"You do know what it means, right?"

Ulysses returned from the distant place in his mind and gave Aria an *'are you kidding me?'* look. "Of course I know what it means. I was pissed and it sounded like a good idea at the time."

Aria opened her mouth, then shut it when the bank's glass doors flew open revealing Garret.

He stopped at the bottom of the steps. "You guys ready? I got the keys."

Asher grabbed Aria's hand pulling her upright flush with him, and then whispered in her ear.

"No. I'm going too," she huffed, throwing her arms over her chest with a stern look. He only shrugged and looked at

327

Tristian. "Let's get to the church before it starts to pour."

"Church?" Aria called after Asher.

CHAPTER 18

*"The mind is its own place, and in itself can make a
heaven of hell, a hell of heaven..."*
John Milton

RELAXING *on the patch of grass in Santa Monica,
Dylan watched the morning tide slide in and out—lazily pulling
back with the moon as it did in each dream. With her arms
wrapped around her knees, she laid her head and closed her
eyes, listening to the soothing waves and the wind's exhale,
blowing a mist of salt on her skin.*

*After the day she had, she needed to see him and know
everything was still okay between them. Her tangled locks
tossed around her face as she sighed, feeling at home, but soon
realized something was different. Flicking her eyes open, she
wrinkled her brow and lifted her head.*

She was alone.

*"Tristian?" she called out getting to a slow and shaky
stand.*

*Her pulse spiked and her eyes searched the deserted beach.
Angry clouds bled, choking the once blue sky.*

*"Tristian!" Lightening crackled in the distance followed by
an explosion of thunder.*

"Tristian! Where are you?"

*She felt a dizzying wave of nausea. She knew in the recesses
of her mind, even dream Tristian had left her.*

"I'm sorry!" she screamed as a wild wind slapped her body

329

with such force she stumbled.

"Please, don't give up!" She jerked her eyes up at the boiling, black sky, swirling with ominous venom.

"Tristian, please! I know where I am! I finally do! It's a place called Zadar!"

"Tristian! Please! Please come back!" Salt stung her eyes from the bubbly spray.

"I'm sorry! I didn't mean to kiss him!"

She fell to her knees in desperation as the wind blew even stronger sucking out her oxygen. She slapped her hands to her throat. She couldn't breathe!

Gasping awake, Dylan woke to a steady stream of tears rushing down her face. Crouching in the fetal position, she wailed, mourning the last piece of home. He was everything to her, everything that kept her moving forward. Even if the dream was tortuous, at least she still had him when she closed her eyes. She lived for her nights with him, the words, the kisses, the love... but now, even he was gone and she was alone.

Utterly and completely alone.

Through her dreams, Tristian embodied everything that was home—her friends, her family, her lover, and her hope to return. She'd lost the only thing tying her back to her roots; the only thing reminding her of what was waiting for her. A part of her knew she hadn't lost anything tangible. It was only a dream. But one so familiar it made her chest ache. She couldn't stop crying and she considered, for the briefest of seconds, if she should call for Silas to hold her.

Literally slapping herself across the face, she immediately sat up.

"I've got to get out of here," she whispered fiercely to herself.

Her eyes were suddenly dry as tears continued dripping off her chin. Was it because of the kiss with Silas that she'd lost her dreams? Rubbing the wetness off her face, she glanced at her wall clock, noting the two a.m. time stamp. Maybe it was just a fluke. Laying her head back down, her body trembled from the violent awakening.

An hour had passed as Dylan tossed and turned. She was afraid to find the truth that perhaps Tristian had truly left. Her mind kept replaying her actions from the day over and over again. Silas' seductive banter; his nimble fingers teasing and coaxing her body into submission; and the way his rumbling groan seemed to travel all the way from her lips to the sensitive seam between her thighs.

"Ughh!" she grumbled, rolling onto her other side and punching the pillow, in hopes to lessen the concrete guilt surrounding her. Squeezing her eyes shut harder, she felt like she'd betrayed him. But why did it feel like she'd cheated on Tristian? Yes, she was in love with him; that was one thing she was sure of these days. But they were never exclusive and besides the text, their last chat was horrendous. Not to mention, he was probably doing way more than heated make-outs with other women, or vampires.

"Oh God," she sobbed.

The thought of Tristian touching another girl made her heart contract with force. The images of that brunette on him were like needles piercing her eyeballs.

Surrendering herself to torture, she closed her eyes once more, needing the comfort of the darkness behind her lids to douse the hellish fire of her days. She needed Tristian to hold her, just one last time.

Twisting onto her back, she shook her head at the colorless void of her skylight.

What was she really doing? It was only a dream! Glancing at the slowest moving clock in all the worlds, she noted it was just past three a.m.

Huffing, Dylan threw off her comforter and walked toward

her armoire. She needed to get out, take a walk, or do a little yoga. She knew at this rate she'd never get to sleep. Stomping out of her bedroom decked in her yoga gear, Dylan commanded her worm to "stay" before making her way to the gym.

An hour had gone by and sweat beaded along her brow. The quiet interior mixed with the violent night flurries pounding outside the glass wall gave Dylan a much-needed sense of calm. It was as if the decked glass enclosure was her personal sanctuary—tucked away in perfect solitude from the demented demons of this deranged palace.

Her mind began to work again; the whole night with Silas felt like such a sham, yet she knew this was the way to get to him. But the way her body had responded to him like it had a mind of its own, absolutely bugged her. Whenever she was around him she'd forget about her agenda and succumb to his desires. His! As if he had some invisible hook in her. She thought about how easily he held her close in the pool, dipped her chair back, and ravished her in the library. She was nothing but a puppet! She thought she was being astute and canny but absolutely played into his hand like a bear succumbing to food from a trap.

The walls around her heart were already cracking and she didn't know if she could keep them erect. Not without her dream Tristian keeping her grounded. It was too easy to get lost in the moment as she did earlier in the evening. That heated kiss lingered in her mind's eye, erupting a flutter deep within her belly. With Silas, her entire mind fogged over like nothing she'd experienced before. It took an insurmountable surge of energy to push him away. She needed to be extra careful.

Lunging, she arched her back and brought her right arm up next to her ear as her other arm scaled down to the back of her straight rear leg in the Reverse Warrior Pose.

Breathing in steady gulps of air, it suddenly hit her: she'd ask Silas to teach her how to use her powers, to train her. He would definitely accept the challenge while Dylan secretly collected information and learned techniques to fight her way out. If she was the most powerful demon as they say, she should be able to conquer this castle, free the servants and— as she opened her eyes moving up to a standing position, and looked at the bitter stormy night—her heart sank. How would she escape in that? There had to be a way. She was sure Silas and Lucia had done it. Datu or Erez had obviously done it, so she could do it. Surely they weren't all trapped here.

Not sure if she would have any chance of succeeding, or if she should just give up, Aria's voice suddenly barged into her thoughts. Back in their freshman year, few weeks had passed when Aria had been moping about her sorority. Dylan finally asked her why she was a part of an organization she didn't like. Her friend had simply looked her up and down and said matter of factly, "Quitting is for pussies."

Feeling the ache of fatigue, Dylan stooped down and rolled up her mat, setting it aside. Looking down, she ran two fingers over the scar on her leg and realized she had forgotten a promise she made to herself only six years ago. Biting her lip, she took a defiant stand, knowing in her heart she wouldn't give up, because she refused to give up. With or without help, she'd find her salvation.

On her way out, Dylan looked at the pool, remembering Silas talk about the 'pull' he felt. She walked towards it still not feeling any pull, but why? Why wasn't she drawn to the elements? Everyone seemed so shocked that she had no idea she reserved these powers without releasing them in some way. Despite her will to keep her emotions in check most of her life, part of her still wondered if maybe they had the wrong demon. She didn't doubt that she was a Collector anymore; but, how did she really know she was an Elementa?

As if her body moved to its own accord, Dylan dove in. If Silas could manipulate water at four-years-old she could figure it out now.

She felt the perfect temperature of the warm waters envelop her body, saturating every fiber, hair follicle, and the surface of her skin. Her body hummed with anticipation as she slowly sank in the deep end—all the way until she met the twelve-foot deep concrete bottom.

Looking around at the vast pool where plastic ropes and pool filters bobbed against the shallow waves of her dive, her eyes fixed shut as she tried to generate her *Unda* as Tristian had taught her not so long ago. Nothing happened. She tried again harder, but still nothing. She quickly ran over the words Tristian had spoken to her at the beach, noting the impending need to breathe.

"Feel for the touch..." his husky voice reverberated throughout her body. With a slight curve to her lips, she began to feel for the touch of the water around her with all her stress, rage, frustration, hope, insecurities and resentment. Each emotion she had felt for the past six weeks—no, for the past fourteen years, in dense waves of current. Her mind ran through the events leading her to this very moment and empowerment swelled within her.

She then surged her *Unda* into the water.

Her nerves were blanketed by tingles, a sparkling experience like nothing she had ever known. The stirring sensation took over her body and mind, humming with energy like an over charged atom jettisoning ions. The floor, her need to breathe, the pressure in her ears all dissipated, leaving her raw, exposed and concentrating on the only thing that mattered, the water.

She felt alive, light, and free. Her face broke into a brilliant smile. She felt in her domain; this was what she was made for. Peeking open her eyes, she immediately shut them. Her heart picked up and her body shook as it began to beg for air.

Opening her eyes once more, they dilated with horror as she

looked around. She wasn't at the bottom of the pool anymore. She was suspended at least thirty feet into the air surrounded by the contents of the pool, touching the soaring ceiling!

This can't be real. She shut her eyes hard squeezing them with all her might.

She prayed she'd imagined the previous scene then opened them again. Panic set in, nothing changed. She slapped her lids back together.

This is how I'm going to die! she thought, willing the water to stay afloat.

She wanted to scream for Silas, or even Lucia, but was too afraid to move or so much as even flinch. Not that it would matter. She knew however hard she screamed it would be worthless; the liquid would muffle her cries.

Oh God! What have I done? I'm so stupid!

Tears threatened under her frantic lids. It was the same feeling she felt just as she attempted suicide. A feeling she vowed to never feel again; it was fear smothered with guilt. An ache deep in her belly rose that made her sick with vertigo. But it was too late, like last time. She couldn't go back. She couldn't restart the night that led her here. Unlike last time though, there was no one here to save her. She felt her body tremble riotously, the weight of the water bearing down on her like an overloaded bench press held for too long; her need to breathe stampeding throughout her mind and body.

She prayed a small prayer for her grandma, for her real parents and her mortal parents. She prayed that everyone that loved her would forget her and she spoke to her mortal parents asking forgiveness for killing their daughter.

With grave resolution, she released her held breath. Her body went slack, and her stomach dropped as she fell with the water.

◇◇◇

Tristian never liked the sensation of his stomach dropping inside a portal. The feeling of falling with nothing to hold onto. It reminded him of the past couple months, since Dylan pushed her way straight into his life. But instead of the feeling of dread on the other side, as he had now, Tristian only foresaw a never-ending line of possibilities—a hope only achievable after he'd found her safe. He wanted to fall as long as it was with her.

He felt the ground form under his boots and a thick, warm breeze toss his hair, bringing with it the scent of the salty ocean mixed with mulch, fish, coconut, and cinnamon. He hadn't experienced this particular combination of smells before and found them surprisingly pleasant.

He focused on his surroundings and for a split second thought he was in a vast, empty canal. But as he looked around, he knew he was on a deserted white beach. Water lapped against his shoes and the sun baked everything it touched. Tristian felt an immediate trickle of sweat drip between his shoulder blades.

To his right, Garret was sitting on the white sand, picking up handfuls of powder and letting the strong gust whisk it away. He looked lost in thought and, as Tristian stepped forward, the werewolf flicked him a glare before returning to his miniature sand storm.

A "grunt" and "oof" resounded. Tristian swung around. Ulysses was rolling in the powder inches from the tide. He stood quickly and shook his body, vigorously spraying crystals towards Garret and Tristian. Ulysses strode up, flashing a smile like he didn't just fall on his ass.

"Damn, how many times does it take to get used to that?" he called to them. "It felt like I dropped out of the sky again."

He continued to brush his shoulders and flap his over-sized blue shirt, refracting the sunlight off the glittering rhinestone koi fish.

"I'm still not used to it." Tristian gave an involuntary

shudder, as his mind did a quick replay of all his portal travels. A string of curses and a loud manly grunt broke his muse as Asher was pulled down into a red and gold tumble with Aria.

"You're squishing me!" she yelped as Asher grinned, landing on top of her.

"Whatever, babe. You know you like it," he panted, pushing himself up and pulling her to a wobbly stand.

"Portal travel feels like skydiving with no parachute!" Aria said excitedly.

"You've done that?" Ulysses asked, looking half shocked, half impressed.

"Yes! That's why I'm standing here before you, having this conversation, and not, you know, dead," Aria chided.

"Then," Ulysses frowned glancing at her through his lashes still picking off random specks of sand, "how do you know what it feels like?"

Asher smirked, folding his arms across his teal V-neck and looked at Aria, waiting for her retort.

"I'm obviously inferring the feel. And I'm sure that's pretty close," she stated, still shaking sand out of her hair. "I don't have special powers like you four. Well, three. Not sure turning into a dog is a special power... unless your evil villain is a cat hyped up on an insane amount of catnip. Then you may really need to bring out your Spike from Tom and Jerry." Garret glared at her and she immediately pulled her bottom lip to the side feeling contrite. "Oh, Garret. I'm sorry, that just popped out-"

"Babe," Asher admonished, stifling a laugh and cupping her cheeks. "I know we joke about werewolves and we do the same for vampires. But Lycanthropes are very strong and have severe senses. They're quite fast, and extremely vicious and hot tempered. Demons *are* faster, but don't reduce him to a

Labrador. He can tear you in two in a matter of seconds."

Aria's face instantly paled and Asher raised his eyebrows to Garret as to say 'you're welcome,' but Garret didn't seem compelled to give thanks. He only nodded to Asher and muttered something else under his breath.

Garret got to a rigid stand and barked, "This way."

Tristian felt the air tense as the four friends followed Garret like obedient school children. Peeling his eyes away from the azure waters and crystalline beach, he focused on the heavy tree line to the right of them, or more like what was in the tree line. A three-story home sprawled about in various levels of cement balconies, Moroccan arches, with jewel-toned tiles and furniture.

It didn't take long to cross the sandy shore and arrive at the back patio connected to the beach. Garret came to an abrupt stop and drew a finger to his lips, listening. Tristian listened as well, but his ears only picked up the heavy beat of his heart. His hearing went beyond the average person, but it still didn't compare to a werewolf or vampire. So, he'd rely on the mutt for this one.

Garret jerked his head towards the right side of the house, apparently sensing movement. He immediately tore across the patio and flattened himself against a stone pillar, peeking over his shoulder sporadically, checking on the sound. Everyone was in curious silence, except for Aria.

"Who the hell does he think he is?" she whispered loudly to their group. "Jack Bauer? Or should I say Garret Bauer. Omigod. Brauer... Like a dog!" She started chuckling as the whole group gave her a silencing glare. "Jeez, sorry," she mumbled. "Don't tell me you've never watched 24."

"Just," Tristian glowered at her, "shut up."

Asher shot him a stern look while enunciating a growl. Tristian rolled his eyes. He was tired of the human hanging around. If she messed this up, he was painfully sure that Dylan would be lost indefinitely. Tristian only shook his head in response as he shifted his eyes back to Garret. Garret who was now missing.

"Shit, where'd he go?"

"Through the open door, genius," Ulysses stated, crouching onto the patio and following the werewolf. Tristian followed suit, as did Aria and Asher. A crash sounded and Tristian left his friends and darted through the open glass door into the massive, two-story, white room scattered with standing bronze oil lanterns, gold and violet silk pillows, and graphic motif furniture with delicate tracery like old lace. Soaring, pewter, stone arches blanketed the exterior walls and each entrance, creating a sexy, exotic, Moroccan theme.

Another crash exploded in the kitchen. Two very different snarls resonated from the same place. Tristian could only imagine the scene of a vampire and werewolf fighting it out.

In a blink, Tristian was standing under the arched doorway viewing a very vulnerable Datu sprawled on the floor face down, clad in white boxers with little jumping frogs.

"Where," grunted Garret, shifting back into his naked human form as he held Datu down like roped cattle, "did you think you were going?"

"Yeah, it's daylight, dumbass." Tristian felt the urge to point out.

"I wasn't exactly thinking," Datu grunted, giving up his thrashes. "I saw a werewolf and my first instinct was to run." He grimaced from being straddled by a naked man. "Man, put some clothes on. You have your sack all over my back."

Ulysses, Asher, and Aria finally appeared next to Tristian.

"Whoa," Aria called out slowly with a smile. "What'd I miss?"

Ulysses and Asher started snickering. If Tristian didn't know any better, he may have thought he saw some color rise in

Datu's deathly pale cheeks.

◇◇◇

Pain erupted in her limp, wet body. Dylan felt something big and hard lying underneath her back and something impossibly sharp slicing her stomach and arm. She wanted to scream from the unthinkable agony, but was unable to wince, move, or so much as even open her ten pound lids. Silently accepting her fate, she listened to the erratic "thump... thump... thump" of her still beating heart as she let everything seep back into the darkness.

Her lids fluttered like broken wings, catching glimpses of scars, burned flesh, blood, and fiery orbs.

Thump... thump... thump...

Feeling someone clutch her, she listened to Silas plead into her neck,

"Temperance, please... please, wake up... please, don't leave me."

Thump... thump... thump...

Her lids bobbed again, but this time she felt the soft cotton of her bed. Part of her hoped with everything she had that this was all a terrible dream. Her very own dark fairytale ending in her death. That she had awakened in her bed at her grandmother's house on that first day of summer before any of the demons existed in her life.

Even before Tristian.

However, a sinister woman's voice crushed her hopes.

"I thought you said she didn't know how to use her powers," the voice hissed.

"She doesn't-" a defeated man's voice replied—Silas.

"This doesn't look like someone without the ability to control their powers!"

"Do you think she was trying to kill herself?" Silas asked numbly.

"I don't know. Nevertheless, we'll need to appoint a new worm slave for her. The stupid creature tried to actually save her." The woman laughed. "All he got was pummeled to death."

Thump... thump... thump...

"You better clean this up!" she warned.

Dylan heard a low growl and a womanly shriek.

"Don't," an unfamiliar, crackling voice boomed. "Don't threaten me, woman. You have no say in anything anymore! I am in charge of this arrangement. You will do as you're told, *Mother*," he spat the last word.

Thump... thump... thump...

Blackness swept across her lids, welcome against the agony of her reality and the pain of her wounds.

Intense light saturated her darkness bringing with it a painful throb across her stiff body.

Ouuuuchh.

She let out a thick groan as she managed to squint an eye open then shut it. She immediately felt a warm hand brush across her forehead, gentle and comforting.

Tristian? Except she knew better than to voice her hope aloud.

"Temperance?" a worried voice croaked.

All she was able to say in response was another groan as she tilted her head into his soothing palm. Despite the hatred she harbored towards the palace and the demons inside, she was happy Silas was there, if only for the company.

"What happened?" she finally moaned keeping her eyes firmly shut.

He continued to cup her cheek with gentle strokes of his thumb. "I thought I'd lost you. I found you unconscious on top of your worm in the shallow end of the pool. Most of the water had splashed out, otherwise you would have drowned for sure."

Dylan whimpered against the searing pain. Her whole body

ached but something was insanely wrong with her stomach. It was radiating white-hot pain and she didn't know if she could breathe through it.

"What were you thinking? Were you trying to..." he started like he couldn't bring himself to say the words.

Pain, pain, pain!

"Were you trying to die?"

She swallowed the ache and exhaled, "No."

Squinting open her eyes again, she studied the disheveled demon next to her. His shirt was blood stained, a heavy line of stubble ran along his cheek, and dark circles encased his mandarin eyes.

She heaved several breaths and coughed, determined to speak without crying. "I was trying to use my powers, like you did." She shut her eyes and ran a slight crease along her brow. "I can't believe I'm alive. That had to be the stupidest thing I've ever done... besides go on a date with a vampire." She chuckled then winced.

She heard a sad laugh. "I'm glad you still have your sense of humor."

"Stomach," she moaned. "What's wrong with my stomach?" Silas' hand left her cheek and inched up her white tank. His finger hovered over the length of her bandage which was the size of a dollar bill.

"Your worm tried to catch you and ended up getting you pretty good here, and your arm, as well as broke your fall."

"My worm saved me?"

"Apparently." He leaned back and rubbed his hands down his face. "We found him crushed under you."

"I told him to stay... when I went to the gym." She knew it was silly to feel a deep sadness for a creature that scared the bejeezus out of her, but she did.

"They're commanded to follow their masters. Even if you

don't see them, they're there."

"Oh," she sighed. "You look like you haven't slept in days."

"I haven't really, not since I felt the castle quake. And to tell you the truth, I was already up... unable to sleep."

"How long have I been out?"

"Just a little over a day."

"No wonder my stomach feels like it's eating itself," she spoke dryly.

He scrambled to the nightstand and poured her some tea. "Drink this. It should help until you feel like eating a meal."

"Thanks," she inched higher in the bed and took the porcelain cup. The steam filled her nose as she inhaled the sweet scent of citrus and mint. Tristian came to mind.

Damn, I've got it bad...

"Silas?"

"Yeah?"

"Can you train me?"

He gave her a skeptical look. "Just focus on getting better and we'll talk about it later," he said vaguely.

"No, Silas." She took his hand and squeezed it to show her sincerity. "Promise to train me." She looked him straight in the eye and gave him the best trusting look she possessed.

He seemed to think for a moment as he returned her stare. Shifting his eyes down to her raw bruised hand tightly grasping his, he nodded.

"I promise."

She gave a weak smile and sipped the tart liquid, savoring the minty bite.

CHAPTER 19

"At some point you have to realize that some people

can stay in your heart but not in your life."

Unknown

THE sun had set over an hour ago and the sky was littered with innumerable twinkling dots. Even on the clearest of nights, Los Angeles didn't have skies like this. The wide canal, fed from the Indian Ocean, was as calm as a millpond. It reflected the white crescent moon, distorting it like two giant fangs waiting for its next unknowing victim.

The atmosphere around him brought an eerie calm over his nerves. He took a deep breath as a gust of wind rushed off the waters, blowing exotic smells of the island onto the patio. The three donkeys that belonged to the property, brayed and barked as they meandered about in the small yard on the side of the house.

Tristian had spent the remainder of the day pacing and going over the questions he had ready for Datu. But one question burned throughout his mind.

Where is Dylan, Datu?

Soon after detaining the vampire, Tristian's withering state became apparent. Asher then extracted Datu's soul without *Unda*, letting Tristian safely inhale the energy. Tristian watched sadistically as the creature screamed in agony. He'd never collected totally without *Unda* and found that even just watching was strangely satisfying.

The weak savage ended up passing out a few moments after Tristian secured the soul, ending the fun. Instead of waking him, the group decided it best to tie him up somewhere and pick an interrogation space.

"Find me, Tristian."

Hell, her voice was still like a broken record, beckoning him to haste. A haste that tested his patience. Part of him wanted to go to sleep just so he'd see her again, to smell that delicious aroma radiating off her skin. Perhaps, he could prolong the dream this time, ending it on a more satisfying note.

Another strong, stinging breeze tossed his too long hair as he noticed the canal churning, erasing the moon's presence until it was merely a blur of light across its surface. The stomp of shoes halted as Garret appeared to his right.

"He's awake?" Tristian asked, keeping his eyes on the small lapping waves of the onyx tide.

"Yeah, squirming like a rodent."

"Good." He felt himself quickly plead to the universe that Datu held the key to her whereabouts; then turned away from the black, soulless waters and headed into the house.

Tristian took the concrete steps two at a time until he reached the third level. He felt the breeze from the top balcony cross his skin followed by a string of curses. Tristian sauntered through the master suite by way of the open double-glass doors. A sheer curtain billowed from the wind. Stepping through the opening, Tristian already knew what he was walking into before he reached the destination.

The balcony was expansive with a knee-high concrete enclosure. Potted plants of exotic flowers and herbs filled the corners and walls. To his left was a hot tub level with the concrete balustrade giving an unobstructed view of the canal. To his right was an intimate group of modern wicker and linen couches. Aria laid sprawled out on the love seat, eyes closed with an arm draped over her eyes, holding an exceptionally

345

large glass of red wine. Ulysses and Asher sat in the matching chairs across from each other, dealing cards and laughing. All were obviously ignoring the worthless existence taking up space in the middle of the patio.

Datu was bound at the wrists and feet, suspended from a bulky metal pergola by the binding on his wrists above his head. He was squirming like a banshee as Garret sidestepped Tristian and punched the blood-sucker straight in the stomach. Datu made an "*huh*" sound as he tried once more to break through the steel chains interlaced with crosses that gripped his body. Apparently Nadia had expected defiance from her vampire lover, so Garret had located the ready-made chains soon after they arrived.

"Relax, vampire," he growled. "This will go easier if you just, *relax*."

Ever the yoga instructor… Tristian rolled his eyes.

Everyone seemed to have snapped to attention as Tristian strode in front of Datu slowly removing his sunglasses, revealing ominous verdant stones. Narrowing his eyes at the revolting creature, Tristian punched him square in the jaw. Aria squeaked as Datu jerked from the blow. Black clotted blood made its way down his chin as Tristian shook and flexed his fingers waiting for his rebuttal.

Datu spit blood, letting his eyes glass over to red spheres. "She's fine," he hissed through dropped fangs. "He wants her as his mate."

"Who," Tristian forced through a stiff jaw.

"Gerion Planto."

"Damn it!" Tristian growled pulling hard on his hair before slamming his foot into Datu's shin. "I knew it!"

Asher stepped forward. "Where or *how* the hell did you get in touch with the Plantos?"

Datu ignored Asher, pursing his lips and looking Tristian in the eyes. If looks could kill Tristian knew he'd be six feet under.

"How do you know," Tristian asked the question with more composure, "that he doesn't want her as a slave?"

"You *demons,*" Datu sang like a petulant child, "always forget about our vampire hearing."

"Get on with it!"

"When I dropped her off, I overheard a man and a woman talking about Gerion having children with Temperance. But he needs her to be committed first. So, that's when I knew she'd be fine. I just still don't know why all the trouble for a mate. Ehh... probably because of his looks." Datu grimaced, his nose already piecing back together from the blow.

Aria's voice carried over the group from her spot on the couch. "Why, what's up with his looks?"

Asher turned around to face her. "He was tortured as a child by his parents. The Omnipotence, our government, found out about it after Gerion killed his father. There was a huge trial, they ruled self-defense for Gerion and cursed his mother and older brother for never stopping the abuse. They can never collect a soul again and have been exiled."

"Tortured?" she asked with a sadness cracking her voice.

Tristian interjected, "His father burned and beat him on the verge of death constantly for years as a child, in order to *shape him.*"

"Oh my-" Aria breathed.

Asher burst into a condescending laugh. "Well, he turned into his little protégé and he's apparently building himself a twisted army."

Aria frowned obviously confused. "What? By marrying and having a baby with our girl?"

"It's not what either of you think," Tristian said, looking from Aria to Datu. "He's not going to marry her with love and devotion. He wants to enslave her for eternity and their children will be super demons. That's what everyone wants her for. Even the OP wants her for their army."

Aria's eyes stretched in realization. "So, he could be raping her to make an army?"

Oh hell, he better not...

Tristian looked down as hollow words fell from his lips. "No, that wouldn't be... appropriate. He needs to make sure she can't leave while pregnant or take their children away at any moment." He pursed his lips not really believing his own words. Because, really, what was to stop him from trying anyway? It had been over three hundred years. The Plantos could very well have changed their motives and culture to something a bit more barbaric.

"So, he needs to enslave her?" Aria said, now standing next to Asher gripping his hand. "Isn't that what's going on now?"

"No, eternal enslavement happens through a signed contract when you're a born demon. It's very rare, but it happens." *And no one, not even the OP, can release this indenture.* He cringed at the thought as something deep inside ruptured.

"You said he's ugly... Dylan will never go for him that way. She's totally into you Tristian. Earlier that night... the one she was taken... she was crying that she... uh, fell in love with you."

Tristian felt his breath snatched straight from his lungs, then looked at her incredulously. Dylan loved him?

You have me enamored, Tristian...

Fuck.

His chest began to spasm with the need to tell Dylan he loved her, too. He loved her too... How was this possible? They had barely spent any time together; yet, he couldn't for the life of him imagine his existence without her.

But before he could interrogate the human for more information, Asher cut in, "You are forgetting the Plantos are shifters."

Aria spoke, "So..."

Tristian's eyes widened as he growled and vigorously itched the stubble that dotted his jaw. He didn't know that about Gerion. How had he not known that?

Datu stopped writhing. "What? What does it mean? He can change forms? Why does that matter?"

Tristian snapped his attention to the vile, repugnant creature feeling the need to start breaking off his appendages. All of this was his fault! But he held back.

"Shifters are the most manipulative of demons. That's without adding the fact that he's one of the most powerful Collectors, in spite of everything!" Tristian roared.

Asher appeared at his side. "Tristian, we could still have time as long as she doesn't talk to him, right?"

But six weeks... is she that tenacious?

Aria suddenly sat on the cool stone floor as Ulysses darted to her side. Asher looked helplessly at the wide-eyed and distraught human.

"Oh. My. God," she whispered, shaking. "We're going to lose her." Her lips quivered as tears filled her eyes.

Tristian's fists began to clench with uncertainty.

"She's stubborn," he mumbled to himself needing hope. "Fuck, Dylan!" he called into the night through surfacing tears.

"Where is she!" Asher screamed into Datu's face.

Datu trembled, "I-I don't know! All I know it's cold, really cold. I was blindfolded and I have to call him."

In a blink of an eye, Asher unbound a single wrist. "Then," he slapped a cell phone into the vampire's icy, swollen hand, "call him."

Datu smirked, "No. I haven't gotten my reward yet."

"Fuck your reward!"

"No!" he spat back at Tristian. "She has to sign that

contract. *I need* her to sign that contract."

"What's your price, vampire?" spoke a surprisingly calm Garret from his seat on the concrete railing. "Millions of humans for blood? I can give you that. Call him."

"No," Datu rebuffed again. "You can't give me what I want."

"What do you want?" pleaded a now bawling Aria as Ulysses smoothed her humid induced wavy locks.

"To be human again," he whispered slowly. "To be free of the bloodlust, to walk in the daylight, see the sunrise-"

A slow sadistic laugh erupted from Tristian's throat.

Obdurate fool!

The vampire snapped a growl his way.

"You moronic vampire," Tristian hissed with disdain. "He can't give you that! Once you go to him for your reward he'll kill you to make you mortal."

"Then why hasn't he killed me yet?"

"Obviously he needs you for more errands," Asher said.

"That's not true," Datu's voice faltered. "I've heard the stories!"

"And they are just that. Stories," Tristian said. "No demon can release your disease. Not even me and I am a healer."

Datu shook his head violently as an inner angst was evident on his face.

"Dammit!" Datu screeched, exasperated as he flexed his neck muscles. Black veins bulged splintering into a web of starved realization. He lifted the phone, dropped his arm, then lifted it again. Everyone stood in silence, mentally urging him to make the call.

"If I do this… you'll have my back? Because there will be no going back once I call. I will have to visit there... earlier than planned."

"That's the plan. Asher and I will follow you there."

Then I'll kill you, you sickening crust of scum. Hell, maybe I'll even let my woman do the honors. This is her life you messed with after all.

Datu nodded and dialed a three-digit number. It rang then he hung up and dropped the phone. Tristian's eyes almost popped out of their sockets with rage.

"You change your mind, vampire?" he hissed with acid laced through each syllable.

"N-no," he stammered. "This is how it's done. He'll call back when he has time."

"Well, let's just hope it's before sunrise for your sake, ass!" Aria barked through a strained voice.

Tristian wasn't sure if it was the overwhelming stress or the fact they may have finally found Dylan's location but everyone, except for Aria and Datu, started to chuckle at Aria's dark omen before it died to painful silence. Datu's phone began to sing as Tristian sucked in a baited breath. Asher bent down and lifted the device planting it back into Datu's palm.

"H-hello? ...Er, yes. Uh, I need to talk... no... no, in person. It's important... Lamu, Kenya... Okay." Datu pressed 'end call' on the screen and after a long second, handed the phone back to Asher.

"There's a portal at the Kenyatta Road Town Centre. We have one hour."

Tristian turned to Garret, "Is there transportation here?"

"One Volkswagen Beetle and three donkeys," Garret spoke with severe composure, ready for duty.

"All right. Asher, Datu, and I will take the beetle. The rest of you take the donkeys and from the portal go home. We'll take it from here. Garret, make sure Aria gets home. And I mean all the way to her apartment and then secure the area."

"Yes." Garret cleared his throat and whispered, "What about the promise to my commander?"

"Don't worry about that." He gave Garret a knowing look.

The werewolf gave a curt nod and turned on his heel releasing Datu of his restraints. The vampire fell then instantly sat up, rubbing the swollen and blood crusted welts on his ankles and wrists. Garret tossed Datu a t-shirt and jeans.

Aria ran into Asher's arms and pulled him to the corner of the patio where they whispered, kissed, and hugged frantically. Tristian watched them with envy as he stuck close to Datu, who was busy slipping on the clothes in human haste. He read Aria's trembling lips as she begged Asher to promise to find Dylan, bring her back, and for him to return to her safely, because she wasn't through with *this* just yet, she motioned between them. Asher cupped her wet cheeks and crashed a fevered kiss on her lips. Feeling like he was intruding on something intimate, Tristian looked away towards the arrogant vampire leaning against the stucco façade.

"We should get going," Tristian said to Datu, but loud enough for Asher to hear.

The vampire nodded and they all exited the villa.

Forty-five minutes later, they arrived at the Town Centre. Tristian spoke to Datu's reflection in the rearview mirror.

"Where are we to go?"

Asher interjected, "I called a friend, the Lamu portal is behind the Old German Post Office."

They left the Beetle in a deserted lot and hurried over to the post office without making a sound. They came up behind the historical landmark and knocked a few times as Tristian kept a watchful eye on their surroundings. At one in the morning, the air was still warm. Cats picked through garbage littered on the street and a slouching Kenyan man, wearing an oversized orange t-shirt, rode a donkey.

The heavy wooden door opened as a tall, lanky, female Portal Keeper talked to Asher and Datu. Her hair was cut close to the scalp and a delicate golden chain hung from her pierced ear to her pierced nose; her light pink dress hung loosely on her body. Other than the red, beady eyes, she was rather normal looking for a warlock.

After a minute or two, they were welcomed into the portal enclosure without passes due to a very generous incentive forked over by Datu. With almost ten minutes to spare, the three discussed the plan.

"Last time their worms came through and escorted me the entire way," Datu spoke softly.

"How many worms?" Tristian asked, feeling for his knives and adjusting his clothing.

"Two. One came through and one waited on the other side." He was starting to fidget and shake as if he was terrified.

"What are you going to tell Gerion?" Asher asked, as he secured his clothes as well.

"I'll ask for my reward." He swallowed and felt his neck. "You guys will have my back... right?"

"Right," the two demons said in unison.

"How are you going to follow without them seeing?"

"I'll need something small and long to keep the portal open," Asher said, eyeing their surroundings while scratching the side of his head. "Hmph."

"Shoe laces?" Datu shrugged.

"Okay, that might actually work." Asher nodded and they bent down to retrieve the string. After tying the six strings together they had about a fifteen-foot "rope."

"Perfect," Asher said as he tied one end to Datu's shoe and held the other.

Glancing at his watch, Asher grinned, "Showtime."

Tristian patted Datu on the back, causing the vampire to flinch. "Don't mess this up," he warned as they disappeared in to the shadows, leaving Datu to wait near the Portal like bait on a fishing pole. Tristian listened to his harsh breathing as seconds ticked by like hours, standing in utter silence. Suddenly the Portal began to swirl and shimmer as a towering golden figure appeared.

Tristian and Asher crouched lower in the shadows, keeping a firm grip on the string, praying their invention would work. The worm, now fully formed, scanned the room and located Datu's quivering figure. Datu grabbed hold of the creature's elbow and the two stepped back through the open portal, the ethereal blue swallowing them whole.

Asher yelped, "Now!"

Tristian rushed after him and they dove into the portal head first. Wind rushed around them as they fell into blue oblivion. The string tugged and the two demons tumbled onto a cold chipped and unpolished wooden floor.

Tristian was still taking in his surroundings when a snarl emanated from above. Opening his eyes, he looked up at the ghastly being holding a sharp axe inches away from his face. His mouth fell slack as the creature lifted it, ready to strike. Snapping himself awake, Tristian rolled to the side just avoiding the blood-crusted axe's decent by millimeters. The wooden floor buckled from the blow and exploded as the worm yanked it free. Tristian looked around. Asher was fighting a similar creature practically hanging on to a gigantic axe while Datu shivered in the corner.

Coward.

Hearing a massive grunt, Tristian tore his eyes away and dodged the worm's second epic swing. The axe drove into the interior wall inches above Datu's head. The vampire about keeled over from fright. Wood rained around them as Tristian searched the cabin for a weapon. Finding none, he remembered, his knives! Freeing his beloved *Argyre*, he flung it straight at the creature, hitting home in the thing's blank white-eye. The creature dropped the axe with a loud thud and threw both hands to the dagger, staggering and yanking the knife, pulling out its own eyeball and guts in the process. Tristian reached for another dagger—black and a couple inches shorter, and jumped on the creature, stabbing it repeatedly to finish the job.

Pushing himself up and wiping the black blood off his face with his collar, he turned to face Asher and Datu. Just behind them, he saw the other worm dead with a broken neck. Asher boosted an eyebrow at the bloody mess in front of him.

"For some reason," Tristian started still wiping his face. "I didn't think about what would happen after we traveled through the portal."

Datu made a snort that sounded squeaky and pathetic.

"Oops," Tristian deadpanned, wiping his blades.

"All right, vampire. Lead the way." Asher swung his arm toward the cabin door.

"What? I don't know where I'm going," Datu flustered. "I told you before I was blindfolded."

"Dammit," Asher spat. "I'm sure it can't be too far. We should head out."

Asher headed for the door, stepping over the large beast and grabbed the handle, pulling it wide open. Wind and ice rushed inside at an angry rate, forcing their arms up to brace themselves.

"Shit!" Tristian barked. "Shut the door, SHUT the door!"

"The wind," Asher grunted pushing the door unsuccessfully.

Tristian found the door and felt his muscles bulge as he helped Asher slam it home. Both demons fell against the wooden frame dusted in fat, white flakes; some still floating in the air. Tristian took a deep breath as he quickly stood.

"When were you planning on telling us there's a damn blizzard!" he screamed in Datu's pallid face.

"Er, I didn't think it was relevant," Datu stammered. "Then

again, my body doesn't feel the cold and I don't think these things do either," he said kicking the foot of the stabbed worm.

"Shit... Shit!" Tristian announced pacing. "Well..." he halted, looking towards Datu. "How long of a walk was it? Surely you'll care to share that!" He shook his head disapprovingly at the insolent vampire.

"About a twenty-minute walk," Datu said, pushing his hands in his pockets. He rocked on the heels of his feet and looked around uncomfortably. "But I don't remember that much wind, just the numbing cold."

"All right," Asher jumped in before Tristian could have a coronary. "We'll wait it out. Once the weather dies down, we'll stake out the area and make a run for it. A twenty-minute walk is only like a mile, so, we shouldn't be too far."

"You came here last time as well?" Tristian spoke through his bared teeth.

"Yeah, man."

Tristian cracked his neck and took a good look around. The exterior walls were still intact and the current room only housed a futon and smashed dining table and chairs.

"We'll probably have about a day before more of these guys come looking for us," Asher spoke, as Tristian stepped over the bloody worm and into the small hallway.

The room to his left was the bathroom—now hardly usable thanks to the behemoth's axe. To his right was a small bedroom—no furniture, only a large mattress. The end of the hall housed a kitchenette, stove, mini-fridge, and a blue plastic water tank. Tristian rummaged through the cabinets and refrigerator. He came up empty save for a gigantic box of beef flavored Ramen noodles. The tank was full. At least they had food and water.

There was a small round window on the right side of the kitchen. Strolling over, Tristian banged his fist against the wall a few times to clear the snow. Once it fell off in a single sheet, Tristian stared at the inauspicious blanket of flurries and fog.

"Find anything?" Asher said, coming up behind him rather soundlessly.

"No," Tristian said, still staring outside. "But we have food and water."

"Hm," hummed Asher, turning around.

The weather broke for a second and Tristian blinked repeatedly. "Well, we found the manor."

Asher was beside him instantly. "Well, damn. They've got themselves quite the little place."

Tristian smirked because the home was anything but little. The palace was nestled between the highest peaks of the snow packed mountains. It was worn with age and crackled with snow, surrounded by rows of jagged black rock remarkably untouched by the ice. The sun was starting to rise behind them, highlighting the gray stone, tired and worn smooth from the many years of harsh weather. Four towers crowned the edges, but the southern tower had crumbled into merely a pile of rubble topped with several meters of snow. The palace seemed like a dreary place to inhabit, but what could one expect from a desolate land such as this?

"Whoa, where are we? Antarctica?" called Datu from behind them.

"Shouldn't you be finding a place to crash?" Tristian said turning to Datu. "Wouldn't want you to get sun burnt."

Datu quickly backed up. "Yeah... I should get to that. Must be the jet lag," he fumbled wide-eyed, disappearing back into the confines of the cabin.

"We're in Zadar," Asher said vacantly, still gazing at the castle.

Tristian raised a questioning eyebrow at him.

"I was here before on a contract." Asher shrugged. "The OP

likes to exile the cursed ones here. I don't know why I didn't think about it before. It's usually a good prison too. But if the cursed happens to be a demon who can create portals... it defeats the purpose."

"Huh," Tristian grunted. "Well, are you familiar with the weather?"

"To an extent." Asher frowned, moving away from the small window. "The blizzards come and go rather suddenly as I recall."

Just then the haze clouded back over revealing nothing but a blanket of white fog.

Apparently so...

CHAPTER 20

"There is no trap so deadly as the trap
you set for yourself."
Raymond Chandler

A couple of days had passed by and Dylan found her wounds healed more quickly than before. Silas explained to her that healing would keep getting faster as she neared her immortal age and how Lucia was able to heal her more severe injuries, like her broken legs and internal bleeding. The insufferable demon left anything superficial, like the two large puncture wounds on her arm and stomach untouched.

While she recovered, Silas constantly sat next to her bed and read to her from a few of the many books the library had to offer. Peppi also stopped by regularly, gossiping about the drama in the kitchen and helped her stay clean and presentable. Dylan began to notice something was wrong with the small girl. She wasn't her usual chipper self, but every time Dylan tried to ask her what was wrong, Silas would make his début into the room, stealing Dylan's attention.

The days went by slowly and she wanted more than anything to practice her yoga and start training.

She enjoyed Silas' visits, but worked extra hard to keep a strong wall around her heart. It was extremely difficult. They always fell into easy conversation, and by the end of their visits a hollow feeling would resonate in the pit of her stomach. It was a mixture of regret, sadness, and disappointment. She wished she could hate him or simply not care whether he stopped by or not, but she could not. It made her feel like a traitor to herself, Tristian, and her friends and family.

Today would be better. She worked really hard on mentally preparing herself for the visit. No matter how much he acted as if he cared for her, Dylan needed to remind herself each hour of each day—*this man is the reason I'm here.* She just couldn't let herself feel for him, not even as a friend. Because what if she had to kill him?

Once she felt comfortable enough with her powers and gently gathered his trust, she'd figure out how to escape. Even if no one was looking for her she would do it all by herself. There was something off about this place and she couldn't put her finger on it. It was something even more twisted than the bizarre family that wanted her commitment. She simply couldn't stay here, even if she grew to love her captor.

"Hey," she said as Silas strolled in looking a bit upset. "Are you okay?"

His frown morphed into his usual million-dollar smile. "Now I am… why?"

"I don't know… you just seemed a bit lost in thought when you came in."

"Oh. Well, actually, two of our worms have disappeared while they were out."

"Really…" *Out doing what?* "They go *out* often?" Dylan inquired, feigning indifference while smoothing the comforter draped across her lap.

"Whenever we need anything or if we receive guests." He sat on the foot of her bed. "But with these blizzards they disappear plenty, nothing to concern yourself with."

If they can't even survive in that weather…Wait, "We're

having a guest?" her voice was a bit too eager and she prayed with all her might he didn't notice her hopefulness.

"No." He slightly narrowed his stare pinning her to the spot. "Just retrieving some supplies."

She only nodded and looked away uncomfortably. She heard him sigh as he lifted the comforter and picked up her feet. She finally looked back at him, shyly, as he began giving her a massage.

"No book today?" she asked just above a whisper.

"Nope. I'm thinking maybe we could take a walk." He smiled apparently forgetting his tension. "You've been in that bed for way too long."

"I a-gree," she said in staccato. She shifted her feet off his lap onto the floor and sat up. Dizziness overcame her causing her to hunch over.

"Are you all right?" Silas asked, rushing to her aide.

She held up a finger, "Yes," she breathed. "Either my body got used to laying down or it's from the concussion." Her spotty vision cleared as she looked into his woeful eyes.

"Probably the concussion."

"That means I've had two in my life and I don't even play sports! I'm a few away from competing with a linebacker." She smirked. "I guess it comes with the package of being a demon."

"Linebacker?" He looked confused.

"You don't know football?" Her eyes rounded, acting shocked although she didn't expect him to.

"What is it? They get a lot of concussions…" he dipped his brow. "Is it like wrestling?"

"It does incorporate wrestling, kind of. More like huge three hundred pound guys tackling each other trying to get an oval ball to each other's goals."

"Sounds entertaining enough."

She took his outstretched hand.

"If you ever get cable, I'll show you a game," she said, favoring her left side as they walked the hallways. "I still don't understand why you have all of these televisions if you don't watch TV."

"Just think of them as monitors," he grumbled.

Dylan felt his mood diving again. "So… where are we going? The North Wing perhaps?"

"There's nothing of value there," he spit out, looking almost resentful, but quickly controlled his temper. "Actually, I thought I'd start your training today."

What exactly is in the North Wing? she wondered.

Her eyes lit up. "Really?" He nodded reflecting her childish grin. "But can I yet… with my injuries?"

"You want to wait a few more days?" He stopped and began turning around. "Because we can go back to your room, *Catcher in the Rye* still has one hundred pages-"

"No, definitely train," she snapped, yanking him back in the direction they were headed, causing him to chuckle. "Don't get me wrong. I really appreciated your reading sessions. It was really sweet. But I was about to go out of my mind. I need some physical activity."

"I'm sure," he said still laughing. "How ever did you manage the first six weeks you were here?"

Dylan got quiet a moment as she thought about the extreme terror she felt because of the man next to her. Silas must have noticed her shift in attitude because he immediately changed the subject.

"So, I was thinking we'd start with the basics." He cleared his throat. "Playing with drops of water instead of, you know, whole pools."

Dylan nodded numbly; *this man is the reason I'm here…*

Silas stopped and gently grabbed her arm. "Look, I didn't mean to bring up that history. I understand your inner struggle.

You're here against your will and you're trying to move past it and just enjoy." He slid a lazy finger down the side of her face, running a paradox of feelings from contentment to disgust. "I'm happy you're here, Tempy, even if you don't want to be. You lighten my days in this icy hell hole." He brought her hand up and kissed it as she finally looked into his exotic eyes.

"It'll take me a while to move past it, but I do enjoy your company." She blinked repeatedly, unable to accept she had just said that.

I need him to think I've moved on. Come on, Dylan, snap out of it!

As she was about to recant her last statement, he lifted her chin and placed a soft kiss on her lips. The simple act sent a rush of heat through her body. Her heart swelled with emotion and she brought a hand to his cheek. Their tongues slipped past each other and she wanted more than anything to melt into his lips but forced herself to pull away.

He bit his lip. "You're going to make me work for it, aren't you?"

Dylan only smiled with a sort of sadness and laced her fingers with his as they walked to the gym. All the while she kept wondering what had she been thinking about before that was so important.

"Again," Silas stated for what felt like the millionth time.

"I can't," she whined falling back on the mat. "I don't understand. It was so easy in the pool."

"What were you doing before you dove in?" Silas asked, grabbing her unhurt arm, pulling her back to a sitting position.

"Crazy spider poses." She reflected his sexy grin. "I was actually really tired when I started to leave... But then I remembered what you told me about the pool, and the next thing I knew, I was sinking in the deep end."

"That's the pull I talked about." He looked smug, which

only seemed to rub her the wrong way.

"I didn't feel any pull. I even recall thinking that, that there was no pull," she chided, crossing her arms.

"It's not a physical sensation, and you fell for it."

"Pull or no pull, why can't I do it now?"

"So, you were calm, and tired, then jumped in. What happened next, give me a play-by-play."

"And you've never watched football?" she smirked as he wrinkled his brow. "Okay…" she shook her head. "I sank to the bottom, felt for the touch of the water, and started sending streams of my *Unda* to the touch." *Just like Tristian taught me.* "Since the touch was all over, I guess I sent out too much? I remember it being intense."

"All right, close your eyes." Reluctantly, she did as he gently placed her hand just above, barely touching the drops. Goose bumps crawled up her arm and she worked hard to keep herself from sighing.

"Do you feel it now?" She nodded, taking a deep breath, slightly confused to which 'it' he was referring. "Good. Now think about the touch and focus on your *Unda* and levitating the drops."

She took another deep breath and concentrated on the tingling touch of the water. Her body went numb as she sent a steady stream similar to before, but only at that particular point instead of her whole body like she had done in the pool. She imagined picking up the drops with her fingertips and moved her palm up. Static charged the air around her as her mind came alive again. She imagined the drops rising, level with her face, when she heard Silas.

"Open your eyes."

She did and watched in awe as the bubbles of water danced near her nose.

"H-holy-" just as she spoke the droplets fell to a splatter,

"Shit."

"Very good, Tempy."

"Thanks." She smiled forcefully, *I really don't like that nickname.* "I should be able to do that with what, dirt, and," her eyes lit up, "fire?"

"Simmer down, Pyro," he laughed. "We'll deal with fire last, after you have basic control of your senses."

She crinkled her nose in disappointment. "How do I manipulate air?" she asked, as she concentrated on the drops controlling them with more ease. She flicked her fingers in a gentle wave watching them dance. It all seemed so surreal.

"The same way the world does, through wind." Her eyes flicked to his as the droplets plummeted to the mat. "So what, can I fly or something?"

"Something like that." He paused a moment as Dylan played with the floating water then flicked it at him. Silas flinched as the water hit his face. Wiping his blinking eye, Dylan suppressed a laugh with her fist.

"Oh, I'm going to have so much fun with this," she said with a wink.

A growl erupted from his throat as he grabbed her injured arm and *twisted* it causing her to suck in a sharp, pained breath. He then yanked her close and on her knees. Her smile was long gone as a jolt of dread rushed down her body. His expression was that of disdain. She swallowed her fear and gave a weak smile, trying to mollify the situation.

"Silas, it was just a joke," she squeaked. Her arm *really* hurt. The verge of blacking out from the pain worked its way back and forth through her mind, mingling with bursts of nausea.

His expression shifted to hunger as he stared at her lips. She couldn't believe this, he was hurting her and looked as though he was about to kiss her! Dylan tried to twist away.

"Silas, please, you're hurting me," she whimpered, but he wouldn't let up.

Her heart beat rapidly. He looked at her wrist where his knuckles were white from his intense grip and let go, allowing her hands to drop to the mat. Blood rushed to her deprived fingers.

Tears burned her eyes as he lifted her chin. She hardened her face as to not let him inside her bleeding heart. A tear escaped and he bent down and *kissed* it. She jerked at the unwelcome touch, but he held her in place forcefully.

"Don't," he growled, "move."

Keeping a numb appearance, Dylan didn't move, only breathed coarsely. Silas slid his lips to her mouth, her salty tear still on his lips. As if on autopilot, her body completely ignored the screaming pleas of her mind—her streaming tears like liquid suffering; the only indication of her true self.

He kissed her with more and more passion mistaking her tearful hiccups as moans of pleasure. Shoving her down on the mat, Dylan cringed. Her whole body still ached and Silas' brusqueness was only making it worse.

He tugged off his t-shirt, tossing it aside as he moved on top of her. She couldn't help but gaze at his perfect body laced with intricate scars—a silver lining on a tarnished blade. He suddenly ripped her tank straight down the middle exposing a black sports bra. She gasped as he fell on top of her, sucking kisses along her neck and collarbone while sliding his hands to remove the bra.

She felt regret attach to overwhelming fear and began to lose her resolve. What had she done? Was she really going to let him do this? She lay there detached from her body as he threw off her clothes, pawing at her breasts. He was brutal and primal as he moved his lips there. He bit and she arched her back as a sobered sob escaped her lips.

Tristian...

"Temperance," he growled against her stomach looking up, surprisingly careful not to touch her bandage. "Tell me what you want."

Her heart hammered so hard that her body shook with each pulse. *What do I want?!* Her mind screamed in rage.

She narrowed her eyes slightly. "I haven't done this before, *remember*?" she retorted with more confidence than she felt. "What do *you* want?" she snapped, unable to look at him without showing her intense hatred for him. She knew it was ridiculous, but she somehow felt betrayed by him.

He kissed her stomach gently. "I want you to be *mine*," he groaned as if it was hard from him to admit. "For the rest of my existence."

Her mind snapped like a rubber band and her breath vanished. She frowned in disbelief. "What aren't you telling me, Silas?" she spoke cautiously.

Could I ever be his?

"Be my mate and I will tell you everything," he spoke, shifting his face just above hers.

Everything? Can I really fake this to obtain information for my escape?

"I'm already yours for eternity," she breathed as her breasts pressed against his perfect chest, "What does it matter if I say yes or no?"

He searched her eyes. "Everything," he said softly, gliding a finger over her bottom lip. "I don't want you to be with me because you have to, but because you want to."

Dylan felt the neatly stacked bricks placed strategically around her heart falter. *What if there's no escaping?* A small voice called from inside her mind. *He's offering his heart on a platter, what will happen to me if I refuse?* The terrifying circumstances of her rejection played about her mind.

He suddenly grabbed her by the nape, fisting her hair with

inexplicable force. She winced, throwing both hands back to the source of discomfort.

"I. Love. You. Tempy," he growled, enunciating each word with a shake of his fist gripping her hair. Her eyes shot open at his statement. Darting her eyes between his, she felt the bricks begin to crumble, revealing her heart exposed and vulnerable. She wanted to scramble and put them back together before anyone saw; but, she was paralyzed by his words. His grip lessened and what she could only describe as desperation worked his features.

"I know this is all so sudden, but after almost losing you… I realized how much I need you in my life. You make this bitter place bearable. No, more than bearable. It's like a paradise when I'm with you." She suddenly noticed the line of red burnishing the outer rim of his eyes, as if he had been crying. "Maybe it's selfish…" he trailed off releasing his hold.

"Would we live here forever?" she asked.

"We can go wherever you would like." He rolled to the side, propping his head up with his elbow.

Anywhere?

This seemed to be her ticket to escape. What would it all really entail? A super fake physical relationship? Dylan's eyes greedily traveled along his naked toned chest straying on a cluster of round white scars. *Burns?*

"After you marry me of course."

She must have choked because the next thing she knew she was sitting up and covering her mouth with one hand and her nakedness with the other.

Silas sat up to pat her on the back. "Are you all right?"

She nodded vigorously, clearing her throat.

Married? She was only twenty-one! Her life had barely begun, let alone the fact that she had an infinite amount of time of her *immortal* life in front of her.

But, the little voice spoke again, *this is your life, no one's looking for you.* She'd either live content with this sad, twisted, but painstakingly beautiful demon next to her or face the repercussions of refusing his love. Taking a deep breath, she knew what she had to do to live, even if it meant to lie and live temporarily, in isolation.

She nodded, "Okay."

Continuing to stare at the floor, she practically heard the crazed smile that broke across his beautiful face. She slowly moved her eyes up to meet his. Without further ado, he pulled her into a slow sinful kiss.

She had caved.

Obviously happy at her assent, his hands landed low on her hips where he began pushing her pants down.

Whoa!

She pulled back and his smirk quickly fell.

"What now?" he grunted.

"I want to wait until after, you know, we're… *married.*" Her mouth was dry and the word came out thick like gauze.

He smiled seductively and nodded. "Whatever you wish, my love."

"Don't ever hurt me again, Silas," she warned, sitting back on her heels.

He looked up as something flickered in his eye and he slowly nodded. Part of her still felt terrified of his unstable mood swings, but this Silas, the one with his heart on his sleeve, this one she wouldn't mind living with here for the remainder of her time.

"So, you have my yes-" she stated unsure where this left them.

"Let's go sign the contract and tell my mother," he said throwing her bra in her face and pulling on his shirt.

Dylan blinked in confusion, "Contract?"

He nodded, wiping up the smeared water.

"Silas, what contract?" she said, severely cocking her head to the side.

"For you to be my mate," he said, as if it should be a given. Dylan slipped on her bra, picked up her ripped shirt and rose to a shaky stand.

"Why do we need a contract? I thought you meant just knowing I'm happy here was enough," she said skeptically.

"It is enough, but," he paused a moment, making Dylan's stomach roll with anticipation.

"But, what?" she snapped.

She saw a flash of expression cross his face like what a person would look like if their own dog had bitten them then watched it contort into a wicked smile. "I want to put it in writing, like a marriage contract in human terms."

"Now? You want to marry me, *now*?" she asked, incredulous and subconsciously twisting the torn tank top with severe force.

"We already want to be together... Why not make it official with the law?" He moved towards her seductively, freeing the death grip she held on the innocent fabric. "It's just a contract, Tempy."

'Just a contract, Tempy,' She mocked inside her head wanting to pummel all the contents of the pool at him. She instinctively grit her teeth at the horrible nickname, speaking through them, "Can I read it before I sign it?"

"Sure, love," as he traced the beds of his fingernails down her cheek. She winced internally at his touch, but outwardly showed no such thing.

This man is the reason I'm here.

The enormous gym felt suddenly as big as a cardboard box, closing in on her and taping up the sides. This was permanent. She didn't think the demon world rescinded contracts. Contracts

370

were the basis of their law. The fundamental pieces that kept demons contained. Those were probably one of the few honest qualities about this life. Not to mention, a large piece of her heart still belonged to Tristian, and this would be a written statement to block him out. What if she did find a way to escape?

Oh God, somehow I need to postpone this.

Her breath quickened and she snapped her fingers involuntarily when a thought surfaced. Silas raised an eyebrow at her action.

"My shirt," she bent down to retrieve her torn tank top. "*First*, I want to change, then we'll tell your mother, like at lunch? Then I want some kind of ceremony, you know *imported* white dress, the whole shebang. *Then* the contract."

That would give me what, a month, maybe six?

He smiled, "You'll have to forgive my insensitivity. In the demon worlds we don't have human weddings, just contracts," he said, then pressed a kiss to her forehead. "Go get changed. I'll meet you for lunch in an hour. We can do the wedding tonight."

He walked past her and Dylan's eyes grew so wide she thought they might actually pop out of her head.

Still standing in the vacant gym, Dylan's thoughts swam laps around her brain.

Tonight. He said tonight!

She was supposed to be the most powerful demon in the worlds, yet she felt helpless. Nothing was any longer in her control. She would marry Silas and she would be forced to... tears pricked her eyes, she couldn't even think it.

"Why couldn't I just have said I'd think about it?" she chastised herself.

Well, because you're stupid, Dylan.

This was her living hell, befit for a soulless demon. Her face contorted into disgust. She hated herself, hated her heritage, this house, this damn gym. She kicked the mat hard with the intent to release her inner rage, only making yet another part of her body ache.

With glassy eyes, Dylan limped away towards her bedroom, retreating in on herself. What could she really do? She wouldn't stand a chance of killing Silas or Lucia. She barely had control over tiny beads of water. What would she do? Flick levitating drops at them until she annoyed them to death?

Standing in front of her bedroom, she released a hopelessly tormented sigh then looked up, shaking her head before entering into what she assumed would be the last day in her private quarters.

Quietly closing the door, she spun around gasping as she threw her hand over her heart at the surprising presence of Peppi Calibri.

"Sorry, Miss!" The girl rushed to her side. "I was setting out your dress for this evening."

"No, it's okay. I was just deep in thought-"

Dylan forgot to finish her sentence when her eyes caught sight of the delicate dress placed carefully across her bed. It was ivory and glossy like polished bone.

Her wedding dress.

She slowly walked to it as if it were a vicious Cobra, liable to bite her at any moment. Touching the rich fabric, she began sucking in several shallow breaths. Her chest felt heavy and tight, as if someone was squeezing her, compressing her lungs into a tiny ball. She ached to run away. But she was trapped. Her legs unable to function and her vision tunneled. Clutching her throat, she couldn't seem to gather air.

Peppi had been pleading something, but Dylan couldn't get the one word out of her mind.

Tonight.

It repeated over and over again, drowning out all noise except the buzzing in her ears.

Tonight.

Dylan's knees buckled and she fell to the floor, yanking the little girl with her.

"Breathe!" yelled Peppi straight into her face.

She gasped, air scraped down her throat, filling her lungs like jagged ice. Dylan suddenly turned to Peppi, staring hauntingly at the little girl, who had worry carved into her features. The word escaped her lips. "Tonight."

"So, this is what I think it is?" Peppi inquired and Dylan nodded.

The girl puckered her brow. "Why are you marrying him if you obviously don't love him?"

"I was—I *am* scared to turn him down."

"I see," was all the little girl said as she stood and walked to the adjacent armoire pulling out a casual teal halter dress fitted at the waist. "Put this on, and get yourself together, Dylan. You need to convince them this is what you want. At least for the next hour. I assume you're joining them for lunch?"

Dylan's shocked face turned to her. "Why?" she whispered, emotion clogging her throat.

"I'll meet you here after. I want to show you something."

The little girl suddenly didn't seem so little anymore. She exuded confidence, far beyond anything Dylan was feeling.

Dylan nodded and stood, taking the little dress. She would do as the girl said. She would get through the lunch and go from there.

Lucia was absolutely beaming at the discussion of a 'merger.' Silas had Dylan's chair close to his and held her hand, interlocking their fingers.

Dylan wanted to hurl.

She was unable to eat very much, but put it off as pre-wedding jitters and wanting to look thin in her dress—things she had seen women say on reality TV. Lucia agreed, telling a similar tale of the day she mated with Silas' father. At the mention of his father, Dylan felt Silas grow rigid. She made a mental note to ask him about it later.

The fake smile she donned was starting to really pain her jaw when Lucia excused herself to grab a present. Releasing her cheeks from their necessary burden, Dylan leaned back against the chair.

"She's really excited about this," Dylan deadpanned.

"Yeah, you could say that." He chuckled and inched closer, sliding his hand from their grasp to her inner thigh and squeezed. "I'm personally excited for tonight," he breathed into her ear and bit her earlobe.

Now she definitely felt like she was going to retch, but she only smiled as he continued to kiss the space below her ear and down her neck.

Just through the meal.

He began to slide his fingers up her thigh. Her pulse skyrocketed and panic set in, but she kept a straight face. However, she couldn't seem to contain her rapid breathing, which he seemed to mistake as a positive sign. His hand grazed her underwear, prompting her thighs to tense.

I can't do this, I can't do this!

Just as she was about to voice the words aloud, Lucia slunk back into the room followed by her worm. Silas reluctantly withdrew his hand as Dylan released a rush of stressed air. She glanced at Silas, who had irritation written all over his face. Lucia sat, placing a small, dark blue box in front of Dylan.

"Temperance, since you have chosen to join our family, I thought it befitting to replace your current ring," she said with a sadistic smile. Dylan's eyes snapped to her only physical possession connecting her to her real parents.

Flustered, she looked to Silas. "P-please. Please, let me keep this ring. I won't wear it, just let me keep it."

Silas looked at her unsympathetically. "Give my mother the ring."

Lucia feigned an overly dramatic, shocked expression. "Dear, let her keep the ring. We'll discuss this on a *different* day."

Silas nodded as he and Lucia exchanged a look and they apologized. He then slid the box in front of Dylan beckoning her to open it. She did, slowly, as though she were turning the lever on a jack-in-the-box—a scary monster bound to pop out at any moment and kill her.

Carefully sliding the top off, Dylan took in the sapphire Planto family ring, all the while keeping a sincere face. She had known what it looked like from seeing Lucia wear it constantly and Silas' intermittent wearing of it.

It was sickeningly ornate as was the house she was imprisoned in. White gold looped and twisted in flour-de-les and flowers around the dark blue rock-like square stone, the size of an ordinary postage stamp. Keeping her Elementa ring on, Dylan slid the Planto ring on her left hand, ring finger.

It fit perfectly.

Silas reached for her hand and kissed it.

"You're going to love being queen of this palace." She frowned and flicked her eyes to Lucia, who seemed intrigued by the red wine in her glass.

Looking for words, any words to say that she could pass off as honest, she came up empty. He started to form a dark expression when Dylan placed a lazy hand on his cheek and kissed him deeply before pulling away. That was the best she could do. He smirked, locking his fingers with her left hand.

After the lunch, Silas walked Dylan back to her room. As she reached for the lever on the door, Silas shifted in front of her, blocking her entrance. He snatched her hips, pulling her until she collided with his chest. With both palms splayed across his hard pecks, she thought about the coming night. She still hurt everywhere and was dreading it. Silas showed no intentions of being gentle. He slid his hands quickly around to her rear, grabbing it and leaning into an intense kiss. Dylan's stomach flip-flopped, and her body instinctively tensed with sharp pain. He picked her up and she was instantly aware of just how much he wanted her.

"I don't think I can wait another second," his voice vibrated against her lips as he blindingly reached for the lever behind him.

Her mind reeled at how she could stop this, but knew nothing she could do or say would keep him from rage. She sent a silent prayer when he found the lever and they tumbled into her bedroom.

Dylan heard a small voice, "Oh! Sorry," Peppi said, pink faced. Silas dropped Dylan. Clutching her stomach, she winced as she hit the floor. Silas' growl at Peppi turned to worry as the he and Peppi huddled around her. Dylan waved them off.

"I'm fine. I just need to rest," she said in a strangled voice. Silas scooped her up and laid her gingerly on the bed beside her detested wedding dress.

Thank God.

"Are you all right?" Silas asked, cupping her face. His honest concern *almost* made her forget her hatred for him.

Dylan nodded and took a risk, "Maybe we should do the wedding when I'm healed. I'll probably be more fun then."

Silas' face was blank. "No," he spat out then lowered his voice, "Cheer up, *my love,* tonight you get to meet the rest of our family. We'll leave you to rest."

Dylan's eyes widened a bit. "No!" She cleared her throat. "I mean, I need Peppi to help me get ready." She stretched a pained smile across her face.

"Fine," he said with a skeptical glare, then turned away and left the room. Peppi held up a finger and tiptoed, lifting her ear to the door. She nodded as Dylan let out a rush of air.

"Ah, thank God you were here, Peppi."

The little girl smiled weakly. "Are you really hurt, or was it just a show for Mister Silas?"

"Definitely hurt when he dropped me. But I may have milked it to get him out of the room," she chuckled. "That lunch was intense." She sat up. "They gave me *the family ring*." She held out her wiggling fingers and Peppi's face contorted into disgust.

"Sorry, but now we have more time," the girl said speedily.

"More time for what?" She raised her eyebrows. "To wait until I'm forced to wear *that* dress?" She jerked her thumb to the adjacent gown.

Peppi shook her head. "What do you know about Mister Silas and his family?

"Well, one," she held up a finger, "that it's weird you call him Mister Silas instead of Planto. Two," she lifted another finger, "he's obviously the one in charge not Lucia. Three," she lifted another finger, "you already know the minor detail about them being my kidnappers and all."

Peppi looked annoyed as Dylan joked a bit exasperated. What else did she have left?

"I'm serious, Dylan," she reproved. "What do you know about *them?* By the way, we're not allowed to call him Mister Planto, his late father's name. And, yes, he is in charge."

"Sorry." She scrunched her face. "I know they can manipulate water and Lucia can heal."

"That's it?" the girl inquired.

"Yeah, is there more?" she cocked her head.

"Quite a lot more that you don't know but should." She

tapped her finger to her chin, making Dylan shift in her seat. "Well… um… I'll be back," she said moving towards the door.

Dylan jumped up impossibly fast and grabbed her arm. "Peppi, what the hell!" she squeaked. "You can't drop a bomb like that and just leave!"

The girl looked at her captured arm then at Dylan. "I want to show you, so you can see for yourself."

Dylan released her immediately and nodded. "Sorry. I'm kind of freaking out… in case you haven't noticed."

"It's okay. I'll be right back," the little girl announced and slipped out of the room.

Alone, Dylan began to pace about. Stopping at the exterior wall and falling against it, she peered up to the dark skylight. It was already night. The days were short and the nights long and dreary, especially without Tristian to lighten her darkness. Nothing was worth living anymore.

"Tristian, where are you? Why haven't you rescued me? I need you. I'm about to be lost forever," she spoke, already dead on the inside, scanning the dark hole of her skylight for signs of life or simply a star.

She felt anger suddenly flood her being. Anger from not including her friends in her life, having a lover that cared, or a family that wasn't afraid to come out of hiding to save her. It seared her vacant soulless void. She kicked the wall, feeling more inclined toward giving up on her pathetic life. Who would really miss her? Silas? She let out a disgusted laugh.

Would I even go to heaven? Is there an afterlife for demons? Tristian mentioned something about living in a void, but was that death or punishment? She shook her head, unable to remember.

The door opened and Dylan gasped, but soon realized it was only Peppi.

"Sorry to startle you, Miss."

"Did you find it?" Dylan inquired, still clutching her chest and feeling the pounding of her heart.

"Um, kind of. But perhaps not the "it" you're thinking of. Come with me," she said oddly.

Dylan frowned at the girl's demeanor.

"Are you okay, Peppi?" she asked, following her down the large corridor.

"Yes. I'm just about to show you something that will disturb you. I wish for your sake, you could continue to live in denial. But as you can imagine, I'm sure Silas will reveal the truth to you after the contract. At least this way you can prepare yourself."

She halted in front of the stone steps leading to the gym.

"It's in the pool." Peppi stated.

"What, Peppi?"

"The real demon you're marrying."

Dylan swallowed, staring at the foreboding door at the top. She slipped off her sandal clogs and took the stairs as quietly as she could with Peppi on her heels. Apprehension tightly coiled her belly as she slowly climbed each dreadful step.

Step.

Who was this demon?

Step.

Why had they kept him hidden?

Step.

Is he what is in the North Wing?

Step.

But why?

Step.

What about Silas?

Step.

Had this been his plan all along?

Step.

Is this more about a contract to keep me, than love?

Step.

Then the thought floated across her mind again. *Could I really live this way?*

Step.

Would death be easier?

She was near the final steps and stopped to seek Peppi's direction. The little girl gulped and stepped past her to lead the way.

If Dylan could aspire to be anyone at that moment she'd pick Peppi Calibri. She didn't know if this little girl was just as terrified because she hid it marvelously. The frail girl with chestnut brown hair and faded teal eyes had more confidence and strength than any adult Dylan knew.

The girls cracked open the door. Stepping through, they padded quietly on the dark blue, industrial carpet. Dylan could already hear someone splashing.

She imagined Silas' gorgeous body flexing and bulging as he slithered through the water in his gracefully perfected butterfly stroke. Except... she somehow knew that wasn't what she was about to witness.

She stepped from behind a wide, ornate column that had intricate designs of withering flowers and swirling lines and strained her eyes as a flashback from her bout of consciousness a couple of nights before enveloped her.

Scars, burned flesh, blood...

Dylan gasped, flattening herself against the stone. She threw her hands up to her mouth. Her eyes wide in utter shock at her sound.

Obviously hearing her, the demon immediately flipped his mutilated bald head in their direction.

In a blink of an eye, he appeared just around the column,

gripping Peppi's throat and lifting her struggling body high off the floor. Being this close, Dylan was able to catch a very quick, detailed view.

His body glistened with several beads of water trickling over the lumps and mounds of his butchered flesh. He had two slits for a nose where his original one had been clearly chopped off. His skin was pink and thin like paper; dark veins bulged over his large muscles and thick neck.

Sucking in slow, deep, trembling breaths, she listened to the demon interrogate Peppi.

"What are you doing here?" he growled, his voice gravelly like crackling fire laced with acid. The brave little girl wheezed from the taut grip on her throat. "Tell me!" he boomed, making Dylan jump and a tear to escape her eye. She clung to the column as if it was her lifeline as the fires housed in the raging candelabras that lit the gym sputtered, threatening to give out.

"M-miss Elementa, requested a yoga m-mat, s-sir," she stuttered.

Dylan heard a thump. A chill ran down her spine and dread licked her insides as horrible memories of her lifeless twelve-year-old body haunted her mind's-eye.

"Very well," he cleared his throat. "Don't keep her waiting, and *no one* is allowed in here while I am."

"Yes, s-sir."

Relief flowed through her and she struggled against almost collapsing to the floor in sheer elation.

Bracing herself, she was utterly afraid to move—that something as small as a twitch would announce her presence. She heard Peppi sob as she tore across the gym to retrieve the mat. The demon was unmoving, glued to his spot when Dylan heard him... sniffing?

Oh God! He can smell me!

She slapped a quivering hand over her mouth as tears now

flowed freely down her face. She could sense him about to round the corner as the flickering fire in the candelabra attached to the column leapt and extinguished—the ember sizzling as it gasped for its last breath of life.

Peppi cleared her throat. "Sorry, s-sir, I know how important the pool time is."

She heard him grunt right next to her ear as she squeezed her eyes shut and held her breath. The next thing she heard was a splash that signaled his return to the pool.

Without looking in the other direction, Dylan dashed out of the gym, only slightly surprised at her wicked speed.

Throwing open her bedroom door, she found herself in the far corner of the room, grasping the small trashcan. Her stomach lurched as the contents of her lunch discovered their way out. She continued to dry heave when a glass of water and a little girl with purpling bruises around her neck appeared at her side.

"Oh God, Peppi!" Dylan squealed. "I'm so sorry! I should have done something, but I was too afraid. Like a big stupid coward!" She sobbed into the small girl's shoulder, holding her tight.

"Shh," Peppi consoled. "It's nothing I haven't dealt with before."

Dylan had not felt the urge to die since her last attempt, but she just couldn't live this way. What was to hold the Plantos back from treating her the same way? Not to mention thoughts of marrying and being intimate with that repulsive creature made her want to slide broken glass across her throat and wrists until she slowly bled out in front of them all. But she knew Lucia would just heal her again; and with her knowledge on the situation revealed, Dylan would undoubtedly lose her privacy and upper hand.

"Was he planning on revealing that... *thing* after the contract?" Dylan asked between sobs.

"I believe so. I overheard him and the mistress talking about your children's power."

Dylan sat back, silent, finally understanding everything.

"That's why they want me."

"You are the most powerful demon in their worlds."

"How do you know all this?" Dylan frowned, suddenly cautious of the innocent Peppi.

"The mistress likes to talk when she drinks, and we have really nothing better to do than to listen." The girl shrugged gently rubbing her swollen neck.

"Why didn't you tell me before?"

"You were so sad and upset. I didn't think you would fall for Silas' manipulations. I saw that look on your face the night before the pool incident. I was planning on telling you the next day; but, I wasn't able to say anything because he was with you constantly after that."

Dylan nodded, still frowning.

"What is it?" Peppi asked.

"I can trust you… right?" she asked with an eerily calmness.

"Of course, Miss."

"I…" Dylan swallowed, looking down at her tightly wrung fingers. "I need you to help me kill myself."

CHAPTER 21

*"Sometimes what you're most afraid of doing is the
very thing that sets you free."*
Unknown

TRISTIAN held his tongue as Datu cursed his pathetic
life, again. Apparently the day wasn't going too good for the
vampire. Tristian felt a continuing lack of empathy for the
creature. He *liked* watching him starve. He liked counting the
splintering, black veins on his skin as it crusted over like a
chipping marble pillar. But the pleasure he derived from the
vampire's misfortune would soon end. It was only a matter of
time before Tristian got to kill Datu, or maybe he would let
Dylan do the honors.

Dylan.

He felt his heart twist with a dire need. Whenever he closed
his eyes all he could see was her. He missed her so damn much
it was hard to breathe. The blackened meat in his chest that only
seemed to pulse in her presence, ached in its stagnation. He
needed their dream, her startling gray eyes and delicious scent.
He just needed her.

Two long days of anticipation had past and to his
disappointment, no dreams of Dylan. He frowned, his knee
bouncing in a tight coil of tension. Perhaps it was due to his
coma. A mere side effect from lapsing brain waves and
flickering synapses of a dehydrated and broken mind; using

whatever it could to fix itself. But that didn't stop him from feeling like he'd lost her. It caused an emptiness inside him that he couldn't even put into words.

Sitting alone on the futon, he gathered his bearings waiting for Asher's cue on the weather in order to sprint to the castle. It was already dark. The weather always seemed to clear at sunrise and midday, both unfortunate times for their vampire companion. It caused them to keep a diligent vigil for changes in the weather. Tristian had debated, quite often, whether or not to just leave without Datu. But Asher had made a good point—they didn't know who would answer the door, and Datu would be expected and more likely granted entrance.

"I think it's clearing!" Asher yelled through the cabin.

Fucking finally.

Two days to wait it out in this weather was overkill. It was only a matter of time before Gerion sent out more worms to scour his real estate for frozen vampires or signs of a threat. But, knowing Dylan was just beyond the mountains increased his willpower to the fullest.

Pushing up from his spot on the futon, Tristian took the living room in three strides and forcefully yanked Datu up to a standing position by the collar of his shirt and shoved him toward the door.

"Shit, fine... Fine!" Datu snarled, swatting him away and stumbling over a split board in the floor.

Asher darted near them and grasped the icy knob. "All right, like we discussed, dart to the closest door, and Datu knocks. Once the doors open we'll all rush in and do what we have to do to get Dylan. Agreed?"

"Yes," answered Tristian in a clipped tone.

"Yup," said Datu in a similar tone.

Asher nodded and threw open the door. Unlike the last time they greeted the world of Zadar, the air was still. The moon lit the powder and sporadic, large, black boulders, casting everything in various shades of blue. Tristian took no time to dwell on the absolute beauty and darted toward the castle that imprisoned his woman.

Dodging and leaping, his vision was tunneled as the blanket of stars, bare trees, rocks, and snow all blurred around him. He was so close. If he thought hard enough, he imagined he could feel her spirit drawing him closer—asking him where he was, why he hadn't come sooner.

Ugh! His legs didn't move fast enough! He pushed harder, running faster than he ever had.

I'm about to be lost forever...

He didn't know why his mind was processing these miserable thoughts, but what he did know was that the snow was starting to descend again—distorting his vision. Ice and wind slapped his face, stinging like bites from a belt. A fog settled in front of him as his heart thundered in panic. He was blind; but, he continued forward conscious of only the few meters directly in front of him.

Suddenly the castle loomed up in front of him like a giant shipping freighter cutting through a foggy oblivion. Knife-like rocks split through his boots, slicing pain into his once numb feet, but he didn't care. He'd endure burns all over his body if it meant he'd find her safe and unharmed so he could take her away to their personal refuge.

Reaching the worn stone siding, he halted only to lean slightly against the frozen slick stone. Asher and Datu followed suit kicking up rubble, ice, and wind. Datu slammed his fist against the large double doors and they waited.

Tristian's body wracked with the throbs of his pulse as the storm began to settle back into its chaotic flurry, numbing and stinging his exposed arms and penetrating the thin fabric of his jeans and T-shirt. With shaky hands, he felt for one of his daggers, the black shorter one for sure. Bending his fingers, pain and stiffness shot up his arm, making it hard to grasp the hilt. Just as he was about to pull out the blade, the doors groaned and the hinges puffed ice. He watched Datu step inside, using a mortal's pace.

Glancing in their direction, Datu nodded in a swift, barely noticeable, movement through the thick blizzard; but, Tristian saw it as clear as day and so did Asher. Dashing through the opening just behind Datu, who seemed to already be feeding on an old woman in a black cotton dress. The woman lay across his one bent knee with a blissful smile and eyes closed. The vampire, while sucking, jerked his head towards the adjacent corridor.

Just as they were about to head in that direction, several worms spilled out of the corners of the castle's foyer, gleaming like tall, golden soldiers, passing a large steel throne and a series of thick pillars. There were so many of them, Tristian didn't even know where to start. Flashing his eyes around the rapidly filling space, Tristian retrieved his short blade. Tightening his hold on the dagger, he watched as at least ten worms power walked towards him, dragging their large bare feet and crusted axes.

"Fuck it," he muttered and launched himself at them.

Grasping the back of a worm's neck, Tristian jumped and threw his knee up to its face—crunching bone and features. He then pivoted around, throwing his blade into the throat of another.

One lunged for him. He ducked and connected a right. It wasn't too long into the fight that Tristian realized the worms didn't care about themselves. They took his beatings; they bled and died as if it were just another day.

A worm toppled over as his axe swung in large, leaping circles, slicing a couple other worms open and shoving three to the hard floor. Tristian chuckled, turning again and with a swift kick knocked another golden figure down. Springing onto a struggling one, he stomped on its neck, pulverizing its windpipe.

Spotting metal in his peripheral vision, he rolled away from a colossal swing of another worm's axe. A glimmer of golden curls rushed in front on him and tackled the on-coming worm Tristian had missed. Asher snatched its axe and began twirling it through the air up and around, slicing the oncoming worms in to several pieces.

Glancing back at Tristian, Asher yelled, "Go find her!"

He almost shook his head "no" unable to leave his friend to fight *his* battle, when Datu appeared at his side, lunging his long nails out in front of him and snatched a worm's neck, ripping its throat out.

Blood and shrieks seemed to emanate all around him as Datu caught his attention. "We've got this! Go get her!"

In that moment, he realized he wouldn't kill Datu. He didn't know if he had forgiven him, but it was a small but solid step in that direction. Tristian nodded with a sincere and panicked look, then bolted to the adjacent hallway leading to his woman.

◇◇◇

Peppi gasped again as she paced the bedroom.

"No, no, no! Miss! I can't!"

Dylan looked at the little girl who was absolutely beside herself at Dylan's request.

"I can't live here anymore." She knew this was the answer. Her heart felt like it was torn to shreds unable to withstand any more of this life. Maybe it was the coward's way, but she knew no other way out. And like hell she'd allow that demon or Silas to use her to mother some demented children or for sexual release. She wanted children, but not like this, not with *that*, and not now.

"My soul."

Dylan snapped out of her dire thoughts. "*Excuse* me?"

"My soul, take my soul." Dylan smiled sadly and shook her head at the selfless child.

"How would-" Dylan stopped, remembering the Shadow Horde.

"That would alert your government, no?" Peppi said wild-eyed. "That way you don't have to die, Miss."

She didn't know.

"It doesn't work like that. And as generous your offer… I can't take your soul. I can't imagine doing that to anyone, let alone someone I have grown to love as family."

Peppi started to cry. "Please, take it and save yourself! My life is this, nothing more and nothing less. A person doesn't need a soul for this life. I won't marry or fall in love. I don't get to have aspirations or an education. I get to have children with the other servants to produce more servants. Believe me when I say I already feel soulless. Make me numb to this life, Dylan."

Peppi's words ate at the scraps left over of Dylan's strength. This wasn't a place for a pre-teen. She should be in gymnastics or dance classes, loathing homework, and gushing over guys like Jacob Mancuso.

"So help me, Dylan." Peppi grabbed her shoulders exasperated. "TAKE THE DAMN SOUL before he comes back in here," she barked.

Without thinking Dylan snatched her wrist. "I'm sorry," she breathed as she sent a quick blast of *Unda* to her small wrist. "Nod when you feel numb... if you can. I don't want to hurt you."

"Okay," Peppi squeaked taking in sharp bursts of air while staring at her arm, no doubt from the strange sensation blanketing her skin. Seconds later, she saw Peppi's eyes roll back in her head as she collapsed on the plush carpeted floor.

"Peppi?" Dylan spoke softly.

When she didn't answer, Dylan swallowed against the burn

in her throat. She had no idea what she was doing as terror burned inside her. She was about to forever change this girl's life as well as mark a hit on herself. Once she started this there was no going back, but what could she go back to? Silas? To that thing? A shudder crept, like countless insects crawling across her body.

"I can do this. No one is looking for me. This is the only way out," she chanted, egging herself to move forward.

Dylan slowly crouched above Peppi as she lay soundless and peaceful. A small smile was on her lips and her hair fanned around her.

Taking a deep breath, Dylan closed her eyes. Instantly assaulted by the deep green abyss that was Tristian's eyes, she thought about the night she spent in his arms at the motel in Santa Monica. Despite everything that had happened, it was the best night of her life. She had never felt the connection she shared with Tristian with anyone else. It was mind blowing and grounding all at the same time. Even though it had been scary as hell, Dylan knew from somewhere deep inside, she was made for him, and he for her. She couldn't imagine being with anyone else, and she didn't want to be.

Half way through the night, she had awakened briefly and caught him staring at her with so much emotion in those gorgeous emerald orbs. His forehead was slightly creased as if he had been studying her features. Seeing her, he quickly slapped his lids shut, feigning sleep. She had wanted to touch him, kiss him, and grasp the inner workings of his mind and heart, but she was still insecure about his feelings, about her feelings. If only she knew what he had been thinking. The way he'd washed her, held, and caressed her, and tried to keep her safe showed how much he cared for her, didn't it? *None of this was a mistake. I do feel it too...* But insecure thoughts plagued her mind that night, keeping her from jumping on him right then and there, but God only knew now, she wished she had.

Retreating further, Dylan thought about her one and only friend, Aria, and the time she dragged her to yoga.

"That's your instructor?" she had asked ready to pounce.

"Simmer down, Wan," Dylan smirked tossing her a yoga mat. "He's actually a really good teacher. Of course the view is a nice incentive." She winked knowing damn well that's all he was. She never thought in a million years he'd ask her out.

"I think I'll ask for a private lesson." Aria gave a gigantic smile, nodding her head and obviously turning those promiscuous wheels in her mind.

"Oh boy," Dylan muttered with a pseudo-roll of her eyes.

"Why don't you ask him out?" Aria whispered even lower as Garret chanted some Mantra.

"Wahe Guru, Wahe Guru, Wahe Guru, Wahe Jeeo"

"What the hell was that?" Aria hollered across the silent meditating class to Garret.

Dylan burst out laughing as Garret tried to keep a straight face, but failed miserably.

"The ecstasy of consciousness is my beloved," he translated with an insecure smile.

Isabel pulled out the two muffin tins practically spilling with fluffy Banana Bread. A treat they had made together. It was the first day Dylan had ventured out of her new room since the accident. Dylan boasted a huge smile that seemed to take up her entire face as she waited impatiently for Isabel's family-famous treat. She couldn't even wait until they were cooled off before diving into the soft dough.

Taking a ravenous bite, she almost gagged as they both realized, simultaneously, that Dylan had accidentally switched the salt and sugar.

Bombarded by a series of overwhelming emotions, tears threatened, but after crying so much for her parents' death, crying over anything else felt superfluous. Even at seven years-old, she felt herself age on the inside. She couldn't enjoy something as simple as a muffin, and she felt like she didn't deserve to. Not after surviving, after letting her family die.

Isabel quickly ate the salty bread anyways to make her feel better, forever calling it Savory Banana Bread. She was always looking for ways to comfort or cushion Dylan's disasters or mistakes, which only made her love Isabel even more. Dylan hated that she was leaving her grandma alone with no family and no one to help go through Dylan's parents' boxes each year. But the worst part was that now she would have to go through even more boxes, Dylan's.

Fireflies flickered all around her as she remembered the area vividly. She was now with her mother and father. They were in their backyard toasting marshmallows over a fire pit in the humid San Diego summer evening. The night was beautiful with billions of twinkling dots sparkling above them. She held the opened, metal clothes hanger, the end stuck with a marshmallow over the crackling heat. She watched as it caught on fire burning the white to a bubbly char.

Dylan had started crying when her mother gently seized the hanger and blew to extinguish the blaze. Tears rolled down Dylan's tiny cheeks as her mother squeezed out the white melted interior onto the graham cracker and Hershey's bar.

"There, there, *ma bichette*," my little doe, her mother crooned. "Remember, changing is not always beautiful, but sometimes necessary to unlock the best part." She smiled, kissing her tears away and handing her the gooey treat.

Opening her eyes, she wasn't sure why her mind was replaying those memories, but she felt strangely at peace. It was almost meditative. She was going to meet her parents. Demon or not, she would knock down Heaven's door to be with them.

Glancing back down at Peppi, Dylan surged just a bit more Unda for good measure. The air was too quiet as she slowly inhaled. Even her pounding pulse had stilled, nothing made a sound, not even the ticking of her silver clock. The same sensation with the rapist began to take form, but this time she felt serene and *invigorated*.

Peppi's body jerked as her back arched off the floor in one fluid motion. Her mouth fell agape and a mist surged through the opening. It shimmered like a thousand diamonds illuminated by a source of light brighter than the sun; it was truly beautiful. The light was both blinding yet inexplicably comfortable to stare at. Peppi's soul was stunning. It glowed with the beauty of who she was. Tears flowed freely from Dylan's eyes as the mist formed into a diamond-encrusted mask of Peppi's small face, then sifted into Dylan's mouth like grains of sand in the wind.

As the light died, Dylan felt a tingling sensation commence slowly in her stomach, a force flowing deliciously throughout her veins like the best drug ever invented.

Then it hit her like a ton of bricks.

Her mind exploded in ecstasy and her body felt like it was floating. Everything around her intensified, saturated in bright colors and amplified smells. The carpet, exceptionally plush between her toes, felt woven by angels. Even the sickeningly sweet vanilla of her quarters smelled rich of toasted beans dipped in sugar.

Her body undulated and danced to the pulsation of her heartbeat as her head fell back. She was so happy, content, *euphoric*. She wanted nothing more than for Tristian to hold her, touch her, kiss her mindlessly; *to jump into his arms and fly far, far away.*

She sighed, collapsing on the sumptuous carpet and lay with her legs at an angle and her arms above her head. She waited for her inevitable death as she cried tears of joy and giggled absurdly.

CHAPTER 22

"New beginnings are often disguised as painful endings."
Lao Tzu

HIS breath came forth in quick pants, his pulse raced, and his hair clung to his forehead as frustration seeped from every pore. He groaned, feeling like he was trudging through syrup; like that dream where no matter how fast you try to run, you just can't seem to move quickly enough or make it to the end of the hall.

Every time he rounded another corner the halls were the same. The same series of floral oil paintings, golden sconces, endless carpet runners, and wood doors. He threw open each door, cautiously at first, then with more force, finding room after dark room of unoccupied bedrooms.

Where was he, a maze?

He bounded another duplicate hallway and came to a junction of hallways. His pulse soared as he stopped and grabbed his hair on the brink of screaming. Unable to decide which corridor to follow, he looked around. Narrowing his eyes, he felt as if he'd entered a fun house. He might as well have been standing in a room full of mirrors as time moved on, racing without him.

Taking a chance, he chose left, feeling his body pulled down a particular hallway. His feet propelled forward as his mind struggled to catch up. He wanted to call out her name but worried he'd alert the Plantos of his location.

Where is she!

Bounding another hallway, he almost ran face first into a golden worm.

"Shit!" he yelled, rolling on the floor, just missing the first of many swings of its sharp talons.

He was *not* expecting that.

It swiped again catching him in the side. He hissed through the sting while trying to regain balance and evade any more damaging strikes. Tristian flipped around kicking the back of its legs, making the creature buckle forward. It elbowed him to the floor. Laying on his back and searching for *Argyre*, he kicked his way back forcing distance between them. The creature wasted no time crawling toward him, his claws slicing the carpet into thin shreds. Yellow drool sloshed out its mouth and its tongue licked across jagged teeth, hungry for blood, *his blood*.

Grabbing the hilt, he tugged, but the dagger seemed caught in his jeans. Pulling harder he heard the fabric rip slightly when the worm swiped again, grazing his leg. Tristian abandoned the task, rolled to his side and stood. The thing instantly lunged without thought, swiping its nails like a deranged cat. Tristian sprung as well, tucking in his head. To his relief, he felt himself collide with damp, sand paper skin as they tumbled together to the floor. Tristian managed to elbow the center of its face as the creature clawed his back. A long rumbling groan burned his throat at what felt like a series of knives dragging across his skin.

Squinting through the thick molasses of pain, he drove his fingers downward and speedily snatched its head; yanking it to the side with all his might, he broke its neck. The creature fell slack to the floor and Tristian momentarily closed his eyes— concentrating on healing his wounds.

He snapped his head up and hastily jumped off the worm.

Darting his eyes about, he tried to remember which room it was guarding. Flexing his jaw, he began throwing doors open, eyeing each space thoroughly.

Yanking open the third door, he rushed in—his eyes searching the room. He saw a young girl unconscious near the far wall. Traveling his eyes further, he suddenly felt the blackness inside him clear into a channel of bright light.

He had found her, *there was Dylan.*

She was lying opposite the small girl, her face flushed and swollen from crying. His breath caught as worry flashed through his mind. He was afraid to move.

What if she's dead?

The door clicked shut behind him and her head flung upright. She blinked repeatedly as if she weren't positive he really stood before her. He suddenly remembered that he was covered in blood and was probably a terrifying sight. The silence hovered for what felt like an eternity. Their chests heaving. A single tear escaped her azure eye.

Snapping time into the present, her eyes widened as she scrambled towards him. Tristian met her in the middle, slapping their bodies together in a strong embrace.

"It's you?" She pulled back, clutching the sides of his face fiercely as if she were to let go he'd vanish in her fingertips. "It's really you?" she searched his face like he was the last thing she ever expected to see and began wiping the blood away.

He nodded, suddenly unable to speak. Tears began to stream down her face as she smiled. She was even more beautiful than he remembered. Without a second more hesitation, he crashed his mouth on hers, melding their lips in perfect alignment. He felt her melt at the touch of his tongue against hers.

She tasted just as he had remembered. They smiled randomly between urgent kisses as something new ignited within his body. He felt whole with her, like she was the soul he never possessed. Nothing else mattered. He had his woman back, finally, *right here*. He wanted to stretch this moment and run away with her. Far away from the Three Kings, the Elementas and everything underworld. She never deserved any of this and he still needed to get her away from the Plantos. At the thought of Gerion, anger rippled through his core in a frenzied attack, but Dylan's frantic voice broke his internal volcanic tirade.

"I thought I was on my own," she cried kissing him eagerly. "That no one was looking for me. He wanted me to sign the contract tonight. I thought I had no other choice." She looked into his eyes for a severe moment then brought her mouth back to his as if starved for her, unable to get enough. Shit, he couldn't get enough.

"I never stopped searching," he pulled away and smiled; so happy he'd finally found her, taking in her beauty once more. Dipping back to her delicious mouth, he spoke to her between kisses, "I couldn't even. Get you out. Of my dreams."

"You were in mine as well. We were on the beach. The same dream. Over. And over. And over. Again," she purred kissing each corner and crevice of his face.

He felt for her hand that rested on the side of his face; traveling his fingers over her knuckles to her fingers, he fused them together and brought her wrist to his nose, inhaling the secret concoction that was Dylan.

She closed her eyes, reveling in bliss.

Could it be? He regarded her as the words fell from his lips. "How is it I fell so hard so fast?"

Her eyes flicked open and beheld disbelief as she answered the question exactly as he'd remembered it ever so seared into his mind.

"I don't know. I've never felt this way about anyone. You've got me enamored Tristian—H-how is that possible?" she stammered. "You were with me the whole time and I had no idea?"

He shook his head, pushing dewy strands of her overgrown bangs away from her face, not quite understanding it himself.

"I promised to never leave you remember?" He chuckled, dipping back to her lips, this time slower, emotion spilling from his heart like honey. He was hers as much as she was his. Nothing could keep them apart now. She owned him and he'd follow her to the gates of hell if need be.

His body felt like it was soaring and his pulse beat to the melody that was hers. He needed her to know she was never a mistake, but the best decision he'd ever made; how sorry he was for leaving her, for his ignorance, and most of all how long it had taken him to rescue her.

His blood boiled with passion as he gripped her slimmer hips, tempted to throw her on the adjacent bed and lick her sweat-covered skin. Sliding his hands up her body, he traced his fingertips along her shoulders frowning at the scars—the same ones he felt in their dream. She parted her wanton lips, needing him.

"I guess I should believe you now," she laughed, biting down on his lower lip and looking into his eyes through lowered lashes boasting the sexiest grin he'd ever seen.

Damn, and she's mine.

"Dee," he groaned, never wanting to break their hold but needing to. He had to get them out of there.

"Oh. My. God," she moaned. "It's so good to hear my name from your lips."

She leaned in to kiss him again, but he grabbed her wrists holding them between their chests. Reluctantly pulling away, he felt something inside him break at the lost contact. Something small but significant. It screamed, threatening to shrivel and implode if he didn't taste her one last time. But he ignored it.

"Dylan, we need to get out of here before-" The door suddenly burst open revealing, what Tristian thought was Gerion's older brother.

Snapping their heads to the doorway, the demon looked at them, narrowed his eyes, and stripped himself of his disguise.

◇◇◇

"You," Silas' voice had grown deeper and crackled like glass ground against pavement.

As he stood, his body began to morph. His perfect skin split like paint cracking on an expanding balloon, only to reveal shriveled rotten flesh underneath. His nose and hair evaporated, leaving holes and mutilated skin. The air bloomed into something awful as the walls began to transform, splintering and oozing, as a red substance throbbed, trying to break free.

Trembling and keeping close to Tristian, she watched as plaster and glass rained around them; as the demon she had almost given herself to, *changed*.

Stretching his body and popping his neck, the disfigured demon from the pool exhaled in relief before snapping his face forward—revealing beady blood-orange eyes.

Silas' eyes.

His pupils winked with every breath, flexing the walls. Dylan smothered a scream into Tristian's chest.

"Gerion," Tristian hissed.

She jerked her head upright and away from the comforting scent of home. Silas narrowed his eyes at Tristian then at Peppi, before flashing his flaming gems back at Dylan, registering what she had done.

Silas marched towards them as Tristian pushed Dylan out of the way.

Silas shoved Tristian propelling him across the room, smashing him into the wall as the plaster broke, pouring chunks and oozing red globs on and around him. He groaned from the impact as Dylan shrieked from a distance.

Silas wasted no time and grabbed her around the neck, cutting off her air. She wheezed and clawed at his hands, her lungs begging for a reprieve.

"You," he growled. "You brought the Shadow Horde. You undeserving piece of-"

But she never heard what she was because Tristian had charged head-on into his side, causing the demon to crash through the wall, ending up in the ornate bathroom. Water sprayed from the broken pipes through the demolished vanity where Silas had landed. She grasped her neck, coughing and sucking in air as she braced her body with her other hand. Tristian immediately turned and rushed to her side. He helped her up as he pushed debris away from her face, examining her with anguish.

"You thought there was no way out," he panted. "That no one was coming for you." She listened as he echoed her words gravely, finally understanding the gravity of the situation.

She nodded wearily, never loosing eye contact. "They're coming to kill me."

"Dylan, we can still leave. I know how to make these things disappear. This isn't over. It can't be over," his voice was shaky and pleading. "I can't live without you. Dee, you have stolen my heart." Tears flowed in gushes down her face and over his hands. He brushed his thumb over her bottom lip. Releasing it, he bent down and kissed her with need and passion. Like the force of a great wave, his love swallowed her whole.

She knew then he was her other half, her *soul*.

He broke their kiss and opened his mouth to say something that she longed to hear but clamped it shut as he caught sight of a form closing in on them from the corner of his eye. It was Silas charging at them yet again. Tristian quickly shoved Dylan out of the way and to the wall, inadvertently making her impact it with a crushing force. Her head burst with pain and a loud ringing reverberated in her head, masking the clash of battle in the room.

She peeled open her heavy eyes, focusing past the agonizing haze and watched as Silas and Tristian tumbled about, breaking everything in their paths. She tried to move, but dizziness and gummy, black spots overcame her. She suddenly felt cold and wet. Pausing, she held up a trembling red hand in front of her face.

Bloody hands, she thought with wide-eyes.

Looking down, she knew the wound in her stomach had ripped open, soaking her dress and spilling down her shivering legs. She felt weak, but managed to push herself up on the oozing wall only to fall again.

Tristian was on top of Silas, throwing punches, *winning*; when he noticed her distress. Losing his focus for only a second, Silas took the opportunity and pounded his fist into Tristian's jaw, knocking him off kilter. Silas laughed and pinned him down, using his beefy legs atop Tristian's struggling arms. Silas continued throwing blow after crushing blow as Dylan noticed Tristian trying to grab something in his back pocket.

Dylan watched Tristian being pummeled but she felt frozen. It wasn't real. None of it was real! A jarring noise split through her ears when she realized she had been screaming. She didn't want to believe it, but she had no other choice. She had to stop him.

Flopping onto her stomach, she tried with everything she had to move more than an inch. Finding momentum, she dragged herself closer, grazing Peppi's feet. Without a second thought, she yanked off Peppi's shoe and hurled it at Silas, hitting his baldhead dead center but, unfazed, he wouldn't stop.

The ringing grew less intense as she listened to him grunt, throwing full force behind each sickening blow occasionally missing when Tristian jerked his head left and right.

Crawling closer in short agonizing puffs, she noticed Tristian finally free what looked like a short knife. He flipped the white hilt and stabbed the closest thing: Silas' thigh. The demon roared, throwing one more punch before yanking the blade free. Blood gushed out of the opening.

Finding some unidentified strength deep within, she dug her nails into the carpet. The ground rippled and cracked. Moisture from the room seemed to affix to her skin like a magnet. She clawed her way across the room and threw herself on top of Silas' scarred back. His skin blistered, bubbling at the contact, causing an agonizing shriek to escape his mouth.

But he continued to break Tristian's face, holding the knife in his other hand. Scrambling to his armed hand, Dylan latched herself on his shoulder flailing for the blade.

Silas laughed bitterly. "Looking for this, my love?" He brought it up, just out of reach and then drove it straight into Tristian's chest. "Go ahead, grab it."

Dylan screamed with horror and, without thinking, bit into Silas' neck—hard.

Silas bucked, but she wouldn't let go, she wouldn't give up on Tristian. Her nails bit into his skin to secure her hold. Bitter blood filled her mouth as the beast bellowed a growl as he stood, flinging her off. She hit the bed and crumpled into a heap on the floor. Her face smashed into the torn and plaster-filled carpet as she struggled to pull herself up; but, she was too weak.

Losing too much blood. In too much pain.

Pain for Tristian, for her aching worthless body, for Peppi, and for not being able to do anything to stop the chaos.

She collapsed once more and stared at Tristian's broken body. A dagger was stuck in the middle of his chest almost flush to the hilt. He coughed and gurgled blood as he brought both hands to the handle trying to pull it free. Silas chuckled sadistically as he brought his foot to the top of the knife and shoved it the rest of the way in. Tristian spasmed, spraying blood as Silas bent down and whispered something in his ear.

Tristian spit in his face, his teeth and lips stained red. "Never."

Silas smirked and strode towards Dylan as she tried to scoot away. He was faster. Silas' scarred knees appeared in her line of vision. He grabbed her chin, yanking it up to his disfigured face. His blood seeped down her chin.

"You *disgust* me," she spat, as he grabbed her injured arm digging his sharp, black nails into her recent wound. She began to sob and he said nothing while pulling her upright.

"I thoroughly enjoyed this adventure we've had," he purred, shifting back into the Silas she knew. "I liked tempting you, watching you, and easing those doubtful thoughts into your mind every day. It was so easy." His grip tightened, digging his nails deeper into her gash and she contracted in pain.

"You are so trusting for such a strong demon." He released one shoulder, snaking a bloodied nail down her cheek. "And you tasted so good. It has been a while since I've sampled another demon." He paused his nail just over her trembling lip. "But no matter what you thought I was... I think, in a way, I really did love you... It doesn't matter, because you are *forever* mine, *Tempy*."

A strange sadistic laugh bubbled up in her throat, which she almost didn't recognize.

"You don't even know what love is." She flicked her eyes at Tristian's still form and tears spilled out of her eyes as her heart began to tear into tiny pieces, never to be fixed again.

No Silas wouldn't ever know love. Love was not being able to imagine a second of your life without the other person. Love was opening up and trusting the person implicitly. Love hurt, but only because it made you feel. It woke the strings in your heart that only the person you loved could pluck. Tristian was that to her. He was her love.

"Every day I was here, *every time* you planted your manipulations into my mind, another piece of me died inside. You've taken *everything*." She brought her bloodshot eyes back to his. "And there is nothing for you to take anymore." Hardening her features, she wheezed, "Silas, or whoever the hell you are, I was *never* yours and I never did nor could I ever love you. *No one could ever love you*," she growled, spitting his stinking blood in his face.

The hot ember in his eyes erupted into black flames.

"Huh," he grunted, using his forearm to wipe where she spat. "Well, it's too bad we never got around to consummating this *marriage*." He smiled, licking a spot of blood at the side of her mouth. She jerked, but he held his tongue there for a beat, enjoying her struggle. "But I think I'll enjoy watching the life drain from your pathetic body even more."

He brought his hand to her throat, lifting her, dangling just above the carpet.

She thrashed wildly. Her toes brushed the ground in frantic spasms.

He smiled.

Giving up, she stilled. "I'm already dead," she rasped and his smile fell. "There is nothing left," she repeated, shooting daggers as an even more disturbing smile broke across his face.

He began closing in on his grip. "As you wish, *my love*."

His crushing strength squeezed her neck. She felt her face flush and her eyes bulge. Letting her body go slack, she closed her lids; several tears freed from her new colorful eyes. She didn't even get to look at them. She imagined they looked like Peppi's. That a piece of her strong soul filled the gaping chasm inside. Maybe with her soul carrying Dylan, she could make it to heaven.

Surrendering, Dylan let go of all that was or ever could be, and let fate finally take its course.

A cracking bang at the door broke her submission. She felt his hands release slightly, allowing air to scramble down into her lungs. Dylan gasped and flicked her eyes open and at Silas, who looked a mixture of panicked and outraged.

Another bang sounded and Silas immediately dropped her. She clutched her neck and wheezed, sucking in deep breaths and willing the fog to clear from her vision.

Gaining clarity, she glanced at Tristian. Her heart felt like it was being torn straight out of her chest, slowly, only to be stabbed repeatedly in front of her face.

This was her fault.

He had come here for her and she didn't wait long enough. She had been selfish to think suicide was an answer, and the fact that she even needed him to save her was her fault. She ignored his warnings, not taking anything seriously until the unthinkable had happened.

Now, he was possibly dead, and she would die soon, too.

She flicked her eyes to Silas and watched him throw his hands against the exterior facing wall. A dark swirling shape appeared as the door shook again, the hinges splintering at their last hold.

She clawed and scooted to Tristian's broken body lifting his limp head in her blood-soaked lap. Her tears fell on his face as she clutched him, sobbing and refusing to let go.

"You're okay." She leaned back, smoothing the hair from his face. "You hear me? You're okay. I promise it's all going to be okay."

She couldn't stop the winded sob that tore from her throat as she tried to stop the relentless bleeding without touching the impaled knife, worried she'd inflict more harm than good. With a heavy heart, she brought his hand to her mouth where she kissed it repeatedly then held it against her cheek.

"*I'm so sorry.*"

His eyes fluttered and she gasped, tightening her hold on his hand. He smiled weakly, sputtering blood and opened his hand to cup her face, he whispered, "I love you."

He brushed his thumb over her lip and she caught a quick glimpse of his beautiful eyes. A flash of ethereal blue glowed in the corner of her eye, pivoting her attention to the snarling Silas.

Tristian's arm fell slack as the door burst open, splinters of wood pouring around the opening.

Turning back to Tristian, Dylan slapped his cheeks lightly, frantically searching for life within him. "My God, please Tristian, wake up!" Shaking her head from side to side when she came up empty, she bellowed a long, agonizing, "Noooo!" She knew in her heart he was gone.

Wiping her nose with the back of her hand, she looked at the door as four demons clad in head to toe black leather uniforms filled the room. They posed, their hoods drawn, shadowing their features. Each was wielding a long sharp blade in a gloved hand. They stood erect and looked exactly like what she thought the Shadow Horde would look like.

Sucking in a sharp breath, she hugged Tristian's body, bringing him limply against hers. "Please, wait for me," she cried, kissing his swollen and split, unresponsive lips. "I'm right behind you. Wait for me, Tristian."

She glanced in the direction of Silas, only to see he was gone. A patch of charred plaster left in his wake.

Looking back at the black army, a man in golden robes sauntered through the solid figures, a wicked smirk smeared across his face.

He had long black hair that grazed his shoulders, thin lips, and black, lizard-like eyes framed by a long jagged scar over his cheek and right eyebrow.

"Temperance Elementa," he beamed, punctuating each

syllable of her name. He slapped his hands together, rubbing them like a true villain as his plan fell into place. He seemed excited and she couldn't fathom anyone being happy right then, or ever. The world was dark again without her light. Now her hope was to see Tristian on the other side. Otherwise, she knew heaven would be dark, too.

Her eyes rounded and she threw her attention back to Tristian—lifting his body against hers as she cried. Her body shook with the absolute realization of his death, her death, and the fact that Silas got away. This wasn't her fairytale, her happy ending. The hero died and the villain had won.

She sobbed, as grunts and moans spilled out of her mouth. She didn't care. All that she could process was the mourning of her soul.

She felt cold, leather-wrapped hands grasp her shoulders and another set of black arms wrap her waist. She screamed and clutched his shirt just above the knife in desperation, her nails digging into the fabric. The action made his body arch and collapse when she let go. She screamed Tristian's name as they lifted her away.

"Bind her," a deep, throaty voice commanded from behind her.

A soldier yanked her wrists together in front of her as she struggled with all her might. But even she knew her strength had been depleted—sucked away with the broken contact from her lover.

The figure bound her with a hot glowing wire, biting into her delicate flesh. Once the wire was fixed, she suddenly felt tapped and fell slack against the shadow soldier holding her wrists.

The soldier seemed startled and braced her before speaking through his dark hood, "Temperance Elementa." She looked up into the blackness of his silhouette, her eyes wide with tears like a small child. "You are in violation of the Collector's Code.

407

You will be tried and convicted for your actions against the Three Kings."

Unable to protest or speak, all she did was blink at the talking being holding her. The man in golden robes was still *smiling*.

"Augusto," the man commanded, as a shadow soldier stood erect waiting for direction. "Check the child and demon for life, will you?"

"Yes, sir," he spoke taking the vast room in two strides. He bent over Peppi first. "The child is alive."

"Good." The man in golden robes smiled wider. "Astrid," he called to another soldier behind him. "Find to whom she belongs and bring them here."

"Yes, sir," she snapped then dashed down the hall.

Dylan's eyes moved back to Augusto and watched him despondently as he leaned his broad form over Tristian's body, hoping she was wrong and that he still lived.

Time stood still as her heart's pounding snuffed out all noise in the room.

"Dead, sir." As the words impacted her brain she grew faint and blacked out.

Fluttering her eyes open, she felt herself lying in someone's arms as two shadows bickered between one another.

"...She just passed out, what was I supposed to do? Let her drop?"

"She's awake." From this angle she could make out an artful neck, roping thick veins, and a tiny scar like a misshapen Y or lazy X. She focused on the tiny blemish wondering how it came to be. If her hands weren't bound, she would have tried to touch it. Whatever the binding was, it made her feel exhausted and unable to concentrate on anything too substantial.

"Why did she pass out? Is she malnourished?" inquired a male voice separate from the two above her. It was a bit higher pitched than the rest, younger no doubt.

Did I pass out? She frowned. *Why can't I speak?* Even in her mind, her words rolled off a cotton tongue.

Maybe I'm already dead?

The other shadow, perhaps death, standing over her shrugged. "I confirmed that Mr. Effingo was dead and she passed out."

Unable to fully scream, Dylan struggled for a breath as she rolled into the man with the scar who was holding her. Tears sprung and fell freely onto his leather jacket.

Tristian!

Oh God, I'm still in Hell...

She wanted to die. No, she *needed* to die. She couldn't move on from this. A memory of her parents' headstones flashed before her mind's eye and she knew then she was broken. There was no fixing this kind of damage done to a single person. Why hadn't they killed her?

"I guess you got your answer," snapped the shadow holding her convulsing body.

The man in golden robes cleared his throat. "All right, Lucia Planto and Astrid are out front ready to leave. No sign of Gerion or his bother Lex. Come on before Ms. Elementa loses anymore blood. We can't afford to let her die before the trial," he said with a twisted sneer.

"My Master," called the younger voice. "Do you want me to bring Mr. Effingo's body with us to the Valley of Ashes?"

Dylan tore herself away from the soldier's chest and watched the man in golden robes, as he crossed his arms, and lightly tapped his chin with his index finger.

"No... Mr. Effingo's family has been deemed rogue against the Court. He doesn't deserve the respect. Leave him here to rot." His voice and attitude were so blithe you would have thought he was ordering dinner, not deciding the fate of her lover's dead body.

Dylan wanted to protest, to kick and scream, and to hold Tristian as she died next to him. But her body was so unresponsive all she could muster were minuscule spasms and jerks.

The soldier gave a solemn, curt nod and stepped out of the room following his *Master*. The demon holding Dylan tried to set her down so she could walk but her legs kept buckling. He grunted a curse as he ultimately lifted her against his chest which smelled of smoke and black pepper. Surprisingly, he held her gently as they exited the room.

Dylan peeked open her eyes from the curled position against the soldier. They focused on the unconscious, selfless Peppi Calibri and a servant she didn't recognize hovering over the small girl, then to the dead love of her life. Then as they rounded the corner, the mansion walls blocked her view.

Another sob broke free from her chest as she clung to the strange demon. She sensed she was suffocating as in the dream after she lost Tristian; except the suffocation was to her heart, caused by the memories flooding her mind of their final words. She felt cold and vacant, her heart lifeless as wind and ice pelted her skin. With a heavy breath, she vowed to never see this place again. Not even in her death.

"In the end, only three things matter: How much you loved, how gently you lived and how gracefully you let go of the things not meant for you."
Buddha.

To my readers,

Thank you for reading my book! I love interacting and hearing from you. Your honest thoughts are highly appreciated. Please take some time and review this novel on your preferred retailer's website. Reviews are the best way to help authors spread the word about their books!

To be updated with the latest info, sweeps, and sales, or to simply chat with me:
Like my fan pages at:
https://www.facebook.com/DNYLPUBLICATIONS
https://www.facebook.com/SMYAIRLEVY
Or follow me on Goodreads:
https://www.goodreads.com/author/show/8331593.S_M_Yair_Levy
Twitter: @DNYL_Books
Instagram: sm.yairlevyauthor

Acknowledgements

My husband, Ori, your great imagination always kept the writer's block at bay. I am incredibly thankful for your constant support and patience during the many nights of being ignored while I barricaded myself away to pour out my heart and soul into writing. You are my rock and best friend. I love you.

My children: Nathanel, Mila, and Jordan, my love for you runs deep to the bone. I love how you constantly keep me on my toes. Every day with you is a new crazy adventure.

My mother, Ruth, you were there every step of the way. Thank you for believing in me and helping me in any way you could, whenever I asked.

My dear friend, Annie, thank you for being my guinea pig in this new adventure and for always believing in me. Your long nights and helpful insights will never go forgotten.

My editor, Carole Gold, I'm so happy we met. Thank you for believing in me and for being such a joy to work with. Perhaps, you've found a new love for the urban fantasy genre?

My cover designer, Noa Yair-Levy, thank you for your patience and for creating a book cover that seriously makes me squeal every time I see it. You are a true artist!

And above all, thank you to all my beta testers and readers/reviewers you guys are the best! <3

S. M. YAIR-LEVY

lives with her husband and three children in Northern Israel. She has an addiction to reading and cherishes a great romance that really makes her swoon.

During her formative years, she pondered the simple question:

"What do you want to be when you grow up?"

Artist, meteorologist, nurse, doctor, tornado-chaser, architect... She had many interests but nothing ever stuck. Ultimately, leading her to a BFA in Architectural Interior Design. It wasn't until after having her first child, that Yair-Levy found she had a lot of time to think and daydream between mountains of laundry and dirty diapers.

Characters blossomed, histories attached and suddenly she felt the gnawing urge to jot it all down. Twenty minutes here, an hour there, in her cell phone or hunched over her laptop. She looked for and took any and every opportunity to write.

With the strong support of her friends and family, she finished her debut novel of The Collectors and cannot believe she's finally found her passion, her calling in life.